THE GIRLS

ALSO BY BELLA OSBORNE

The Library

THE GIRLS

Bella Osborne

An Aria Book

9 7 5 3 1 2 4 6 8

A CIP catalogue record for this book is available
from the British Library.

ISBN (E): 9781801100496
ISBN (PB): 9781801100519

Cover design © Tatiana Boyko
Typeset by Siliconchips Services Ltd UK

Printed and bound in Great Britain by
CPI Group (UK) Ltd, Croydon CR0 4YY

MIX
Paper from
responsible sources
FSC® C171272

Head of Zeus
First Floor East
5–8 Hardwick Street
London EC1R 4RG

WWW.HEADOFZEUS.COM

For Cheryl

I

PAULINE

Pauline didn't usually drink vodka at lunchtime. But then it wasn't every day you committed suicide. If she was honest she wasn't entirely sure today was that day. It wasn't that she was doing it out of despair or even boredom, rather a sense of inevitability. She glanced around her. Her small kitchen table still bore the marks from many a smashed plate, but he and his anger were long gone. And so, it seemed, was the person she used to be before him. The husk of her remained, as did the rickety table. The rows of neatly laid out white tablets were quite satisfying in their own way. Uniform and orderly. She liked things neat and didn't like the thought of leaving a mess for someone else. She'd planned this out and put everything in order. Hoovering and dusting the tiny flat had also given her something to do. She didn't have much of anything to do these days. Nothing to do and no one to miss her.

Pauline unscrewed the lid on the vodka and picked up a tablet. She stared at them both. She felt calm in a way she hadn't on all the other occasions she'd reached this step. Perhaps that meant this was the right time. She opened her mouth. The doorbell screamed at her and she almost dropped the pill. Some people would interrupt anything. Could you not even kill yourself in relative peace? She could ignore it. Although if she was to do a proper job she didn't want to be found too quickly. She didn't fancy having her stomach pumped again.

She was sixty-eight with no family and lived alone so the person at the door wouldn't be for her. It never was. It would likely be a door-to-door thing – she hated those. The inability to say no made those interactions particularly tricky. Or a delivery for a neighbour. They were all out at work and persistent delivery drivers liked to try all the buttons until someone responded. The doorbell screeched again. It really was an unpleasant noise, like someone strangling a parrot. She closed her eyes and tried to concentrate on the matter in hand. Death. Escape. Peace. She'd imagined leaving the worries and torment of life would be serene. Two more shrieks from the doorbell told her something different. Whoever was at the door was quite tenacious. She had no idea who it was and yet she didn't like the idea of keeping them waiting on the doorstep. It was no good. She was too British – she'd have to answer it. She positioned the pill back in its place in the neat row and went to answer the door.

'Blimey, that's got some lungs on it,' said the postman with a chortle. Pauline frowned. What was he on about? 'The doorbell. It's loud,' he added. She'd put new batteries in it as part of her plan to put things in order. Prior to that, like virtually everything else in the small rented flat, it hadn't worked. She realised she was staring at the postman. He gave her a quizzical look like he was working out if she was a bit dim or not.

'Oh, yes. It is a bit loud. Sorry.' Her words came out as a croak. She'd not spoken for some time. Days in fact. Probably over a week ago when the lady at the supermarket till had asked her if she was having a good day. It had been a difficult question to answer. So she'd settled on 'Fine thanks.' When fine was the last thing her life was.

'Post for you.' He presented her with a pearlescent envelope. She tried to find a smile but she was out of practice. 'You need to sign for this one,' he added. Pauline gingerly took the envelope from him. She usually only received bills. Actually, she only ever received bills. The mail for the previous occupant had stopped some months back. She stared at the pretty envelope. 'That is you, right?' asked the postman tapping the letter and breaking her gaze. The name was written in thick black swirly pen, like someone had attempted calligraphy with a sharpie. Only it wasn't her name – well not entirely. It was her maiden name. 'I reckon you've won something. Premium bonds maybe. It's got that quality feel to it. That or someone is seriously early for Christmas.' He belly-laughed at his own joke. When Pauline didn't react he coughed. 'Suit yourself. Sign here.'

'Right. Thank you,' she said, not wanting to come across as rude. He didn't know he'd interrupted her third suicide attempt of the month. Third time lucky – she mulled that phrase over. As she signed her name with the stylus she realised her hands were shaking.

The postman nodded at the envelope. 'You going to open

it then? See if I'm right?' He seemed keen and this was one of those times Pauline would struggle to say no.

'Oh, yes. Sorry.' She pushed a bitten thumbnail under the corner edge of the envelope and gently began tearing. The postman's nose was hovering above. She feared he was going to be disappointed. 'I don't enter competitions,' she said, now starting to wonder what it was. She pulled out a thick piece of card with the same pearlescent sheen as the envelope.

'Ooh,' said the postman skim-reading the invitation before Pauline had a chance. 'Surprise party. That'll be a posh do if the invitation is anything to go by. Shame it wasn't the premium bonds. I might have got a tip.' He laughed as he walked down the concrete steps and carried on up the road.

Pauline continued reading the invitation, slightly dazed. 'Bye,' she said, belatedly. She shut the door and went back to the kitchen table. She was almost surprised to see the little white pills waiting patiently for her. She put down the envelope and scooped all the tablets back into their tub. Today wasn't their day. She pushed the tub and the vodka bottle to the far edge of the table. Then she remembered the invite and pulled the bottle back towards her. There was a good chance she might still need it. But then if she drank that now she wouldn't have any to wash down the tablets. She wasn't good at making decisions.

Maybe she'd have a cup of tea instead. She liked tea. It was cheap and warm, unlike her flat. She waited for the kettle to boil with her back to the Formica worktop, keeping a safe distance from the envelope. She took her tea to the table. Should she have a proper read of the invitation or

4

return it to the envelope and forget about it? Alternatively she could put it in the bin. But she'd just emptied the bin. This was inconvenient. It wasn't even addressed to her. It was for the person she used to be. That was one thing she was certain about – that Pauline didn't exist anymore.

2

JACKIE

Jackie picked the invitation up and kissed it. Then really wished she hadn't because now the prettiest thing to land on her doormat was emblazoned with Defiant Coral lip marks. It was already a good day because it was the last of her working week and she was seeing Stefan later but, with the arrival of the invite, it had just got a whole lot better. The thought of the party had filled her with excitement. She had danced around her kitchen when she'd opened it and something inside her was still dancing. She popped it in her pocket, fluffed up her hair, checked she didn't have lipstick on her teeth and left for work with more than a spring in her regulation flat shoes.

Jackie signed in at the care home and tried to listen as the carer going off shift handed over to her but her mind was elsewhere. In her head she was already at the party. Although her outfit kept changing. She knew she had nothing in her wardrobe suitable and anyway a party was always a great excuse for a new outfit, however maxed out her credit card was. This was going to be a special night and she wanted, no *needed*, something exceptional to wear. She'd go up the West End on her day off and see if any of the designer shops had a sale on. She needed to look the part.

'...mils of insulin, Jackie. Did you get that?' The woman was scowling at her.

'I'm sorry. Something on my mind.' Jackie pulled a troubled expression.

'Sorry to hear that. But you can't get this wrong.' She tapped the page where she'd underlined a resident's insulin dosage.

'Absolutely not. You can trust me,' said Jackie. The other carer didn't look so sure.

There wasn't much in life that Jackie took seriously but one thing she was serious about was her job. She'd worked hard to get her diploma and, who knew, maybe if she'd come to the profession earlier in life perhaps she may even have qualified as a nurse. She'd tried out a lot of different roles in search of her niche and something that suited her talents. It was thirty years before it dawned on her she was simply drifting from one crap job to another. Becoming a carer had at least stabilised things on the job front, even if the rest of her life was still somewhat unreliable. She was diligent, worked hard and the residents loved her – and considering what she got paid they were pretty lucky to have her.

Once the handover was complete she popped in to see Mr Wiggins. She shut the door behind her. Mr Wiggins was in his wheelchair reading a neatly folded newspaper. He put it down and a smile grew on his face.

'How much did I win?' he asked, rubbing his hands together.

'Eighty-seven pounds,' she said, in a hushed voice, quickly handing over the cash. 'Put it away before anyone sees.' She straightened his bedcovers out of habit.

'Jackie, you're a star. Here you go.' He passed her a ten-pound note.

'You don't have to,' she said, slipping it in her uniform pocket. She never asked but he always saw her right out of his winnings. The bookie's was near where she lived so it wasn't out of her way to pop a bet on for the old boy. Residents often had to make huge compromises when moving into the nursing home. Helping them find a bit of enjoyment was, in her mind, all part of the job.

'Now can you put these on for me?' He held out a slip of paper and a twenty-pound note.

'Shhh,' said Jackie. 'You'll get me shot.' She took them from him. 'No problem. I'll bring your tea through later.'

'You seem extra happy today,' he said.

'I am. Take a look at this.' She took the invitation from her other pocket.

Mr Wiggins put on his reading glasses and gave it a thorough read. 'A party at the Dorchester Hotel, no less. I say Zara Cliff. As in THE Zara Cliff, the actress?'

'The very same,' said Jackie, proudly. 'We're old friends. We go way back. Shared a place together in the Seventies.' Not that she'd seen or heard from Zara in years but here was a chance to reconnect. Perhaps to be part of a different world again. One full of glitz and glamour rather than dentures and bed pans. The thought of it made her giddy.

'Blimey, the Seventies. That is way back. Even I was a whipper-snapper then. That's fifty years ago.'

'No!' said Jackie, rather sharper than she meant to. Her

brain was trying to do the maths. 'It was the mid-Seventies, that's like... forty-six years ago.' Her voice had turned to a whisper. How could so much time have passed? It was as if someone had fast-forwarded her life. It didn't feel that long ago that she'd been young, single and living it up in the heart of London with her friends. But as Mr Wiggins had unwittingly pointed out it was, in fact, a very long time ago indeed. Not much had changed inside her head. She was still the spontaneous, flirty, fun-loving person she'd always been but even she had to admit she'd noticed a change on the outside. Greying locks, wrinkles and hairs popping up in unwanted places.

'Should you be showing people the invite if it's meant to be a secret?' he asked, pulling her out of her thoughts.

'They just say that to make it seem more exciting. I'm sure she knows about it. Now did you fancy a change of scenery? Mrs Nossington is in the day lounge shuffling cards like a card sharp waiting for someone to play rummy with her.'

'She only plays for ten pence a game,' he said, with a huff. Jackie gave him her schoolteacher look. 'Ahh, go on then. Wheel me through.'

3

VAL

Val checked her diary. She was free. She added the party, along with a couple of run-up reminders to make sure she would be well prepared for the social event and sent her reply by email to Zara Cliff's agent. She picked up her phone and dialled what she hoped was still Pauline's number. She heard Pauline clear her throat before speaking.

'Hello?'

'Pauline, it's Valerie Chapman. It's been a while. How are you?'

There was a slight hesitation. 'Oh, Val, how lovely to hear from you. I'm… fine. How about you?'

'I think I'm little bit in shock if I'm honest. I've just had a blast from the past and I'm wondering if you've had one too.'

'Ah, the invitation to Zara's party?'

'Exactly. I couldn't quite believe it when I opened it.' Val rearranged a few cushions and settled herself on the vintage leather sofa for a chat.

'I know. It's been a while since I've heard from her too.'

'Not that. She's eighty! She always swore blind she was younger than me when in reality she was nine years older. Nine years!' Val tried to keep her annoyance in check but it felt good to vent. At least Pauline would understand her frustration. 'You could have knocked me down with a bald feather. All these years she's kept that a secret. It's even wrong on Wikipedia.'

'I wonder if it's a misprint on the invite.'

'Pauline, you're too kind. You always have been. You try to see the good in everyone. But I'm afraid I don't think that's the case here. I think Zara has lied through her teeth for years about her age.'

'I guess it's hard being an actor. Didn't Zara always say they either want orphan Annie or Miss Marple but nobody in between?'

'She did. Goodness, I can't believe that was all decades ago.'

'Nor me,' said Pauline, and the line went quiet.

'Look, I hold my hands up to not having been in touch apart from Christmas and birthday cards. Work was a big part of my life and then I sort of got caught up with all these charities. But that's no excuse. I'm sorry, Pauline.' Val hoped Pauline knew her apology was genuine.

'It's fine. Any of us could have made the effort but we didn't. No one person is to blame. And I really appreciated the cards.'

'That's decent of you, Pauline. But like I say, you've always been too kind. I take it you'll be going to the party.'

'Um. I don't know at the moment,' said Pauline. 'I've got stuff on and things planned.'

'And these things clash specifically with that three-hour window do they?' asked Val.

'Always to the point, Val. You've not changed. No, you're right. I don't have anything that clashes specifically.'

'Then you'll come?' Val needed clarity.

There was a long pause. 'I'd like to but it's been a long while. And the Dorchester. I mean that's fancy. I know this will sound pathetic but I honestly don't have anything I could wear to something like that. And I'm really not a social sort of person anymore. The thought of it is actually bringing me out in hives.'

'Pauline, don't exaggerate and stop looking for excuses. This isn't a red-carpet affair, it's a gathering of Zara's friends. Whatever you're wearing right now will be fine.'

'Christmas pyjamas and a tea-stained dressing gown,' said Pauline, flatly.

Val laughed. 'You've still got that dry sense of humour of yours. But I'm serious. Dig out a little black dress, sling on some heels and you'll be good to go.'

'Oh, Val. That takes me back but I'm afraid I've put on a few pounds since then. It's a lovely thought and you know what? I'd love to hear all about it after you've been but I think I'll give it a miss.'

Val didn't like her ideas being dismissed. Especially not when she knew best. She needed to be less directive and more persuasive. 'It'll be like a reunion.'

'I hate those.'

'Come on, Pauline, I'm sure you've got fond memories of when we all lived together. Surely it's worth us reuniting if only to relive our youth.'

'Jackie was a big part of that.' It was Val's turn to go quiet.

'Sometimes it's better to leave the past alone. Remember the good parts. It's been lovely speaking to you again though, Val. Thanks for calling.'

'Oh, no you don't,' said Val. 'This feels like something monumental.'

'That's not helping my anxiety.'

'Well, what I mean is - this is a pivotal point in our lives. The four of us have gone off in different directions and here is Zara pulling us back together. I don't think we should miss this opportunity. One last hurrah, what do you say?' There was another long pause. 'Are you still there, Pauline?'

'I guess so, for now.'

4

PAULINE

A few weeks later Pauline was questioning her life choices. Darting through the streets in an Uber she watched London change before her eyes. The concrete high-rises and scattered bins were soon left behind for glass and splendour. Old and new creations side by side vying for attention. She glanced down at the birthday card on her lap. It had taken her ages to choose it. She'd thought a lot about Zara and the girls since her phone call with Val. She'd picked up a card with *80* emblazoned on a rosette-style badge but on seeing the price she hastily put it back – she figured Zara wouldn't wear the badge anyway. The other cards talked of relaxing, gardening and putting your feet up and hadn't seemed appropriate. Zara was still working, attending film premieres and hosting parties. Zara didn't fit the mould of the average eighty-year-old.

They drove past Buckingham Palace, a sight that never failed to make Pauline feel proud to be a Londoner. She clutched her bag. She'd not been *out* out for such a long time. She took a deep breath to try to steady her pulse. It didn't work. As they neared Park Lane, Pauline lost her nerve. This was madness. She couldn't do this. What had she been thinking?

'I'm sorry... I've forgotten something. Can we go back please?'

'I've got rides backed up tonight, love. Are you sure?' replied the driver.

'Certain.'

He muttered something under his breath and whilst shaking his head he did a slightly dangerous manoeuvre into a side street. There was more traffic and he was unable to get out again. Trapped in a dead end. It was like a metaphor for her life. Was she doing the right thing by giving the party a miss? She didn't feel any less anxious at that moment, but she would calm down once she was home and safely back at the flat with a cuppa in her hands. She could get out of the dress she'd found on eBay. She glanced down at herself. It was a little black dress, just like they all used to wear. The four of them had all dressed identically but at the same time had all looked very different. Zara had been the glamorous one with big hair and lots of accessories. Val the tall, slim and sensible one. Jackie the busty, exuberant one with expertly applied make-up and then there had been her. Which one was she? Pauline didn't know. She ran her hand over the dress.

'Bloody traffic,' mumbled the driver, finally pulling out and getting hooted at. He replied with a hand gesture.

'I'm sorry,' said Pauline, automatically. He glanced in the rear-view mirror but the look he gave her wasn't particularly charitable. She'd upset him now and she was definitely going to upset Val. She'd confirmed to Zara's agent that she'd be there but would they notice if she wasn't? Probably not. Not many people noticed Pauline. She looked down at the card. She could always post it.

Pauline felt her mobile vibrate in her bag. She pulled it out and answered it. It was Val.

'What's going on?' asked Val.

Pauline needed to think of an excuse fast. 'I've got a headache, possibly a migraine. It's best I stay in bed.'

'Pauline, you are in the Uber I booked for you and I am tracking your progress on the app. Would you like to think of a better excuse?'

'Hmm. How about there's a tornado heading for Hackney?'

'Seriously, why are you heading home? I was looking forward to seeing you. For us to all be back together. How we used to be.'

'I'm sorry, Val. It's just...' What was it? Why was she running away?

'I've seen a few celebrities go in already,' cut in Val. 'Nobody will be looking at us I promise you. We'll find a corner and we'll chat.' She listened to her friend. 'Come on, Pauline, I don't want to be a doomsayer but none of us know how long we've got left. We should be enjoying it.' She had a point. 'Please come. For me.'

Guilt landed heavy on Pauline. 'I've already upset the driver once.'

'Tell him I'll give him a decent tip and five stars if he turns around again.' Pauline's palms prickled. She sighed into the phone. 'Please, Pauline.'

Against her better judgement she said, 'Okay. But stay on the line so I don't chicken out.'

'Of course. I'm not going anywhere,' said Val.

Pauline apologised every few minutes for the rest of the journey with no response from the Uber driver whose annoyance was radiating off him and emphasised by the many angry gesticulations he was throwing at other vehicles. As they neared the Dorchester Hotel Pauline changed from sorry to thank you and continued to repeat it until she was on the pavement.

'Would you look at you,' said Val, striding forwards and wrapping Pauline in a hug. The Uber driver sounded his horn. Val rolled her eyes. 'Let me sort out his tip,' she said. Val did something on her phone and spoke to the driver. Pauline missed what she said but he seemed placated and even waved as he left – one of the few hand gestures she hadn't seen him share with his fellow road users.

Val turned back to face Pauline and unexpected emotion took her breath. It was unbelievably good to see Val again. They'd not seen each other since Pauline's wedding. Her friend was older, but she was unmistakably Val. Tall and smart wearing an elegant navy trouser suit that accentuated her stature. Her short hair was many shades of grey and brushed off her face. Her eyes sparkled above sharp cheekbones – she was still a good-looking woman.

'You decided against the dressing gown then?' said Val, with a smile.

'It can gape a bit.'

'In that case you could have worn it. My word there's a lot of flesh on show.'

Pauline pulled her black cardigan tighter around her. 'Is the neck too scooped?

'From the other partygoers I mean,' added Val. 'Not you. You look marvellous.'

'I thought I'd stick with plain old black.'

'Understated suits you.' Val linked her arm through Pauline's and guided her towards the entrance. 'Let's party.'

'Should we not wait for Jackie?'

'No,' said Val, continuing inside. 'Who knows what time she'll show up.'

5

JACKIE

Why was the underground so buggery far under ground? she wondered, removing herself from a sweaty commuter's armpit. Escalators and heels were a no-no. Her feet were throbbing already. It was a relief when she finally emerged from the tube station at Hyde Park Corner. It was mid-May and whilst the day had been balmy the fading light was taking the warmth with it. She started walking around the edge of Hyde Park. It felt like her shoes were trying to devour her from the toes up. They had looked divine in the shop. Granted they hadn't exactly felt comfortable when she'd tried them on but it was only for one evening, she'd reasoned, telling herself they'd be fine. How wrong she had been.

Five minutes of walking and she was ready to hail a taxi. And she would have done if she could have walked closer to the road but she'd made her choice and she needed to stick with it. She focused her thoughts on the many cocktails that would inevitably be waiting for her at The Dorchester.

She checked her watch. She was going to be cutting it fine. As long as she didn't arrive at the same time as Zara that'd be okay. Not because she didn't want to spoil any surprise, but because Zara would be planning to make a grand entrance and she wouldn't want to get in the way of that.

Jackie was pleased with her outfit. It had cost a bomb even though it was from the designer sale rail but it fitted her like a glove, showcasing her assets to the max. Adorned with black sequins it was actually quite weighty and was making her overheat. All she needed now was a bloody hot flush and she'd completely melt. A bit further on and she could see the hotel. It was like an oasis in the desert and she was the desperate traveller overjoyed to see it. Only she was expecting jugs of cocktails instead of water. Just a few more painful steps.

As she reached the entrance a doorman approached her. 'Are you here for the party?'

'I am,' she said proudly, straightening herself.

'It's the entrance around the side.' He indicated where she needed to go.

'You are frigging kidding me.'

The doorman was momentarily alarmed at her response but recovered himself. 'I'm afraid so, but it's probably quicker than going through the hotel.'

'Thank you,' she said reluctantly and set off again.

The ballroom entrance was less impressive although the two limousines she saw leaving made up for its discretion. At least she wasn't the only one on the drag. She wondered if she had time to redo her lippy.

'Hello, welcome to the Dorchester and Zara's party. Can

I take your name please?' asked a slim young woman with wavy hair.

'Jacqueline Heatley. But only my mum calls me Jacqueline. Well, used to, before she died.' The woman was giving her an odd look. Sometimes she overshared. 'I might be down as just Jackie.' The woman returned her eyes to her list.

'Yes, here you are.' She ticked her off. 'Please go through; help yourself to champagne. Zara's a little delayed, which is good. It gives us time to assemble everyone.'

'Fab,' said Jackie. 'Where's the loo?' The woman gave her directions.

The toilets were sumptuous and there was a possibility that Jackie had overdone the free hand cream. The smell was overpowering her own liberal dousing of perfume. She headed to the party whilst trying to rub the cream in, although probably looked as if she was wringing her hands like Scrooge on counting day. Someone ushered her into the ballroom. It took her a few steps before she looked up and took in her surroundings. The room was vast and teeming with beautiful people. A huge sparkling chandelier dominated the ceiling and a myriad of mirrors reflected its brilliance off every surface. Even the floor shone. It was stunning.

Jackie had only ever seen this many famous people in the same place at awards shows on the telly. A giant screen was showing clips of Zara in her most famous roles and the other end of the room was festooned with white and gold balloons and a large banner wishing Zara a happy 80th birthday.

A young man followed her in. She looked him up and down. Very smart but not anyone she recognised. Shoes were a bit pointy but otherwise he looked good. She smiled. He tried to do the same but didn't quite manage it. She watched him make his way through the crowd and pop up again on a raised platform where there was a microphone.

'Is this on?' he said and it echoed around the room, grabbing everyone's attention. 'I think that answers my question.' A smattering of laughter rippled through the guests. 'Hi, I'm Jules. For those of you who don't know me, I'm Zara Cliff's agent. It's me who sent you the secret invitations and has been hassling your publicists for confirmations. Please accept my apologies for that. Anyway, I know Zara will be thrilled to see so many of you here tonight. She's on her way. Fashionably late as always.' A few people nodded at this. 'When I get the signal from the door that she's here, we're going to dim the lights and that's your cue to go silent. And then a round of applause as she comes through those doors would be nice. Okay?' He gave a thumbs up to a couple of photographers. There were mumbles of agreement and the volume rose as everyone went back to their conversations.

Jackie wanted to take her shoes off but feared she'd leave sweaty footmarks on the highly polished floor. A waiter offered her a tray of champagne; at least that might dull the pain. 'Thank you and one for my friend,' she said, taking two glasses. She wandered into the crowd and began celeb spotting. She wished she'd not got both her hands full, now she couldn't take any photographs on the sly. Jackie thought she spotted George Clooney on the far side of the crowd so she hastily made her way through, apologising as she went. She was almost there when the lights dimmed and someone grabbed her shoulder, making her jump.

6

VAL

Her trademark blonde hair was piled on top of her head and pulled so tight there was no need for plastic surgery, too much eye make-up and a cleavage barely contained by a dress that sparkled more than the chandelier – it was unmistakably Jackie. Val had hoped seeing her again would prove to her that their issues were in the past but a flood of emotion told her that wasn't the case. Jackie spun around and liberally doused a tall gentleman in champagne.

'Whoops. Sorry,' said Jackie, her voice now ringing out as quiet descended.

There was a chorus of 'Shhhh.'

'Sorry,' she whispered, before finally she saw Val. 'Bloody hell, Valerie. That's the move you put on a shoplifter.'

'I wouldn't know,' said Val. She'd been keen to intercept Jackie before she disappeared into the crowd but now they were face to face, and the room was hushed, it all felt quite awkward.

Jackie held up her two champagne flutes. 'I would give you a hug but I've already spilled loads.'

'I know,' grumbled the man she'd spilled it on.

'Still got your priorities right, I see,' said Val, stepping to one side as Pauline rushed forward and stopped Jackie replying.

'Jackie, you look amazing,' she said in a quiet but excited voice as she kissed her lightly on the cheek. 'Are you here with someone?' she asked, eying the glasses in her hands.

'No... I—'

'I think we need to be quiet now,' said Val, leaning forward. Pauline scuttled back to Val's side. Jackie shrugged and turned to face the door. There was a lengthy delay. The ballroom door opened a crack.

'It's a bloody imposition, Jules!' Zara's voice carried into the ballroom. 'Dragging me all the way down here for some tin-pot film that may or may not have secured funding.' The door opened fully and Zara stepped inside still conversing over her shoulder. 'Bloody drama queen. I suppose you told him—'

The lights went up. 'Surprise!' One person led the shout and a sort of verbal Mexican wave followed along with a hearty round of applause.

Zara jolted like she'd been momentarily tasered. The shocked look on her face was only there for a fraction of a second before her experience kicked in. A broad smile appeared and she opened her arms wide. 'Oh, my darlings, what a tremendous surprise.' She blew kisses to the crowd. She stayed rooted to the spot as people surged towards her and a series of air kisses and hugs followed. Val saw her glance at the banner and immediately return her gaze to the people in front of her.

'Same old Zara,' said Jackie.

'She looks amazing,' said Pauline. 'Like she does in films.'

'Professional make-up,' said Jackie.

'I think I'm just going to pop to the loo,' said Pauline.

'Again?' Val tilted her head.

'Nervous bladder,' Pauline whispered.

'Is that code for you're terrified of pissing yourself?' Jackie hooted a laugh.

Pauline flushed crimson. 'I'll only be a minute.' She almost ran from the room.

'Have you spoken to anyone famous yet?' asked Jackie, scanning the backs of numerous heads.

'Not really been looking,' said Val, trying not to stare at Jackie's sparkling dress. She looked like a walking glitterball.

'Do you think it's okay to ask for selfies?'

'I don't think that's really the done thing at an occasion such as this. These people aren't working, they're guests at a friend's party.'

Jackie twisted her lips. 'That's a bugger. Maybe if I take a couple of over-the-shoulder snaps.'

'That's worse,' Val said, confounded.

Pauline made her way back to them. 'I just dried my hands next to Judi Dench.' She opened her mouth in a silent, excited scream.

'Actresses have to pee too, you know,' said Jackie. 'Actually that's a great idea. I might hang around the loos. Where are the gents?'

'Not a good idea,' said Val. 'And anyway we're here to see Zara – no one else.'

'Oh yeah. Course.'

'Anyway, how are you?' asked Val, feeling she needed to be the bigger person.

'Marvellous, apart from my feet feeling like they're on fire. Are there any seats?' Jackie swivelled her head in various directions.

'There's a few over there but I assumed they were for when the buffet arrived,' said Val.

'Sod that.' Jackie was already making her way to where four tablecloth-draped tables were surrounded by chairs. Val followed and they sat down.

'Ahhhh.' Jackie let out a sigh.

'Still wearing the killer heels, I see,' said Val.

'Standards, Valerie. The day I stop wearing heels is the day I—'

'Break a hip?' suggested Pauline, joining them.

Jackie laughed and the tension was broken. 'Don't say that. It makes us sound old.'

'We are,' said Val, checking the situation with Zara. She was still surrounded. She would go over once the crowd had died down.

'Speak for yourself. I'm in my sixties. That's nothing these days.' Jackie finished her first glass of champagne and moved on to the next.

'Late sixties,' pointed out Val.

'I'm sixty-four!'

'But we're all a lot younger than Zara.' She nodded at the sign.

'I know,' said Jackie. 'That was a bloody surprise. She always was a sly one.'

'I always thought Zara was lovely,' said Pauline, following

Val's gaze. 'She looks amazing. You'd never think she was eighty.'

'She's had work done. I read about it online.' Jackie kicked off her shoes and rubbed her foot. Val tried hard not to scowl.

'And everything online is completely reliable,' said Val, giving her a look she knew belonged over the top of half-moon glasses.

'You look terrific too,' said Pauline to Jackie.

'Thank you. I look after myself. Stefan keeps me young, if you know what I mean.' She gave an elaborate wink.

'Is he your husband?' asked Pauline.

'He's my current lover. Nobody has managed to tie me down.' Jackie sipped her champagne seductively.

Val fought hard not to roll her eyes but it was a challenge. 'And how old is Stefan?' she asked.

'Forty-five,' said Jackie proudly. 'Recently divorced. As fit as a butcher's dog with a bone to match.'

'That's some age difference,' said Val. 'Doesn't it worry you that he'll find someone his own age?'

'Why on earth would he do that?' Jackie swept a palm over her body and the sequins shimmied in the light.

'Because all the others clearly have.'

7

PAULINE

'Please don't,' said Pauline, looking from Val to Jackie and back again. 'Let's not do this.' Confrontation made her tense and she was already stressed just by being there. She had zero confidence at the best of times and being in a posh hotel full of celebrities did not improve that. Her recent trip to the ladies hadn't helped because the mirror had reminded her how dull and dowdy she was and standing next to Judi Dench had made things even worse. She wished now she'd done something about the grey hairs rampaging through her mousy brown locks. It was somehow more ageing than Val's shock of platinum, which in its short, neat style showed off her cheekbones. Hers showed off a wonky fringe and her inability to blow-dry it into a discernible style.

'Don't look at me,' said Jackie, raising a palm. 'I'm only here to have fun.'

Pauline looked at Val and she gave a curt nod. 'Fine,' said Val.

Pauline took a deep breath. 'You are the best friends I ever had. And it's been such a long time since we saw each other.'

She saw Val's shoulders relax. 'We have left it far too long to get the four of us back together.'

'Looks like that's about to get sorted.' Jackie waved a glass towards the entrance. Zara was making her way towards them and looking a little unsteady on her feet. Perhaps she'd already been at the champagne.

Pauline stood up to greet her and Zara took hold of her hand. Her grip was fierce and as she leaned forward Pauline had to support her. 'My darling girls! You're all looking completely gorgeous.'

A series of hugs, kisses and happy birthdays followed. Pauline wanted to commit this to memory. A moment that was a world away from her everyday life. A life that had once seemed to drag and yet now she looked back some things had raced by. The good things had been fleeting. Only the bad times had lingered. Her time with these women had been the very best she could remember. Something fizzed in her gut. It was an odd sensation but one she had vague recollections of. For the first time in so long Pauline felt happy. The kind of happy that blossoms inside and makes you smile without thought. She realised she had a grin to rival the Cheshire cat's and she didn't care. It made a pleasant change from feeling alone, worthless and generally crap.

'Thanks for inviting us,' said Pauline.

Zara checked over her shoulder before lowering her voice to a whisper and making them all lean in. 'You're the only people here I trust. I'm going to be completely honest with you.' She left a dramatic pause. 'This is my worst nightmare. I will murder Jules.'

'Not what you were expecting then?' asked Jackie.

'I was expecting a meeting with a film producer. Not a sodding surprise party. And especially not for that ludicrously high number to be emblazoned everywhere.'

'Is it a mistake?' asked Pauline.

'It's an abomination,' said Zara.

'How can we help?' asked Pauline, concerned by the look in Zara's eyes.

'Get that down and then we'll plot how to murder Jules,' she replied, letting go of her hand to stab a finger towards the signage before taking hold of the table.

'Leave the sign to me. You will have to sort out Jules,' said Val, already on her feet.

'I used to date a hitman,' said Jackie, in an everyday tone that made the statement somehow more worrying to Pauline.

'Useful to know,' said Zara.

'Unfortunately he's dead now,' added Jackie. 'He was shot by a hitman. Quite ironic really.'

In a swift movement Val pulled down the banner, rolled it into a ball and deposited it under the nearest table. Pauline adored how ballsy Val was. She'd love to have just a scrap of her confidence. Although being back with her friends was definitely giving her a boost. A bit like the day she'd mistaken the vitamin D for aspirin.

Val strode back to join them. 'What else do you need us to do?'

The three women waited while Zara appraised them all. 'Please don't judge me or worse still pity me but I need to

sit down. I can't let all these people see that I have some…
issues. I don't want to look like an old woman.' There was
a moment where she did look frail and vulnerable but then
in a flash Zara straightened her spine and pasted on a smile.
'Thank the stars I'm wearing my longest kaftan so my puffy
ankles are hidden.'

'Sit here with us,' said Jackie retrieving another chair
from the next table. 'This looks like you're being sociable.'
Jackie moved Emma Watson to one side and put the chair
next to Zara. Pauline had a feeling Jackie hadn't recognised
her.

Zara took hold of Pauline's arm and gingerly lowered
herself onto the seat. 'Oof, that's better. Thank you.' She
gave Pauline's arm a firm squeeze.

'No problem.' It worried Pauline how much of an effort
that small movement had seemed to be. Zara was obviously
struggling with mobility issues that she was keen to hide.

A short man scurried over. Threw his arms around
Zara and turned his back on the others. 'Zara, you've not
changed,' he said.

'Flatterer,' she said.

'Must dash. I'm on *The Graham Norton Show*. No rest
et cetera.' He guffawed in a slightly alarming way.

He gave Zara another hug. Over his shoulder she
mouthed to the others. 'Who the hell is this?'

Jackie became animated. 'Mr Trout, I'm a huge fan.
Could I have a sel—'

'How lovely. Bye now,' he said striding away.

'That was Nigel Trout?' Zara was shaking her head. 'He
had one line in a film thirty years ago. How the blue blazes
did he get on *The Graham Norton Show*?'

'Because that one line has made him famous. He's a meme,' explained Jackie, showing Zara a picture on her phone.

'The world's gone mad,' said Zara. 'And that woman there in the long pink dress used to make me cups of tea.'

'I think she's in *EastEnders* now,' said Jackie. 'I remember seeing her wearing that dress to the Television Awards.'

'Recycled dress.' Zara tutted. 'But the boobs are new,' she added, giving the woman a cheery wave. 'I think I'm going to need a stiff drink to get through this.'

'I'll get you one,' said Val, getting to her feet.

'Ooh and another one for me and one for my friend,' said Jackie. Val looked like she was going to say something but thought better of it and went in search of refills. Pauline had hoped the friction between Val and Jackie would have ebbed away with the years but it appeared nothing had changed. They were two big characters who had frequently clashed.

Val returned and handed out champagne including just one for Jackie who pulled a face at the single glass.

'Thank you, darling.' Zara took a swig. 'That's actually better than the usual house shite. At least Jules thinks I'm worth decent fizz.' She took another sip and savoured it. 'Laurent-Perrier I believe.'

Pauline wondered how much champagne you must have to drink to be able to tell them apart. 'It's all rather lovely though. All these people in a swanky hotel to celebrate your birthday.' Now she had the others all around her she was beginning to relax a fraction. They brought with them a long-missed sense of safety.

'But surely everyone knows the best parties are at

Claridge's.' Zara glanced at the assembled crowd. 'And these people. Vultures picking over the carcass of my career. I haven't seen or spoken to most of them in years.' There was an awkward silence. The women all looked at each other. Pauline bit her lip. Zara seemed to belatedly realise her faux pas. 'No offence. I am genuinely thrilled you are all here. *Surprised*. But thrilled.' Zara reached out and squeezed Val and Pauline's hands.

'How could we miss our friend's special birthday?' said Val.

Pauline could feel the arthritic bumps on Zara's knuckles. The years had left their mark on each of them. Some in more obvious ways than others. But to feel the touch of another human being, of a friend was quite moving. At that moment she was immensely glad she'd come. 'I wouldn't have missed it for the world,' she said and could feel Val's eyes boring a hole in her skull.

A tear formed in the corner of Zara's eye. 'Thank you.'

Jackie was drinking her champagne whilst scrolling through her phone. She seemed to sense eyes were on her and she looked up. 'What? I'm seeing if anyone is posting selfies.' She knocked back the rest of her drink. 'I could drink another one of those,' she said tipping her head at Val.

Val ignored her. A grey-haired man approached them and focused on Zara as if she were sitting alone.

'Zara, hi, *Daily Mail*. I need to make a move. There's a Leicester Square Premiere. Can we get a couple of photographs? Perhaps you with your banner?' He did a double take at the space where the banner had once been.

'I'm afraid I have a confession to make.' The reporter leaned forward. 'In the very early days of my career I lied about my age so I'm afraid that's way off. And we wouldn't want you printing something incorrect or libellous now would we?' Zara laughed theatrically, making the reporter wince. 'How about a photograph with my girls?'

'These your kids?' He was frowning hard at Val.

'No, they're my girlfriends. We go way back. We were children in the Seventies together.'

He checked his watch. 'Yeah, okay.' He nodded at the photographer to take the picture who then rearranged the women around Zara. Pauline felt instantly underdressed, scruffy and desperately self-conscious. She wanted to run for the door. Her smidgeon of comfort had been erased by a couple of sweeping looks from the photographer.

'In a bit closer, ladies,' he said, waving his camera. 'Lean forward a fraction.'

Val stood tall. Jackie flirted with the photographer. Zara straightened her back and posed beautifully. Pauline's head started to swim. She couldn't do this. What was she doing at an event like this anyway? She was about to bolt when she felt Val's hand in the small of her back. She darted a look in her direction. Val gave her a warm smile. 'It's fine, Pauline. We're all back together.'

8

JACKIE

Jackie was excited at the thought of appearing in a national newspaper and had already shared that news on all her social media platforms. 'Ooh, Zara. You're trending on Twitter.'

'Why? Has someone said I've died again?' Zara rolled her eyes.

'No. There's a hashtag. Zara's party.' Jackie showed Zara her phone screen.

'Can't see a bloody thing without my glasses,' said Zara, before she was interrupted by a group of women approaching the table. Jackie was side-lined as Zara held court. 'Darling, thank you so much for coming...'

Jackie tuned out of Zara's conversation. Chatter and laughter rang in Jackie's ears as a steady stream of people fawned over Zara. The volume of talking was quite something; the sound from Zara's film clips was completely drowned out. Waiters armed with bottles of champagne skittered between the many small groups but their visits to their table were less frequent than she'd have liked. Jackie noted there was a distinct lack of male talent in the under-sixty category but that was the same wherever she went. And all hopes of a selfie with a film star were fading. She'd been hoping to at least score on one front or the other.

At last a waiter approached the table and refilled their glasses. He was quite cute. 'Can you refill my friend's glass too?' She smiled. He topped up the champagne and hurried away.

Val and Pauline were chatting. Zara had her fan club. Jackie took a long draw from one of her glasses and surveyed the room. This was an opportunity even her aching feet couldn't deny her – a chance to track down a decent man. Of course she had Stefan who bulged in all the right places but he didn't have what she was really looking for – a bulging bank account. 'I'm going to mingle,' she said, to nobody in particular. Pauline nodded. 'Assuming I can get my feet back in my shoes,' she added.

It was a struggle and her toes protested but she managed it. It would have to be a brief mingle if she didn't want to end up on crutches. She took her empty glass with her and it was quickly refilled by a waitress. She wished she'd brought both glasses. She joined a small group of mixed-age women.

'Hello, I'm Jackie. How do you all know my old friend Zara?'

There was a chorus of greetings. 'I'm Cynthia, we worked in the West End years ago,' said one.

'Hi. June. We were on *The Benny Hill Show* together.'

Jackie spluttered a laugh. 'I'd forgotten she did that. Blimey that's one she won't want to be reminded of.' No one else was smiling. Maybe it was time she moved on.

'Ooh look Noel Edmonds,' she said and left the group as fast as her aching feet would let her.

Jackie found herself with a young group: a mix of YouTubers and stage actors who had apparently been told to come by Jules as they were with the same agency as Zara. But they were a fun crowd and gave her some top tips about taking selfies and which were the best filters to use. She was particularly pleased with one that made her look like a puppy and completely removed all her wrinkles. If she could have worked out how to remove the dog ears she would have dashed down to Max Spielman and had the thing printed off.

She was enjoying herself. She glanced across at Zara and the others. Val and Pauline were still chatting and Zara was surrounded by a different group of people. Jackie had been excited to see the others but it had been a shock. The same shock she had every time she looked in a mirror. They were getting old and she was struggling to face up to that. She didn't want to see them with grey hair and crêpey skin because she didn't want to be reminded of how she was ageing. Although thankfully she was the youngest of the group and that was a small mercy. She needed to hang on to that.

Next she chatted with a group from *Emmerdale*, although she was pretty sure none of them were still in it, but it was fun to get a few photographs. They were top gossips and although she barely knew who they were talking about she was enthralled. They talked about how hard they'd all been working but what did they know about real work? They just pretended to be someone else, swanned about and got paid shedloads for it. She'd worked hard all her life and for what? A waiter topped up her glass for the umpteenth time and she realised she had no idea how much she had drunk although she did know that she needed to sit down. She made her apologies and headed for the safety of the table.

Zara intercepted her and gripped her arm. 'Hang on. Jules is doing a speech.' Zara turned to face the stage but kept a firm hold of Jackie's arm. Jackie felt herself sway. She wasn't sure who was holding who up. Val and Pauline appeared and Zara let go of Jackie. She chose one of the others to steady her. One of the reliable ones.

'Good, because I'm not sure I'm capable of—'

Jackie was interrupted by Jules tapping the mic. 'I just wanted to say a few words. Firstly thank you to everyone for coming and an even bigger thank you for keeping today a secret. I think it's fair to say Zara was surprised.' His expression looked pained as if he was now realising his mistake. 'With a little help from Zara's personal assistant I got hold of a guest list for a celebration arranged in 1978 for Zara's run in a West End play...'

'I remember that,' said Jackie, marvelling at the slur in her words and the sway in her knees. They'd gone all rubbery. She downed the rest of her glass, which it appeared had been refilled again – it was like magic.

'Shhh,' said someone from *Emmerdale*. She swatted them away like a fly. More waiters were circling but they were carrying cones of what looked like mini fish and chips. She needed some food.

On stage Jules continued. 'Since then Zara has been a constant presence either on stage, television or film and I, and the agency, wanted Zara to know how much we all care about her. How much of a national treasure she is and that she will go down in history as—'

Jackie didn't hear anymore. She made a lunge for a waiter's tray. She toppled and she couldn't save herself. She heard a dull thud as everything went black.

9

VAL

'**B**loody typical that the one medically trained person in the room is the person who needs the medical attention,' said Val, kneeling on the floor next to Jackie who was out cold.

'She damn near took me down with her,' said Zara, holding on to the back of a chair.

'Here,' said Pauline, appearing with a cold wet flannel. 'They have them in the ladies loo to dry your hands on,' she explained.

'Thank you.' Val placed one on the large bump coming up on Jackie's forehead. Immediately she stirred.

'Fish and ships,' mumbled Jackie.

'Thank heavens,' said Pauline.

Val puffed out a sigh. She and Jackie had had their differences and had parted on bad terms but there was an undeniable bond the four of them shared. Seeing Jackie crash out the way she had had unfurled something inside Val. Whatever had happened between them or however many years they had been apart she'd never stopped caring about these women.

'She's fine,' said Zara. 'Can we move her somewhere?'

'Give her a minute to come round,' said Val. She could see Zara wasn't impressed by the floor show but it was fairly typical Jackie behaviour. Wisdom hadn't come with age in her case. 'Why don't you enjoy the party and leave Jackie to us?' suggested Val. Zara nodded, slapped on her showbiz smile and greeted the *Emmerdale* crowd as if they'd just teleported into the room.

Jules appeared with his mobile at his ear. 'Yes, she's breathing.' He pulled it away for a moment to speak to Val. 'An ambulance is on its way.'

'What? Cancel it. She's drunk that's all. She just needs a sit-down and lots of coffee.'

Jules looked like someone had put him on pause. He blinked. 'I thought she'd had a heart attack or something?'

'Because she's not twenty-five you think it's got to be medical?' Val held his gaze.

'No, I just... hang on...' He disappeared whilst apologising into his mobile.

'She did bang her head though. Do you not think a paramedic should take a look at her?' said Pauline, stroking Jackie's hand. Jackie snored, jolted and woke herself up. 'Hey, you,' said Pauline.

'How many fingers am I holding up?' asked Val.

'Two, you rude cow,' said Jackie.

Val was relieved. Any situation where someone collapsed was never good and there was always a chance of injury. 'How do you feel?' asked Val. 'Anything broken?'

There was a long pause before Jackie lifted up her hand,

which was still gripping her phone. 'No, thank goodness,' she said, narrowing her eyes with the effort of trying to focus on the screen. 'Did I miss the food?'

'Yep, come on. Let's get some coffee into you.' Val helped her onto her knees and then onto a chair.

Jules appeared with a cup of espresso. 'Thanks,' said Val, taking it from him. 'Two more of those please.'

'And some chips,' said Jackie, sounding sorry for herself.

Jules looked puzzled but he didn't query the request.

Pauline pulled up a chair next to Jackie and took her hand. 'It's just like old times,' she said with a wistful smile.

'Too much like old times,' said Val, holding the damp flannel in place. She could all too readily remember the occasions they'd had to get Jackie out of situations thanks to one too many at a party. She wasn't an alcoholic – well, she hadn't been when she was younger. She was someone who had an all-or-nothing approach to drink, which was never going to end well.

'Hi, do you want me to take a look at her?' asked a familiar-looking man with a Hollywood smile.

'That would be brilliant. Thank you. Are you a doctor?' asked Pauline.

'I did over ten years on *Grey's Anatomy*, which is more training than most doctors,' he said, with a practised chuckle.

Val shook her head. Actors were absurd. 'I'm not sure that's—'

'McDreamy?' said Jackie, blinking at the actor.

'Yes,' he said, proudly.

'Can I have a shelfie?' slurred Jackie.

'Thanks,' said Val to the actor, 'but I don't need an episode of *Grey's Anatomy* to tell me she's had one too many glasses of champagne. She's fine.' He shrugged and went to have his picture taken with the video screen now showing stills of Zara, which was odd given that the real-life version was standing just a few feet away. 'Jackie, drink.' Val tipped up the espresso.

Within half an hour the coffee had done its job and Jackie was taking photographs of celebrities while holding a bag of ice on her bump. It turned out that was proving to be a good icebreaker as she'd already got pictures with some daytime TV personalities and Colin Firth. Val and Pauline had a bit of a tag team thing going where one of them was keeping an eye on Jackie whilst the other enjoyed the party. Although Pauline didn't stray far on her own.

After a lifetime as a solicitor Val was fascinated by people and this room had more than its fair share of interesting characters. She was also watching Zara, who seemed to have got over her initial annoyance about the banner and was now enjoying the attention being lavished upon her. She'd found a way to lean on the back of a bar stool that made her look more casual and less like she couldn't stand for long periods, which Val was realising was the real issue.

She joined the group Zara was talking to and interjected into their conversation occasionally but mainly she listened. 'Do you remember when we toured with that ropey play?' said one and the others laughed including Zara.

'That awful B & B we got chucked out of for making too much noise,' added Zara.

'To be fair, we were a rowdy lot,' said the first woman. 'I'd have hated to have been staying there. I can't stand noise now.'

'Nor me,' said Val. 'I think you appreciate peace more as you get older.'

'I agree,' said the woman. 'I love my grandchildren. Honestly I do, but the racket they make drives me up the wall.' The others agreed. Val felt a twinge of something in her gut at the mention of grandchildren. She often wondered if she had any. The conversation moved on to current projects and Zara turned to Val.

'So you've embraced peace and quiet. Are you living out in the sticks now?' asked Zara.

'Still in the city, well on the outskirts really. Best of both worlds. I've got good neighbours and it's quiet. I like that. Actually I think I *need* periods of silence.'

'I agree. I love my place in Belgravia being right in the thick of things. But I escape to France to recharge.'

People began making their apologies and soon the room was looking sparse. Jackie seemed pleased with her haul of celebrity selfies despite the large bump on her head. Zara appeared to have enjoyed it more than she was expecting and Pauline hadn't run for the hills. They had all migrated back to the table. The friends eyed each other.

'Right.' Zara rapped a knuckle on the table. 'We four need a proper catch-up and I need some gin. Back to mine,' said Zara. 'Jules, call my driver.'

IO

PAULINE

Pauline wasn't entirely sure how they ended up at Zara's swanky Belgravia townhouse but she was sipping a cup of tea and sitting on the comfiest sofa her bum had ever graced, feeling quite proud of herself for having survived the party. She'd even enjoyed parts despite it being quite different to her usual evening of making a cheese-spread sandwich and reading a book.

Zara kicked off her diamanté flip-flops. 'That was an ordeal. Bloody Jules.'

'He'd obviously gone to a lot of trouble to arrange it and to track everybody down.' Pauline was feeling sorry for poor Jules. Zara had given him a tongue-lashing before they'd left.

'Bloody whippersnapper,' grumbled Zara.

'Didn't Ed wotsit used to be your agent?' asked Jackie, who was unashamedly picking up and inspecting Zara's ornaments.

'I remember Ed taking us all out for drinks and we ended

up at the American bar at the Savoy,' said Pauline. She recalled the larger-than-life American who seemed wowed by life and saw everything as an exciting opportunity. He was also generous to four young women.

'Sadly Ed died. And I didn't have any Hollywood agents banging on my door. I've had a couple since Ed but Jules came along and was with a big agency and very keen. But this party stunt is unforgivable.'

'I'm sure he was trying to do a nice thing,' said Pauline.

'Here you go,' said Val, handing Zara a large gin and tonic.

'Val, you're a lifesaver.' She closed her eyes and took a sip. 'Ahhh bliss.'

'Water or coffee?' Val asked Jackie who was looking longingly at Zara's G&T.

'No more coffee. When I burp I smell like Starbucks.' Jackie stifled a belch.

'Too much information,' said Val.

Jackie pulled a face. It made Pauline smile. Jackie still had a carefree air about her, like they all had at one stage in their lives. They'd all met thanks to an advert for rooms to let at the local college. Pauline tested her memory by trying to recall what classes they were each taking. She had been learning shorthand because it was her master plan to get herself out of the typing pool she worked in. Zara was taking pottery as research for a play she'd been cast in and she wanted to get into character. Pauline chuckled at how serious Zara had been and how much they'd pulled her leg about the misshapen pots she'd brought home.

'You okay?' asked Val.

'I am. What was the evening class you were taking when we met?'

'French. I was considering switching to French law,' said Val. 'You were doing shorthand. Zara was throwing pottery—'

'Literally if I remember right,' said Jackie with a snort. 'Didn't you lob some clay at someone?'

Zara rolled her eyes. 'I got a bit cross and the clay missed my turntable and landed in someone's lap. Years later the ruddy woman sold a highly fabricated account to a tabloid.'

'And Jackie…' Val paused. 'For some bizarre reason was taking a course in sailing.' They all laughed apart from Jackie.

'It was a skipper's course and it was theoretical. I figured if I wanted to land a bloke with his own yacht it'd give me a head start.' She gave the briefest of pouts before joining in with the laughter. The sound transported Pauline back to a happy time of banter and shared discovery.

'And did that course land you a sailor?' asked Val.

'Did you get much use out of your French?' Jackie countered.

'I didn't take up French law, if that's what you mean, but it's been useful for business trips and holidays.'

'If it wasn't for those courses we wouldn't have met,' said Pauline. It amazed her how life was simply a string of random interactions, some of which determined life paths and others that derailed them.

'Anyway, weren't you getting drinks?' Jackie nodded at Val, who turned and left the room. Jackie looked around as if seeking inspiration for a new subject. 'This place must have set you back a bit, Zara?'

'Husband number...' Zara pretended to count them off on her fingers. 'Three. He was the grandson of a baron and an investment banker with a gift for speculating and a weak heart.'

'Perfect combination.' Jackie slumped into a large circular chair and it turned slowly. 'Please tell me it's the chair moving and not the room again.'

'It's the chair,' said Zara. 'Some designer thing. Looks fabulous but completely impractical. I was once trapped in the sodding thing for two hours. Penelope Keith had to come round and rescue me.'

Val re-entered the room, put her foot against the side of the chair and it stopped spinning. 'Here. Drink some water,' she instructed, handing a tall glass to Jackie.

'Thank you,' she said, whilst turning her nose up. 'Any ice?'

'There's ice in it.'

'No, for my head. That bump is still throbbing.'

Val returned with a smaller version of Zara's drink, some ice in a tea towel for Jackie and took a seat next to Pauline, which she was grateful for. There was something reassuring about Val. She was one of life's organisers. Totally reliable, if not a little forthright, but someone whose presence she found soothing. She wasn't sure everyone would feel that way about Val. As a solicitor she'd most likely scared the bejesus out of many but she was one of the few people who didn't scare Pauline. She pondered why for a moment. Maybe it was because Val hadn't scared the old Pauline; perhaps if she met her for the first time now she'd be terrified of her. There was one lady on the supermarket checkout who Pauline always avoided because she'd snapped at her more than once. Val was scarier than her. But Pauline knew Val's softer side, knew that her stern approach came from a point of caring. Maybe the checkout lady had a caring side too – somehow Pauline doubted it.

Pauline looked around the room. High ceilings, ornate plasterwork and soothing pale yellow walls – it was like being in a magazine photoshoot. In fact she had a feeling she had seen one that Zara had done in this very room. She felt Zara's eyes on her. 'I love your house,' said Pauline.

'It's wasted really. Four floors and I can barely manage the front steps. But I can't do hotels anymore. No privacy.' Zara fanned her kaftan and Pauline caught a glimpse of her swollen lower limbs. Zara sighed. 'Look at us.' She paused, which Pauline took to be an instruction. She cast her eyes around each of them. Val straight-backed and thoughtful. Zara resplendent, holding court. Jackie crashed out and spinning gently. And they each in return surveyed her and smiled. She wondered what they were each thinking. The unhelpful voice in her head told her they could see a pathetic individual utterly devoid of purpose.

'You were quiet at the party, Pauline,' said Zara. 'You used to be the life and soul of things like that.' Zara gave a little wiggle.

For a moment Pauline wondered what Zara was on about. She would almost have laughed if it hadn't felt so tragic. She was right – once upon a time Pauline would have been in her element at a party. She had loved to dance and have fun. She'd never been as in-your-face as Jackie but she did used to know how to enjoy herself. But a lifetime had passed. That person had packed her bags and left a long time ago. 'Not anymore.'

'Why?' asked Jackie as the chair picked up momentum and she completed a full turn.

'Life.' Was all Pauline could think to say. How did you explain that people had left you battered and bruised until the person you were had disappeared without a trace?

'That's obtuse,' said Zara. She scrutinised each of them. 'I expect you're all up to date with each other's lives.'

'I didn't do much chatting tonight,' said Jackie, with a yawn. 'But my Insta is rocking.'

'But I assume you three see each other regularly.' Zara eyed them over her expensive-looking gin glass.

There were some furtive looks. Pauline stared into her tea. 'None of us kept in touch,' said Val, sticking a toe out to halt Jackie's chair.

'Really? That does surprise me. And there was me thinking I'd been the odd one out all these years.' Zara sounded wistful. She raised her glass. 'To the girls being back together.'

'The girls,' they all chorused.

I I

JACKIE

Jackie's head was starting to throb – she blamed all the coffee. The ice had taken her bump down. She was still gutted about missing out on the mini fish and chips. She flicked through what she'd posted on Instagram. Being drunk in charge of social media was never a good thing. She'd had to delete the selfies she'd taken with the few decent celebrities who had agreed to one, because she looked like a drunk old woman with a record-breaking number of chins. And all the photos she'd taken on the sly were either out of focus or completely off target. But she'd got seventy-three likes for the glass of fizz she'd posted, which was something.

'So, Jackie, where are you living these days?' asked Val. 'Didn't you move to Spain?'

Val's questions still had a whiff of solicitor about them. Jackie put down her phone. Her mind raced back to 1989 and the heady summer she'd spent in Majorca. 'That was a while back. Boy did we have fun. I flew out with a Juan and came home with a Greg.' Pauline smiled. Val looked nonplussed. 'I've got a place in Leytonstone; it's handy for work and the city is only a few stops on the tube.'

'You're still working?' Zara looked like she would be frowning if only her forehead could crease.

'Yeah. I love it. I'm nursing at a private care home.'

'Still scouting for potential husbands?' asked Val.

'Blimey no. They're far too old for me. But they are sweethearts. It pays the bills and the few quid cash in hand here and there for running errands helps.'

'Sounds like you're running a racket,' said Zara, with a twinkle in her eye.

'Just a few bets on the horses. And the dogs. A bit of contraband alcohol. It all brightens up their days. I'm doing a public service really. And if they want to tip me for helping them out then I'm fine with that. Some of them never have a visitor and the little bit I do brightens up an otherwise dull existence.'

'That's nice,' said Pauline. 'It's kind of you.' Bless Pauline – she was still as lovely as ever. And probably as naïve, thought Jackie.

'How about you?' Jackie nodded at Pauline.

Pauline's eyes dropped to the table. 'I lived on Mersea Island for a while. But now I'm back renting a place in Hackney. It's small but fine. I can afford it, which is a bonus.'

'Any men in your life?' asked Jackie. Pauline had always struck her as perfect wife material. Exactly what men were really looking for. They liked girls like Jackie for fun and sex but when it came to marriage they wanted someone nice, ordinary and dependable.

'Not since I lost my husband.'

'My condolences,' said Zara, reaching out and patting

her arm. 'I've lost a few. Granted most of mine were in the divorce courts but it still stings.'

Pauline nodded. 'Heart attack.'

'I'm sorry,' said Val, squeezing Pauline's shoulder.

'That's awful,' agreed Zara.

'Horrible,' said Jackie. 'Sorry, Pauline.'

'It's okay. He wasn't the nicest person...' With a shaky hand Pauline took a sip of her drink.

'We've all been there,' said Zara and the others nodded in unison.

'You should get a pet,' said Val. She caught Jackie rolling her eyes at her. But this was typical Val. Always telling people what they should do. She'd not changed either.

'Definitely more reliable than a man,' said Zara. 'Probably better housetrained too.'

'I'm not sure. I like cats but it's a responsibility.' Pauline returned to staring into her mug.

'Zara, you've always got a man on your arm. Who is it at the moment?' asked Jackie.

Zara sighed. She tilted her head before speaking as if delivering a performance. 'Sadly nobody. I am all alone. The men dried up a few years ago. Partly their decision and partly mine. I'm afraid something switches as you get older. Maybe it's the business I'm in but once you stop looking beautiful...' She paused and then waved away their protestations of her beauty that eventually came. 'They see you simply as a bank account. Rogues and charlatans are all I seem to attract these days. And nobody wants a decrepit old woman with the memory of a stunned goldfish. I'm better off alone.' She turned her head and gazed out of the tall windows with dramatic effect.

'Val,' said Jackie, and Val stared her down as if daring her to ask her the same question. But Jackie had never been afraid of Val. 'Still no men in your life?'

'No,' said Val. They glowered at each other until Pauline cleared her throat. Pauline had never liked it when they'd bumped heads but for Jackie it was sport.

'You've had some fabulous roles,' said Pauline, fixing her gaze on Zara in a clear attempt to distract them.

Zara pulled a face. 'I have in the past. But not these days. I get the odd cameo. Some voice work, which is good because I can do it from pretty much anywhere in the world. I don't get invited onto chat shows anymore as they're purely for actors with something to sell. It's not about who the audiences want to see interviewed. You can't really call them interviews anymore; they're chatty adverts.'

'Surely you've retired,' said Jackie. Given Zara's look of surprise that she was still grafting in a care home she'd assumed Zara had stopped treading the boards and was now living in the lap of luxury. Zara was minted. She'd had peaks and troughs in her varied career but it was something Jackie had paid close attention to, especially all the interviews from far-flung residences. Photographs of holidays on yachts and generous donations she'd made to charities littered the celebrity rags. She didn't like to think of herself as a jealous person but it was hard not to think that maybe you'd got a raw deal when you saw a friend's life go off in a much better direction than your own.

'Darling, I'm an act-or.' She laboured the vowels. 'We never retire; they simply stop offering us work. Acting… isn't just what I do; it's who I am. It's everything really. Where I feel at home and what I truly love. Without it I'm quite lost.' Her voice trailed off at the end. The mask slipping for a moment. 'Anyway, it doesn't do to be maudlin. That leads to frowning and that breeds wrinkles and goodness knows they are already virulent. More drinks please, someone,' she said, downing the rest of her G&T and offering up her glass.

12

VAL

Val took the glasses and went to refill them. There were plenty of mixers but little food in the fridge and even less in the freezer – only ice. She figured Zara was perhaps due to jet off somewhere. Val didn't begrudge Zara her lifestyle one jot. She was quite proud to be able to call her a friend even if it had been a while since they'd spoken. No, she wasn't envious of Zara. It was more that her own life was lacking a little something and it had been ever since she'd retired. Work had been all-consuming, which she acknowledged probably wasn't entirely healthy but, like Zara, she had loved her job. For a long time it was all she had and she'd clung to it.

As a family solicitor she felt she had helped people through a difficult period in their lives and hopefully had got the best results for everyone. It had in some way helped to ease her own family situation by knowing that she was helping others. Because despite her best efforts her own family was lost to her.

She made the drinks and returned to the living room where the conversation had moved on to memories of their time sharing a house.

'Val, you remember when I locked myself out after that big awards dinner. Don't you?' asked Zara, trying to suppress giggles. 'When Roger Moore climbed in through the window and Jackie thought he was the Milk Tray man!'

They all hooted with laughter.

'I thought he was a rubbish Milk Tray man because he'd forgotten the chocolates,' said Jackie. She eyed the iced water that Val handed her with disdain. 'I don't suppose there's any gin in that?' she asked.

'Nope. You still need to flush your system out,' said Val, offering around the other drinks.

'I remember that party we had where I couldn't get to work the next day because people were sleeping on the stairs and blocking the front door,' recalled Val.

Jackie shook her head. 'Don't remember that.'

'You were probably still in bed... with someone,' said Val.

'Probably,' said Jackie, with a shrug. 'I knew how to party. And I still do.' She raised her iced water in a toast.

'Was that the party where Lionel Blair was trying to teach us to tap-dance?' asked Zara.

'Yes,' said Val, clicking her fingers. 'And Cilla was getting cross with him because he was going too fast.'

More laughter filled the room. The celebrity stories flowed now, sprinkled with gossipy snippets from Zara, which Pauline and Jackie lapped up. Val had never been that wowed by the famous folk Zara socialised with. They were still just people after all.

'I remember us living on jacket potatoes and beans,' said Pauline, when there was a pause in conversation.

'Apart from on a Sunday when we went to that place up Brompton way that did a massive Sunday roast,' added Val.

Jackie was frowning. 'I remember you forcing me out of bed dead early on Sundays to get there.'

'Early?' queried Val. 'It was last meal orders at two o'clock and we only ever made it by the skin of our teeth.'

'You could ring your order in nowadays. Or do it via an app.' Jackie waved her phone. 'I wonder sometimes how we ever managed without mobiles. The youth of today haven't got a clue how lucky they are.'

'I remember waiting by that old Bakelite telephone we had in the draughty hallway for my mum to call on a Sunday evening,' said Pauline.

'And Zara walking up and down the hall carrying it as she spoke,' added Jackie.

'And you…' Zara pointed at Jackie. 'Chatting for hours to your latest bloke and hogging the line when I was waiting to hear about parts.'

'They were simpler times,' said Val, feeling a little melancholy. She wouldn't drink any more tonight. Alcohol always sent her blood sugar haywire and as a diabetic she had to be mindful of that.

'Bloody marvellous times,' said Zara. 'No aching limbs, no getting up in the night for a pee, no wondering if your next breath would be your last.'

'Wow, that turned dark really quickly,' said Jackie, with a snigger.

Val scowled at her. She was starting to get a feeling that

all wasn't well with Zara. 'Is there something you're not telling us?' asked Val.

Zara sighed loudly. 'I'm getting old and I don't like it,' she said.

'Sadly we're all more Mary Berry than Halle Berry,' said Jackie. Val shot her a look. Why did she always treat everything like a joke?

Val turned her attention back to Zara. 'We're all getting older and to my mind it beats the alternative.' She smiled at Zara in the hope it would lift her spirits.

'The alternative being death?' asked Jackie. 'Bloody hell, Val. You're such a mood hoover.' She shook her head.

'Stop,' said Zara, waving a ring-bedecked hand. 'You can't turn the clock back and be young again. I know that. But what if you could recreate it?'

'Go on,' said Jackie, sitting up and setting the chair off on another slow spin.

'I'm thinking out loud here,' said Zara, becoming animated as her hands joined in the conversation. 'We're all on our own. No family to speak of. Why spend our lives alone when we could be together?'

'For like a holiday?' asked Pauline.

'I was thinking permanently,' said Zara. There were confused looks all round. 'Think about it. Why be alone for our twilight years when we could have fun every evening like we have tonight? We're not getting any younger and one by one...' she pointed at each of them in turn '...we could have problems if we're on our own. But together we could look out for each other.'

'You're serious?' Jackie smirked over her glass.

'Totally!' Zara threw up her arms. 'It solves all our

problems. It's perfect. And none of us end up in some stinking nursing home.'

'Hey, I already spend most of my time in one of those stinking nursing homes,' said Jackie. 'Well, you know what I mean.'

Pauline gave an uneasy chuckle. 'You're joking.'

'Never been more serious,' said Zara, and she knocked back her gin.

Val recoiled and was thankful the others didn't seem to notice her silence. Today had been lovely but she wasn't ready to move in with them. She'd worked hard to be mortgage-free and she needed her own space. Granted she was occasionally lonely. She'd been estranged from her parents and they'd died a few years back. Her sister lived in New Zealand but she had clubs and friends nearby. She had a life. Zara's idea was fraught with problems. 'There are quite a few issues with shared property ownership,' said Val, trying to take the practical angle and hoping she didn't sound too negative.

Zara laughed. 'No, you don't need to sell up. I meant move in with me. I have a big place that I rattle around in. You don't need to pay any rent or bills. You can even rent your places out, make a bit of money.'

Zara was off on one of her fantasies. They had been more elaborate when she was younger and she had been expert at whisking them all up with her. As it turned out Zara's life had turned out quite like the fantasies she had imagined. But Val still had her feet firmly on the ground.

'I'm not sure,' said Pauline, swallowing hard.

'I think it's the drink talking,' said Jackie, looking a little disappointed.

Zara turned her attention to Val. 'You're the sensible one. This makes sense from a financial perspective because you'd all have more spare cash. They bang on about mental health these days; being together would definitely improve that. From a caring perspective there would always be someone on hand to raise an alarm if one of us was unwell and also it would stop any of us spending our last days alone. And if we're all honest doesn't that scare you the most?' She raised her chin and appraised the impact of her little speech.

'I'm sorry, Zara. As lovely as that fantasy is, I think we're all settled in our lives. It's not really for me,' said Val.

Zara slumped back into her seat, the hint of a pout on her lips. 'It was merely a suggestion. More for your benefit than mine.' Zara yawned into the back of her hand. That was their cue to leave.

13

PAULINE

The days after the party had been quite good. Well, good in comparison to a standard day for Pauline. She'd relived the party and the chat back at Zara's afterwards a thousand times. She had been buoyed by seeing her friends but now she was back in the dull routine of life. Her pointless little life. Her tiny flat seemed to have grown smaller. The walls squeezed the air from her lungs. She wiped down the battered table again. She'd move into the lounge in a few minutes but not before three o'clock. It was like a little reward to have a change of scenery for the afternoon. Even if it was swapping bland walls for four more bland walls. At least she had cushions in the lounge.

She'd had a few texts from Val since the party. It was nice to have someone to communicate with. She knew Val sensed something amiss which, she suspected, was why she was finding excuses to message her. Val was checking up on her. Pauline quite liked that. There was nobody else in her life who would be bothered if she was alive or dead. When she'd left Mersea she left behind the few friends she'd made there. A couple of them had persisted but had soon got bored with chasing someone who didn't respond. Breaking ties with them was for the best though. After Ivan's death she'd needed to get away from the small community and wagging tongues of Mersea Island. But all she knew was London, which left her little choice. Her options had been further whittled down by the cost of renting in the city.

Pauline had really liked Zara's house. She'd enjoyed history at school and she liked the thought of all the different people who might have lived in the Regency building. She'd thought about Zara's pie-in-the-sky suggestion that they all move in with her. Whilst she loved the idea of it she also feared change. Her flat wasn't much but as long as she paid the rent it was a roof over her head. If she moved in with Zara what happened if they fell out? She'd be homeless. As a child who had spent her life in the care system she'd always felt she was one wrong move away from the streets. It was her greatest fear: that and prison. A shiver went through her. One day her past would catch up with her – she knew that. She banished the dark thoughts from her mind. Perhaps she would move to the lounge earlier today. She put the kettle on to make her third cup of tea of the day and the last one for that teabag.

The doorbell screeched. Another parcel for next door, she thought as she went to answer it. Zara was the last person she expected to see on her doorstep. She was standing there dressed to the nines and inspecting her finger as if by pressing the doorbell she may have picked up a communicable disease.

'Zara. Hello.' Pauline was beyond surprised to see her

and more than a little self-conscious of her home. She pulled the door to behind her to hide the shabby interior. *Please don't want to come in*, she thought wrapping her cardigan tightly around herself.

'Darling,' said Zara, giving her elaborate air kisses. 'I can't stop. I'm on my way to do a radio interview about this whole age debacle. Bloody Jules. It's blown up into quite the media storm.' Zara looked thrilled at the prospect.

Pauline pushed her hair back behind her ears. She knew there was no need to feel underdressed on her own doorstep but she did. 'What can I do for you?'

'I thought about what you said and I made a few phone calls. And guess what? A friend of a friend had one left. She needed someone to take it off her hands. And I knew you were thinking about getting one.'

Zara wasn't making sense, that or Pauline had finally lost the plot. Pauline scanned Zara's hands. She wasn't carrying anything. 'One what?' As she asked she spotted Zara's driver carrying things up the path.

'A cat,' said Zara, looking delighted.

Shock coursed through Pauline's system. 'Oh, um, I don't think that—'

'He's weaned and has had all his jabs. He's even got a passport. Here you go.' Zara pulled a wodge of paperwork from her designer handbag and handed it to Pauline.

Pauline scanned the papers. 'But I couldn't. I've not got—'

'Everything you need is in that box,' said Zara, as the driver handed it over. It was heavy so all Pauline could do was reverse back inside and put it down.

'Look, Zara. It's a lovely thought b—'

'You don't need to thank me. My friend said he was left

behind because he was the runt of the litter and I thought of you. Poor thing.' Pauline wasn't sure who Zara was referring to. Zara seemed mightily pleased with herself as she took the fancy wicker cat carrier from her driver and thrust it into Pauline's arms.

Pauline was about to protest again but from deep inside the carrier two big eyes were looking at her. Eyes full of something she recognised – fear.

'I've got to go. But we must meet up again soon. We should have a conference call – the four of us – or a video chat. I'll get my P.A. to set something up. Ciao, Pauline.' Zara was already at the car as she blew a kiss and her driver helped her into the back seat.

Pauline stood there for a few moments after the car had pulled away clutching the carrier to her chest. The grey tabby kitten let out a pitiful yowl. What on earth had just happened?

14

JACKIE

Once she'd got over her monster hangover the party looked a lot better. It had provided her with umpteen stories to share with the care home residents. All of them getting more and more elaborate each time she told them and the celebrity guest list was also increasing. It didn't do any harm and it certainly seemed to cheer people up, and that was what she liked to do. Her mum and dad had both ended up in a home. She wished now that she'd visited more often. They'd died, in quick succession, a couple of years ago but only after their nursing care had devoured all their assets.

'Hey, Mr Wiggins, how's tricks?' she asked, entering his room. 'You had a cracking win yesterday didn't you?'

She handed over the cash. 'Jackie, you're a star. Here, take this. Treat yourself.' He passed her back a handful of notes. She didn't count it. She needed it for her colossal credit card bill, which had just landed with an almighty thud. The party might have been fun but the cost of the outfit wasn't looking smart now and she couldn't seem to shift the thing on eBay either, which wasn't helping.

'You're too kind. Now what's the smart money on today, Mr W?'

'Dogs,' he said, handing her a list and forty pounds of his winnings.

Jackie picked up his empty teacup. 'No problem. Leave it with me. Tea and a biscuit?'

'Yes please, Jackie.'

She had a smile on her face when she opened the door to leave but the face that met her quickly made it slip away.

'Jackie, we need to talk. My office,' said the care home manager, turning on his heel and not giving her a chance to reply.

He was a bit abrupt but then he was a serious sort of man, so it could simply be about wanting her to do extra shifts. She hoped that was what it was, because the additional money would be very timely. At worst it was probably about her not cleaning something properly or leaving cups in the sink – she was always getting reminded about that. He pointed to the chairs opposite his desk and she sat down.

'How are you?' she asked, with a friendly smile.

He frowned at her from across the desk. 'It has come to my attention that you are taking money from residents.'

'What?' Jackie sat up straight. 'I've never stolen a thing. Whoever said that is lying. That's libel.'

'Slander,' he replied.

'That too.' Jackie was furious. She'd never even nicked a biscuit. She was lots of things but a thief wasn't one of them.

'Could you turn your pockets out please?'

Jackie gulped. 'You can't make me do that.' She wasn't entirely sure of her rights but she knew as soon as she put the notes on the table she was as good as admitting it.

'No, but if you have nothing to hide then you'll put the contents of your pockets on the table.'

'That's not the point. It's a civil liberties thing.' She was grasping at straws. Her pulse was starting to race. This was not a good situation.

'Fine,' he said. 'Then I need to remind you that it's against our policy for staff to accept gifts of any sort from residents. And we have it on good authority that you have been taking money.'

'Oh right. That's a bit better than being accused of thieving. But I didn't realise that. I'm really sorry.' She obviously did know she wasn't meant to take the tips but it was the top-up her meagre salary needed and it wasn't doing anyone any harm. 'It won't happen again. I promise.' She gave him her most sincere smile.

'No, it won't because I'm afraid it's a dismissible offence. Consider your contract terminated with immediate effect.'

'What?'

'I said—'

'Yes. I know what you said. But you can't sack me for that.'

'I can and I am. This home has a reputation to maintain and besides that relatives get very upset about this sort of thing.'

'Hang on. I'll give back all the money.' All the tips she'd had over the years flashed through her mind, making her reword her offer. 'I'll return the money in my pocket.' She clarified. 'And I promise I won't accept any more. So we can just go back to how we were. Okay?' She nodded in the hope it would encourage him to join in.

'I'm sorry, Jackie. I don't have any leeway here. The owners are explicit about this sort of thing.'

'Come on. You can turn a blind eye if you want to. Please. I need this job.' Jackie didn't like to beg but she was fast running out of options.

'My hands are tied. But if you want to return the money I think that would be a nice gesture.'

'Stuff off. I bloody well earned that.' She stood up abruptly, making the manager do the same. She was furious, mainly at herself for getting caught. She was also scared of what this meant. Where was she going to get another job at her age?

'You'll be paid up until yesterday. If you could post your uniform back that would be helpful.'

'If I'm posting it anywhere it's up your arse!' she said, as she stormed out of his office slamming the door behind her.

15

VAL

Val's house was lovely but the outside space was a little sparse. She turned her garden chair around but it was still in the shade. Pretty much the whole courtyard was in the shade after about two o'clock. She'd made it nice with pots and a couple of climbing plants but she would have loved to have had a garden to potter in now she had the spare time. She closed her eyes and listened. London hurried about its business. She'd thought a lot about what Zara had said after the party and couldn't help wondering what was driving such a suggestion. It was true that Zara did a lot for charity and had always paid her way but in Val's experience there was often an underlying reason for her generosity. She felt a little bad for thinking it but it was a niggle that wouldn't go away. So she was more than circumspect when her laptop sprang into life on the nearby garden table, reminding her of the video conference call Zara had set up.

Val found the email from Zara's personal assistant and clicked on the link. Up popped four windows. There was a chorus of greetings as everyone spoke over each other, apologised and then laughed.

'My darlings,' began a radiant-looking Zara, from behind designer sunglasses. 'Look at you all looking gorgeous...' Val studied the screen. Jackie looked tired or possibly hungover and she could only really see the top of Pauline's head and a lot of Artexed ceiling. She checked her own image. She looked fine.

'Pauline, can you angle your camera down a bit?' asked Val.

'Oops, sorry,' said Pauline, coming into shot for a second and then immediately tilting it back towards the ceiling. Perhaps it was a pyjama day for her.

'I am over the moon that we could do this,' said Zara. 'Now we have reconnected it is important to me that we keep in touch. I've been busy, busy, busy what with radio and television interviews. Jules is finally earning his money and set up a couple of hush-hush conversations I can't possibly disclose. But enough about me; what have you all been up to?'

They were all quiet. Val hated that. 'Well, I went to a wine tasting last night with some friends, which was fun, and I've been pottering in the garden today.'

'Val, you must come out to France. They have the most amazing vineyard tours – you would love them. Forget the substandard bottles they ship over to poor old Blighty; the wine they keep for themselves is incredible.'

'That sounds good,' said Jackie. 'Maybe I could get a job picking grapes.'

'Like a busman's holiday?' asked Pauline's fringe.

'No, like I've been sodding well sacked and if I don't get

a job in the next week I'm going to miss my rent payment and I'm already behind with the credit cards – basically, I'm screwed.' Jackie stared into the camera and lifted a mug to her lips.

'That's unfortunate, Jackie. I hate to ask but did they have grounds to sack you? If not I could give you some advice,' offered Val.

Jackie puffed out a breath. 'Kind of but it's all been blown out of proportion. I used to run errands for some of the residents and apparently them tipping me a couple of quid is against the rules.'

'Ah,' said Val. 'I'm afraid there's little I can do then. You need to register for benefits.'

'Yeah, that's easier said than done. Loads of forms and it all moves slower than an arthritic snail. No offence.' Val hoped Zara didn't pick up on Jackie's thoughtless comment.

'Jackie, that's awful,' said Pauline, her eyes – briefly coming into shot – full of concern. 'Is there anything we can do?'

Jackie shrugged. 'It's my mess and I need to sort it. But if you've got a spare room I can bunk in that would be handy as a back-up. You know, in case the worst happens.'

'Umm I can't help you there,' said Pauline. 'My landlord has given me a month to either get rid of my cat or move out.'

Zara's hands shot to her face, making the many bangles on her wrist jangle. 'Oh no, Pauline. I am so sorry.'

'It's okay really. It's not your fault.' Pauline's eyes scanned the other faces. 'Zara got me a cat a few weeks ago and he's been a revelation. Having something else to care for gives you a purpose. He's a proper little character too. The thought of parting with him breaks my heart.' Emotion caught in Pauline's throat.

'What are you going to do?' asked Val, who could see only one option.

'You can't give him up – he's the runt,' said Zara. 'Poor little soul has already had a tough start in life. There must be properties that take pets.'

'Not as many as you'd think,' said Pauline. 'I've been looking but there's nothing in my price range.'

'Any friends who could take him?' suggested Jackie. 'Then you could at least get updates.'

Pauline appeared to wipe away a tear as she shook her head. 'There's no one.'

'Darling, don't worry.' Zara reached a hand towards the screen. 'We'll think of something. We'll save little... what did you call him?'

'Brian,' said Pauline. Jackie laughed and almost choked on her drink.

'Jackie, maybe you should mute yourself,' suggested Val. Jackie pulled a face but did as Val suggested.

Pauline continued. 'I named him after Brian May from Queen. He was my first love.'

'Did I introduce you?' asked Zara.

'I've never met him. He was the first person I had a crush on,' explained Pauline, her forehead puckering.

'Oh, I see. Well, darling. We can fix that. Bri and Anita often holiday near Nice, which is a stone's throw from my villa.'

Pauline's full face came into view her eyes big and round. 'Seriously?'

'Absolutely,' said Zara. 'So, Valerie. How are things with you?'

'Good thanks,' said Val.

'That's lovely to hear. I've been thinking since we met up...' Here it comes, thought Val. 'And I know it was a spur-of-the-moment crazy suggestion but now with what you've told me, Jackie, about losing your job and, Pauline, your issue with Brian. Perhaps it wasn't that crazy after all. We did have a wonderful time when we lived together. Didn't we?' Everyone nodded. 'I just want to say that my offer is genuine. You only need to say the word and I'll get the place ready.'

Jackie put her mug down and started speaking but there was no sound. 'You're still on mute,' said Val.

'—king thing,' muttered Jackie. 'I hate to be the one to ask but how much would the rent be?'

'Nothing,' said Zara. 'I was thinking that perhaps if we all utilised our skills. All do our bit, that would be enough.'

'How do you mean exactly?' asked Val, keen to understand what her friends might be committing to.

'Well, Pauline, you're a trained secretary, right?'

'I was. I mean I'm a bit rusty.'

'I've been asked to write my autobiography and I was thinking that you could type while I dictate. And I know that's a one-off thing but I've also been offered a magazine column. You would be using your skills and in return you would have free lodging. We both win.'

'What would you want from me?' asked Jackie, leaning into the camera.

'I'm on all sorts of medication,' said Zara. 'I could do

with a medic around the place. Someone to make sure I'm taking the right pill at the right time.'

'Administer tablets – that's all?'

'And reassure me when I think I'm having a stroke or a heart attack,' said Zara, with a hollow laugh. 'Val, I could also do with someone I trust to keep an eye on my financial affairs.'

'Then you need an accountant,' said Val. She wasn't getting sucked in to this fantasy, that appeared to be spiralling out of control before her eyes.

'It's more keeping an eye on the accountant and also the legal documentation for pensions, shares and invest-ments that I find quite dull but really should pay more attention to.' There was a pause and Zara appeared to be scanning their faces. 'What do we think?'

'I'm in,' said Jackie. Just like that without any thought – it was completely reckless and typical Jackie.

'Fantastic!' Zara clapped her hands together and the bracelets jingled happily. 'Pauline? You and Brian would be most welcome.'

Pauline's tiny kitchen came into view. Drab Seventies units in orange glared into the camera as Pauline bit her lip. 'I don't know. I am tempted, really I am. But it would be such a big upheaval.'

'But if you're keeping Brian then you've got to move somewhere anyway,' chipped in Jackie.

'I guess.' Pauline closed her eyes. 'Let me think about it.'

'So, Valarie,' said Zara, removing her sunglasses and speaking directly to the camera. 'One for all and all that. Are you up for getting the girls back together again? Are you in?'

'Thanks, Zara, but it's not for me,' said Val, although she couldn't deny she already felt like she was going to be missing out.

16

PAULINE

Pauline had treated herself to a trip on the train as it was quite a way to Val's place and would have taken hours by bus. The fact that they were technically both living in London obscured the fact that they were fifteen miles apart and easily an hour and a half's car journey. Not that she had a car.

She felt something of a marvel. Here she was, Pauline Crozier, travelling across London by train all on her own. And yes she was scared and her palms were sweaty but she was out and she was doing it. Something had changed in Pauline. Since the arrival of Brian in her life she had a reason to get up in the morning. She knew a lot of people would mock her for it but she didn't care. Life now seemed to have a purpose. Brian relied on her for food, shelter and affection and in return he gave her love, a purpose and quite a few judgemental looks. The latter were actually quite helpful. He had scanned her up and down that morning with the critical eye of a fashion designer.

'What?' she'd asked him. 'I'm only going to Val's.' She had scanned her sweatshirt and leggings ensemble. Brian had been right: she could do better. She had returned to her wardrobe and after rummaging in the back she'd found some boot-cut jeans and a cotton jacket, which both fit. She couldn't do up the jacket but it was warm outside so she could get away with wearing it loose.

Having Brian wasn't a miracle cure. She still had her demons who worked hard to bring her down. Things she regretted had become shadows that haunted her dreams – letting her know she'd never be able to forget what she'd done. The fact that she was soon to be homeless was also wreaking havoc on her state of mind but Zara had thrown her a life raft and she was clinging to it.

It was a bit of a walk from Richmond station to Val's place but the sun was out and the blue sky was dotted with wispy clouds, making Richmond far prettier than Pauline had realised. Val had given her good directions and even sent her an annotated map to follow so she didn't have to use up her phone's data on maps.

Val's house was in a neat terrace. Next door's garden was a little overgrown but the 'let' sign lying on the lawn was likely the reason for that. There was music coming from somewhere nearby but otherwise it was a serene place – especially for London. Pauline knocked the door and waited.

'You found it,' said Val, opening the door and ushering Pauline inside before giving her a brief hug of welcome. 'Come through to the garden.' Val marched off.

Pauline followed her through a hallway and an extended kitchen, the like of which she'd only seen in magazines.

There was a walk-through utility room and then they were out in a small courtyard garden.

'Tea?' asked Val. 'Or coffee? I've got a machine that does lattes from pods. It's not the same as shop-bought but it hits the spot.'

'Ooh yes please. A latte sounds lovely.' Pauline took a seat and admired her surroundings while Val went to get drinks. There were lots of flowering plants and sunny patches. Brian would love an outdoor space like this, she mused. She could picture him stretched out in the sunshine. She'd not had a chance to look at the outside of Zara's house after the party but she was guessing it probably had a garden, which would be much better for Brian than the main road she currently lived on – not that she'd actually let him outside yet. She'd been too scared of losing him, partly because of the busy road but also because she feared if he realised there were better places to live he'd move.

Val returned with the drinks. 'Now if you've come here to persuade me to join you and Jackie in this frankly quite mad trip down memory lane then I'm afraid you're wasting your time.'

'Oh,' was all Pauline could manage, quite taken a back. It was stridently forthright even for Val.

'I'm sorry. I don't want to upset you, Pauline, but I also don't want to feel blackmailed into joining you.'

'Heavens, no. That wasn't my intention.' Although now she thought about it, from Val's perspective that might have been exactly how it would have looked.

'Grand. Is it all going ahead?' asked Val, appearing genuinely interested.

'Well, I've only had a few messages from Zara's P.A. but

it all seems to be happening. Any large items like furniture that I want to take with me are being collected a couple of days before and then on the day it's just me, Brian and a case.' A shiver went through her as she said it out loud for the first time. 'It's all moving quite fast really.'

'Pauline, please don't be railroaded by Zara and Jackie. They are strong characters. Are you sure it's what you want?'

'I don't really have a lot of choice,' said Pauline, voicing what was troubling her. 'But at the same time I quite like the idea of having company.'

'Haven't you got Brian for that now?' Val arched an eyebrow.

'I guess.' Pauline picked her mug up and then put it down again. 'Look, Val. I'll be honest with you. When we shared a place you were the one who kept me sane. You stopped me getting caught up in Jackie and Zara's fights and hare-brained schemes and whilst I'm sure they've grown out of that—' Val's expression said she disagreed '—I'm still apprehensive about living with—' She stopped as a drum solo kicked off at full volume from the neighbouring house. Pauline turned to look but there was nothing to see. 'Blimey that's loud.'

Val's jaw tightened. 'New neighbours.'

'Phil Collins is it?' Pauline had lived through more than her fair share of noisy neighbours. 'That's not good.'

'No. I've spoken to them and they are really lovely people but they don't seem to realise the amount of noise they make. I now spend a lot of time out here.'

'That won't work come the winter,' said Pauline.

'It won't. The place was sold recently and almost

immediately it was let out. I fear this could be a cycle as different tenants come and go. I'm hoping my strongly worded letter to the letting agent will have an impact but I'm now thinking that I'll have to involve the local authority.'

'They might be gone in a few months. Then you might get a nice family.'

Val looked alarmed. 'Families aren't quiet either.'

'Someone who doesn't make any noise then.'

'I truly hope so.' Val sighed. Pauline felt for her. She remembered how important peace and quiet was to Val. How she used to take herself off to her room for what she called 'thinking time'. Jackie used to scoff but Pauline understood how she felt. There were only so many times you could tell Jackie and Zara to keep it down. 'Anyway, you were saying?' prompted Val.

Pauline had to have a think. 'I was going to own up and say that I had come here to ask you if you'd come over to Zara's. I don't expect you to move in but I thought if you came over regularly that might... I don't know...' Pauline shook her head. She wasn't sure what she was asking for. 'I just liked the idea of all of us being there. Four is balanced. Three means two against one – that someone gets overridden or left out. Please don't be a stranger.' Pauline sipped her coffee – it was divine. 'Mmm this is lovely, thank you.'

Val eyed her from over her mug. Pauline could almost hear Val's brain whirring. Was she considering what she'd said? 'I want to help you, Pauline. I really do. I understand probably better than Jackie and Zara that this is a huge change for you. I'm not a million miles away. You'll be in

Belgravia – which is forty-five minutes give or take – so yes, I will come and visit for a coffee but I can't hold your hand.'

'I understand,' said Pauline. She was a bit deflated by Val's statement but she knew she was right. They weren't twenty-somethings anymore. She needed to steel herself for the change that was coming. She just hoped it was for the best.

17

JACKIE

The move really couldn't come soon enough for Jackie. Her credit card juggling was Barnum-worthy and she'd sold off anything of value either through the local Cash Converters or eBay. She had been surprised how well her old clothes had sold once she'd labelled them vintage and classic. She'd become a regular at her post office, taking down parcels on an almost daily basis. The chap behind the counter there was quite sweet too, which made for a nice interlude in an otherwise dull day.

She was missing her job. Not the side she called 'mucking out' but the rest of it. The residents at the home had been like friends. Regular faces and, she now realised, she got as much from their daily interactions as they did. Whilst she'd always thought of it as her updating them on what was happening in the outside world she now wondered if it had been more about her needing to share with another human being.

Finding herself in dire financial straits had also shown

her who her real friends were, as the few she did have had gone awfully quiet of late. She suspected they feared she may turn up on their doorstep with bin bag in hand. She wasn't quite at that stage yet but if Zara didn't firm up a date soon she was going to have to do something. She'd suggested to Zara's P.A. that she move in now but was told that because Zara was away working for a couple of weeks that wouldn't be possible. Jackie didn't like to point out that she'd seen Zara post on social media that she was recording an audiobook in London but she couldn't afford to upset her new landlady.

A couple of people had asked about her plans – one of those being her landlord. And she had been happy to share that her good friend the famous actress, Zara Cliff, had invited her to stay indefinitely as part of a package as her new medication supervisor. She'd come up with the job title herself after an evening on Google and a couple of polls on Twitter. But if she was honest with herself she had some doubts.

Looking back was always lovely when you had your rose-tinted specs on but some of her memories of that time were less than perfect. Four young women with different jobs and ambitions, varying moods and vastly different back-grounds had led to many shouting matches, slammed doors and hurtful words. Whilst she could see that they had all got older she was pretty sure the same women were lurking underneath the wrinkles and it wouldn't take too much for them to reappear. At least if Val wasn't joining them that was a help. She and Val had rubbed along okay for the most part but a massive falling-out had ended their friendship and that wasn't a scab she wanted to pick.

At least she still had Stefan. He was a twinkle of light in the gloom. He'd been busy of late with work and dates had to fit around his schedule. It was Thursday, the weather was good and she'd just sold an Eighties rara dress for more than she'd hoped for. Watching things sell was actually even more addictive than bidding and winning things. She decided she would package up the dress and get it straight in the post. That would hopefully get her a nice five-star rating from the recipient to balance out the one star for the customer who had been unhappy with the 'crop top' that had lost its label and thanks to a quick spin in the tumble dryer had come out a couple of sizes smaller than it should have been.

Jackie decided that after the post office she'd pop into the supermarket and grab whatever meat was on offer, some salad and rolls and she'd get a barbecue going for when Stefan got in from work at about six. She wasn't much of a cook but she could grill stuff and for some reason people always seemed impressed if you did that outside, less so indoors. She could probably stretch to a bottle of wine, which would make for a lovely evening.

Armed with her discounted sausages Jackie had a spring in her step as she let herself into Stefan's flat. She put the wine on the worktop and was opening the fridge when she was aware of a noise elsewhere in the house. She stopped and listened – it was probably coming from next door. Or maybe it wasn't. It was a two-up, two-down, which wouldn't take much checking. Still carrying the sausages, she inched her way upstairs now somewhat aware that she could be about to face a burglar. Perhaps she should have checked the back of the house for a forced entry before she went all Dempsey and Makepeace.

By the time she reached the top step she was pretty sure she could identify the sounds and where they were coming from. Unless of course Stefan had gone to work and left the *Fifty Shades of Grey* DVD on repeat – oh how she wished that was the case. Jackie nudged the bedroom door and it swung open to reveal a large mass jiggling rhythmically underneath the discounted duvet cover she'd bought him. She froze. Should she wait until they'd finished or cough politely? Then she remembered that she didn't really go in for all that sort of thing and she hurled the sausages at the writhing lump. The lump stopped moving with the pack of sausages now precariously balanced on top.

'What the shitting hell is going on?' she asked. Rage swept through her. She was ready for a cat fight. She strode forward, grabbed the duvet and wrenched it off, ready to slap whichever tart was underneath her Stefan.

But she wasn't faced with a pretty younger model of herself as she'd expected. Instead it was the opposite. Two hairy bottoms.

'Jackie, I can explain,' said Stefan as the other gentleman covered his head with a pillow. It would amuse Jackie later that at that precise moment it was his head he chose to hide.

Was Stefan her long-term plan? Of course not - but they'd been going out for months and he'd made her happy. How easily her happiness was snuffed out. A plethora of abuse she could hurl at him raced through her head. But what was the point? Whatever it was she thought she had with Stefan was over and unfortunately any happy memories would now be replaced by an image that would be hard to erase.

She took a breath. 'I was going to ask if you like your sausages well done but I think I have my answer.'

18

VAL

It was Sunday morning and after very little sleep, thanks to additional drum practice next door, Val had decided to take a walk around Richmond Park. There was a light mist hovering, giving the park an almost ethereal feel, and it was calming to her fractious soul. High-spec earplugs hadn't been able to drown out the noise. When she'd been driven to the end of her fraying tether and had marched around in her dressing gown to bang on their door, they hadn't responded – most likely they couldn't hear her pounding over the drums.

Joggers and dog walkers dotted her walk. Sounds of the breeze tickled the leaves and the birdsong soothed her. She checked a bench for any unwelcome substances and gave it a rub-over with a glove she found in her coat pocket and sat down. Now she was calmer she could think. She was seventy-one and she had fought other people's battles her whole adult life. She was tired. The thought of fighting with her neighbours drained her. But she knew she couldn't simply do nothing. It wasn't in her nature and any more sleep deprivation and she'd start to go the full clockwork orange.

Zara's offer gave her an option. And if it was her decision perhaps that felt a little different. She was, and always had been, fiercely independent and that wasn't going to change. She didn't need a rent-free place to stay like Jackie or a roof over her head like Pauline – that made her situation distinctly different to theirs. She wouldn't be going because Zara was demanding it or even because Pauline made her feel guilty. She would be moving in because it suited her.

Val knew there were downsides, Jackie being one of them. She clearly hadn't changed. The rift between them wasn't something likely to be healed but in a house the size of Zara's there was space to get away from each other. The thought of helping Zara with her investments also interested her. She'd done a bit of consulting to keep her hand in and stay up to date but the legal world was high-stress and she didn't need that. She did enjoy investigating things though. And to be able to do it at her pace was definitely appealing.

When she got back to the house there was no sound of drums. Instead some foul-mouthed rapper was being blasted from speakers. She could almost feel the vibrations. That was the deciding factor. She picked up the phone and took it through to the garden, dialling Zara's number on the way.

The call was answered but Zara wasn't speaking to her. 'That goes with nothing at all. We'll have to redecorate. Tell them we need something to go with distressed orange.' Val heard a mumbled reply. 'And remember I need my diary cleared for the rest of the week except for lunch on Thursday with Elton because if I cancel on him again I won't hear the end of it.'

Val cleared her throat. 'Zara, can you hear me?'

'Darling, I'm sorry. How rude of me. It's bedlam this end. We're getting everything sorted for Jackie and Pauline moving in. Their furniture has just arrived so we're having to make a few adjustments.'

'That was what I was calling about,' said Val, feeling apprehensive. She wasn't one for snap decisions. She liked to weigh up the pros and cons of everything, preferably in a spreadsheet.

'Please tell me you've reconsidered and you're going to join us?'

'I'm considering it.'

'Marvellous!' hooted Zara. 'You've made my day.'

'I said *considering* it, Zara. I think I might be the only one who remembers the good *and* the bad of when we lived together.'

'Of course. We have all mellowed with age, which should mean fewer hormonal outbursts. I don't want to force you into anything. But then I wouldn't be – you have your own property you could return to at any time. So what's troubling you?' She made a good point.

'Well, for one thing how quiet is it?'

'Exceptionally. Half the time the neighbouring properties are empty. Business folk fly in and out and I barely see them. But then I guess I do the same.' She chuckled. 'The permanent residents on either side are about our age.' Zara was running fast and loose with 'our age' but Val let it go. Zara continued. 'All delightfully quiet people.'

Val was struggling to see a downside. 'When are the others moving in?'

'Saturday.'

'That's two days away. I don't think I can sort things that quickly. But I guess we don't all have to move in at the same time.'

'Aw, I was planning a little welcome dinner on Saturday night. You only need to throw a few things in a case. You can go back and sort the rest out later on. I know Pauline would be happier if you were here from the get-go. What do you say?'

'I think I'd like to give it a trial. Say three months. To see how it goes. I don't want to commit to something I later regret.'

'Very wise, which is exactly what I'd expect from you,' said Zara. 'And if you decide to stay you can easily rent out your house for an additional income. Top up your retirement plan.' Val did like that idea and as the rapper rose to a foul-mouthed crescendo her mind was made up.

19

PAULINE

Pauline was ready hours before the car arrived to collect her. Brian wasn't. Brian had decided that the cat carrier was to be avoided at all costs and seemed to quite enjoy the game of hide-and-seek that had followed. When Pauline did manage to corner him and try to pop him in the basket he appeared to double in size and grow extra limbs. At least it felt like that. Whichever angle she tried Brian had a leg stuck out to thwart her attempts. He was part cat, part octopus. She resorted to upending the carrier and almost dropping him in and received a scratch and a hissed protest in reply. Brian was now sitting hunched up at the far end of the carrier with his back turned to Pauline. They were not talking.

She'd had little in the way of large items to send on ahead to Zara's. Her small bookcase and a box of treasured tomes along with a blanket box of her grandmother's that had followed her from house to house. She'd taken pleasure in evicting the scarred kitchen table, which had sat on the pavement for all of six minutes before someone had walked off with it. Most of her stuff was old, battered and not worth keeping – just like her. Her mother had given her up as a toddler so it was nothing to do with age; nobody had ever wanted her. When she looked back through her life, at all the people she'd considered friends at one time or another, who was still in contact? Only Val had bothered.

The few things that wouldn't fit in her old suitcase she'd dumped in a box and sent on with the bigger items. She didn't have many clothes but it appeared she had quite a few pairs of shoes. Unlike her dress size, her shoe size had remained static and she didn't like to scrap shoes if they still had some wear in them. That was her all packed up. One suitcase, one handbag and one cat.

She looked around the small kitchen as if seeing it for the first time. She'd cleaned it and kept it tidy but that didn't detract from the fact it was a dump. She was looking forward to being somewhere nice. It made her sound superficial but the drab, unloved flat was partly to blame for her state of mind. That and being alone. Pauline had been alone most of her life really. She thought maybe one day she'd get used to it but she hadn't. At least there was nobody she needed to give her forwarding address to – every cloud, she thought. This move was a milestone. She hoped it would mark her return to a happier self. The demons were still there. But if she had some friends around her she could keep the demons outnumbered. The shriek from the doorbell made her jump. That was something she wouldn't miss.

A man in a white shirt and dark trousers was on her doorstep and a large black car was at the kerb. 'Pauline?' he asked and she nodded. 'Zara sends her best wishes and

is looking forward to seeing you. Let me take that for you.'
He reached in and took the case from her. She was grateful
as it wasn't one of those posh wheelie cases.

She put Brian's carrier down on the step while she locked
the door and posted the keys through the letterbox. The
end of an era. A really shitty one, she thought. She picked
up Brian and got in the back of the car. The driver wasn't
chatty and that suited her. The traffic was bad and he kept
checking his watch. A couple of times he turned the car
around and dashed off down a side street to try to outwit
the jams.

Eventually they pulled up at a row of terraces. A red door
opened and out came Jackie. She was wearing an orange
patterned top, leggings with high-heeled boots and was
pulling a large case brazenly decorated with bright red lips.
It was a lot bigger than Pauline's but then she had sent on a
box as well, she reminded herself.

'Hey, roomie,' said Jackie, as the driver opened the car
door for her.

'Hi, Jackie. You look terrific.' Pauline put Brian's carrier
on the floor, freeing up the seat next to her.

'Thanks. I'll be a while yet. I've got loads more.' The
driver looked worried. She turned and headed back inside.
A few more trips and Jackie declared that was everything.
She jumped in the car and sat next to Pauline.

'I didn't think to ask how big the bedrooms were,' said
Jackie doing up her seatbelt. 'I bloody hope they're huge
because I've got a king-size bed and all that lot.' She tipped
her head towards the boot where the driver was still
struggling to get it all in.

Jackie was chatty. She seemed excited at the prospect

of moving in with Zara and a little of her enthusiasm was threatening to rub off on Pauline. 'I mean we'll practically have the place to ourselves I reckon. She's always here, there and everywhere. She's got at least two other properties. And her P.A. says she has a cleaner and a part-time cook. I'm telling you, Paul, we've landed on our kitten heels here.'

The driver got back in. 'Right, next stop Belgravia. Don't worry we're a little behind schedule but I've called Alina, Zara's P.A., and she says it's fine.' He grinned at them both and they smiled back.

'Thank you,' said Pauline. She was unsure why it was all being done to a strict schedule but perhaps that was what happened when you paid people to sort things out.

Jackie relaxed into the seat. 'This is the life,' she said, looking around the car's leather-clad interior. Her eyes landed on the cat carrier. 'Is this who got you evicted?'

'Yes. He's sulking.' Brian twitched an ear but didn't move.

'He'll be fine when he's eating smoked salmon off of Royal Doulton,' said Jackie. 'He won't be sulking then.'

Pauline recognised the road as the car turned in. A neat square surrounded by stucco townhouses. The driver found a gap in the many expensive cars a couple of doors away from Zara's. He got out and walked off.

'I hope he's not expecting us to carry all that stuff,' said Jackie, undoing her seatbelt.

Jackie got out and Pauline followed. She looked up the street and was thrilled to see a familiar figure standing on the pavement.

'Oh, look it's Val.' Pauline waved. How lovely of her to be there when they arrived. The driver was walking back whilst talking into his phone. Val waved but stayed where she was.

The driver paused his conversation. 'Would you ladies mind speaking to your friend? I think there's been some confusion. I'm just trying to sort it out.' He pointed to his phone.

'Of course,' said Pauline, and she carried Brian down to Val with Jackie clip-clopping beside her in her heeled boots.

'Good morning,' said Val. 'Surprise,' she added rather half-heartedly.

'Does this mean what I think it means?' Jackie didn't sound best pleased.

'I *was* moving in too,' said Val stepping to one side to reveal a medium-sized black case.

'Oh, Val.' Pauline was overcome with emotion. Any last worries she'd had about the move dissolved. She hugged her friend. 'Thank you.'

'Was?' questioned Jackie.

'I thought it was me who was going to be the surprise today but apparently it's Zara.'

'Why?' Jackie looked up at the house.

'She's not here,' said Val.

'Never mind.' Jackie shrugged. 'I figured she wouldn't be about much anyway.' She started up the steps.

'She won't be here much because this isn't where she lives.'

'It is,' said Pauline. She didn't like the look on Val's face. Something was wrong.

'I'm afraid not,' said Val. 'Which also means this isn't where she has invited us to move to.'

Pauline was sensing a familiar black cloud descending. 'Where does Zara live, Val?'

Val sucked her bottom lip. 'France.'

20

JACKIE

Jackie spun around and headed back down the steps, which wasn't easy in her boots. She couldn't have heard that right. Could she? 'You what?'

'According to the driver Zara lives in France. She rarely uses this property. Your stuff has been shipped out to her villa there. And we are all due on a flight this morning.' Val held up her palms as if to indicate she had nothing else by way of explanation.

Pauline put the cat basket down with a bit of a thump and the creature inside let out a howl of protest. Pauline sat down on the steps, her breathing was noticeably faster.

'Are you all right?' asked Jackie.

'Obviously she's not,' said Val, sitting down beside Pauline.

'There must be some mistake,' said Pauline, shaking her head. 'I can't move to France. We...' she pointed at Brian's tail swishing inside the basket '...can't go to France.'

Jackie's brain started to join a few dots and answer a

few niggling queries she'd had but had dismissed along the way in her keenness to escape her financial situation. 'That's why Alina said we had to have valid passports,' said Jackie, pulling hers from her handbag and tapping it.

'I wondered about that too. But I assumed it was for identification purposes for any legal documents Zara wanted us to sign,' said Val.

'I thought she was joking,' said Pauline, in between gasps. 'Like she used to say bring spare pants and your passport.'

That memory made Jackie giggle. Zara had used to say that a lot. Then a thought struck her. 'But you've got a passport haven't you?' asked Jackie.

'Yes, it was the only thing I had with a photo ID so I've kept renewing it. And Brian has a passport too.'

'Who the hell is Brian?' asked Jackie.

'My cat. He came with his own passport.'

Jackie took a moment to order her thoughts while studying the splendid Regency building she'd thought was going to be her new home. The idea of having a posh address definitely appealed. She'd even thought about getting back in touch with her brother just so he would know she'd moved up in the world. Now she wasn't going to have a Belgravia address, although she'd still be living somewhere rent-free and knowing Zara her French pad wasn't going to be a dive.

'Ha!' said Jackie a little louder than she'd intended making Pauline flinch. 'This is frigging brilliant.'

'Is it?' asked Val, with her trademark scowl.

'Yes. France. Come on. It's warmer than here for a start. They have great food and more booze than you shake a baguette at. It's going to be like being permanently on holiday.' Jackie was struggling to see a downside. 'I know you're both surprised right now. Me too. But this is a good surprise. I wouldn't wonder that Zara even planned it like this.'

'I bloody well hope not, or I'll be furious with her,' said Val. 'Although her P.A. did seem confused when I said I would meet you both here this morning. She kept talking about the driver needing to pick me up but... anyway that's all irrelevant now. The situation has changed and we have decisions to make.'

'What are we going to do?' asked Pauline, her voice barely more than a whisper. 'I've handed my keys back. Brian and I are homeless.'

'Perhaps we could ask Zara about getting the keys to this place.' Val pointed at the house behind them.

'Why?' asked Jackie.

'So you two have a roof over your heads for tonight at least.' Irritation was seeping into Val's words.

'But Zara isn't here and that was kind of the main point of us all living together – for us to keep an eye on Zara.'

'Ladies,' said the driver and they all spun in his direction. 'I've spoken to Alina and she apologises profusely for any confusion. She assumed you all knew it was the French property. And I'm sorry to pressure you but you are all booked on a flight to Nice that's due to leave in just over two hours' time.'

There was a moment of stunned silence, punctuated only by Pauline's deep breathing.

'Well, I'm all for going to France,' said Jackie. She'd loved her time living in Majorca and that had all been on the cheap. Here was an offer to live in the lap of luxury rent-free. She really could see no downside. But if Val didn't go, then it was likely that Pauline wouldn't, which would leave her on her own with Zara. Not ideal – they were a bit too much alike. They needed the others to dilute their personalities. 'Val, are you staying in dreary London or are you coming for the time of your life in France?' Jackie felt a little bit of a sales pitch might help the decision-making process.

Val ignored Jackie and turned to Pauline. 'Pauline, what do *you* want to do?' she asked kindly.

Pauline took a shaky breath. 'Would you come to France?'

This was it. Crunch time. Jackie held her breath. She couldn't quite believe she was willing Val to say yes, but she was.

Val looked up to the clouds and then slowly back down at Pauline. 'Why not?'

Val always questioned everything so it wasn't obvious if she was agreeing or not. 'Is that a yes?' asked Jackie, wanting to be sure.

'Yes. I'll go to France with you pair of reprobates,' said Val, with a laugh. She looked surprised by her own decision.

'Yes!' exclaimed Jackie clapping her hands together and making the cat basket jump. 'We're only going to live in bloody France!'

'Great,' said the driver. 'Can we all get back in the car now? And quite quickly please.' He waved his hands as if trying to shoo chickens into a coop.

21

VAL

Val spent most of the forty-five-minute journey to the airport wondering what on earth she was doing. Although a tiny part of her was quite excited. Excitement was a sensation she hadn't felt for a while, not since she'd stopped practising law. Generally she wasn't a spontaneous person, never had been. She liked to take her time and weigh up the options. Being forced to make a hasty decision would usually be uncomfortable for her but this time, for some reason, it felt okay. Perhaps knowing she had a back-out plan helped. If it was truly awful she could be on a plane and home within a few hours. Although she knew from experience that Nice wasn't awful. In fact Nice was beautiful. She had stayed there for a few holidays and it said a lot that it was one of the few places she had returned to. The thought of being a couple of hours away from sitting in a pavement café with an espresso in her hand and the sea breeze on her cheeks brought a smile to her face.

'So Nice,' said Jackie. 'Is that near Paris?' She looked hopeful.

'No, it's in the south of France,' replied Val. 'The French Riviera.'

'Yeah. That's right.' Jackie nodded as if she was well aware of the location. 'Near the beach?' she asked.

'It's on a beautiful bay, with the alps behind it. It's a particularly pretty part of the country,' said Val. 'It has some fabulous museums and art galleries. There's also the Opera de Nice for ballet, classical concerts and, of course, opera.'

'Uh-huh, what's the shopping like?' asked Jackie.

Val had a think. Shopping wasn't really top of her list of things to do on holiday or any time, come to think of it. She wasn't one of life's shoppers. Clothes performed a function like a pencil or a hairbrush; they weren't something she spent a great deal of time over. 'The flower market is lovely.'

Jackie pulled a face.

'Ooh that sounds nice,' said Pauline, who appeared to be a little calmer.

Val was starting to picture places she'd been in the area. 'There are some quaint little boutiques dotted around and some big shopping centres but I've not visited those.'

Jackie perked up at the mention of shopping centres. 'Great because I sold my bikinis on eBay. I didn't think I'd have a use for them. Damn it. I would have had a full wax if I'd known.'

'Too much information,' said Val, with a shake of her head.

'I suffer from excessive hair. Well, I have done of late. It's like my body is actively trying to repel men. Do you think

Zara will have her own pool? Maybe I could pick up some Veet at the airport.'

Val shrugged and looked out of the window as they were approaching Heathrow. It felt odd and a little out of her comfort zone to be going to an airport for a trip where she wasn't in control of the booking. She knew that these days she simply had to show up with her passport but Val still liked to print everything out as proof - just in case.

A few minutes passed and she realised they had veered off their route to Heathrow. Perhaps the driver knew a quicker way. Pauline now had Brian's carrier on her lap and was hugging it. She wasn't sure whose comfort that was for.

'Does Brian have to go in with the luggage?' asked Pauline.

'I think they have a separate section for animals,' said Val.

'I hope he'll be all right.' Pauline was peering into the carrier at the rear end of the cat.

'It's a short flight. By the time we're up we'll be coming down again.' Val really hoped that sounded reassuring.

'I hope not,' said Jackie. 'I like to get a few gins in me on a flight.'

'Are you a nervous traveller?' asked Pauline.

'No.' Jackie looked puzzled by the question.

Val glanced out of the window and was surprised by what she saw. 'RAF Northolt?'

'Ooh men in uniform,' said Jackie, twisting in her seat to look out of the window.

They drove up to a barrier, where the driver spoke to someone but Val couldn't hear because Jackie was telling a story about someone she'd dated who had been in the territorial army.

'...and you can't beat a man in uniform. It has that *Officer and a Gentleman* vibe about it,' she said with a happy shudder.

'What's going on?' asked Val, although as they drove past a hangar she had a pretty good idea. They were soon facing a large expanse of tarmac. The driver was out of the car and the boot was open.

'Wow, an aeroplane,' said Jackie pointing out of the window like a four-year-old.

'Are we meant to be this close to the planes?' asked Pauline.

Val got out and looked around. 'Private jet?' she asked the driver.

He heaved Jackie's case from the boot, making his voice taut. 'Yeah.'

'Bloody hell, is that Zara's?' asked Jackie.

'No, but she uses this company regularly,' he replied, taking out the remaining luggage. 'I'll make sure these get on board. You need to show passports over there.'

'What about Brian?' asked Pauline, holding up the cat carrier where a quite cross-looking feline was staring out.

'Just show his paperwork and he can go on the plane with you.'

'That's such a relief,' said Pauline, puffing out a breath.

'Not if he craps himself mid-air it won't be,' said Jackie, twitching her nose.

'Come on,' said Val, leading the way.

It was all very casual. Their passports were checked and a few papers were ticked and before they knew it they were choosing which cream leather seat to sit on. The inside of the plane was quite small but lavishly decked out. Lots of leather, chrome and polished wood and one smiley air stewardess. She introduced herself as Melanie and explained that as she hadn't received any specific requests they had gone with Zara's usual menu of chicken Caesar salad and scones with jam and cream.

'Is there no booze?' asked Jackie, her mouth already sagging.

'There's champagne, gin, beer, or soft drinks, which are—'

'Champagne please,' said Jackie but the words hadn't left her lips before Melanie was offering her a glass.

'Sorry, I usually wait until everyone is seated,' explained Melanie.

Val shot Jackie a look. Could she not even wait until everyone was sat down before she started necking alcohol? 'You remember what happened last time you drank too much champagne?'

'Yes. And wasn't that a blast?'

Val was already starting to have regrets.

22

PAULINE

Pauline sat down opposite Val and popped Brian on the seat next to her. Melanie came over and made a fuss of Brian through the basket. 'I've got him some tuna and there's a litter tray in the toilet.' She pointed to the back of the plane.

'Thank you,' said Pauline.

'Bugger me, talk about thinking of everything. Brian's flying furs class,' said Jackie, who had discovered her chair could move in different directions and was making it tilt and turn at the same time.

'If you could keep your seat in the fixed position for take-off, please,' requested Melanie.

'Sure,' said Jackie, trying to return it to its original position.

'Good morning, ladies,' said a disembodied voice. 'My name is George Darcy and I am your pilot for this flight.'

'Ooh Mr Darcy,' said Jackie, with a hoot. Val glared at her. Pauline feared she was going to witness this scene playing out on a regular basis and not just on the flight. The pilot continued. 'I am talking to the control tower and we're expecting to be given authorisation to take off in the next five minutes. Our flight time to Nice is approximately two hours. Please ask Melanie for anything you may need and enjoy your flight.'

Pauline had never enjoyed a flight before and despite the lovely interior and free-flowing drinks she doubted today would be any different. She'd only ever been on a plane a handful of times, the only reason she even had a passport was for ID purposes. For someone who contemplated suicide on a regular basis she was really quite afraid of dying. Or more the pain associated with it. Or being trapped. Injured and trapped – that's what she was afraid of. Images of death and destruction flooded her mind and her pulse started to race. She took a deep breath and did up her belt with shaking hands. She needed to force herself to relax. But perhaps that was counterintuitive.

Pauline glanced into Brian's carrier. She hoped he wasn't afraid of flying. Brian appeared to have forgotten his earlier irritation and was now sitting with his face up against the mesh, studying the new surroundings. She pushed her fingers through to feel his silky fur and he rubbed around them. Instantly she felt a little bit calmer.

Jackie leaned back in her seat and savoured a sip of her champagne. 'I could get used to this.'

'It's mind-boggling, isn't it?' Pauline couldn't take it all in. Discovering she wasn't moving to the other side of London had been a shock but if this was the level of luxury she was about to experience it was certainly a sweetener. France felt like a long way away. Although she really didn't have anything or anyone to stay in England for. Maybe she could leave her demons behind. Well, some of them at least. Perhaps when she'd processed all that was happening and made it to Nice in one piece she'd start to feel better about everything. She hoped that would be the case. Goodness, was that a little positivity creeping in? Whatever was she thinking? She smiled to herself.

The plane began to move. It trundled off across the tarmac. 'Excuse me.' Pauline waved to get Melanie's attention and she was at her side in an instant. 'Is my cat okay in his basket? Should it not be restrained at all?'

'Or in an overhead locker?' suggested Jackie. Val scowled at her. 'What?'

'He's fine in there for take-off. We'll pop him on the floor for safety,' she said, moving the carrier. 'Once we're in the air I've got a small harness he can pop on if he wants to come out of the carrier and sit on the seat next to you or on your lap. We can't let pets walk around the cabin because they're a trip hazard.'

'I used to go out with a bloke who liked to wear a harness,' said Jackie, absent-mindedly gazing out of the window. Pauline ignored her and Melanie appeared to be trying to do the same.

Pauline was amazed by how geared up they were for animals. 'That sounds great. Thank you.'

'You're welcome. We have pets on our flights all the time. Is there anything I can get anyone before take-off?' asked Melanie.

'No, thank you,' said Pauline and Val shook her head.

'Have you got any of those little packets of peanuts?' asked Jackie.

'Sorry, we're nut-free due to airborne allergies. But I've got crisps, pretzels and some mini cookies.'

'Yes, they all sound perfect. And a quick top-up, please,' said Jackie, pointing to her glass. Melanie smiled sweetly and quickly returned with the champagne and a trayful of snacks. Jackie's eyes lit up.

Melanie took her seat and strapped herself in. Pauline checked her seatbelt was secure for the fourth time. The engines fired up and she gripped the plush armrests. She was sure that the harder she grimaced the more Melanie smiled back.

The plane left the ground. She held on tighter to the seat. Brian gave a wobbly meow. Pauline felt like doing the same. After a couple of minutes the plane levelled off a little and either the engines were quieter or her ears had gone fuzzy – either way the sound wasn't as violent. She looked out of the tiny porthole-style window and glimpsed the ground disappearing beneath them. That was it; she was leaving England behind. For the first time she realised this would put her a long way from her past. The things that haunted her were from years ago but the fear of them rearing up again had been ever-present. Moving to a different country put miles and the North Sea between them. That could only be a good thing. She glanced down at Brian and he was looking up at her. Did she dare to dream that this could be a new start? Pauline wasn't known for her positivity – but perhaps she could change that. If she searched deep inside could she find the person she used to be?

'Are you okay?' asked Val, getting a book out of her handbag and putting on her glasses.

'I think I might be,' replied Pauline with a smile.

23

JACKIE

Jackie couldn't believe her luck. On the few occasions she'd flown it had always been cheap flights. Which had been fine at the time. They had got her to her destination for very little money and in very little comfort. It was the price you paid to end up somewhere for a holiday. But this was a world away from any flight she'd ever been on. She was almost disappointed that the flight was only two hours.

There was a bong sound and Melanie undid her seatbelt. 'You're free to move around the cabin now. I'll be back with some food shortly.'

Jackie looked across at Val reading her book. 'That's the trouble with these budget airlines. No in-flight entertainment,' she said with a grin.

'I'm so sorry, here you are,' said Melanie, leaning over Jackie, opening a flap next to the arm of Jackie's seat and pulling out a screen on an arm. She pressed a button and it lit up. 'Films, TV, podcasts – whatever you fancy.' She passed Jackie a plastic bag with headphones in.

For once Jackie was speechless. 'Thanks,' she said belatedly. It didn't seem enough. Melanie went to the back of the plane. 'This literally just needs Pierce Brosnan and it's my ideal fantasy. Maybe throw in some whipped cream.'

'It is really lovely,' said Pauline.

'Imagine travelling like this everywhere you went.' Jackie liked the idea a lot. Hopefully Zara would continue to travel. All she had to do was convince her that it would be wise to have a health professional travel with her and the world was her oyster. Not that she wasn't excited about France. She was. The first thing she was going to do was take some photographs and text them to her brother. Bragging rights counted, however old you were.

'I think I'll be staying put in France once we get there.' Pauline glanced out of the window and looked away. She seemed a bit tense.

'Drink your champagne, it'll calm you down,' suggested Jackie, knocking back hers. She still wasn't sure that she liked champagne all that much. She enjoyed telling people she'd had champagne but it would never be her first choice in the pub – not that she could afford it.

Financially she still had a lot to sort out. The credit cards weren't spiralling anymore but she wasn't out of the woods yet. Whilst this solved the issue of not having somewhere to live it didn't provide her with an income. Now she was going to be living in the sunshine she might need some spending money. She had over a year until she could claim her state pension. She didn't like the thought of being pensionable age but she did like the idea of an income. She just had to work out how she was going to manage in the meantime.

Perhaps she'd have to find herself a retired gentleman friend with deep pockets.

Her mind drifted to her fantasy version of Zara's villa. Her version had topless waiters and she stifled a snort. The others looked at her. 'Do you think we'll have a drinking game to choose the bedrooms like last time?' she asked.

Val put her book down. 'I'd forgotten about that. But I haven't forgotten that I won.'

'You got me on a technicality.'

'You vomited,' said Val.

'And that was the technicality. I'd still drunk more than you,' pointed out Jackie.

'I can't believe you're bringing this up again,' said Val.

'She did on the night,' said Pauline, miming being sick. They all laughed.

All four young women had been doing evening classes for various reasons and had seen a notice for rooms to rent. The tutor whose house it was had invited them all round at the same time to view the rooms. It was a steal, so despite not knowing each other they had all agreed to it. That left the issue of who had which of the three bedrooms and the downstairs room that was really the dining room but had been converted – meaning it had a bed in it rather than a table. Jackie had had the great idea for them to play a drinking game to determine who had which room. It was something in which she was sure she would have an advantage. Despite being the youngest she'd been brought up in a pub and her father liked to joke that she'd been bathed in Guinness as a new-born and weaned on bitter. The former was true, thankfully not the latter, but she had been sneaking alcohol for a great many years.

However, her plan hadn't worked. Zara commandeered the downstairs room, which nobody else wanted as the bathroom was upstairs. It had a beautiful bay window and the space she said she needed to practise her lines. That left the three of them to fight it out for the upstairs rooms. As it turned out, Val could hold her drink.

'I loved my room,' said Val.

'Of course you bloody did,' said Jackie light-heartedly. 'It was huge and had bloody fitted cupboards. My room was smaller than the airing cupboard.'

'I hope we don't have to choose,' said Pauline. 'I think that could cause a row.'

Jackie disagreed. 'I should get the biggest room as I had the smallest last time,' she suggested. It was worth a try.

'Somehow I think Zara gets to choose which room is whose,' said Val.

She was probably right.

24

VAL

'So, Val,' said Jackie. 'Are you still gay?

Pauline looked the most alarmed by the question and Val waved a palm to show her it was okay. 'Yes, Jackie, I am *still* gay.'

Jackie shrugged. 'I thought I'd best check. Can I still say gay? Everyone has gone so PC I don't know anymore.'

'Gay is fine. Bisexual would be more accurate.' Val picked her book back up in the hope it would stop Jackie but it didn't seem to work.

'That's greedy.' Jackie chuckled at her joke. 'Any wives in your past then?' she asked.

'No wives... no.' Val saw Pauline look over. And Melanie's ears had pricked up too. Val wasn't keen on personal conversations at the best of times but when they were being conducted in public they were a definite no-no. 'I'm happy being single, thanks.' *Unlike you*, she added in her head. Jackie had never been without a man the whole time they had lived together. She was always lining up the next one in case the current one went off the boil as they invariably did.

Val wasn't being entirely honest when she said she was happy being single. She was fine on her own but that was different to happy. She enjoyed her own company, had many interests and could amuse herself. She also had a good number of friends in varying degrees of closeness so she wasn't short of company. But there was still something missing in her life. Whether that was the lack of a partner she'd probably never know.

Melanie brought over the harness and some tuna for Brian.

'The cat gets served first?' Jackie rolled her eyes.

Brian made a noise crossed between a meow and a loud purr and rubbed against the mesh. Pauline opened the carrier and while he tucked into the tuna they put the harness on him. He gave them a couple of sideways glares while he ate his food but otherwise seemed happy with the deal.

Melanie brought out everyone else's food and it was as delicious as Val had expected it to be. Zara had always enjoyed the finer things in life and, according to the gossip columns, since the divorce from her last multimillionaire husband some years ago she had been doing exactly that. Val had done a little online research to try to ascertain how much money might be involved in the investments Zara had mentioned she wanted Val to scrutinise. Thanks to multiple film deals Zara had grown her own bank balance but she had made the real money from her husbands.

They were all quiet while they ate – even Brian who was receiving the odd piece of chicken from Pauline on the sly.

'I couldn't eat another thing,' said Jackie, patting her rounded stomach.

'Coffee and mints?' asked Melanie.

'Ooh yes please,' said Jackie, pouncing on the sweets as soon as they were put on the table.

Val smiled to herself, some people didn't change, she thought and then she looked across at Pauline and realised how wrong that statement was in her case. Pauline had changed and drastically so. The once vivacious woman had been reduced to an indecisive and anxious person and it hurt Val to see it. She hoped there would be something she could do over the next three months to help Pauline.

Val was viewing it as a three-month experiment. If she compartmentalised it like that it helped. Despite the noisy neighbours she was still sad about leaving her lovely home but she also hated missing out and if she hadn't joined the others in France she would always have wondered. This was the best of both. She could dip her toe in the water, hopefully physically as well as metaphorically, and enjoy some time with old friends whilst also taking action against her neighbour from a safe and far quieter distance.

Brian was now on Pauline's lap, marching up and down to a rhythm only he could hear. He turned around three times, got himself and the cord on the harness in a proper tangle and settled down for a nap. Val decided to join him in a quick snooze before they landed and their new lives could properly start.

25

PAULINE

Melanie came round with lollipops just before they came into land, which were meant to relieve the pressure in their ears. Pauline hadn't had a lolly since she was a child and it was a useful distraction to the thoughts of plummeting to the ground. When the wheels were finally back on tarmac Pauline tried to breathe normally again. They'd made it to France.

Brian seemed to quite enjoy his first flight. He'd certainly enjoyed the tuna but had been nonplussed by the view out of the window and had slept for most of the trip. He hadn't been keen on going back into his carrier but she promised him it wouldn't be for long.

Melanie directed them into the General Aviation Terminal where they were processed quickly and reunited with their luggage.

'What happens now?' asked Pauline. She was feeling adrift again.

'That's a good question.' Val was already on her mobile.

'Hi, Alina, we've landed and I was wondering… uh-huh… yes. I see him. Thanks.' Val ended the call. 'Looks like we have another driver.' She pointed to a man in full chauffeur's outfit holding a sign that read 'Zara's Girls'.

Jackie's trolley teetered with her piled-up luggage. 'I bloody love this.' She waved at the driver, who nodded in response and came over.

'Welcome to Nice. Zara is looking forward to seeing you all,' he said, his French accent strong. 'Zis way,' he added taking control of Jackie's trolley. Pauline and Val followed them outside.

As they left the air conditioning the sunshine seemed to envelope Pauline like a warm hug. It was bright and the airport was busy with people trundling cases in and out.

'Zee car is parked over 'ere,' said the driver.

'And what's your name?' asked Jackie.

'It is Gabriel.'

'And aren't you an angel!' said Jackie gleefully. 'And isn't that a beautiful accent?'

'Thank you, madam, but 'ere it is you who has zee accent.'

'I guess you're right. I bet we have cute English accents, don't we?' she asked.

'Er, *oui* if you like,' he said, concentrating on pushing the laden trolley across the road. Jackie gave Pauline the thumbs up. Jackie's approach to life was vastly different to her own but it did make her smile.

'I'm really pleased you came,' said Pauline, to Val. 'Thank you.'

'You're welcome. I wouldn't have missed this,' said Val, nodding at Jackie trying to keep up with the driver and have a conversation with him as he strode off with the baggage.

When he stopped by a stretch limousine Pauline couldn't believe her eyes. 'Crumbs,' she said.

'Would you look at this?' Jackie was already taking selfies with it and surreptitiously trying to get the driver in the frame. 'My Insta is going to light up.' Jackie pouted into the camera.

The driver opened the rear door and they all filed inside. There was an ice bucket and a bottle of champagne, which the driver expertly opened, and then he poured some into the three waiting flutes.

While they were chinking glasses and giggling like schoolgirls he got in the front. 'It is five kilometres' journey. Relax and enjoy zee view, ladies,' he said, before buzzing shut a partition between them.

Pauline had to admit she was impressed, and with Val one side of her and Brian the other she was feeling more at ease than she had done in a while. The limo was the height of luxury – vast inside and swathed in leather and full of gadgets that Jackie was quick to uncover, although Val had muttered under her breath something that ended in *ostentatious*. Pauline tried to commit it all to memory and not just what she was seeing – she wanted to grasp and savour the feeling too. There was excitement and hope in her gut. None of it felt real and yet it was.

'Cheers,' said Jackie for the umpteenth time as she held out her glass and they clinked yet again. 'Is this not the best thing ever?' She didn't wait for a response before continuing. 'Apart from the private jet obviously. But a stretch limo. I've always wanted to go in one of these. Hang on,' she said buzzing down the window nearest to her and sticking her head out like a spaniel. 'Woohoo!' she yelled and a few pedestrians glared at her and shook their heads.

Even Val cracked a smile before reverting to being the sensible one. 'Jackie, pull your head in.'

'I've a better idea.' Jackie pressed a few more buttons and eventually the sunroof opened. Jackie climbed onto the seat and thrust her top half through the roof and resumed her hollering.

'Well, that's one way to acquaint yourself with the locals,' said Val.

'Come up,' said Jackie. 'It's awesome. Look at this place.'

Pauline was tempted but she felt safer seated and buckled in. Instead she watched out of the window. Large houses gave way to greenery.

Jackie bobbed down to speak to them for a moment. 'There's only a bloody castle. You don't think Zara lives there do you?' Her eyes were wide.

Pauline peered out of the window in the direction Jackie was pointing. There was indeed a large castle-like structure in the distance.

'It's a fort,' said Val. 'So no, that's not Zara's house.'

Jackie pulled a disappointed face before returning to sticking her head back out of the roof. Pauline realised the driver had said the journey was five kilometres and now she wondered exactly where they were going.

26

JACKIE

When the driver put his foot down it was quite blustery with her head and torso stuck out of the sunroof. She feared her hair would soon resemble dreadlocks but she didn't care. She was quite tipsy after champagne on the flight and the recent top-up but she was buzzing with excitement. She felt twenty again only this time it was better – one of her friends was rich. The speed increased a fraction more and Jackie had to admit defeat. She came back inside the limo and flopped onto the seat.

'I feel like Cinderella and I'm finally going to the ball,' she said, buzzing the sunroof closed.

'I won't ask what that makes us,' said Val.

Jackie laughed. 'Can you even believe this?'

'I wonder where we're going,' said Pauline. 'We've left Nice behind.' She was peering out of the window.

Jackie looked out the other side and as they slowed for a junction she read the sign as best she could, her pronunciation very English with hard consonants. 'Saint

Jean Cap Ferret I think it said. Ferrets are those nasty weasel things aren't they?' Pauline nodded in agreement. 'Blimey, I hope this isn't where they come from.'

'I'm not sure your logic works,' said Val. 'I don't think Leighton Buzzard is known for its birds of prey or that a large striped feline has ever run free in Tiger Bay, Cardiff.'

'Right. Is that a no then, Val?' asked Jackie. Sometimes a straight answer was hard to come by.

'It's a no, and it's pronounced Cap Ferr*at*,' explained Val.

'Never heard of it,' said Jackie. 'Maybe we're just passing through.'

'Not likely,' said Val. 'Cap Ferrat is a peninsula. It's an extra piece of land, like a geographical dead end. I think this must be where Zara lives.' Val looked quite pleased although it was sometimes hard to tell. She wasn't a jump up and down sort of person. Not prone to getting excited but that did have its plus side as it also meant she didn't panic either. Whatever happened Val usually remained calm.

Jackie was a little disappointed they weren't staying in Nice. She'd heard of Nice and that meant people she knew would have heard of it too. She wanted people back home to know she was somewhere posh. 'Is it near the sea still? Because I've totally lost any idea of which way we're facing now.' She wanted to get maps up on her mobile phone but she'd done that a couple of times on a bus and it had made her feel queasy and after all the booze she didn't want to risk getting travel sick – that would be an unpleasant way to end a fantastic journey.

'It's virtually surrounded by sea. Imagine it like a tiny island that is still attached to the mainland by a small piece of land and a road. That's Cap Ferrat.'

Almost as Val spoke Jackie caught her first sight of the sea and just like when she'd gone on holiday to Great Yarmouth as a child she pointed and shouted. 'I can see the sea!' Pauline flinched and put a protective arm around Brian's basket. They all stared out of the window. And what a first sight it was. The sun was glistening off the brilliant blue of the ocean dotted with white boats of varying sizes.

'It's beautiful,' breathed Pauline, her nose inches away from the glass.

'It really is,' said Val.

Jackie was dumbfounded but only for a moment. 'I've never seen sea that colour. Not in real life. When the celebs post photos it looks like that but I always assumed they were photoshopped.'

'Which they are,' cut in Val.

'True,' she agreed. 'I've seen it on David Attenborough but even then I wasn't sure it could ever really be that blue. It's like it's in competition with the sky.' They rounded a bend and the sea was replaced with bushes and then a few villas. 'Blimey, I bet they've got cracking sea views.'

'And I bet they pay for them too,' said Val.

For the rest of the journey they were all fairly quiet. Each trying to catch glimpses of the water through the urban sprawl. The car eventually slowed and pulled in close to a wall and opposite a bus stop.

'I'm hoping it's not a joke and we have to get a bus back to the airport,' said Pauline.

'I can't see any houses,' said Jackie looking out onto a fancy seafront.

The driver opened a door. 'We are 'ere, ladies. I am afraid, I must stop 'ere. This car will not make the tight bend onto the driveway. Please head on up and I will bring your luggage.' He gave a brief pause. 'That may take a few trips.'

'Fab, thanks, Gabriel,' said Jackie, getting out first. She looked up and down the street. It was lovely. The sea was right in front of them with a long promenade stretching in both directions but she didn't have time for sightseeing now; she could do that later. She desperately wanted to see where she had moved to. And she hoped it was Insta-worthy. She was looking about, working out where to go when Gabriel pointed to the wall. There was a CCTV camera above an iron gate, behind which were some steep stone steps. 'Come on,' she called to the others and she headed up the steps hoping like hell that whatever was waiting for her at the top was worth the effort.

27

VAL

The steps were a bit of an ordeal and Val was wondering how Zara managed them when she found herself joining Jackie and Pauline, all breathing heavily at the top. They were standing in beautifully manicured gardens with a strong tropical theme – palm trees and yuccas were dotted around an immaculate lawn, bordered by beds overflowing with vibrant flowers. Gabriel appeared looking slightly red-faced from hauling up Jackie's huge case. 'Zis way,' he said.

Val caught a glimpse of a colourful bird in a tree and pointed. 'Look at that.'

'Do you think someone has lost a pet?' asked Pauline.

The driver followed her gaze. '*Non*, madam. This is a wild parakeet. We have a lot of them. They are love birds.' He left them studying the bird.

'They're beautiful,' said Val.

'Damn sight prettier than pigeons,' agreed Jackie. 'Do you remember that awful manky parrot Zara used to have?

Who used to say, "Show us your knickers."' She started to laugh.

'Toby,' said Val. 'And *you* taught him to say that.'

'That's it. Toby. After some blooming pretentious shite play she loved.'

'Shakespeare's *Twelfth Night*,' said Val, feeling offended on Shakespeare's behalf.

'I hated that parrot,' said Jackie. 'He used to squawk through all the best TV programmes, important phone calls and he'd wake me up dead early in the morning.'

'Oh, I quite liked him,' said Pauline.

Val loved the theatre but was indifferent to the bird. Her memories of Toby were of a poor African grey missing most of his feathers. He'd been a sorry sight.

They followed after Gabriel along a winding path, which took a turn around some sculptured hedging to reveal a villa – side on.

It sat perfectly in the gardens and was in some ways simplistic with its terracotta-tiled roof and white-painted façade. It didn't look huge but it was still impressive with ornate wicker chairs scattered across a large covered patio area.

Gabriel whistled and they all hustled after him as he disappeared around to the front of the house. It was picture-perfect with yellow shutters and matching door.

As if on cue the front door opened and with a flurry of multicoloured kaftan Zara appeared. 'Welcome to Maison Floraison,' she declared, taking one step outside and spreading her arms wide.

There were hugs and air kisses and words of appreciation.

'My girls,' said Zara, appraising them Miss Jean Brodie style. 'You must be exhausted after your trip.'

'Not really,' said Val. 'It's hard to be tired when you're waited on hand and foot.' She stood to one side to let the driver go past with yet another case.

Zara let out a tinkle of a laugh. 'Come inside, the air conditioning is divine. And my chef has prepared some lunch when you're ready.'

'We ate on the plane, thank you,' said Pauline.

'But I could squeeze something in,' said Jackie predictably.

'And, girls, firstly let me apologise about the confusion. I've lived here so many years it didn't cross my mind that you would think I was inviting to you live anywhere else.'

'No worries,' said Jackie.

'I think this is nicer,' said Pauline. 'Not that I don't like your Belgravia house. I really do.'

'Pauline, stop worrying,' said Val, and they followed Zara inside.

Zara elegantly twisted her hands in different directions as she pointed out rooms. 'On the ground floor we have the living area, kitchen, office, snug and dining room. Downstairs there's a gym, cinema room and laundry.' They walked past some closed doors and into a vast living space. She waited while they all took in the huge room. Light flooded in from the giant glass doors and bounced off the gleaming floor and white walls. It was a total contrast to her Belgravia residence.

There was a screech and Pauline jumped. 'Sorry, that sounded like my doorbell.'

They all looked at the source of the unpleasant noise.

A gold domed cage was in the corner of the room and an African grey parrot was preening itself.

'You all remember Toby,' said Zara waving an arm in his direction.

'He got his feathers back,' said Pauline, sounding delighted.

Jackie blinked. 'That can't be the same parrot.'

'It is,' confirmed Zara.

'He must be...' Val was trying to work out his age.

'He's fifty this year,' said Zara. 'I thought we might have a party to celebrate.'

Jackie gave Val a look and made a twirling motion at the side of her head just out of Zara's eyeline and Val waved at her to stop. They didn't want to upset their host on day one.

If the villa was traditional at the front it was the opposite at the rear. An extension ran across the back – predominantly glass panels. They stepped outside where the gardens at the back were even bigger, and tucked round the other side of the villa was a small swimming pool.

Jackie spotted something else. 'Wow. Is that a hot tub?'

Zara turned as if to check. 'Yes, I don't use it now. But you can.'

'I bet you've had some famous bums sat in there,' said Jackie.

'Jackie, really,' said Val. 'I don't want to be thinking about whose backside has been in there before mine.'

'Johnny Depp,' said Zara, surveying her gardens.

'You can't even see the neighbours,' commented Pauline.

'Probably for the best.' Zara screwed her nose up.

Jackie was on it like a sniffer dog at a rave. 'Ooh are they famous. It's not Ozzy Osbourne, is it? I always thought however much money you have some poor sod still lives next door to him – or is it a royal?'

'Celebrity lawyer over there, hedge fund manager that side and jewel thief the other.' Zara pointed in various directions before a swirl of kaftan announced her departure. 'Come and see your rooms.'

'Did she say thief?' Pauline was looking anxious.

'Jewel thief is a different class of thief,' said Jackie. 'Like the Pink Panther.'

'She's probably exaggerating,' said Val, although her interest was piqued.

Zara was making her way back through the living room. It seemed there were strategically placed pieces of furniture to aid her journey. The others followed her inside. She pressed a button on the wall and a lift opened.

'Bloody hell,' said Jackie, but to be fair it was what they were all thinking.

'You've got a lift in your house?' said Pauline.

'The old legs aren't what they once were.' Zara seemed sad but only for a moment. 'But they danced across the stage at the Royal Palladium with Bruce Forsyth so they've done me proud.' The lift opened and they all got in. It was small but there was space for the four of them.

Upstairs they stepped out in front of a picture window, looking out over the ocean, and while Zara took Pauline and Jackie off for a tour Val took a moment to take in the view. It was spectacular. The promenade was just visible and then a line of beach before the deep blue of the ocean and the lighter contrast of the sky – it was like an exquisite painting.

'Val,' called Jackie. 'You're okay if I have the bigger room this time, right? Because my bed is already in there.' She beamed a cheesy grin in her direction. But Val didn't care what room she had; she'd found her kind of heaven.

28

PAULINE

Pauline really didn't mind which room she had. They were all bigger than the one she'd left and she was fairly sure the largest room was bigger than the whole of her old flat.

'Well, there's nothing that can't be moved around. You can decide amongst yourselves. They are all en suite...' said Zara.

'En suite,' mouthed Jackie.

'But the largest is at the front of the house and has no balcony, which the other two do,' Zara explained.

'Aww,' said Jackie like a spoiled child. 'No view then?'

'It's of the hills. I'd quite like that,' said Val stepping into the room for the first time. 'This is fabulous.'

'It is and my bed looks good in it too.' Jackie waved her hand at the large bed with an orange painted headboard that had seen better days.

'It does,' agreed Pauline. Val was frowning hard so Pauline kept talking in the hope Val wouldn't make a disparaging comment. 'I don't mind which room I have,' said Pauline. She didn't want there to be any friction. 'But if Jackie's bed is in here then I think she has to sleep in here tonight.'

'You're right,' said Val, exiting the room and checking out the other two.

Pauline followed her through the next bedroom and out onto a balcony with a glass balustrade so as not to interrupt the amazing view. There were four sun loungers, two at each end.

'We can all lie out here and admire the view,' said Pauline. 'It doesn't matter who sleeps in which room.'

'I guess.' Jackie didn't sound convinced.

Pauline took a deep breath. The air was warm and fresh. If she concentrated she could hear the waves breaking on the shore. This truly was paradise. Zara joined them and they stood side by side on the balcony looking out across the water. The colour of the sea was vastly different here. It wasn't just one blue; it was varying shades from deep ink blue to bright azure. Not the dark navy or muddy grey she was used to on Mersea Island or anywhere at home. Home. That was something she would have to realign in her mind. This was home now. It would take some getting used to even though her previous place had been easier to leave behind than she'd expected. When she thought of home she still pictured Mersea. But the picture always brought with it a sense of foreboding – not like any home should at all.

She was here now. Miles away from Mersea and a world away from what happened there. All the shouting, the pain and what had ended it all. Although it hadn't ended; it had continued to follow her. To haunt her.

'This is a beautiful place, Zara. Thanks for inviting us,' said Pauline. Val and Jackie agreed.

Zara waved their thanks away. 'My pleasure. Thank you for coming. It's good to have you all here. Quite wonderful in fact.' She looked at each of them and then out to sea. 'Tonight we will talk but for now we should, eat, drink and be merry,' she declared and she left the others on the balcony all puzzling over what she meant.

'She's not lost the theatrics, I see,' said Val.

'Sounds ominous,' said Pauline, already worried about what it was Zara wanted to talk about.

'Chill out, Pauline,' said Jackie, leading them off the balcony and through the bedroom. 'It's only Zara wanting to hold court. By talk she means she talks and we listen. I can live with that if I get to bunk in a room like this.' She splayed her arms out.

'I thought you wanted the bigger room,' said Val, a twitch of a smirk on her lips.

'I do but I also want a balcony. Let's get some lunch – that might help me think.'

Downstairs Pauline found Zara holding on to the back of a chair. 'Zara, what should I do about Brian, my cat? I'm worried about Toby.' At the sound of his name he let out a screech.

'Quiet now, darling boy,' said Zara. 'That's a good point. I expect you'll want to keep him indoors until he gets his bearings.'

It was a relief that Zara was on the same page. 'Yes. It's all new for him.'

'One of the staff have set up a litter tray in the boot room and he can have the utility as well. Maybe put a note on the door to remind everyone.' She turned to go.

Pauline caught her arm and noted how thin it was under her billowing kaftan. 'Zara, I don't think I said a proper thank you for Brian. So, thank you. He means the world to me.'

Zara placed her hand over Pauline's and gave it a gentle pat. 'That's good to hear.'

Pauline let Brian out in the boot room and with a swish of his striped tail he had a mooch about. It wasn't a big room but with the utility next door he had space to stretch his legs. It would only be for a couple of weeks until she was happy he'd settled and wasn't going to run away. She found some sticky notes and a laundry marker in a drawer and made a polite note to stick on the door.

'Pauline, could you fetch the others?' asked Zara as Pauline was sticking up the note.

'Of course.'

She found Val staring at the view and Jackie trying to measure rooms by walking in a wobbly line. When they all returned to the kitchen a grey-haired man in chef's whites was chatting to Zara. 'Ladies, I want you to meet my chef: Christian.'

Jackie was giving the tall Frenchman the once-over. 'As in Christian Grey? There's not a red room in the basement is there?' She gave a girlish giggle.

Christian pouted in a typically French way. 'He is here Tuesday to Saturday and makes the most amazing meals,' said Zara. 'He can whip up pretty much anything you can imagine.'

'Ooh,' said Jackie. 'I could murder a toasted cheese sandwich.'

Christian recoiled at her words and looked like there was something he'd like to murder too. When he spoke he had a light French accent but his words were hard. 'I am a trained chef. I create cuisine. This is not a cheap beach café.'

Zara waved her palms to calm him down. 'Christian, she was joking. They will all love your food.'

'Then, my apologies,' he said, but he and Jackie were locking stares.

'Anyway we'll be on the patio,' said Zara and went to turn but instead seem to wince and freeze.

'Everything all right?' asked Pauline.

'Yes, I'm fine. Totally fine.' Zara regained her poise and headed outside. Zara appeared to be in pain and was trying to mask it, although her acting skills weren't quite up to the job.

29

JACKIE

Outside it was gloriously hot. The contrast from the air-conditioned house was drastic. Zara sat down in a large wicker chair with a high back fashioned like a peacock's tail.

'Blimey, that's like the one from *Game of Thrones*,' said Jackie.

'But without the swords,' said Val, with a condescending look.

'I was offered a part on that,' said Zara. 'Turned it down. It clashed with me filming *Midsomer Murders*. Did you see that?'

'Yes,' said Pauline. 'I really enjoyed that episode and the eccentric character you played. You were terrific. Until you died.'

'Wasn't that just one episode?' asked Jackie, stretching out on a sun lounger. One thing she was keen to do was get a decent tan. People always knew you were having a good time if you had a tan in photographs.

'One episode is virtually two hours long. That's film length and takes months to shoot,' explained Zara.

'Right. Still. *Game of Thrones* had eight seasons. I'm thinking that might not have been...' Jackie sensed Zara was glaring at her. A quick glance confirmed it, so she changed tack. 'But what do I know?' She needed to tread carefully where Zara's ego was concerned. It was as fragile as a recently dunked biscuit.

'I guess nobody knew how big *Games of Thrones* was going to be before it aired,' said Pauline. After all these years she was still the one to smooth over the waters.

'It was a book first, so actually...' started Jackie but Val interrupted her.

'This is lovely but I'm conscious that we are not on holiday and I for one would like to understand what your expectations are.'

'Now, Val. I want you to relax. It's the weekend and I don't expect anyone to be working at the weekend.' Zara adjusted her sunglasses.

'Great,' said Jackie, getting herself comfortable. The less work the better. This was going to be an easy ride – exactly what she'd hoped for.

'Actually, Jackie, you may be the exception to that rule as I might need medical support at any time,' said Zara. That was bloody typical. Jackie gave her a lazy thumbs up from her horizontal position and puffed out a breath. Trust the other two to get let off.

'That's very generous of you.' Pauline was getting in a muddle trying to adjust the sun lounger next to Jackie. Jackie reached out and with one hand lifted the back up, making it lie down flat with a jolt. Pauline squealed and they both started to laugh.

'I think we should ease into our new set-up,' said Zara.

'I think that's wise,' agreed Val. 'Although, I'm also keen to get started.'

Jackie huffed. Val had always been a goody two shoes. The only one of them in the Seventies to have a proper career.

'How do your days pan out here, Zara?' asked Val.

'I'm amazed you get anything done,' said Jackie, feeling her whole body soaking up the sun's rays and her armpits start to sweat. Getting a bikini really was a priority.

'I'm woken at seven o'clock...' Jackie eased her sunglasses down to have a proper look at Zara to see if she was joking. Unfortunately, it appeared she wasn't. 'Then a light breakfast followed by lemon and hot water under the pergola where I do a little yoga and Tai Chi.' Jackie had to fight to hold in a snort of laughter. Zara continued unaware. 'I spend the morning seeing to my correspondence but I will be turning over most of my mornings to writing my memoirs.' She waved at Pauline.

'I'm a little worried about my typing skills. It's been a long while since I've done any.' Pauline was searching faces for a response.

'Don't worry,' whispered Val. 'I'm sure it will all come flooding back to you. It'll be fine.'

'Then lunch is either out here or in the dining room apart from Sundays when I go to Table du Royal at the Royal-Riviera hotel...'

'Is it a carvery like we used to do back in the day?' asked

Jackie, sitting up on her elbow. She loved a Sunday roast. But only if someone else was cooking it.

'Gosh, no. I remember that place. There was so much meat, they had to put the vegetables on top,' recalled Zara.

'I know. It was bloody wonderful,' said Jackie, salivating at the thought of it.

'Table du Royal is a traditional French and Mediterranean fusion restaurant,' explained Zara.

'What's that then?' asked Jackie.

'Too posh for you,' said Pauline and Jackie took a playful swipe at her.

Zara cleared her throat. 'And then on Mondays I'm a bit more flexible and see where the mood takes me.' She swirled her hands around. 'There are many fabulous cafés and restaurants in the area I'm... well, *we* are really blessed.'

'Amen to that,' said Jackie, propping herself up again. 'Actually...' A thought struck her. 'Are these places pricey? Because I currently don't have an income. And it's okay because I'm planning on getting a little job but at the moment things are a bit tight.' The last thing she wanted to do was pile things back on the credit cards when she'd had to sell virtually everything of any value she owned to clear them.

'I'm sure we can come to some arrangement,' said Zara.

Jackie nodded although she had no idea what Zara meant. 'And would that involve me having some cash for lunch and other essentials?'

'I'll be covering things until you're all properly settled in.'

'Fab,' said Jackie and she settled back on her sun lounger. 'I was hoping to check out the shopping at some point. Val said there were some good shops around here. Maybe we could all go and it'd be like old times, trying stuff on. Who's up for that?'

'That would be nice. Not sure that I'd buy anything but I'll come with you,' said Pauline.

'Not really my thing,' said Val.

Zara spread her arms wide and her kaftan sleeves swished as she spoke. 'I've found my look, darling, and I'm sticking with it,' she said in a thespian voice and they all laughed.

'I loved it when we used to borrow each other's clothes,' said Jackie. 'My parents used to think I was earning loads because of all the different clothes I rocked up in.'

'But the clothes swapping did cause arguments between us,' said Pauline.

'It didn't always work out well did it?' said Val. Jackie knew without looking that Val was staring at her.

'You not over that yet?' she said.

'If you mean you losing my sheepskin coat then yes, I am. But if you mean what you said to my parents, then no, I'm certainly not over that.' The sun moved behind a cloud but the chill that descended was disproportionate. Jackie had wondered how long it would be before Val starting dragging this up.

'Lunch is served in the dining room,' said Christian, appearing on the patio. Saved by the bell, thought Jackie. She couldn't believe that Val was still harbouring a grudge after all these years. Actually on second thoughts she absolutely could believe it – that was *very* Val.

'Magnifique! Merci, Christian,' said Zara. 'You girls go on, I'll only be a moment.'

Val and Pauline were on their feet, following Christian

inside. Jackie was about to join them when Zara reached out a hand to stop her. 'Could I have a quick word, Jackie?'

'Sure,' she said, but she was watching where the others were disappearing to because she didn't want to miss out. She was surprisingly hungry given what she'd eaten on the plane.

'Jackie. I can easily sort out your financial issues but in return I need you to do one thing for me.'

'Name it,' said Jackie. This got better and better.

'When the time comes I need to know that you will... help me on my way.' Zara fixed her with a cold gaze.

She had to be joking. 'Blimey, Zara, you're not ready to shuffle off just yet.'

'No, but when I am I need to know that you'll *help* me.'

Jackie swallowed. It had turned very dark all of a sudden and it wasn't the weather. 'Do you mean what I think you mean?'

Zara lifted her chin. 'If you're thinking euthanasia then yes. That's exactly what I mean.'

30

VAL

Val opted for one of the balcony rooms, unpacked her things and put them in the fitted wardrobes. The few clothes she'd brought looked quite sad in the vast cupboard. Given the vagaries of the British weather, Val's wardrobe was an efficient mix of items that could cope with most conditions. She had a few things that had sufficed a week's holiday in warm weather but it still left her with scant choice given she was now in the South of France. Perhaps Jackie would persuade her to go shopping yet. She opened one door to reveal a dressing table and lights came on around a large mirror in the style of a theatre dressing room. It made Val smile.

Zara was an unusual combination of flamboyant flair and joie de vivre that managed to keep away from tipping over into kitsch. There was a painting on the wall that reminded her of something. She stepped back to study it. She'd seen it before somewhere. It was a beach scene or more specifically waves breaking on a shoreline. It came to her. It had used to hang in their living room all those years ago. Zara had seen it in a gallery window and coveted it for many weeks before she'd started filming a big role and received a pay cheque. Val had gone with her to buy it, as at the time Val had been the only one with a car. She could remember them trying to get it in the boot of a mini and having to put it on the back seat.

It surprised Val that Zara had kept it all these years. She'd always had Zara down as a dispassionate person who embraced new trends but this showed a level of sentimentality she'd not expected. It was a lovely painting and it made the room feel familiar and homely. She was going to be fine living here, especially if it was only for three months.

That evening Val realised she was having a surprisingly nice time. The morning's location mix-up was forgotten, she'd settled into her room without any arguments with Jackie, and she was now sitting outside in an ambiently lit garden with a chilled glass of champagne in her hand. Christian had excelled himself with the welcome meal; the food was up there with any top London restaurant she'd eaten in. It was a headily warm evening and she could hear laughter on the breeze from the surrounding villas.

'Top-up?' asked Jackie, although she was already refilling Val's glass.

'I've never drunk this much champagne,' said Val.

'Apart from Zara's eight—' Jackie seemed to check herself. 'Big birthday bash. And that time at a Bond film after-party,' said Jackie, clicking her fingers as if trying to spark her memory.

'*The Spy Who Loved Me*,' said Val, pleased that her

recall was still strong. It wasn't a competition but so far that evening she had remembered more details than any of the others.

'Yes, that was the one.' Jackie was shaking her head. 'Blimey I was ill that night.'

Pauline covered her mouth. 'Oh my goodness. That was the night you vomited on Barbara Bach's shoes,' said Pauline.

'Don't remind me. That has haunted me ever since. But in a good way because it's helped me learn when to stop drinking.' Val gave her a look – she was about to remind her of Zara's party. 'Okay, most of the time.' Jackie sniggered. 'Poor Barbara Bach.'

'Barbara deserved it,' said Zara. 'A few years later she stole Ringo from me.'

'You did Zara a favour then,' said Val, looking between the two of them.

This had been pretty much how the evening had gone. Someone would say something that triggered a memory, which in turn triggered another and sent them off in another direction. Memory lane was generally a happy place to be. For Val there were a few dark alleyways but if she steered clear of those she was fine. She'd found it hard to come to terms with her sexuality as a young woman in the Seventies in a career where men dominated and being a woman was enough of a handicap. Anything else out of the ordinary would have sealed her fate, as her husband had pointed out to her in no uncertain terms.

The more they reminisced the more Val realised how much they had done in the few years they had lived together. Living life as carefree twenty-somethings with no idea of where life was going to take them or what it had in store. She suspected they would have done things differently if they knew which routes their lives were to take – in which case she reasoned it was probably best they hadn't known. The memories played out like scenes from one of Zara's films.

'Jackie did do me a favour that night with Barbara,' said Zara. 'But then that's what we girls do for each other.' She raised her glass. 'To looking out for each other.'

They all clinked glasses. Was Val mistaken or did Jackie hesitate?

'But you can't have one person doing all the heavy lifting. That's not fair,' said Jackie.

'We'll help,' offered Pauline quickly.

Zara was giving Jackie an odd look. 'I'm sure we'll all pull together.'

'I guess we'll see,' said Jackie, her eyes firmly fixed on Zara.

Val could see there was obviously something up. 'You okay?' she asked Jackie on the quiet as Zara regaled them with a far too detailed account of her bedroom antics with Ringo Starr.

Jackie frowned. 'Yeah, I'm fine. Why wouldn't I be?' There was an edge to her words.

'No particular reason. I just thought... I don't know. It's probably the champagne.' Val got the distinct impression there was something brewing. As youngsters they had all fallen out at one time or another. It was only a matter of time before that happened again. As a solicitor Val had a sixth sense when it came to people. She had often wondered how she would have fared as a police detective. The conversation segued from Ringo Starr to celebrities in rehab and before they realised it was almost two o'clock in the morning.

'I'm going to bed now,' said Zara. 'Jackie… could you give me a hand please?'

Jackie finished her glass of champagne and it felt like everyone was waiting for her to answer.

'Sure,' said Jackie and she helped Zara to her feet.

'Good night, girls. I believe this is what the youngsters call hashtag living your best life.'

Val watched them walk slowly across the patio and into the house. Zara using Jackie as support.

'I'm going to check on Brian and then go up,' said Pauline. 'Night, Val.'

'Night,' she said, but her mind was still on the already strained relationship between Jackie and Zara. Maybe she'd be grateful she was only staying for three months.

31

PAULINE

Pauline had the best night's sleep she'd had in years. The bed was like sleeping on a giant marshmallow. She was blown away by the size of her en suite. The shower was huge and so powerful she felt like she'd had a massage too. She had to stop herself from grinning like the Joker when she joined the others for breakfast.

After a round of good mornings they helped themselves to an array of fruit, cereals and pastries in the dining room.

'Did you all sleep well?' asked Zara.

'Really well,' said Pauline, refraining from being too gushing.

Zara's gaze rested on Jackie. Something passed between them. Pauline felt momentarily anxious. She feared they'd had words. 'All right,' said Jackie with a shrug.

'Very well, thanks,' said Val. 'I love the sheets.'

'Egyptian cotton, one thousand five hundred thread count,' said Zara.

'Wow, I didn't know it even went that high,' said Pauline, who was more used to threadbare than thread count.

'I don't know what a thread count is,' said Jackie, helping herself to more orange juice. 'But it soaked up my menopausal night sweats a treat.'

'Eww,' said Val.

'And *you* didn't get them?' Jackie's tone was challenging. There was definitely something wrong.

'I did,' said Val. 'But the thought of... actually you're right, menopause is tough. If the sheets are helping then that's good.' Val returned to eating. Pauline could sense the antagonism radiating from Jackie.

'Just ask any of the housekeeping staff and they'll change the sheets for you,' said Zara.

'Thanks,' said Jackie. 'I think I'll take this outside.' She picked up a croissant and her drink and left the room.

'Is everything all right?' asked Val.

Zara placed her palms on the table and slowly lifted her head. 'I fear the reality of what Jackie has signed up for is weighing heavy on her. I hope you don't both feel the same.'

Pauline shook her head. She was having a great time. Mentally she felt the best she had done in years. She was living somewhere absolutely beautiful, she no longer had any money worries and she was actually looking forward to working with Zara on her memoirs. If last night's stories were anything to go by it was going to be a tell-all tome that would likely sell in its thousands, which even if all she did was type the words was most definitely the closest she would ever get to success.

'I don't feel like that,' said Val. 'But then my situation is different, as is Pauline's. We have pensions. I also have some investments. Jackie has neither. That makes her dependent on you. That's never going to be a comfortable situation.'

'You're right, Val.' Zara was nodding sagely. 'And it's something I'm addressing.' Zara checked her watch. 'What time is it?' she asked.

'Almost eight o'clock,' said Pauline checking her own.

'Damn, I'm late,' said Zara, gripping the arms of her chair and trying to haul herself upright.

'Here, let me help.' Pauline stood up and supported Zara one side and she unsteadily rose to her feet.

'What exactly are you late for?' asked Val, looking puzzled as she sipped her juice.

'Tai Chi and a little one-upmanship.' Zara winked and shuffled off.

'Should we follow?' asked Pauline.

'Definitely. My interest is piqued,' said Val, going after Zara.

They found Zara at the ocean side of the house under a vine-strewn pergola. She was holding on to one of the wooden struts with her other arm outstretched.

'Help yourselves to a slice of lemon and hot water,' she said, nodding at the table nearby. Pauline marvelled at how the staff seemed to move about almost without being seen, like the house-elves from *Harry Potter*. It both fascinated and saddened her at the same time that these invisible people did such a good job.

'You all right?' asked Jackie, joining them. 'Do you need a hand?'

'No, I'm fine.' Zara repeated the same arm stretch again.

Pauline took a place next to Zara and began doing some stretches. She wasn't entirely sure what she was doing but it was warm, the view was amazing, and she wanted to fully embrace her new lifestyle.

'Don't we need mats for yoga?' asked Val, helping herself to a slice of lemon and water.

'Well, it's more Tai Chi,' said Zara.

Pauline realised Zara hadn't taken her eyes off the promenade. It made her look in that direction too. It was quiet. Too early for most people, especially holidaymakers.

'Woo-hoo!' someone called from the street below. They all looked down at a petite woman in a pink tracksuit waving as she race-walked past.

'Good morning, darling,' called back Zara. 'Late night with my city friends but it doesn't halt the routine,' she added, before lifting her chin and repeating the same arm stretch yet again.

'How lovely,' said the woman. 'Cheerio.'

'Ciao, darling,' said Zara.

Val was leaning forward. 'Is she that actor—'

'Yes, Felicity bloody perky bottom,' said Zara, letting go of the pillar and flopping into a chair. She held out a hand towards her glass but she was clearly too far away to reach it. Jackie rolled her eyes and leaned towards it a fraction but Pauline got there first and passed it to Zara.

'I thought she was meant to be lovely,' said Pauline, hovering while Zara took a sip.

'She is but that just makes what she did even worse.' Zara was glaring towards Felicity's retreating back, now a pink splodge in the distance. 'Okay, I might as well tell you.' She said it as if they'd been pleading with her to explain.

'In the Seventies I was a shoo-in for Derriere of the Decade. Back then it was sponsored by a jeans manufacturer. All of a sudden, Felicity was strutting around on TV in jeans and, what do you know, they gave her the award instead of me! Now don't tell me that wasn't premeditated. Totally unforgivable.'

'Derriere of the Decade is a bit of a joke award. Isn't it?' asked Jackie, craning her neck to get a look at Felicity.

'An award is an award,' said Zara, bitterly.

'I don't think anyone remembers,' said Val.

'Really?' Zara twitched her head to one side.

'Not now,' said Pauline.

'Still, she shouldn't have stolen it.' Zara sipped her water and Pauline wondered how perfect Zara's life was if that was a genuine concern.

32

JACKIE

Jackie shrugged, put on her sunglasses and leaned back in her chair. Zara was potty. That was the only conclusion she could come to. She'd not been there twenty-four hours and she'd already witnessed enough to make that deduction. Zara couldn't be in her right mind. That was the only explanation – or at least the only one Jackie wanted to contemplate. Yesterday's conversation had been beyond bonkers. And whilst she wanted to dismiss it she found it was taking up a lot of space in her head.

She had witnessed that while Zara's acting was useful in putting on a show, behind the façade, her health was not in great shape. She hadn't got to the bottom of what exactly was wrong with her but there were definitely mobility issues as well as occasional shortness of breath. However, nothing that implied she was terminally ill so perhaps Zara's request was more theoretical. Either way she needed to think through how she was going to respond because Zara was expecting an answer.

'Anyway, enough of bloody perky bottom.' Zara passed her glass back to Pauline who was continuing to do some half-hearted stretching. 'I've got something fun planned for all of us today.'

Jackie sat up. Now she was interested.

'It's Sunday and you said you always have lunch at the um... Royal table?' Pauline wobbled precariously before righting herself and sitting down.

'Ah, you're right – usually I do but not today. The car is picking us up in half an hour. Sling a few things in a bag and I'll see you out here shortly.'

'The stretch limo?' Jackie was already wondering if she could get a shot of her lying on the bonnet.

Zara tinkled a laugh. 'I hire that for high days and holidays. My own is a fraction more modest but has room for all of us.'

'Where are we going?' asked Jackie, trying to hide her disappointment. Given Zara's age and the rickety state of her body Zara's idea of fun and hers were most likely quite different.

'Sorry, it's a surprise.' Zara tapped her nose. The exact same thing she'd done the day before when telling Jackie that she wanted her proposition to be kept between themselves. It seemed Zara was racking up the secrets.

'What things should we bring?' asked Val.

Zara paused for a moment. 'I'm not going to give the game away so pack for a day at the beach.'

'I've not got a swimming costume.' *Bloody typical,* thought Jackie.

'I have plenty in an array of sizes. My weight has always been a challenge for the screen,' said Zara. 'Come up to my room with me now and you can choose something while I grab a couple of things. Hats, girls, you'll all need a hat.'

Jackie shrugged. She knew she was acting like a teenager but that was how she felt. She was hormonal thanks to the lasting effects of the sodding menopause and she was being controlled again. It was exactly like being a teenager but with less sex. At least that was how it felt. That ever-looming presence her parents had over her was exactly why she had left home and moved in with the others aged eighteen. Here she was again in exactly the same situation but this time there was no escape. She had no job, no pension for over a year and nowhere to live.

She'd hardly slept at all thanks to the bombshell Zara had dropped yesterday. She needed to talk to her about it but getting an opportunity was quite difficult. It wasn't something Zara wanted to discuss with the others around – she'd been clear about that. But until she spoke to Zara properly questions would continue to swirl around her brain.

Pauline joined them in the lift and was chattering about sun cream. Pauline peeled off to her bedroom, Jackie and Zara entered Zara's room and Jackie closed the door. 'Zara, we need to talk about…' Wording this was trickier than she'd thought it would be.

'Ah, bikinis and costumes, here we are.' Zara opened a drawer and sat down in a nearby chair. 'Have a good look through and help yourself.'

'Thanks. Look the whole…' Jackie lowered her voice '…euthanasia thing isn't something you can just lob into a conversation like a hand grenade and then walk away from. Unless you were asking theoretically.'

'I thought I was quite clear that I need someone I can trust to end my life when I deem the time is right.' Zara was completely composed and unemotional. 'And I will reward you for it. In advance.'

'You realise what you're asking me to do.'

Zara eyed her thoughtfully. 'Yes. I do.'

This was madness. 'Are the laws different in France?' asked Jackie.

'No.'

'If the law is the same as the U.K. I'd basically be committing m—'

A tap on the door stopped her finishing the word – something she was actually quite relieved about. Saying it out loud would have made it even more real.

Pauline popped her head around the door. 'Val has got some factor fifty sun cream but you might want something with a lower protection if you're after a tan. Anyone got any spare flip-flops?' she asked. 'Or hats. Neither Val nor I have got one.'

'Don't worry, we'll stop at a beach shop on the way and you can grab anything you're missing,' said Zara. 'It's going to be a wonderful day out together. Live each day as if it were your last; that has always been my motto.'

'Here's one you could try. You can't always get what you want,' suggested Jackie.

'Ooh Rolling Stones?' asked Pauline coming into the room.

'That's the one.' Jackie nodded.

Pauline hummed the song. 'Great. Have you picked a costume?' Pauline started to look through Zara's beachwear.

Jackie couldn't take her eyes off Zara. She felt she was being backed into a corner. Or worse still a prison cell.

'This one is nice.' Pauline held up a swirly orange one-piece.

'Not really me,' said Jackie.

'How about this?' Pauline pulled out a bikini with a peacock feather pattern.

Jackie glanced at it. 'At what cost I wonder?' Her words aimed at Zara.

'Nothing. This is friends helping each other out. It's what we do.'

Jackie scrunched up a shoulder. 'I'm not sure I want to risk it. I'll be fine in my undies.'

'There might be a law against that,' said Pauline, looking aghast. 'This is France.'

'Then I suppose I don't have much choice.' Jackie took the bikini and walked out.

33

VAL

After a quick stop at a boutique beachwear shop they all came away with anything they were missing from hats to beach shoes and sunglasses while Zara waited in the car. Their choices were quite interesting to Val. She went for a reasonably priced floppy sun hat and a striped beach towel. Pauline chose a baseball hat with *Cap Ferrat* embroidered on it and some cheap flip-flops. Jackie bought the largest sun hat in the store, some Jackie-Onassis-style sunglasses, a tasselled sarong and factor fifteen sun oil.

There was a frisson of excitement that even Val couldn't ignore. When they stopped a second time it was actually not far from the villa if Val's bearings were correct. They were at the port. Gabriel got out and helped Zara from the car. She elegantly rested a hand on his arm and led the way.

'When I was a child we used to do crab fishing off a jetty like this one,' said Val.

'I bloody hope that's not what we're doing,' said Jackie,

lifting up her exceptionally dark sunglasses as if checking where she was going.

All around them were boats and yachts of various sizes and shapes, their rigging tinkling like Christmas bells in the warm breeze. Up ahead someone shouted and they all looked.

'Ahoy, me hearties!' hollered a young man in shorts who was standing on a large white yacht.

'Locals are friendly,' said Jackic. 'Well, hi yourself,' she said appraising him over the top of her sunglasses.

Zara stopped when she reached the boat. The man jumped down and kissed her on both cheeks. 'Zara, looking fabulous as always. And these must be the girls.' He offered his hand and they each shook it in turn.

'This is my good friend Raphael.'

'I'm your skipper for the day,' he said, helping each of them up a small step and on board.

'If you need a hand I believe Jackie is qualified,' said Val. Perhaps her evening class was going to come in useful after all.

'That was sail boats rather than motor boats. You know, the sort with a boom,' said Jackie.

'I know all about booms,' said Raphael, with a cheeky wink.

'I can tell today is going to be a good day,' said Jackie, holding on to his hand a fraction longer than was necessary. But Val had a feeling she was right.

Raphael gave them a quick tour of the impressive motor yacht. Like everything they had experienced so far it was the height of luxury. Fifty-eight foot of top-quality cherry woodwork, elegant furnishings with such things as an aft sun deck, wet bar with barbecue and sunbathing pads. There were even toilets, showers and a hidden ironing board. He pointed out the cabins including one for crew, which brought on one of Jackie's hot flushes.

The crew settled them all on deck where sumptuous leather-clad seating made a horseshoe around a gleaming table and it wasn't long before they were motoring out into the open ocean. The salt spray hung in the air as the boat picked up some pace, cutting through the calm waters with ease.

Raphael had two other crew members who were equally attentive and they soon found themselves moored offshore looking back at Cap Ferrat with cocktails in their hands, the yacht bobbing gently.

'This is something else,' said Val, admiring the view. But it was the calm and tranquillity that was utter bliss to her. Zara told a story about Stirling Moss and Jackie Stewart but Val wasn't really listening. She was savouring the peace that was all around her. She liked the idea of being in the middle of nowhere and the Mediterranean Sea fitted that brief perfectly. When they'd finished their cocktails they set off again, which was sadly all too soon for Val. She could have happily stayed there for the day just breathing in the clean air and revelling in the tranquillity. The boat sped across the water and Jackie almost lost her new hat. While the wind in her hair was certainly blowing the cobwebs away, Val was already pining for the stillness of the earlier hour.

The coastline was pretty and Raphael pointed out some key sights along the way. It was a lot greener than Val had been expecting. Having spent time near the coast on holiday she'd always felt you had to go into the heart of France to find lush areas, but she was happy to be proved wrong. She closed her eyes and listened to the rhythm of the sea against the hull.

A shrill whistle brought her back. 'Starboard!' hollered Raphael pointing to his right.

Jackie was there in a flash. 'It's only bloody Flipper,' she said pulling out her phone.

Val went over and watched as a couple of dolphins darted through the water whilst keeping pace with the yacht. One of the dolphins treated them to a display as it leaped out of the water. It really was a sight. Jackie almost fell in trying to get a selfie but was saved by Raphael. If Val was being uncharitable she may have thought Jackie had done it on purpose.

'Thank you. You saved my life,' said Jackie.

'And her bargain sunglasses,' added Val.

'You're welcome,' said Raphael.

'I love this boat. Is it worth a lot?' asked Jackie.

'It's a few years old now so around eight hundred thousand euros.'

'Wow. You must have a bob or two,' said Jackie, fluttering her eyelashes.

Raphael laughed. 'It's not mine. I'm just hired crew.'

'Shame,' said Jackie, looking genuinely disappointed.

'It belongs to a friend of mine,' said Zara. 'To be honest with you we had quite a choice. Virtually everyone on Cap Ferrat owns a boat of some description. Can't move for the bloody things.' She laughed.

They had barely recovered from the excitement of the dolphins when the boat appeared to be heading towards land. Val felt a pang of sadness that the trip was coming to an end. She watched as they drew closer to another port. This one was bigger and had some seriously impressive yachts anchored.

Zara made it to the front of the boat. 'Are she and Raphael going to have a *Titanic* moment?' asked Jackie.

'Why? You jealous?' asked Val. Instead of a witty retort or comeback Jackie just shook her head.

'Welcome to Monaco, girls,' said Zara, pointing at the dock as they glided in. They moored between two larger vessels, one of which seemed to be hosting a party.

'Wow,' said Jackie. 'Wall-to-wall beautiful people.' She wasn't wrong.

After a few formalities on entry to the principality they were given a guided tour in two 2CV cars. Val was paired with Zara and a young enthusiastic driver. 'I used to have one of these cars,' said Val, as it took a bend quite fast.

'I know,' said Zara from the front. Her thoughtfulness was quite astonishing. They did the full Monaco Grand Prix circuit, Palais du Prince and the cathedral before they were set down outside a swish-looking restaurant. 'Lunch,' declared Zara. 'Then I will stay here and you can all gamble away your life's savings in the casino or stroll the harbour or whatever turns you on. Raphael will be ready to take us home whenever we're ready.' Val was starting to think that perhaps her three months could be extended a little.

34

PAULINE

After lunch they left Zara sipping cocktails and set off together to hit the casino because Jackie said it had to be done. Despite the casino being quite stunning with its chandeliers and artwork, after a couple of spins of the roulette wheel Pauline was itching to get back outside and explore. Her fifty euros had disappeared in the blink of an eye and she wasn't prepared to lose any more. Jackie had managed to win on her first spin, convincing her she was on a lucky streak.

Pauline and Val followed Jackie around for a bit. 'Jackie seems to have cheered up,' said Val as Jackie whooped and punched the air.

'This is definitely her sort of place.' Pauline looked around at the well-groomed people betting stacks left right and centre, and it made her head spin.

'But not yours?' asked Val.

'Not really.' Pauline didn't want to sound ungrateful.

'I mean it's amazing to experience but now I'd like to see more of the town.'

Thankfully Val revealed that she felt the same. They left Jackie with the new friends she'd made on an erratic move to the blackjack table and went to investigate more of Monaco. They took a bus up to the palace as they had already established that the prince wasn't home thanks to Zara explaining that there had been no flag flying.

For a modest entry fee they were transported into a lavish world of Monaco royalty and the history of the principality. Pauline had never seen anything like it and Val had to keep nudging her to move on to the next room – each one grander than the last. There were vast amounts of silk, velvet and marble. One of Pauline's favourites was the one where the wall coverings matched the furniture in a deep royal blue. The pictures of Prince Rainier and Princess Grace brought a lump to her throat. The love was virtually radiating from the photographs. *Oh, to have ever been loved liked that*, she thought.

When they'd seen it all they decided to walk back to the casino, which took them down one hill and up another, but it was worth the effort as the views were magical. Pauline tried to pick their yacht out in the harbour but it was tricky as from a distance they all looked very similar. She was getting a bit sweaty under her baseball cap so she took it off for a moment. She'd chosen the cheapest hat in the shop – force of habit. The warm breeze ruffled her hair and it struck her how much her life had changed in just a couple of days.

'I keep expecting to wake up,' she said to Val. 'But then I've never even had a dream as amazing as this.'

Val gave her a warm smile. 'You've had a tough time, haven't you?'

'No more than anyone else.' Pauline focused on the view as they walked.

'I think losing your partner is pretty tough.'

Pauline concentrated on her answer. 'He wasn't a nice man. At the start he was but then they all are, aren't they? Even on the honeymoon the cracks were starting to show. I should have spotted the signs, not been so blinkered. It was my own fault really.'

'I doubt that,' said Val. 'Making you think it's your fault is the sign of a grade-A manipulator.'

Pauline shrugged. 'It's history. Not worth going over.' She didn't want to think about it. It was locked away in a dark corner of her mind and that was where she wanted it to stay. But Val didn't look like she was going to drop the subject.

'Was he violent?' she asked.

'A few times... more towards the end. I seemed to wind him up quite easily.'

Val stopped walking. 'Pauline, have you had any counselling for this?'

She shook her head. 'Val, it was almost eight years ago. I'm fine.'

'I'm not sure you are.' Val was always blunt. 'I think you are still harbouring some blame and you shouldn't be. None of it was your fault. There is no excuse for violence.'

'Well, I—'

'None,' said Val quite forcefully, making Pauline blink with the vehemence of her word.

'I know you're trying to help. And that's kind of you, really it is. But I am all right.' She was tempted to add *now that he's dead* but decided against it. 'Come on,' she said, setting off again. 'They'll be wondering where we've got to.'

As they neared the casino they both received a text from Jackie saying she was at the beach. They carried on walking but, as they reached the Café de Paris, Pauline had a pang of guilt. 'I think I should join Zara,' she said, checking her watch. She'd been on her own for a few hours and that somehow didn't seem right. 'You go to the beach and join us when you're ready.'

'Are you sure?'

'Of course. I'm hoping this won't be the last time we come here.'

'Good point. Okay. See you later.' Val headed off towards Larvotto and Pauline went inside to find Zara.

Pauline spotted her sitting in a sumptuous sculpted booth under a giant chandelier and was about to bound over when she realised that behind the large sunglasses she was sleeping. She went to the bar and ordered herself a café au lait and was quite pleased that her O-level French was still passable. Pauline took care not to wake Zara as she joined her on the luxurious velvety seating. It was quite a good spot for people-watching and the waiters were attentive.

She watched Zara snoozing and wondered at what the ageing process had done to her friend. Without her theatrical mask she seemed elderly and vulnerable, and Pauline was glad she was there. Not only in her decision to detour from the beach but glad she had moved countries. Just thinking about it made her marvel at what she'd done. She, little never-amount-to-much Pauline, had moved to a whole new country. She was quite proud of herself. Whilst she had done it for her own benefit she could see now how she could repay Zara's kindness. Zara was old and she didn't want to face it alone, and with the girls back together she wouldn't have to.

A champagne cork made a bit of a pop and Zara jolted awake. She took a moment to come to and at the sight of Pauline the mask was back. 'Pauline, what time is it?'

'Almost five,' she replied.

'Oh, darling, what on earth are you doing here? You should be exploring.' Zara made a shooing motion with her hands.

'Val and I have been to the casino and the palace but I wanted to spend some time with you. I think I'll visit again because it's utterly beautiful. Not on a yacht or anything that grand but perhaps I could get the bus here.'

'The bus?' Zara scoffed. 'You take my car. It's what it's there for. I'm paying for Gabriel anyway. Bus fare would be a waste of money.'

'Thank you. And not only for that but for all of this. It's incredibly generous of you. I just wanted to make sure that you knew how much I appreciated it.'

Zara reached across and took Pauline's hand. 'It's my pleasure. But there is a little something you can do for me...'

'Of course. Anything,' said Pauline, keen to try to balance the books on Zara's kindness.

'Excellent,' said Zara. 'My body is letting me down, Pauline, and it's only going to get worse. You wouldn't want to see me suffer. Would you?'

'Of course not.'

'That's good.' Zara squeezed her hand. 'I knew I could rely on you, Pauline. As you know I have had the most wonderful life. I've graced the silver screen, been immortalised on film and have a loyal fan base. And I can't let those fans down. They don't want to see a decrepit old woman wither away in a nursing home. Can you imagine the field day the press would have with that?' Zara looked alarmed at the thought. 'I want to die on my own terms. Which is why when the time comes I need to know that you will do whatever's necessary to help me on my way. To end my suffering.'

A wave of nausea swept over Pauline and she thought she was going to faint. But she didn't and was mightily disappointed.

35

JACKIE

Jackie soaked up the sun on a beautiful soft sand beach. This was the life she had always dreamed of. Cocktails on a yacht, fabulous lunches in swanky restaurants, reckless abandon in the casino followed by chilling out in the sunshine. She couldn't help but feel a touch of jealousy that Zara had been living a life like this for all these years and not bothered to get in touch. All the holidays Jackie could have had. Why was it always rich people who got to have free holidays at places their other wealthy friends owned? The world was all skew-whiff. It was expensive to be poor. She'd watched people in supermarkets merrily stock up on three-for-twos when she had to think carefully which credit card wasn't at its limit. She'd seen colleagues buy expensive boots that would last a lifetime when Jackie had to go with the cheapest she could find and be happy if they lasted the season without springing a leak.

But she was here now and she needed to keep that at the front of her mind. If she wanted to enjoy her new life to the max though, she needed cash and that meant sorting out a job or landing herself a rich man. She knew which option she preferred. She was sick of fighting her way through life on her own. Raphael was gorgeous but what she really needed was someone wealthy. Sadly the men with the money were usually old. She was contemplating which film star she would like to date when Val joined her. 'You're turning the colour of a cooked prawn,' said Val.

'Good,' said Jackie. 'I don't want to post too many pictures of me looking like the Bride of Dracula. I'm aiming for that sun-kissed look.'

'Currently you look more sun-slapped. Like you've been boiled.'

'I'm fine.' Jackie adjusted her borrowed bikini top.

'Still, I'd put some cream on those shoulders.' Val handed her the factor fifty from her bag and sat down on the sand next to her.

Jackie pretend-huffed and sat up. 'Okay, Mum.' She moved her sunglasses to the top of her head, took the proffered tube and started applying lotion to her shoulders. 'Why aren't you on social media?'

'Why would I want see into the lives of the superficial?'

'Because it's fun. You can stalk all your favourite celebrities and people like your photos.'

'I don't need strangers to validate me.'

'Nor do I,' said Jackie, slightly miffed by the insinuation. Val took things too seriously. 'You do feel good when you get a hundred likes though.' Jackie liberally smothered her hot shoulders with the high-factor cream.

'I'll take your word for it. I suspect my life is too dull

to generate any interest from strangers and that's exactly the way I like it.'

'It's not dull anymore though.' They both looked at the scene before them: sand stretching around the bay, happy families and couples dotted about, the sea in a postcard shade of blue gently lapping the shore and the sun coating everything in warmth. 'This place is something else isn't it?' said Jackie.

They both looked out across the water. 'It really is. I can't help wondering what the catch is,' said Val, fixing her with a look that made Jackie scratch at her neck.

'None that I can see.' She returned the sun cream and put her sunglasses back on. It was easier to have this sort of conversation when the other person couldn't study you too closely. Especially someone like Val who was used to interrogating people for a living. 'Are you stripping off and going for a dip in the sea?' asked Jackie, keen to change the subject.

'I would but I'm not sure I can be bothered.'

'I know that feeling. I think it's the sun that makes you feel like that. And my wobbly bits.'

'You don't have any,' said Val. 'You're looking in great shape.'

'Thank you, Valerie. As someone who is somewhat a subject matter expert on the female form I will take that as a compliment.'

'You're welcome.' Val sighed. 'I'm no expert though. I've been just as much of a failure with relationships as you have.'

Bloody cheek, she thought. 'Hey, I'm no failure on that front. I've had plenty of great fellas.'

'Perhaps we have different criteria for success. All I meant was I would have liked a long-term partner.'

When she put it like that Jackie wasn't quite as offended. 'Yeah. Me too,' said Jackie. 'Although, I wouldn't have changed my youth for anything. But if I had uncovered the perfect man while I was having fun that would have worked out better.'

'It's not too late to find someone,' said Val.

Jackie hoped she was right although her extensive research on the subject told her it was unlikely. She'd had a good look around the casino but most men were flanked by protective wives who knew what they'd got. And the others who she'd found attractive were not interested in her.

'You missed some fun at the casino,' said Jackie, moving up onto one elbow and regarding Val who was sitting hugging her knees.

'Why's that? Did you win enough to buy a yacht?'

'I wish. No, but I did win back what I lost.' Val gave her a look. 'More or less.' She was about fifty quid down overall. 'This woman at the blackjack table stopped me changing more money for chips. Told me the odds were stacked against me and not to put down anything I couldn't afford to lose.'

'And you needed a stranger to tell you that?'

It had been quite addictive and with the heady setting she'd been caught up in it all. 'Well, no. I guess I got swept along and everyone else was betting such large amounts.'

'Because they can afford to lose it.'

'Yes. Oh wise one. So we got talking and turns out this woman knows Zara.' Jackie paused while she recalled what she'd been told. 'Actually, she said she knew Zara a few years ago when she was a regular at the casino. She said she used to hold these amazing parties, which got my interest because who doesn't love a party?' Val's expression was undecided. 'Anyway, this woman said everything changed about a year ago and of late Zara's become almost a recluse. She'd heard she'd been ill.'

'You're the nurse. What's her health like?'

'Between you and me?' Jackie waited for Val to nod her agreement before she continued. 'From what I can tell, not great. Her ankles are swollen so that's circulatory, which implies heart issues. And her arthritis is severe.'

'Yes, I'd noticed that. She looks like she's in a lot of pain.'

'She shouldn't be with the number of tablets she's taking. She's got English and French doctors dishing them out. I'm going to have a sort through everything. But not today.' Jackie returned to her horizontal position.

'Do you think we should be heading back to the restaurant?' asked Val.

'Not until I've gone the colour of a conker.'

'About ten more minutes then,' said Val. They'd not always got on well but Jackie did appreciate Val's dry sense of humour. Her forthrightness was irritating but she was a reliable person. She reasoned there were worse people to have around.

36

VAL

Val eventually managed to drag Jackie off the beach. Back at the Café de Paris Zara insisted that they stay for one round of drinks. It took them an inordinate amount of time and far too much laughter to get themselves all seated on bar stools. Hopping onto a bar stool had once been something all of them would have done without a second thought. However, in advancing years it was easier said than done. At one point Val thought they were going to have to get a winch for Zara. Instead a joint effort between her and Pauline had managed to get her in place, whilst Jackie discovered yet another seat that she could twirl around on. After such an effort, once they were all in place they had no intention of moving for a while. The cocktail menu was enticing and Jackie found the barman to be equally so, which meant she had more cocktails than anyone else. The prices were eye-watering but Zara just waved a gold credit card.

'You know you don't have to pick up every tab,' said Val,

although she was well aware she was the only other one of them who could have afforded it.

'Darling, you're going to go through my finances so you'll see that I really don't need to budget. I can barely keep on top of spending my interest although I do try my hardest.' She gave a little wink.

'It's still very generous of you though,' said Val. 'Thank you.'

'You're welcome.' Zara linked arms with her. 'Let's head homeward.'

They took a leisurely stroll, partly due to Zara's difficulty in walking but also due to Jackie who kept doubling back to take photographs of herself with an array of expensive cars and almost got herself run over twice. She'd take a few steps forward, look at the photograph and realise it was either blurred or she had her eyes closed, and then dash back for another attempt. By the time they had walked back to the yacht, the light was fading. Raphael was waiting to help them aboard.

'On deck or down below?' he asked.

'Ooh down below. That's cheeky,' said Jackie, giving him a friendly slap on the arm and leaving her hand resting there.

'It can get chilly on deck,' he said. 'But I have blankets.'

'Blankets all round,' said Zara, clapping her hands together. 'You have to see the coastline by night; it's an absolute picture.' Val surmised Zara wasn't mobile enough to manage the spiral staircase down to the plush lounge area and cabins below. She'd struggled enough getting onto the boat, which was only a few steps.

'Come on.' Val steered a slightly wobbly Jackie away

from Raphael to the seating at the stern. Something was swaying and it wasn't the boat. Zara took Pauline's arm and they joined them. Everything about the yacht was luxurious but even at almost twenty metres in length it was dwarfed by far bigger vessels moored around it. Many had jet skis strapped to them and one even had a helipad. Zara called them floating gin palaces. Raphael pointed out a couple that he'd crewed in the past. Val wondered how much the others cost and then decided she'd rather not know.

They were soon settled with blankets and steaming mugs of coffee although Jackie and Zara had gone for Irish coffees, which weren't going to help in the sobering-up process.

Raphael came to check they were all okay before they set off. 'You can sit by me,' said Jackie, patting the seat seductively.

He smiled kindly. 'Sorry, ma'am, I'm at work.'

'Leave the lad alone,' said Val, when he'd returned to the wheel.

'Lad? He's an adult – that makes him fair game,' said Jackie, her words a little slurred.

'You've got underwear older than him,' said Pauline, who had been rather quiet.

'It's not my fault that Marks and Spencer's make them to last.' Jackie jutted out her chin. 'Anyway I'm young at heart and that's what counts. I'm down with the kids. I still listen to Radio One. Don't get on my case just because you're more BHS than BTS.'

A discussion followed about who or what BTS was and Val tuned out and savoured the moment. Sitting up on deck of a luxury yacht, huddled under a warm blanket and sipping hot coffee whilst watching the lights come on across Monaco, was something she wanted to commit to memory. She wouldn't have missed this for the world. She was really quite grateful to her noisy neighbours for giving her the motivation she'd needed to do this. It was quite unlike her to do something spontaneous, although she knew she could hardly count a few weeks of mulling something over as spontaneous – although it was for her. She'd used to be far more impulsive but that had got her into trouble. She'd learned that thinking things through and adopting a measured approach were the far safer bet.

'Here we go,' called Raphael as the engines started and the boat left the jetty.

'Woo-hoo!' shouted Jackie before dissolving into laughter. Val wasn't sure what was funny but they all found themselves laughing.

They quietened down as the boat got going and whipped up a breeze, but the blankets were warm enough to keep them comfortable. Val admired the twinkling lights on the land. It was like a Christmas scene but without the snow and the clawingly saccharine verse.

'Good day?' Zara asked her.

'Really lovely, thank you. Do you come to Monaco regularly?' Val watched closely as Zara considered her reply.

'Not as much as I'd like to. I used to come to escape the paps. Oh how I wish they were an issue now. Monaco has a strict no paparazzi policy, which was a blessing at times. They were wild and happy days.' She let out a deep sigh as if remembering. 'I'm glad I was able to share a little of the fun of Monte Carlo with you all. I've enjoyed today immensely.' Zara looked at each of them, making Val do the same. Pauline was staring out to sea, Jackie was blowing kisses to Raphael. Zara cupped her mug with two gnarled hands.

'How's your health, Zara?' asked Val.

'Could be worse.' She gave a bright smile. 'The Mediterranean climate is much kinder to my arthritis. Just twenty-four hours in Blighty and I can feel myself seizing up. I'm far better here. Especially now I have all of you.' She let go of her mug with one hand to give Val a one-armed squeeze. The mug toppled. Val was quick to grab it and stop any spillage. Zara returned to holding it with two hands and no more was said.

The lights of Cap Ferrat drew closer and Val felt a little blue that their trip was over. She had enjoyed everything about it, especially the company. They moored up. Val felt the night air chill her shoulders as she relinquished her blanket.

Raphael helped them from the boat. 'Ring me,' called Jackie making a sign like a phone with her hand. Raphael nodded.

It must have been a good day because Val noted she was even entertained by Jackie. 'Leave him alone,' she said, steering her away. Jackie hadn't changed a bit but unfortunately nor had the age of the men she went after. Together they made their way along the wooden jetty back to the waiting car.

'Did you not see the connection we had?' Jackie made fists with her hands and then pinged them open to emphasise her point. 'Sparks were flying.'

Val guided her into the car. 'Yeah, nylon does that,' she said.

37

PAULINE

As soon as she got inside the villa, Pauline headed to the utility. She shut the door behind her and leaned against it like she was escaping the enemy. Brian yawned and stretched. She picked him up and hugged him to her. She needed some comfort. He let her hold him for a moment and then he started to wriggle. He liked affection but it was on his terms. She put him down and he went and sat next to his food bowl. She was pleased to have a distraction but trying to open the cat food with shaking hands was difficult. She took a moment to try and calm herself down. Brian meowed his impatience. She was reeling from the conversation she'd had at the Café de Paris with Zara. It wasn't images of the past that were haunting the darkest corners of her mind now. Her brain was conjuring up vivid pictures of her smothering Zara with a pillow. It made her gasp. She took a breath and concentrated on opening the food pouch.

The door flew open. She jumped and dropped the cat

food. The meaty contents spewed out of the packet and Brian immediately set to work on tidying it up.

'Did you want a tea or coffee?' asked Val, surveying the scene.

'Whoops.' Pauline tried to mask how she was feeling with her best attempt at a smile. 'Er, no I think I'll head off to bed thanks.'

'You all right?' Val nodded at the mess.

'Oh yeah. You know me – butter fingers.' She grabbed a cloth and began wiping up, much to Brian's annoyance.

Val paused and Pauline avoided eye contact. 'Night, then.' Val left and closed the door behind her. Pauline's shoulders slumped as the tension abated. This was a nightmare. The past she thought she had left behind in England was now tapping her on the shoulder or at least that was how it felt. Did Zara know what she had done? Was that why she had asked her? But she couldn't possibly know. Could she? Pauline took a deep, steadying breath. Brian batted the pouch about in an attempt to get the rest of the food from it.

'Here,' she said putting his bowl on the floor and decanting the rest of the cat food. Brian gratefully tucked in. She stroked his silky fur. It was going to take more than Brian to calm her down this time.

Up in her room she uncovered one of the bottles of pills she'd brought with her. She'd hoped she wouldn't need them. She unscrewed the top and tipped one out. There was a knock on her door, making her jolt and tip a load more out into her palm.

Jackie stuck her head around the door. 'Are you sure you don't want a cocktail?'

'Cocktail?' Pauline's brain was fried.

'Did bloody Valerie offer coffee? She's obsessed with everyone sobering up. I have no idea why.' Jackie walked into the room. 'We're basically on holiday which means sun, s—' Jackie's eyes finally focused on Pauline's hands. 'Are they antidepressants?'

'Yes.' There really wasn't any other way to answer such a direct question.

'Shit. What are you doing?' Jackie's eyes widened in alarm.

Pauline looked down at the handful of tiny white pills. 'Oh, no, I just tipped too many out.' She put them all back in the bottle apart from one, which she popped in her mouth and dry-swallowed.

'Bloody hell, Pauline, you gave me a fright.' Jackie held her hand to her chest.

'Sorry.'

Jackie sat down on the bed next to her. 'You on those for depression?'

'I have ups and downs but lately, since Brian moved in, I've been okay. I thought I could wean myself off them but today was a bit...' There was no way she could explain any further.

'Today was an amazing day.' Jackie was looking puzzled. Pauline could understand why. Right up until her conversation with Zara, Pauline would have placed today as one of the best days of her life. Off the top of her head she couldn't think of a day to rival it. Even her wedding day hadn't been that great. Arguments, rain and a groom too drunk to share their first dance. Yes, today was a front runner.

'What was it about today that's got you reaching for those?' Jackie was looking mystified. 'Was it all a bit too much?'

'I guess. It's a lot to take in that this is my life now. Last week I was in a dingy damp flat eking out my teabags and this week I'm sipping thirty-pound cocktails with abandon.'

Jackie sucked air in through her teeth. 'Yep, yeah...' She started to laugh. 'It's freaking amazing ain't it?'

Usually her laughter would have been infectious but now it felt inappropriate. 'I think I'll turn in.' Pauline checked the top was tightly back on the tablets and returned them to her bedside drawer.

'Okay, it's up to you. Zara is digging out some of her old films.'

'That's nice.'

'No, it's not,' said Jackie with a snort. 'She lives for an audience and that's us now. She's basically paying us to massage her ego. How twisted is that?'

'I think it's nice...' She struggled to finish the sentence because her automatic response of how she'd felt earlier in the day – that her friend Zara was a selfless, kind individual – was no longer true. But she couldn't let on to Jackie that anything had changed.

'You would think that.' Jackie squeezed her shoulder affectionately. 'Goody two shoes Pauline. Always sees the good in everyone.'

Jackie got unsteadily to her feet. 'Well, a large cosmopolitan and a dull film are calling me. With any luck I'll fall asleep before we get to Zara's part.' Jackie sniggered. 'Night, Pauline. Sleep tight, mind the bed bugs don't bite.' She left the room but didn't close the door.

Pauline puffed out a breath. How on earth was she meant to get to sleep? Then she remembered she had a tablet for that too.

38

JACKIE

Jackie woke up to find herself on the sofa with a blanket half covering her. She blinked a few times and as she looked around she remembered where she was. She looked over her shoulder and a chink of bright light stung her eyeballs as it cut its way through the gap in the blinds. Surely at some point in life you became immune to hangovers? There had to be some benefits of getting old, although she hadn't found any as yet, but then she wasn't old. Not really. If forty was the new thirty then sixty-four was fifty-something... She stopped herself. Even fifty-something felt too much.

She slumped back into the sofa. How the hell had she got so old? It felt like her school years had lasted forever. She'd longed to be an adult and be old enough to drink and have sex. School had been interminable. Her teens had stretched out. And the few years the girls had lived together had seemed much longer than they actually were. But then what? The next thirty years had been a blur of work, scraping by and losing men. It was like someone had fast-forwarded her life. And now, here she was, sleeping on a sofa at sixty-four.

'Good morning,' trilled Zara exiting the lift. 'Blinds open,' she said and they slowly rolled away on her command. Light flooded the room and Jackie pulled the blanket over her head. Whatever time it was, it was too early.

'Good morning, Toby darling. You'll speak to Mummy, won't you?' Jackie heard Zara remove the parrot cage cover. Toby screeched and flapped his wings. That bloody parrot.

'Morning,' mumbled Jackie, peeking out from under the blanket. She probably looked a sight.

'You're not dead, then,' said Zara, twisting to look at her. 'I was all for waking you last night but Val said given how much you'd drunk it was better to let you sleep. There was no way we could have carried you to bed. You only made it up from the cinema room with Val's help.'

'I didn't drink that much. I was tired, that's all.'

'As tired as a newt,' said Zara, with a chuckle.

'I'm fine.' Jackie decided to front it out. It was nothing some coffee and paracetamols couldn't fix.

'That's good to hear, Jackie. As today is officially day one in your new job.' Zara gave a wide smile.

Shit. She'd kind off forgotten about that. 'Yeah. I don't think we ever agreed any formal working hours or a contract though did we?'

Zara's grin faltered. She gave a hollow laugh. 'We don't need anything formal; this is an arrangement between friends.'

'Still, it might be best for both of us to know where we stand.' Jackie sat up and her stomach lurched. 'I'm going for a shower.' She rearranged her gaping top and straightened her dress that was all twisted around her. Her shoes were by the sofa but she knew she couldn't bend down without throwing up so they'd have to stay there. She fake-smiled at Zara and tottered into the kitchen. Priority number one was to rehydrate. Then after paracetamol and a shower she'd tackle her new job.

As it turned out she spent an okay morning with Zara going through her medications. She'd had to look a couple of things up – mainly because they were in French – but she had worked out what each tablet was meant to be doing and when they should be taken. Pauline helpfully typed out a list but seemed a bit disappointed with her typing speed, which was interesting because Jackie thought she was super-fast – her fingers were a bit of a blur.

Jackie went out to find her new boss in the garden and presented her with the list. Zara read it solemnly. 'Now you know what I'm taking and why,' said Zara, regarding her from behind her sunglasses.

There was nothing she wasn't familiar with. 'Tramadol and codeine painkillers for the arthritis, aspirin for your heart, statins for cholesterol, fluoxetine for depression, furosemide for high blood pressure and the oedema in your feet and ankles, and donepezil for… Alzheimer's,' said Jackie.

'It's a wonder I don't rattle.' Zara sighed heavily.

'I've moved the painkillers to your bathroom cabinet, by the way.' Jackie was concerned that it was too easy to unintentionally take a deadly cocktail especially if she was suffering from Alzheimer's. Although from what Jackie had witnessed she was coping well on that front as it wasn't obvious even to her.

'Keep them where you like. I can't open the bloody childproof bottles anyway.'

'There's a reason for those.' Jackie watched Zara struggle to adjust herself in her chair. Zara's earlier request was making more sense. As her health deteriorated it took with it the option to finish things for herself.

'It's not a great outlook is it?'

'I've seen people cope with worse,' said Jackie.

'My bloody ailments are eroding me. Like a slow torture as I watch little pieces of me disappear. My last blasted doctor said I should consider a nursing home. What a bloody insult.' Her eyes widened in alarm. 'Can you imagine the field day the papers would have with that?' And there was the real issue. The thing that clearly terrified Zara more than any of the illnesses ravaging her body was the fear of how the papers would portray her.

'Zara, your health is more important than your image.'

'Huh. In my job there is *only* image.' She looked out across the garden and Jackie saw she was watching a man clipping the hedge. 'I used to love pottering in the garden here. The sun on my skin. You get a great sense of achievement from nurturing plants. But one by one all the things I get pleasure from are being taken away from me. Some days I can barely walk. I can't stand for long and now my mind is turning to mush.'

'The tablets should help.' Jackie wasn't sure what else to say.

'But they don't fix anything do they? It's like sticking a

plaster on an amputated limb. Bloody pointless. Well, I'm determined to keep going but when the end comes, as it will, I want to be here.' They both surveyed the beautiful gardens and the sea beyond. 'I can't go into a home.'

Jackie could see it was distressing her. 'You can have professionals to nurse you at home, Zara.'

'I won't have strangers. There's always someone willing to pay for a story. That's why I need people I can trust. That's why I need my girls.'

39

VAL

Zara had been occupied with Jackie for most of the morning. Val, with Zara's permission, had tried to be proactive and track down information on Zara's investments. What they had sent through was actually quite straightforward and Val wasn't entirely sure where she was going to add value. Although she had already started to document everything in a spreadsheet. Zara had asked if they could discuss it another day as it was lunchtime.

The car was waiting for them as they walked out of the front of the house. The air was heavy with the scent of bougainvillea and Val breathed it in.

'Morning,' called a man wielding a hedge trimmer.

'Walter, darling, these are my girls,' called back Zara.

'Ladies, it's a pleasure.' He nodded at them and returned to work.

'He is the loveliest man,' said Zara. 'Wife dropped down dead. Terrible. He does a fabulous job with the garden though.'

They all agreed that he did and filed into the car. Jackie paused for a moment. 'I bet he was cute when he was younger,' said Jackie, watching as he bent over.

After a short air-conditioned drive they were deposited outside a striking cream building which was a restaurant called Les Voisins where they ate the most delicious lunch. It was one of those occasions when everyone's food looked amazing and Val wished she could try it all.

Zara paid the bill and rose unsteadily to her feet. 'I think yesterday wiped me out. The rest of the day is your own, girls. Feel free to use the car, gym, pool, cinema room – all my classics are available. Pretty much all my work is there. You can come back with me or did you want to have a look around Beaulieu-sur-Mer?'

'What's Beaulieu-Sue-wotsit when it's at home?' asked Jackie, squinting.

'It's where we are,' said Val. 'We're in the next village on from Cap Ferrat.'

'Cool,' said Jackie. 'Does it have any shops?'

'A few,' said Zara.

Val, Pauline and Jackie looked at each other as the lunch things were cleared away. As if waiting for one of the others to make a decision.

'It's a beautiful day,' said Pauline. 'What do you both think we should do?'

'I'm going to explore Cap Ferrat,' said Val, pushing back her chair.

'When you say explore…' began Jackie slowly. 'Do you mean walk aimlessly – or worse still museums and stuff – or are we talking shopping and bars?'

'I was thinking it would help us to get our bearings if we

made our own way back to Cap Ferrat...' Jackie rolled her eyes. 'Maybe work out where the good cafés and bars are for us to try in the future,' suggested Val.

'It's a beautiful walk along the prom, about half an hour, maybe a bit longer. I used to adore that walk.' Zara sounded wistful. 'I'll take the car; you three enjoy yourselves. Look out for David Niven's place. It's bright pink – you can't miss it. Remind me to tell you about the parties we had there. Just call Gabriel if you need picking up. Ciao.' She walked unsteadily out to the waiting car.

'I feel like I've been let out of school early,' said Pauline, scrunching up her shoulders.

Jackie was scrolling on her mobile. 'There's a handful of shops and a casino here. That's about it.'

'Let's wander back then,' said Val, making a move.

Zara had been right. The walk back to Cap Ferrat was indeed breath-taking and thanks to a level promenade it was really quite enjoyable, if not a little warm in the afternoon sun. Some of the villas they passed were stunning and dwarfed Zara's.

'I'm beginning to think we're living in the cheap seats,' said Jackie, when they found the giant pink villa Zara had told them about.

As they strolled along the prom at Cap Ferrat, they all agreed it was time for a sit-down and coffee. A delightful little café with tables outside took their eye and they found themselves seats in the shade where they could look out at the many boats bobbing in the marina.

It was busy and it took a while for someone to serve them but they really didn't care. '*Bonjour*,' said a harassed-looking young woman.

'*Bonjour, trois cafés au lait s'il vous plait,*' said Val.

'Hang on,' said Jackie. She leaned into Val and lowered her voice. 'How much is coffee?'

'They're on me,' said Val.

'Okay, great. Carry on.' She smiled at the waitress. 'Large ones please.'

'*Grande, s'il vous plait,*' added Val.

'*Oui bien.*' The waitress dashed back inside.

'How was your morning with Zara?' Val asked Jackie. They'd been shut away in Zara's bedroom for most of the time.

'Well...' Jackie let out a sigh. 'She knows me well enough to know I'm going to blab to you both and she didn't tell me not to so...' She shrugged. 'As well as the crippling arthritis and the heart issues, she's also got Alzheimer's.'

Pauline gasped. 'Oh no, poor Zara.'

'It's early days I think from the medication she's on and, to be honest, I've not noticed any issues with her memory but then we've really only been talking about the old days, which are often the last to go.'

'That's awful,' said Pauline, going all wobbly-lipped.

'It makes a lot of sense.' Val had felt there had to be an underlying reason for Zara's apparent generosity. She was saddened that Zara's health was failing but pleased to be proved right that there was something other than magnanimity driving Zara's actions.

'She's terrified of going into a home and the press getting hold of the story. She trusts no one,' said Jackie.

'The question is what level of care is Zara expecting us to provide and for how long,' said Val.

Jackie looked uncomfortable and then perked up as the

waitress approached. 'Ooh they look good.' She nodded at the approaching large cups of coffee.

But Val now had bigger things to ponder.

40

PAULINE

On the way back from the café loo Pauline spotted a corkboard with a myriad of leaflets and handwritten notes pinned to it. Her French wasn't up to much but thankfully there were a few items in English and one of them caught her eye. She unpinned it from the board and took it back to their table. She placed it in front of Jackie.

'What's this?' she asked, peering over the top of her sunglasses at the handwritten note.

Pauline read it out. 'A high-profile English couple are looking for a guardian to take care of their seafront villa in St Jean Cap Ferrat, France. It is a part-time residence, where the principals spend around three to four months a year (mostly in the summer and some occasional weekends). When the principals arrive, they bring temporary personnel with them (a chef and one to two stewardesses) who the guardian will have to guide and oversee. Blah, blah, blah. One thousand euros per month plus accommodation in a two-bedroomed fully furnished annex in the grounds.'

Jackie almost snatched the note from her. 'You're kidding right?'

'Not at all.' Pauline sat down feeling rather pleased with herself.

'Do you think it's Posh and Becks?' asked Jackie looking excited.

'No. But it looks promising,' said Val, rereading it over Jackie's shoulder. 'Although you're committed to Zara now, which poses a conflict.'

'How could it?' Jackie was frowning at the suggestion.

'Didn't Zara want you to be on hand at all times in case she had any health scares?' asked Val.

'Yeah, but I'd only be up the road.'

'Where is it exactly?' asked Val.

'No idea but Zara said herself Cap Ferrat was tiny so it can't be far away. I could call Gabriel to come and get me. That would work.'

Pauline was starting to feel uneasy and wished that she'd left the note pinned to the board. 'I think you'd need to talk it over with Zara first.'

'She'd say no and we have no formal contract.' Jackie turned to Val. 'You're the legal eagle. I've not signed anything. She can't force me to stay, can she?'

'Verbal contracts are binding,' said Val. 'Which means it's as enforceable as a written one. Especially when there are a number of witnesses to it. The only shaky ground would be the detailed terms of that agreement because there aren't any written down.'

'I thought you got people out of stuff like this?' Jackie pouted.

'No, I specialised in family law.'

'I'd be mad not apply for this. A grand a month for doing literally nothing. Pauline, you're a star.' Jackie patted her on the arm, got out her phone and started dialling the number.

'Don't rush into something.' Pauline could feel her stress levels rising. 'Please.'

'I think you need to sleep on it at least,' added Val.

Jackie put her phone to her ear and waved for them to be quiet as someone had answered. She introduced herself and gave them a thumbs up before leaving the table to take the call out of their earshot.

'This is all breaking down already and it's only day three,' said Pauline, chewing her thumbnail and wishing that she'd never laid eyes on the advert.

Val appeared to ponder the situation for a moment. 'Try not to worry. Despite it being a note on a café board I suspect they will be doing rigorous background checks on someone who will be living in and taking care of their property. In which case when the subject of references comes up I think our Jackie will have a few issues.'

'She can't ask Zara and she was fired from the nursing home,' said Pauline, thinking aloud. 'Thank heavens… sorry that makes me sound like a right cow but that all spiralled super-fast. I saw it and thought of Jackie and then when I really thought about it I realised it was a bad idea and…'

'Breathe,' said Val, giving her wrist a gentle squeeze. 'It'll be fine.'

Pauline took a shaky breath. 'Thanks, Val.'

'No problem. It was a kind thought. Jackie does need to get a job and, let's face it, we know what she's like. So one where she doesn't actually have to do much would be ideal.'

'That's probably unfair. I think she liked her job as a carer. Maybe she could find another role like that here.'

'You're right. But again, anything in that field will require references.'

Jackie marched back to the table and slammed down her phone making Pauline jump. 'Problem?' asked Val.

'There's one thing we overlooked. They won't do anything without a CV detailing my experience and references from my last employer. I can't believe it. That was my perfect job.' Jackie shook her head and picked up her coffee. 'I need a proper drink.' Pauline felt bad as relief washed over her.

Val raised her index finger. 'You've been open with Zara about needing some paid work. Why not suggest to her that she ask her local contacts if they have anything suitable? That way Zara is on your side and you are far more likely to get something based on a personal recommendation.' Jackie was either scowling or thinking – it was hard to tell the difference. Val shrugged. 'It's simply a suggestion.'

'It's not a bad one,' said Jackie, at last. Pauline exhaled deeply. This was turning into a stressful afternoon. 'But I've just lost my dream job so I definitely need a drink first,' Jackie added picking up the bar menu.

41

JACKIE

A couple of days later and Jackie was feeling slightly better about things. Although she wasn't really sure why because she still had no money and hadn't got around to asking Zara if she had any friends she could work for. The reason she hadn't broached it was the fear that requesting a favour of Zara would raise the still unanswered question that hung over them regarding the favour Zara had asked of her – euthanasia. But she and Zara had settled into a routine of sorts, which left her with a huge amount of free time. She couldn't really grumble. However, as she walked into the living room and Toby screeched in alarm, grumble was exactly what she did with a few swear words thrown in. She really hated that parrot and his incessant screeching. There was no need for all the fancy burglar alarms and CCTV Zara had installed. How Zara had stuck living with the noisy bird for fifty years she had no idea.

Jackie was hoping to lie out on a recliner but she spotted that Zara and Pauline were out on the patio. They had started work on Zara's memoirs although given Zara's nature she had informed Pauline she could only work on it when the muse was with her. Jackie had thought you only had one of those if you were writing fiction but what did she know? Zara spotted her through the glass and beckoned her over. She could hardly pretend she hadn't seen her so she went out.

'How's it going?' Jackie asked.

'It's marvellous,' replied Zara. 'Quite therapeutic to be able to regurgitate my life experiences and try to make sense of them.'

'We're still on her childhood,' said Pauline, with a tight smile. She was sitting at the small bistro-style table with the laptop inside a cardboard box to keep the sun's reflection off the screen. Poor Pauline – she really had got the short straw.

'Morning, ladies,' said Walter, the gardener, striding past with the lawnmower. He was clearly quite fit even if he was pushing seventy. He was friendlier than the other staff but then he was English, which helped. Jackie had tried chatting to the others but her French was non-existent, making conversations limited. With Walter it was different, easier.

'Morning, Walter,' called Jackie and he gave her a wave and a broad smile.

Zara cleared her throat. 'I'm glad I've got you all together,' she said. 'I've been thinking about that party we talked about.'

Jackie had no recollection of a conversation about a party but she wasn't going to argue because she absolutely loved parties and it might be a great opportunity to meet people and widen her friends circle, which she was currently finding quite restrictive.

'Would it be here?' asked Pauline.

'I was thinking about hiring a marquee. We've had them before and they work rather well. People get to see the house but not trash it. I was thinking Saturday.' Zara rested her hands on the arms of the chair.

'I'm in,' said Jackie. 'Do I need a new outfit? Will it be dead posh?'

'That's a bit short notice for whoever is organising it, and for people to respond,' said Val, getting out of the hot tub in a surprisingly fluid motion and putting on a bathrobe over her swimming costume.

'I've organised them in far less time,' said Zara.

'*You* have?' asked Val with the emphasis on *you*.

'My P.A. has. Oh come on, it can't be that hard. Marquee and booze – what else do you need?' Zara looked at them like they were making a big deal.

'People?' suggested Val, pulling up a chair.

'I guess we could help,' said Pauline, looking at Jackie.

Jackie instinctively started shaking her head. This was exactly what Zara wanted. She was feeling more and more like Zara's puppet and it got her back up. 'Not really our place though, is it?' replied Jackie.

'That's the perfect solution.' Zara clapped her hands together. 'I'll tell my P.A. to liaise with you three. Now all we need is a theme. Any suggestions?'

'Slave and Master,' said Jackie and Val scowled at her.

'Sounds like a bondage party,' said Zara, looking aghast. 'No, I was thinking a golden theme.'

'The age or the colour?' asked Val.

'I did mean the colour but now you say that I'm thinking

the golden age of cinema.' Zara splayed out her palms in arcs like the parting of Tiller Girl fans.

'That would be when you were in films would it?' Jackie couldn't hide her rancour. She was remembering now why Zara used to wind her up. Everything was about her. She had to be the centre of attention and it left no room for anyone else.

Zara uttered a stage laugh. 'That was way before my time. I think it was between the wars. And anyway I've had plenty of Zara-Cliff-themed parties in the past.'

'I bet you have,' muttered Jackie under her breath but given the pained look Pauline was giving her it was likely it was louder than she'd intended.

'Do people still dress up for parties?' asked Val, drying her legs with a small towel.

'You've obviously not been to one of Elton's,' scoffed Zara.

'Not recently, no,' said Val. 'But then that's Elton and this is you.'

'True.' Zara pursed her lips. 'I wouldn't want to upset him.' She shook her head. 'Golden in colour it is then. You can all have some fun with that. Help me, Jackie.' She reached out a hand.

Jackie hesitated. 'Are we *all* tasked with organising this bash then?'

'Yes. With the help of my P.A. Alina.'

'I think we need more information,' said Val. Always one for the detail. *Hopefully she'll find a loophole to get me out of it*, thought Jackie.

Zara shrugged dismissively. 'Here. Saturday evening. Gold theme for Toby's fiftieth birthday.'

'Toby?' Jackie had to stop herself from swearing.

'Obviously,' said Zara, looking mildly irritated. 'We talked about it being his big birthday and needing to celebrate that.' She impatiently waved a hand at Jackie and she reluctantly helped her to her feet. Once Zara was upright and steady Jackie went to let go but Zara continued to grip her arm. 'You can walk me to the lift, if you would.'

'You really need to get a stick or a frame,' said Jackie. She heard Pauline gasp unhelpfully behind them.

Zara made a half-hearted attempt at a laugh. 'Jackie, Jackie, Jackie. Always the joker.'

When they got inside and the door was closed Zara halted, making Jackie do the same. 'Perhaps we could have a rule that you don't suggest things like that in front of anyone else?' said Zara, her voice surly.

'A rule?' The phrase instantly put Jackie's back up.

'Yes, Jackie. A rule – is that okay with you?'

'You hired me to be your medication supervisor; I don't remember any mention of there being rules.'

'And I don't recall giving you the title of medication supervisor.' Toby made a sound like canned laughter.

Once she'd deposited Zara at the lift Jackie returned to the others outside and flopped into Zara's vacated chair. 'How the hell did we get stitched up with organising a party for a bloody parrot?'

'You're not a fan?' asked Walter, appearing as if from thin air and making Jackie do a double take.

'He's just very screechy,' she explained. 'You a bird fancier?' she asked.

'Do I fancy birds?' he asked, with a smirk. 'Some more than others.' His eyes swept over Jackie.

She liked a bit of harmless flirting. Even if he was on the older side, it still gave her ego a little pep. 'With or without feathers?' she asked.

'Toby didn't used to have any feathers,' said Pauline, making Walter turn in her direction. 'When he lived with us before.'

'Ah, the London years,' said Walter, with a raised eyebrow.

'Zara told you about those?' Jackie was intrigued that Zara had shared stories with the staff.

'Only the PG-rated bits. Who do I come to for the really juicy stuff?' he asked.

'Well, that would be me,' said Jackie.

'I was hoping you'd say that,' said Walter.

Val cleared her throat in an unsubtle fashion and widened her eyes at Jackie. What was her problem? She was only having some harmless fun. Was that against the rules too?

42

VAL

Val had to admit she was quite pleased about the party. Not the actual party itself because she was indifferent about those but she did love to organise things. And whilst she'd gone down a few rabbit holes on Zara's investments she had yet to find anything untoward or a cause for any alarm so she had plenty of time on her hands. She was enjoying relaxing and found she was sleeping well, having a walk along the promenade before breakfast when it was cool and quiet and mixing up her day with a little work and pleasure meant she felt everything was balanced. Generally she did a bit of work in the morning, enjoyed a leisurely lunch with the others and then she read a book or had another walk in the afternoon. It was blissful.

Val was back from her walk and the house was still quiet. She decided to check a few things before the others appeared for breakfast. Zara had given her access to her computer but the filing system was vast. Val gave Zara's P.A. Alina a call. Alina was based in Nice and seemed to work all hours but rarely visited the villa. Val understood why because she'd seen first-hand Zara's ever-growing list of demands. Val wanted to talk through responses for the guest list Alina had drawn up but Val couldn't find it anywhere.

'It's on the shared drive,' said Alina.

'Right. I've not got access to that,' said Val.

'No problem. I can add you.' Val could hear fingers tapping on the keyboard at the other end. 'There you go. I've sent you a link. Just log in as you would to the computer. I've set up a party file and everything is in there.'

'Excellent. Thank you.' Val decided to have a browse while Alina was still on the line in case she encountered a hitch. 'Did you get anywhere with the cake?'

'No, it's a nightmare. Nobody in the area can do what she wants in the timescale. I've tried her favourite London bakers but at such short notice I'd have to get it flown out by private plane and if the journos got hold of that they'd have a field day. Zara has been clear about what constitutes dismissal.'

'I can imagine,' said Val, adjusting her reading specs as she scanned the filenames. 'Right, I've got it. Let me see if I can source a cake locally. We may have to make do with one of those photograph onto icing ones instead of the 3D model of Toby in chocolate she wanted. I'm sure Toby won't be bothered. Thanks, Alina.'

'Great, if you're sure.' And she was gone. Val got a feeling standing up to Zara wasn't something most people did. She looked through the party files. Alina was efficient. Val jotted down a couple of actions and closed what she was working on. She scanned some of the other names further down the filing structure on the shared drive in case there was anything investment-related and one filename caught her eye: Chapman. Her surname wasn't the most unusual but she was intrigued enough to click on it. She was shocked by what she found. A few more clicks later and she was looking at copies of her divorce papers. Confusion and temper vied for first place. She printed off the documents, snatched them from the printer tray and went to confront Zara.

She knocked on her bedroom door but didn't wait to be invited inside. She was too cross to follow formalities like manners when her personal life had been dug up. And for what? Zara's entertainment? Her mind was spinning.

Zara's eyes popped open. 'Val?'

'What is going on?' Val threw the printed sheets across the bed at Zara.

She glanced at them. 'What is it?' she asked meeting Val's stare.

'Copies of my private documents that I have just stumbled upon on *your* computer drive. Would you care to explain? Not that I think for a moment you can come up with any reasonable justification as to why you would have them.'

'Ah, I was going to talk to you about that.' Zara remained calm and tried to shift herself upright but it appeared to take more energy than she had.

'You had no right, Zara. This is a gross invasion of privacy.'

'There isn't anything on that drive that's not in the public domain, and anyway don't you want to know why I did it?'

Val was still furious but Zara was right – she did want to know. 'Go on.'

Zara slowly drew in a breath, eyeing Val the whole time.

The dramatic pause was annoying. 'I did it because I wanted to help you.' She fixed Val with her pale green eyes.

'How is you digging up my personal life going to help me?'

'Because you're not in touch with your daughter are you?'

Val was wrong-footed by the statement. It was like a body blow. She thought nobody knew about her child. She'd not gone out of her way to keep it a secret but the question hadn't come up. It was easier to say she didn't have any children than to admit she didn't know where her daughter was. She'd reasoned not having her daughter in her life amounted to the same thing.

Val's anger hitched up a notch. 'That is none of your business.'

Zara patronisingly waved a hand for Val to calm down. 'Your husband took her away when she was what, two years old? And despite court orders and investigations you never managed to find her, did you?'

Val's blood felt like ice in her veins. How on earth had Zara found all this out and who else knew? Her limbs started to shake so she sat down on the bed with a bit of a thump. A door to a long-closed part of her life had opened up and it appeared other people had been snooping around in there. She had to swallow a few times before she could speak. 'No, I couldn't find her.'

Zara perked up. Like the turning point in a film. Her expression went from grim reality to fairy tale. 'Well, I've found her, Val. I had a private investigator track down your Wendy.' She opened her bedside drawer and pulled out an envelope. 'Here.' She offered it to her. 'All the information is in there. Her address, her new surname, job and a couple of photographs. I was waiting for the right time. But here.' She waved the package.

Val was struggling to process what she was being told. She'd spent the last forty-seven years of her life searching for her daughter. How could it now be so easy as to accept the envelope that Zara was holding and have all her questions answered? She reached out to take it with a shaky hand. But initially Zara held on tight. 'There's just something I'm going to need from you in return.'

Val was immediately hesitant and withdrew her hand. 'Zara, I'm not one for game playing. If there's a cost involved, that's fine.' She knew it wouldn't be cheap and didn't expect Zara to be out of pocket but Val could realise some money with a little notice.

Zara gave a tinkle of a laugh. 'I don't want your money. All I want in return is a promise from you that you will do something for me in the future.' She tilted her head at a jaunty angle but there was something about her expression that bothered Val.

'When you say something… Is that a general request or another specific role you'd like me to perform?' Val had to admit hers was the loosest remit. Pauline was typing her memoirs, Jackie was supervising her medication and general health. Val's task around the investments hadn't amounted to much. Clearly Zara wanted more payback.

'Quite specifically…' There was another pause but this time Val could see Zara was choosing her words carefully. 'I would like you to ensure that I don't suffer at the end of my life.'

'As Jackie takes care of your medication I'm assuming you don't mean that.'

'I don't.'

Val knew what she was asking but she wanted to be clear. 'Are you asking me to facilitate your demise, Zara?'

'Yes. I am. Do I have your word?' She fixed her with her gaze and offered the packet again.

'Absolutely not.' She stood up and left the room because she feared if she stayed the temptation to take the envelope would be too much.

43

PAULINE

Pauline entered the dining room where she found Val ripping apart a croissant. 'Morning. How are you?' she asked.

Val scowled so hard in her direction it made her jump. On seeing Pauline's reaction Val seemed to soften a little. 'Sorry. Ignore me. Good morning, Pauline. How are you?'

'I slept well. And without any tablets or anything.' She was really pleased that she was easing herself off the sleeping pills. It was nice to know they were there but even nicer that she felt she wasn't relying on them and that didn't just go for the ones that made her sleep; she was gradually reducing the antidepressants too.

'And how are you finding life here in France?' Val popped some of the butchered croissant in her mouth. She seemed tense.

'You know what?' Pauline sat down opposite and helped herself to freshly squeezed orange juice from a cut-glass jug. 'Much better than I could ever have dreamed I would.

Everything here is lovely, the weather is glorious and I'm enjoying the typing, too. It's really interesting. Zara has had the most amazing life. Sometimes she repeats herself but when I point it out she says we can pick it up in edits. It's all going really well. Don't you think?'

Val seemed to ponder the remnants of her mutilated croissant. 'Mostly, I'd say it is.'

'And we're all getting along well.' She almost added *even you and Jackie* but feared that would be tempting fate. There was one little fly in the ointment – Zara's end-of-life request. She feared a repeat of the Café de Paris conversation every time she was alone with her. It hadn't happened yet, which was a relief, but it also meant the unanswered question was hanging over her. Was it wrong of her to hope Zara's memory would fail and she would forget about it?

'I suppose we are.' Val seemed to be pondering something. 'Do you think—'

'Another day in paradise,' trilled Jackie, sashaying into the dining room. 'Have you seen the sky? There literally isn't a cloud in it. It's pure blue.' She poured herself a coffee and sat down. 'What are your plans for today?'

'Sorting Zara and this party out,' said Val. Her jaw seemed tight.

'Good luck with that,' said Jackie. 'After I've argued with Zara about her medication, re-enacted a couple of scenes from *Holby City*,' she said, with a wink. 'Then I think I might go shopping. Anyone fancy it?'

'No, thank you,' said Val.

'Sorry. I can't,' said Pauline. 'But there is something I'd like you to get for me if that's okay?'

'Name it,' said Jackie.

'I was thinking about dyeing my hair. What do you think?' She'd been considering it for a while and now seemed as good a time as any to try it.

'Great idea. A rich auburn would suit you. Or blonde – everyone looks fabulous with blonde hair.' Jackie ran a hand through her own.

'Nothing brash, just the colour it used to be,' said Pauline, quickly.

'You should go to a hairdresser, Pauline,' said Val. 'Get it done properly.'

It had been a very long time since she'd had her hair done professionally. And the thought of it wasn't a comfortable one although it didn't fill her with fear like it once would have done. 'I'll think about it. I can't go today – I'm letting Brian out for the first time.' Pauline nibbled at the edge of a nail. 'It's been two weeks. Do you think that's enough time for him to have settled?' She looked to Val for reassurance.

'I've no idea,' said Val, standing up, dropping her serviette and striding from the room.

'What's up with her?' asked Jackie, ladling fruit salad into a bowl.

'I don't know. What do you think about Brian?'

'Who? Oh the cat. I can't wait to see him go after Toby,' she said, gleefully.

'I'm a bit worried about that too.' For a moment Pauline feared she'd be back in the position she was before: facing eviction. If Brian jumped on the parrot's cage poor Toby could die of fright at his age.

'What are you worried about?' asked Zara, almost in the doorway. She beckoned for Jackie to come and help her.

Jackie rolled her eyes for Pauline's benefit but slapped on a smile and went to help Zara.

'How Brian and Toby are going to get on,' said Pauline.

'Or not,' added Jackie, patiently supporting Zara for the last few steps to her seat in the dining room.

Zara gave an involuntary huff as she sat down. 'Well, my last husband would have said they have two chances.' Pauline was alarmed. Was this a two strikes and you're out policy? 'Don't look so worried, Pauline. What it means is, they either will get on or they won't. If they do, then great.'

'And if they don't?' asked Pauline. Her voice had gone all wobbly.

'Brian has the utility rooms and all of the gardens. Worst case, he doesn't get to roam the rest of the house alone but he has all of the outside at his disposal and an inside space for shelter. You're also welcome to take him up to your room.'

Pauline released a heavy breath. That would work. 'Thank you.'

Zara leaned over and patted Pauline's hand. 'There's always a solution. That's what friends do – they help each other.' Zara smiled but Pauline wasn't sure she was still talking about the cat.

44

JACKIE

Jackie's morning pretty much played out as she'd thought it would. She was trying to introduce some light physiotherapy to help ease Zara's arthritis and Zara was beyond sceptical. To be fair, Jackie didn't know too much about it. She'd only been on the first day of a five-day course when she'd been sacked. She figured the other four days would be mainly practising and repeating what they learned on day one. She'd tried a little gentle manipulation of Zara's joints, where Zara huffed a lot, but Jackie had decided she was going to persevere. Arthritis couldn't be cured but if she could make things a little more comfortable for Zara she wanted to try. It would all look good on her new CV she was drafting ready for landing herself an actual paid job.

Jackie had arranged with Gabriel to pick her up after he'd deposited Zara in Nice for a lunch date with some old friend from her West End days. From what Jackie could make out they basically drank wine, ate croque-monsieurs and pulled apart any actors who were doing well at the moment. It was important to have a pastime at their age, reasoned Jackie.

She was standing out the front of the villa waiting for Gabriel. They'd arranged that he would honk and she would walk down to the gates to save him having to reverse the thing up the steep narrow driveway. Jackie was checking her account balance on her phone. It was nice to see that she had one, even if it was modest.

'Hey there,' said Walter. Where the heck had he sprung from?

'Hiya.' She put her phone away. 'You clocking off?'

'Yes, that's me done here for the day. I've a few tasks I've been meaning to get around to so today is their lucky day. How about you?'

'I thought I'd pop into Nice and check out these shopping areas I keep hearing about.' As if on cue there was the sound of a car horn. 'That'll be Gabriel. See you later,' said Jackie, with a wave.

'Hang on, I'll cadge a lift into Nice if that's okay? That's where I'm heading too. Save the planet and all that,' said Walter, walking in step with her.

She couldn't really say no. It wasn't like it was her car and driver although she had been planning on pretending exactly that. She forced a smile. 'Of course. The more the merrier.'

'Great.'

It was a short trip to Nice and Walter made it entertaining by pointing out landmarks and local stories of wild parties and even wilder celebrities. Walter said Jackie's needs took priority so they visited three different shopping areas and had a thoroughly good time. Jackie got quite the thrill when people clocked Gabriel opening the car door for her. The Centre Commercial Nicetoile was a swish shopping mall, decorated with giant chandeliers and shiny surfaces with a mix of tourists and wealthy locals who were easy to tell apart. In her mind she wondered what category she fitted in – neither it seemed.

Walter was patient and had a good eye for women's clothes, which he blamed on trailing after his spouse for over thirty years. He spoke warmly about his wife, who Jackie learned had died six years before. It was nice to hear about someone who had enjoyed a long and happy relationship. This was something she and the other girls had missed out on.

Jackie bought a dress for Toby's party and accessories but she was mindful of her cashflow, or lack of it, so hadn't hit the credit cards with abandon like she would have done in the past. It also helped that Walter knew a few bargain shops. Gabriel took her bags and while Walter went off to do whatever it was he'd come into Nice for, Jackie went for a stroll along the Promenade des Anglais.

The sun was high in the sky as Jackie strolled the palm-tree-lined walkway with the ornate palace-like buildings on one side and the glittering Mediterranean a stone's throw away on the other. There was a mix of life here: tourists taking photos, couples walking hand in hand oblivious to the beautiful view, and the odd jogger and skateboarder weaving around them all. And here she was, Jackie Heatley – the girl who wouldn't amount to much.

Her parents had always struggled financially but it was all behind a thin façade. They had a little house in an average area and her father was extremely proud that it wasn't rented. But that house, and the mortgage it came with, were all they had. It had been a stretch too far but they never saw that because they were desperate to drag themselves out of the poverty they'd been born into. More than once they'd been faced with eviction. She remembered rows, tears and unhappiness. Her father taking all the overtime he could at the factory and her mother working two cleaning jobs. All for what? To compete with the neighbours? They'd been strict, telling Jackie how she should behave and who she could be friends with. But making friends didn't work like that. Jackie was always the kid in the second-hand clothes. The one who didn't quite fit in. She'd fought all her life to do better, to not to have to worry about paying bills. And whilst she was now in the most beautiful surroundings, the fight wasn't over yet.

'There you are,' said Walter, jogging up to her. The gardening clearly kept him fit. Maybe she should actually do some swimming the next time she was in the pool. Having a live-in chef was starting to impact her waistline. 'Val's sent Gabriel off on an errand. We can either get a taxi back or if you've got time for a coffee...' She liked the way he looked expectantly at her. She realised all too frequently it was her asking others, and by others she meant men, to spend time with her. It had been a long while since it had been the other way around.

'I've got time,' she said.

Walter beamed a smile that she couldn't help but mirror. 'Splendid. I know just the place.'

45

VAL

Val was so cross she had to go out. She'd tried occupying her mind but there was no remaining space. Her head was full of the conversation she'd had with Zara. Jackie had gone shopping, Pauline was giving Brian a lengthy talk on reasons why he wasn't to stray far from the villa and she couldn't even look at Zara. Val had grabbed her sun hat and stormed out – although she wasn't even sure it was storming out if nobody noticed.

What she'd intended to be a stroll had turned into a power walk. When she noticed people flinch as she marched by she decided she needed to calm down. It was rare for her to let anger take over like this and she admonished herself for it. Usually she maintained an outward composed exterior but not today. That's how far Zara had pushed her. But entwined with the anger was also a mass of emotions she'd been suppressing for too long and more than anything she feared them breaking the surface. The anger helped to keep those at bay. Because once they'd breached her defences she would once again be vulnerable and she couldn't have that.

Val made for a bench up ahead and sat down. She took a moment to calm her breathing. She'd exerted herself but still hadn't managed to burn off her temper. She took some deep breaths and placed her shaking palms on her knees. She replayed her conversation with Zara. The one that was on a constant loop in her brain. Zara had found Wendy. Pictures of her baby girl swam in her mind. Her chubby little cherub. Her cheeky toddler taking her first steps. And then she was gone. She swallowed hard. These were hard memories to be reacquainted with. They stabbed at her heart as they had always done but now there was new hope. Wendy was alive and Zara knew where she was.

However, there was a huge price to pay for getting hold of that information. How could Zara even ask her to do such a thing? Her a lawyer, for goodness' sake. It was beyond ridiculous. Val took a moment to think. Was Zara really that desperate? She seemed to be coping okay, although she knew her variety of ailments were only going to make her deteriorate. It wasn't a nice prospect. Val could sympathise with how she must be feeling.

She couldn't, however, understand why anyone would try to blackmail someone and use their estranged daughter as bait. The temper started to bubble again. This was completely unacceptable. Zara had information and Val wanted it and she wasn't going to be coerced into a crime to get hold of it. With renewed energy, Val got up and strode back towards the villa, oblivious to the people recoiling as she passed.

*

'Ooh look, Val's back. Hiya,' called Jackie. 'I have found the cutest little café just off the Promenade des Anglais where they do *the* most amazing pineapple cake. Walter—'

'Where's Zara?' asked Val, striding across the patio, her eyes searching in all directions. She was ready to face Zara. She had it all planned out in her mind. She'd gone over and over what she was going to say. How she was going to put her foot down and demand the information about Wendy, and if that failed offer to pay for it. She was also planning to talk to Zara about euthanasia facilities, which were available across the border in Switzerland, where it was all legal and above board. She knew Zara's immediate counter would be the press attention but Val was confident, with enough planning, they could transport her undetected when the time came. She felt she had all bases covered.

'Eww, you're all sweaty,' said Jackie.

Val scowled at her. She didn't have time for Jackie and her superficiality right now.

'Zara's been called away at short notice,' said Pauline, rather more helpfully. 'She's probably already on a flight to London.'

'What?' Val hadn't been gone an hour.

'The actor previously cast in some period drama died suddenly,' said Pauline.

'Zara was bloody thrilled,' added Jackie.

'The production company wanted her to hotfoot it to Shepperton Studios,' explained Pauline.

'There's some very warm dress slippers that need filling,' said Jackie, with a chuckle. Pauline gave her a look and she tried to turn her laughter into a cough. 'Poor unfortunate woman. Terribly sad.' Jackie returned to her sunbathing.

Val was floored. 'I can't believe she's swanned off like that.' And with her she'd taken the wind out of Val's sails.

'Yes, you can,' said Jackie, from her horizontal position.

'Come and sit down,' said Pauline, concern all over her face. 'Can I get you a camomile tea?'

'Bloody hell, Pauline,' said Jackie. 'Zara's only gone to London, not joined a monastery. Oh, hang on, that's monks. What's the one that nuns join?'

'Convent,' muttered Val, distractedly. She turned to Pauline. 'Didn't she say anything…' Her sentence petered out. Of course she hadn't said anything to the others. This was Zara's plan. Put Val in a difficult position. Manipulate her. She wasn't going to have shared that with the others. But at least that meant they didn't know about Wendy. She definitely wasn't ready to open up about having a daughter she hadn't seen for forty-seven years.

Pauline pulled forward a chair. 'Zara did say to give you a message.'

Val sat down gingerly. 'And what was that?'

'Zara said to tell you that whilst she's in London she's going to make arrangements to have lunch with someone and that you would need to do the thing she'd asked you to do.' Pauline gave a little shrug as if not understanding much of what she'd just relayed.

'Blimey that's earth-shattering news,' said Jackie.

'Please be quiet,' said Val. Jackie stuck her tongue out at her. 'Who's she meeting for lunch, Pauline?' asked Val.

'Oh sorry,' said Pauline. 'Someone called Wendy.'

46

PAULINE

Pauline had hoped Zara being away for a few days would be a good thing and generally it was. With Zara in London there was certainly less tension in the air but without her they were like the pages of a book left too long in the sun – without the glue they came apart.

For the last couple of days Val had been preoccupied with Toby's party. She'd been very busy, even getting a specialist company in to clean the villa from top to bottom because the housekeeping staff insisted they only deep-cleaned twice a year. It was a bit over the top but whatever products they'd used had left a nice scent in the air and everything was extra shiny – even the parrot cage. Now party day had dawned Val had become even more forceful than usual, resulting in Jackie calling her a bossy cow and the two of them having a stand-up row in the living room. Pauline had escaped out the back and been spotted by Walter. 'Trouble in Paradise?' he asked nodding towards the villa where raised voices were shouting over each other, but Jackie's voice was winning and her sentences consisted mainly of her repeating the word *arseholes*.

'Sorry.' Pauline couldn't bear arguments. They put her on edge and made her want to flee. Which was exactly what she had done at her earliest opportunity.

'Not your fault. Those two don't really see eye to eye do they?' he observed.

'No. They're both strong women.' Pauline felt that was both a good explanation and a compliment.

'I know. Val told me I was doing the lighting and electrics for the marquee and then tasked Jackie with supervising me.' He puffed out his cheeks.

'Sorry,' repeated Pauline. There really wasn't much else she could say. 'Good luck,' she added and she made her way around to the front of the villa to the waiting car.

Pauline wasn't sure how she had found herself supervising the catering and the cake for the party but she hadn't exactly had a choice. Val had been fraught and had been dishing out tasks in all directions including hers. Zara had sent a few messages via Alina who had been up to the villa to pass on a string of last-minute party requirements and now Val was ready to blow.

The bakery was in La Trinité, north-east of Nice, and the owners were completely lovely. The language barrier had been a small issue and Pauline had apologised profusely for her poor French but then it wasn't often that you needed to ask for an African grey parrot to be immortalised in cake. They had insisted on carrying the boxed-up cake to the car, which was good because it appeared rather heavy. Gabriel had wanted it to go in the boot but Pauline couldn't stand the thought of it careering around in there as they took the twisty roads back to Cap Ferrat. At least on the back seat with her she could hang on to it if the worst happened. Pauline peeked inside the giant cake box. It looked all right to her. It wasn't exactly to Zara's specifications, or Val's for that matter, but it was a cake and there was a bird on it. She would have been over the moon if someone had got it for her.

The thought of the party made her a little anxious but she noted it wasn't the abject terror she'd felt at receiving the invite to Zara's party all those weeks ago. She knew with her friends by her side she could get through it, maybe even enjoy parts, and afterwards they could go back to it being just the four of them. Well plus the staff, oh and Toby and Brian. Zara had even agreed that a cat flap could be fitted so Brian could come and go as he pleased and save them having to keep letting him in and out. Zara seemed open to most suggestions at the moment but that only fuelled Pauline's worry about Zara's request and that when the time came she wouldn't be able to refuse.

Gabriel drove around to the front of the house. Val appeared and opened the car door. 'Have they done it right?' she asked, her eyes darting over the large box.

'Let's get it inside and then we'll have an unveiling,' suggested Pauline. She had a bad feeling that if Val saw it in the car she'd simply send her back to the bakery with it. The three of them moved it carefully from the car and through to the kitchen.

'We can't take it into the marquee until the last moment because it's like a sauna in there and I'm having trouble keeping the flaps open to let it cool down.'

'Still having trouble with your flaps, Val?' asked Jackie, appearing and lifting the cake box lid as they were still carrying it.

'Jackie!' snapped Val.

She backed away with her palms up in surrender. 'Blimey, you need to chill out.'

They safely deposited it in the kitchen. Gabriel made good his escape and Pauline couldn't blame him for that. She tensed as Val lifted the lid and Jackie stuck her face inside the box.

'And that's what exactly?' asked Jackie.

'It's a tree,' said Val, blinking rapidly. 'It's a cake with a tree...' Her lips were still moving but there was no longer any sound.

'It's bougainvillea which is Zara's favourite and here.' Pauline guided Val round to her side. 'Here is Toby in the bougainvillea.'

'I can't deal with this right now,' said Val, roughly handing the lid to Pauline and stalking off.

'It's just his head,' said Jackie. Her grin widening.

'I know but it is rather good. It's 3D like Zara wanted and if we have it that way round people should see Toby.'

'They might if we add a very large sign and an arrow,' said Jackie, no longer trying to hide her amusement.

'What's this?' asked Walter coming into the kitchen and washing his hands.

'Toby's cake,' said Pauline.

'The bird has been immortalised in icing. I'm going to bite his head off later,' said Jackie.

Walter snorted a laugh and joined them to peer at the creation. 'I can only see flowers.'

'Stop it,' said Pauline, starting to feel panicky. 'He's there.' She pointed.

Walter leaned forward and squinted. 'You're right. There he is. He was hiding.' Walter gave Pauline an encouraging smile. 'I'd hide too if someone was throwing me a party.'

'Would you?' asked Jackie, leaning on the countertop. 'And there was me thinking you'd be the life and soul.'

'I'm more of a sit in the garden with a glass of red wine on my own sort of guy.'

'But you could be persuaded to shake your tail feathers. Couldn't you?' asked Jackie.

'That would depend on who was asking.' Walter was watching Jackie closely.

Jackie gave a slow pout. 'I might. I might not.'

Pauline looked closer at the image of Toby on the cake and a sense of dread shot through her. 'Is it me or is that parrot cross-eyed?'

47

JACKIE

It had been nice to have the villa to themselves for a couple of days without Zara playing Queen Bee. And for Jackie to have time off although Val had tried to fill her every waking hour with party duties. She'd been busy all day supervising Walter and a few of the housekeeping staff as they'd set up the marquee. Walter was quite a laugh and very helpful. He'd sorted out all the lighting while she'd been directing an arrival of tables and chairs. She could look herself in the eye and say she'd done her share of the workload – well for today at least. Tonight she was going to look and feel amazing.

She'd had her hair done at a cute little salon in Villefranche-sur-Mer and Val had lost her rag yet again because she'd taken Gabriel and the car when he was meant to be collecting table linen. She checked her reflection in the mirror. Her floor-length golden gown was nothing short of stunning. She had a good figure and it hugged every curve thanks to its stretchy velvet-like quality. The low back had meant she couldn't wear any of her bras under it so she'd had to go for a stick-on version, which felt quite peculiar but did the job. This time she had comfortable shoes too. They still had a decent heel on them but as they were hidden under the dress she had opted for something that wouldn't cripple her.

She was hoping Zara would introduce her to some of her friends at the party and that hopefully these new contacts would lead to a job. She'd decided her approach was going to be to drop into conversation that Zara had head-hunted her from the U.K. to be her carer. Even as she thought of it she knew she'd need to be careful how she worded it and who was in earshot, because if Zara got wind of that she would be furious. Although she had never been scared of Zara. She was all drama and no awards.

Jackie smiled at herself in the mirror – she'd had her make-up done for free thanks to a trial in one of the malls. With any luck she might also find herself a man tonight; then she wouldn't need Zara or any other job. She sighed a little. She wanted someone like Walter but with money. Jackie checked her watch. She probably needed to investigate how the preparations were shaping up before guests started to arrive.

She came downstairs to find the house was a hive of activity. It was full of strange people dashing about. She did recognise most of them but the staff at Zara's kept themselves to themselves and just appeared to clean, change beds, do laundry and clear away plates. Jackie spotted Pauline biting her nails outside and went to join her. The sound of a band tuning up inside the marquee gave her a little shiver of excitement.

'Where's Valkyrie?' she asked.

Pauline spun in her direction looking anxious. 'She's been looking for you,' she said, her eyes wide.

'Why?'

'The decorations for the marquee. Weren't you down to sort them all out?'

'I ordered balloons.' Now she thought about it, Val had said something about bunting, fairy lights and a banner but that had slipped her mind. Oh well, too late now. Jackie shrugged.

'Wasn't there meant to be more?' asked Pauline, picking a different nail to demolish. 'I asked Walter who found some Christmas lights and—'

'Jackie!' Val's voice pierced the warm afternoon air.

'Yes, sergeant major, sir,' said Jackie, standing to attention and saluting.

'That's not going to help,' muttered Pauline, taking a step back.

'Here you go,' said Walter, his timing faultless as he and Gabriel approached with a giant banner. In gold lettering emblazoned on black were the words 'Happy 50th Toby'.

'Walter, that's perfect,' said Pauline.

'Careful it's still damp,' he said.

'It'll have to do,' said Val. 'Can you put it up above the stage, please?'

'You're an absolute angel. You've saved my bacon,' said Jackie to Walter under her breath. She didn't want to show any sign of responsibility in front of Val.

'My pleasure,' he said. 'Just don't let her see what's on the reverse.' He turned to show her the other side which read 'Saint Jean Cap Ferrat Jazz Festival'. She laughed as he winked at her.

'Where are the rest of the decorations?' asked Val. 'I've been having a nightmare while you've been dolling yourself up.' Val looked like she was going to spontaneously combust.

'Calm down. Your blood pressure's probably sky high and that's not good for a diabetic,' said Jackie.

'I'm fine,' snapped Val.

'You're not,' said Pauline. 'But that's okay. We understand.'

'Look,' said Jackie. 'There are balloons and a fabulous sign. There's nothing else we can do now. Guests are arriving in like an hour. You go and get showered and changed and I'll oversee everything here.' She took the clipboard from Val's grip.

'Go on,' encouraged Pauline. 'You've done an excellent job. Zara should be made up and if she's not then it really isn't your fault.' Pauline splayed out her arms. 'Look at what you've achieved in just a few days.' As if on cue the fairy lights came on and the marquee sparkled beautifully. Jackie would have to thank Walter for sorting those too.

Val took a deep breath. 'Right. Christian is managing the caterers and the serving staff. He and Francine have dressed and laid all the tables and the centrepieces.' Jackie wondered for a moment which one was Francine and then she tuned back in. 'The whole house has been cleaned and the floors polished. The bar is in place and we have two cocktail mixologists.'

'Ooh are they cute?' asked Jackie, leaning to see if she could catch sight of them.

'Yes, very cute.'

'Excellent.' Jackie was instantly keen to get a cocktail and check the mixologists out.

'And they're both female,' added Val, clearly getting some pleasure from Jackie's incorrect assumption.

'Shame,' said Jackie. 'Basically we've done everything. It's time to relax and enjoy the party.'

'Zara needs collecting from the airport and there's something else I've forgotten, I'm sure of it.' Val sucked her lip.

'Gabriel is going to the airport as soon as he's helped Walter hang the banner,' said Pauline. 'And I don't think you've forgotten a thing.'

Jackie could see she was tense. 'It's just a party, Val,' she offered.

Val let out a breath. 'You're right. I need to get some perspective. I'll go and get ready.'

'There you go,' said Jackie. She tapped the clipboard to show she was in control. 'We'll cover everything from here.' As soon as Val had disappeared into the lift Jackie handed the clipboard to Pauline. 'She's uncharacteristically stressed isn't she?' Val liked to be in charge but there was a reason for that – she was good at it. Not that Jackie was going to admit that, but it was true. Val usually relished something like this where she could boss people around and then take credit for the end result but today there was something amiss, or perhaps things were more stressful when you got older. Jackie had to keep reminding herself that Val was knocking on too.

48

VAL

Val had been stewing for days. Having found Zara's bedside cabinet empty she was desperate for information about her daughter. Zara had sent a message via Alina for Val to stop calling and messaging her as she was on set and therefore unable to respond. Val knew it was Zara calling the shots and she loathed it. She was desperate to know if she'd met with Wendy and, if so, how it had gone. Val didn't have a great imagination but she'd nevertheless played out the scene a thousand times in her head and the disastrous version where Wendy stormed off was winning.

Val needed to focus on getting ready. There was nothing she could do until Zara arrived. She was titivating her hair when the thing she had forgotten flashed into her mind. 'Toby.' She'd forgotten that the parrot needed to be centre stage. She rushed downstairs and when she reached the bottom she was grateful she was holding on to the bannister as her foot slipped a fraction on the highly polished surface and she almost tumbled.

She dashed around trying to find someone to help her lift the cage. She found Jackie flirting with the band in the marquee.

'That was quick,' said Jackie, giving her the once-over. 'You look good though.'

'Thank you. I need you—'

'Have you seen this ice sculpture?' said Jackie. The giant ice replica of Toby peered down on her. 'You pour your drink through it and it chills it down. It's even got a tray hidden underneath to catch drips when it melts.'

'I know. I ordered it,' said Val, flatly. 'Jackie, I need a hand with the bird cage.'

Jackie made a move towards her and then stopped. 'In this dress? You must be joking. Get Walter to give you a hand,' she said, looking around. 'I don't know where he's got to.'

'He's also going to need to sort out the tray and run-off for the ice sculpture. It's going to melt quicker than we hoped in this heat.' Val could see more jobs racking up before her eyes.

Pauline joined them wearing what she'd worn to Zara's party but she'd had her hair done earlier in the day and now she'd put on lipstick. 'You look fabulous,' said Val.

'Thank you,' said Pauline, touching her hair and going shy.

'Watch out, she's only after someone to help her with Toby's cage,' warned Jackie.

'Oh, I'll help,' said Pauline.

Val and Pauline carried Toby's cage into the marquee and set it down near the entrance away from the speakers. 'He can greet his guests from here,' said Pauline.

'Careful, you're starting to sound barmy,' said Jackie, sashaying over.

Val's phone pinged and she pulled it out of her bra. 'Damn it.'

'Now that is something I wish I'd thought of,' said Jackie. 'Quick thrill with every text. Genius.' Val gave her a death stare. She didn't have time for her stupidity.

'Problem?' asked Pauline.

'Zara's flight is delayed.' Val looked at her watch. 'Guests will be arriving soon.'

'Not a problem,' said Jackie. 'We can entertain them.'

'Good evening, ladies,' said Walter. They all turned to see him wearing full dinner suit and bow tie. He looked remarkably different. They all stared a moment too long without saying anything. 'Am I too early?' he asked, a little frown darting across his forehead.

'No, it's fine,' said Val, checking over her shoulder. Everything and everyone was in place. 'Can you keep an eye on the ice sculpture overflow tray tonight?'

'Sure,' he said. He turned to the others. 'Your new hair colour suits you, Pauline. And you all look...' His eyes rested on Jackie. 'Amazing.'

'Thanks, Walter, and you've gone the full James Bond yourself,' said Jackie, not hiding the fact she was giving him a once-over.

'I'll take that as a compliment. Fancy being my Bond girl?' he asked, offering her the crook of his arm.

There was a moment's hesitation while Jackie glanced around. Val wondered – uncharitably, she knew – if Jackie was checking there were no better options before she took his arm. They all walked further into the tent and Toby screeched a welcome.

The party got off to a good start. Jules and Alina arrived and offered their help when there was literally nothing else left to do. Guests arrived in dribs and drabs and they wandered in and out of the marquee. Walter seemed to know everyone, which was handy. But as time marched on her head was spinning with possibilities about Zara's meeting with her daughter. If it had gone ahead how had Zara handled it? Had she assumed Val would agree to the deal and therefore talked her up? Or had she destroyed any hope of her ever having a relationship with Wendy? There was still no word from Zara and now she was panicking.

'Excuse me,' said Val, interrupting Jackie's conversation with a lavishly dressed older couple.

Jackie glared at her as Val steered her away. 'I was just about to ask them if they'd got any need for a carer,' said Jackie, looking genuinely miffed.

'You can't ask people that.'

'Why not? I'm a professional.' Jackie looked affronted.

'Because it implies they look infirm, which is rather insulting.'

'I guess. But I need to get a job. Looking this fabulous costs money.' She gave a little shimmy before scanning the early guests. 'And my other idea of finding a sugar daddy is disappearing fast so I need to focus on a job.'

'My heart bleeds.' Val wasn't in the mood for Jackie's trivial dramas. 'I can't get an answer from Gabriel. I've no idea if Zara's flight has landed or not.' Val was aware that she was wringing her hands so she stopped. What she wasn't telling the others was the fact that it wasn't Zara who was causing her palpitations but the information she was desperate to hear.

'Chill out,' said Jackie. 'Have you had a cocktail yet?'

'No, but—'

'No buts. You should be enjoying the party too.' Jackie took her firmly by the arm and walked her to the bar where they were greeted by a smiling young woman. 'She likes gin, champagne and white wine but nothing too sweet,' said Jackie. 'Can you whip something up for her?'

'Certainly,' the mixologist replied.

Val was impressed that Jackie remembered her tastes. Maybe Jackie cared more than she let on. If that was the case she was certainly good at hiding it.

Pauline dashed over. 'Zara's here. She's in a foul mood.'

'Thank goodness.' A new wave of angst swept through her. 'I need to speak to her,' said Val, making a move to leave.

'I wouldn't. She's spitting feathers. We'd best keep her away from Alina. Everything was wrong with the flight. I've no idea why she flew scheduled and not private jet.'

'Too short notice. It was extortionate what they wanted,' explained Val.

'And Gabriel had gone to the loo at the exact moment Zara came through customs so he's in trouble and the lift has stopped working.' Pauline bit her lip.

'What the villa lift?' asked Val.

'Yep. But then she was bashing the buttons like an angry chimp so it might be user error,' said Pauline.

Val looked over her shoulder at Walter who was nearby waiting for a cocktail but was clearly listening to their conversation. 'On it,' he said, good-naturedly. 'You can have my cocktail when it's ready,' he added to Jackie.

'What is it?' she called, as he walked off.

'Hanky-Panky,' he shouted and half the guests turned in his direction. Jackie giggled.

'I should go with him,' said Val, but Jackie gripped her arm firmly.

'Why? Zara will just rant at you. Let her calm down. At least if we wait for her to join the party she'll be in showboating mode.' She had a point. Pauline picked up one of the many ready-made cocktails invented especially for Toby's party. Val and Jackie took their drinks and together they went to stand at the entrance to greet new arrivals. There was a flurry of guests who they had a brief chat to and then directed them to the alcohol.

'Were they famous?' asked Jackie, craning her neck to follow the two women who had clearly had a lot of facial surgery.

'No, they're from the yacht club,' said Val. She was struggling with the small talk. Her mind could think only of her daughter. She was meant to have been meeting with Zara that afternoon but maybe she hadn't. What happened now?

'I spoke to someone else who knew Zara from the yacht club,' said Pauline. 'She's not been for a while but apparently she was a regular even though she doesn't own a yacht anymore.' Pauline sipped her cocktail.

'Fascinating,' said Jackie, sarcastically. 'What is that?' Jackie nodded at the grey mixture in Pauline's glass.

'It's an African grey surprise. It contains blue curaçao, gin, blackberry liqueur and lime juice – I think.' She smacked her lips. 'It tastes better than it looks.'

'It would have to,' said Jackie, sipping Walter's Hanky-Panky.

Val sipped her drink but barely tasted it. Her head was too full of questions for her to concentrate on anything else. Had Wendy and Zara met? And if they had what did that mean for Val's side of the bargain?

49

PAULINE

Pauline was quite relaxed but then she was on her second African grey surprise of the evening. She had a little chat to the guest of honour as she felt bad that everyone was ignoring Toby.

He was a handsome bird and looked distinctly better now he had all his feathers back. A conversation with Zara had revealed that the reason he had lost them as a young bird was because they weren't feeding him the right foods. Given they had struggled to feed themselves anything nutritious, it wasn't a surprise that the parrot had been undernourished too. Pauline was fairly sure they used to give him peanuts on a regular basis. 'Happy birthday, Toby. Can you say happy birthday?' she asked.

Toby loved having attention; in fact, he thrived on it. And when he didn't get it he screeched his displeasure. Pauline mused how very like his owner he was. 'Happy birthday,' she repeated.

He climbed up the side of his cage using his beak and

ruffled up his feathers, before puffing out his chest. 'Feck off,' he said.

'Who taught him that?' asked Val, spinning around although Jackie's wobbling shoulders probably held the answer.

'For crying out loud, Jackie, how juvenile – and tonight of all nights.' Val ran her fingers agitatedly through her hair.

Pauline stifled a giggle. 'Actually it is pretty funny.'

'Feck off,' repeated Toby for his audience.

Jackie hooted with laughter, unable to hold it in anymore. They were chortling together when there was a crash from inside the villa.

'For heaven's sake. What now?' said Val, putting down her drink.

Walter came rushing outside. 'Quick, call an ambulance! Zara's had an accident.'

Pauline had only had a few moments in her life that had played out like they were in slow motion and this was to be another of them. Glasses had been discarded as the three of them hurried inside to find Zara laying prostrate at the bottom of the stairs.

'Oh my goodness,' said Pauline. Her heart raced as adrenaline flew through her system.

Jackie went into nursing mode; immediately dropping to her knees next to Zara and talking to her softly. For all her faults, Jackie was actually very good at what she did. Zara wasn't moving or making a sound. Her ankle was at an odd angle.

'Get towels and blankets. We need to make her comfortable,' said Jackie, taking Zara's pulse. Val shot off upstairs.

'Has someone called an ambulance?' asked Walter.

'I'll go,' said Pauline before dashing to the office. With shaking hands she dialled 112. In terrible French she requested an ambulance and gave the address of the villa. They assured her they would be there soon. Pauline returned to the others.

Zara was now on her side and conscious which was a huge relief. Although the blood on a towel Jackie was wielding didn't bode well.

'What can I do?' asked Pauline.

'Keep everyone away,' said Zara. 'I don't want anyone to see me like this.'

'It's fine. I don't think anyone—'

Zara slapped a hand on the shiny floor. 'KEEP. THEM. AWAY.'

'Okay, I'll make sure nobody comes in.' Pauline went and closed the doors with her on the other side so she could direct people away from the scene. Jules rushed over and she explained what had happened. He insisted on going inside but was soon dismissed by Zara. After a few minutes Pauline heard a siren and shortly afterwards ambulance crew appeared but without the ambulance, most likely thwarted by the tricky turn into the steep driveway.

She directed them inside and fielded concerned questions from a few guests. Walter joined her. 'You okay?' he asked.

'Fine, how's Zara?'

'Hopping mad.' Pauline raised her eyebrows. Was now the time for jokes? 'Sorry, no pun intended. She's furious that we called an ambulance.'

'Oh great, I'll get the blame for that,' said Pauline.

'No, you're all right. Jackie has already told her she's got to get herself checked over at the hospital. She's great isn't she.'

'What Jackie?' He nodded. 'Yes, she's one of a kind.'

A few more guests came over as word was spreading about the accident and they were now trying to look through the giant glass windows for a gawp at poor Zara. 'We need to do something,' said Pauline, hoping that would bring an idea to mind. 'Food. I'll see if Christian can start serving something.'

'And I'll get the band to start,' said Walter. They both sped off in opposite directions.

Christian was accommodating, having been made aware of the situation with Zara, and great platters of food were soon winging their way out to the marquee. Pauline paused at the bottom of the stairs to see if there was anything else she could do.

'Yes, tell them I don't need a bloody ambulance,' said Zara, with a flinch as she batted away another attempt to check her over. The medics were looking frustrated and repeatedly doing the classic Gallic shrug. Pauline decided she would be most helpful policing guests and keeping out of Zara's way.

When she returned to her post by the windows the party was in full swing. More guests had arrived, music was playing, and from her vantage point she could see people dancing. Walter emerged from the marquee carrying two cocktails.

'I got you an African grey something. It looks crap but apparently it tastes all right according to Felicity.' He handed her the grey cocktail.

It felt a bit odd to be enjoying a drink and chatting amiably to someone when Zara was in her current predicament, although the fact that she was barking at people was always a good sign.

Jackie tapped on the window and Walter opened it for her. 'Any chance of a Hanky-Panky?' asked Jackie. 'That woman is insufferable.'

'Here, have this to tide you over,' said Walter, handing over his African grey surprise and heading into the marquee.

'Thanks.' Jackie took a long draw. She regarded the glass with disbelief. 'That's actually all right.'

'How is she?' asked Pauline.

'Belligerent, demanding, infuriating... Oh you mean after the fall? Belligerent, demanding—'

'Jackie,' said Pauline, in her most stern voice.

'I'm certain she's broken her one good wrist. And she's done something to her ankle but it's hard to tell because she won't let anyone near it and it's hugely swollen anyway from the oedema. She's also complaining of pain all down her right side so possibly a cracked rib or two. And Val's not helping.' Jackie took a larger swig of the cocktail.

'Why what's up with Val?' Pauline peered inside. Val was pacing up and down and waving her arms about. She certainly looked agitated.

'She seems preoccupied with what Zara had for lunch, which all feels a bit irrelevant.'

'Maybe she's just worried.'

Jackie downed the rest of the drink. 'I don't know. But there's something going on that you and I aren't privy to. I guarantee it.'

50

JACKIE

The ambulance crew eventually gave up trying to persuade Zara to go to hospital. She was a stubborn old bat. After a heated discussion where Zara insisted she was fine to go to the party and everyone else pointed out that she couldn't stand on her injured ankle, Walter, Jackie and Val helped her up to bed. Walter had managed to fix the lift. Apparently the problem was simply that it was reminding them that it was due for servicing so needed someone to override the controls. It had taken the three of them to virtually carry her to bed. Jackie had dosed her up with painkillers partly because she'd been yelling for them and partly because Jackie hoped she'd zonk out. But Zara had still been ranting when Jackie had snuck out, leaving Walter and Val to it.

She felt she had done her bit by trying to ascertain her injuries and giving her some advice, which she blatantly ignored. She'd dressed the wound on her elbow where she'd broken the skin. It was more that the thin skin had come away than a gash but it had bled profusely. She'd only just dodged getting blood on her lovely dress. She'd done all she could and she wasn't missing out on a fabulous party just to be yelled at.

'Come on,' said Jackie emerging into the garden. Pauline looked around. 'Let's have some fun.'

'What about Zara?' Pauline looked concerned. She was a far better person than Jackie was. Pauline genuinely cared about people.

'She's resting and she's ranting at folk so she's perfectly happy.' Pauline didn't seem convinced. 'Don't fret, Val's with her.' Jackie took her by the arm and they joined the party.

The marquee was hot. A combination of a balmy June evening, the lighting and lots of writhing bodies. The alcohol and music had clearly worked their charms and people were laughing and dancing and generally having a good time.

'Ooh look, it's that racing driver,' said Pauline, pointing to a tall man, presumably dancing with his wife.

'Yeah, Val said there were a few of them on the guest list. They all live in Monaco.'

Pauline looked back towards the villa with a deeply worried expression. 'Are you sure there's nothing else we could do to help?'

'No, we have done everything.' Jackie took Pauline's drink off her, set it down and beckoned her onto the dance floor. She was a little reluctant at first but once Jackie started dancing Pauline joined in. The tunes were mainly golden oldies of the Seventies and Eighties and Jackie felt the years melt away. Or that could have been the effects of more cocktails. She danced with abandon.

Sometime later Walter joined them and soon lost his dinner jacket and bow tie. The band took a short break and Jackie was glad to have a chance for a quick sit-down, not that she was tired but she definitely needed another drink after all the grooving. She'd missed dancing. It wasn't like she was going to be the next *Strictly Come Dancing* professional, far from it, but she'd always enjoyed dancing. Unfortunately, opportunities had reduced as she got older. Nightclubs were for the young. Invitations to weddings had petered out in her thirties leaving only milestone birthdays and anniversaries, which she'd noticed had increasingly been celebrated with boring meals rather than parties.

'You've got some moves,' said Walter.

'Why thank you, kind sir,' said Jackie.

'You put Cate Blanchett to shame,' he added nodding to the woman visibly catching her breath in the corner.

'These youngsters can't cut it.'

'You certainly can.' Walter held her gaze. He was a handsome man and there was something else that attracted her to him. He seemed genuinely interested in her and that was an aphrodisiac in itself. In another time or place she would have really gone for Walter, but however lovely or attractive he was he couldn't offer her what she needed most – to not have to worry where the next euro was coming from.

'I do my best,' Jackie did a half-hearted curtsey.

'More Hanky-Panky?' he asked, his eyebrow slightly arching suggestively.

'Oh, go on then,' said Jackie, who'd been thinking he'd never ask. It didn't do to look like a drunk even if it was in front of the gardener.

'Pauline. Another one?' he asked.

'No thanks, I'm bushed,' said Pauline.

'You're not ducking out at…' Jackie checked her watch '…eleven o'clock.'

Pauline puffed her cheeks out. 'It's knackering, dancing like that. But hopefully I should have lost a few pounds.' She patted her stomach. 'I'd best go and check on Zara.'

'You're okay. I think we're about to get an update.' Jackie nodded towards a harassed-looking Val making her way through the throng of beautiful people.

Val took a seat next to them and sighed deeply.

'How's Zara?' asked Pauline.

'In a lot of pain. She's desperate for more painkillers. She can't use her wrist. She'd be popping all sorts if she could open the bottles herself. She really should have gone to hospital.'

'I know,' said Jackie. 'But she won't listen to sense. Or to me for that matter.'

'It is a worry though,' said Pauline. 'If she won't go to hospital how will she get better?'

'That is a very good point.' Jackie was starting to realise that Zara's fall was going to have far-reaching consequences for her and her workload. 'I should have insisted she went. Now she's going to expect me to be nursing her twenty-four-seven.' She flopped back in her seat.

'Not just you,' said Val. 'I suspect the spotlight will be on all of us.'

'Here you go, ladies,' said Walter, returning with a tray of drinks. 'I saw you'd escaped, Val, so I got you a champagne and a mojito. I wasn't sure which you'd want.'

'Thank you, Walter,' she said, taking the champagne.

'Leave the other – it won't go to waste,' said Jackie.

'How's the party going?' Val asked scanning the room as the band returned to the small stage.

'Cracking,' said Jackie, taking a long drink of her cocktail. Despite the drama with Zara she was enjoying herself.

'Look around you,' said Walter. 'Everyone is loving it. The food went pretty quick, which is a good sign because half the folk here are on permanent diets or have had their stomachs stapled.'

'I've had nothing to eat,' said Val, as if remembering.

'Sorry, Simon Cowell just beat me to the last of the hors d'oeuvres,' said Walter. 'But I could ask Christian to rustle you something up.'

'That's kind. If you don't mind, Walter?'

'My pleasure. Back in a mo.'

'He's really quite lovely. Isn't he?' said Pauline.

'He earns his money, that's for sure,' said Jackie. They sat in silence for a while. Sipping drinks and watching the other partygoers. Jules and Alina seemed to be getting friendly. Jackie was still celeb spotting.

Walter came hurrying back to the table. 'Quick,' he said. 'I think we've got another casualty.'

'For crying out loud,' said Val getting to her feet.

They all followed Walter who stopped by the entrance and pointed at Toby's cage.

The bird was hunched up on the bottom of the cage and breathing heavily. He really didn't look very well. The last thing they needed was the ruddy parrot to cark it.

'He looks as sick as a parrot,' said Jackie, but apparently she was the only one who found that funny.

51

VAL

The rest of the night had been a bit of a blur. Apparently there had been a stand-up row between a racing driver and some veteran singer but it had all passed Val by. She'd made a call to the vet. Thankfully they spoke English because whilst her French was good it did have its limitations and she quickly found they were in the area of describing how sick a parrot looked.

For an exorbitant fee a young female vet came out and checked Toby over. She diagnosed it was possibly a mild poisoning from disinfectant and had taken him into the surgery to keep an eye on him. She'd had a lovely reassuring bedside manner but she'd declined Jackie's suggestion of her giving Zara the once-over.

It was Sunday morning and Val heard someone moving about the villa so decided to get up and get a cup of tea. She was still processing the scant information she'd managed to gain from Zara the previous evening. Wendy had agreed to meet Zara for lunch but had not shown up. Zara had waited and then not remembering that there was a cut-off for everyday flights, having been used to travelling by private jet, she was too late to board the plane. Hence her delay due to having to wait for the next flight and her extreme level of annoyance.

It had probably also contributed to her reckless decision to use the stairs rather than waiting for Walter to fix the lift. She was so cross at being late for Toby's party she'd got changed and headed downstairs a little faster than was safe and had slipped. Val feared the cleaning products were also to blame for the incident.

She walked into the kitchen and found Pauline fully dressed with Brian on her lap. Val yawned. 'Morning. You both okay?' She started making tea.

'Yes, we're fine. How's Zara?'

Val looked over her shoulder. 'I've not checked on her yet. If she's still sleeping then that's probably a good thing.'

'I heard her call for Jackie in the night,' said Pauline. 'And I heard them arguing.'

'Me too. It sounded like it was over painkillers. I have to say Jackie really stepped up last night.' Val had to concede that Jackie had done her best to ascertain Zara's injuries and encourage her to get proper treatment – and all in the face of a verbal onslaught.

Pauline nodded her agreement. 'I'm not looking forward to Zara's mood today.'

'I'm also not keen to tell her about Toby.'

'At least if Zara stays upstairs she won't notice he's missing.' Pauline gave Brian a head rub.

'What if he doesn't make it?' Val had been pondering this unfortunate possible outcome.

'Ah, good point. Maybe just tell her.'

'Tell who what?' said Jackie entering the kitchen. Her hair looked like she'd backcombed it with a hedgehog and she still had a full face of make-up although it was now rather patchy and smudged, giving her a certain Dalí-esque quality.

'Tell Zara about Toby being poorly,' explained Pauline.

Jackie nodded her understanding. 'Large coffee for me, Val.' She went to the large fridge, opened it wide and lifted up her strappy pyjama top.'

'Why are you boob-flashing the sausages?' asked Pauline.

'Hot flush. They're always worse after alcohol,' Jackie explained. She finished with the fridge, pulled out a chair and sat down. 'Well, last night was a blast.'

Val scowled at her. 'Last night was a total and utter disaster. Zara has multiple fractures and Toby got poisoned. That's not what I'd call a blast.' She shook her head at Jackie's shallow view of everything. More than anything she wanted to tell them her disappointment about Wendy but she didn't know where to start. She could hardly slip it into conversation.

'Apart from Zara's accident, and almost removing my nipples along with that stick-on bra, I had a good time,' said Jackie. 'My nipples are hair-free now, which is a bonus.' She inspected her nails. 'And I'm fairly sure I snogged Johnny Depp.'

'He wasn't even at the party,' said Pauline, with a chuckle. 'But there was a rough-looking bloke with eyeliner who was eating food off of unattended plates. Walter thought he was a gatecrasher.'

Jackie narrowed her eyes. 'Well, when I repeat the story it will definitely be Johnny Depp.'

Val passed the others their drinks and joined them at the table. 'What do we do about Zara?' she asked.

'Let her sleep,' said Pauline.

'Not just for now. I mean longer term. What do we do?' She looked from one to the other and waited for a response. Her eyes rested on Jackie. She was the closest they had to a medical expert.

'Why are you looking at me?' She sipped her coffee and winced. 'No sugar?'

'In the cupboard.'

Jackie shrugged and took another sip. 'Look it's not down to me. I'm not her carer.'

'Er, I think that's exactly what you are,' said Val. She was fed up of always being the one to sort things out. This wasn't her responsibility and for once she was not going to take it on just because others were happy to let her.

Jackie leaned forward. 'She's an adult. If she refuses medical attention I can't exactly force her.'

'She does have a point,' said Pauline, breaking eye contact and shifting uneasily in her seat, making Brian scowl at her.

Val drank some tea and tried to master her thoughts. Zara was incredibly stubborn. If she didn't want to do something they weren't going to be able to force her. But she was still nursing a number of injuries, which they couldn't ignore. 'Then I think all we can do is look after her between us. But with you taking the lead.' She eyeballed Jackie.

Jackie puffed out a breath. 'You're overreacting as usual.' Val began to protest but Jackie held up a palm to halt her – it was very annoying. 'I suggest we encourage her to rest and get her a surgical boot and a wrist support off the internet. Apart from an x-ray, to confirm the damage, that's all a hospital would do. As well as give her painkillers, which she has in truckloads.' Jackie leaned back.

It did sound like quite a sensible suggestion. 'Only one problem,' said Val. 'There is no way Zara is going to wear a surgical boot.'

52

PAULINE

The situation with Zara was worrying but there was a little bit of light in the darkness because, with Toby at the vet's, Brian was allowed to have the run of the house. However, Pauline was reluctant to let him off her lap as she found stroking him comforting.

Staff began arriving so the women vacated the kitchen and relocated to the living room. The empty cage in the corner was a reminder of who was missing. Pauline let Brian follow them and he immediately headed for the cage to investigate.

'Parrot's not on the menu for today's breakfast,' quipped Jackie as Christian appeared from the kitchen and scowled at her.

'How is Zara?' he asked.

'Well, we've not checked on her yet,' said Pauline, feeling instantly like the worst friend ever.

Christian looked surprised.

'I'm sure she's fine,' said Jackie. 'It's better she rests.'

Christian headed back to the kitchen shaking his head as he went.

'Actually, I will go and see how she is,' said Pauline. 'Can you keep an eye on Brian?'

Val nodded. Jackie appeared to have zoned out.

Pauline went upstairs and tapped gently on Zara's door and waited. There was no reply. This was awkward. Should she knock again and wait or go in? She tapped again a little louder and waited. Nothing. 'Zara?' she called. She started to feel a little anxious. Silence was rarely a good sign.

She opened the door. 'Morning, Zara.' The room was in darkness and Pauline's eyes took a little while to adjust as she edged closer to the bed. Zara was lying on her back with her eyes closed – her complexion pale. Pauline's pulse quickened. She walked around to the side of the bed nearest to Zara. Her hands were over the top of the covers. She looked almost like she'd been laid out. Pauline wished she hadn't come to check on her own. Her heart started to thump. Had Zara died in her sleep?

Feeling hesitant she reached out a hand to touch Zara. At that moment Brian leaped onto the bed.

'Shit!' exclaimed Zara, jolting awake.

'Argh!' shouted Pauline her hand going to her heart.

'What the blue blazes is going on?' Zara was blinking. Brian ran across the bed, jumped down and dashed out of the bedroom.

'Sorry, Zara, I did knock but you didn't answer so I crept in to check you were all right.'

'Of course I'm all right. Apart from having the bejesus scared out of me by people creeping around my bedroom.'

'Sorry.' Pauline's heart was thumping hard in her chest.

'Blinds open,' said Zara and the room flooded with light.

'How are you feeling? asked Pauline.

'Like I've done a few rounds with Muhammad Ali.' She tried to sit up and winced.

'Can I help you?' Pauline stepped forward and Zara waved her away.

'Don't touch me.'

'Are you in pain?' she asked.

'Every limb, every inch and every fibre of my body is emitting some degree of pain. You wouldn't keep an animal like this.' The thought of the lovely female vet shot into Pauline's mind but she quickly dismissed the image – it wasn't helpful.

Pauline daren't suggest a doctor. She bit her lip trying to think of something useful or a way that she could leave the room and hopefully hand over to Jackie. 'I'll sort you out a cup of tea and maybe some breakfast.'

'Hang on.' Zara patted the bedcovers and winced as she did so. Pauline moved a little closer but didn't sit. She had an uneasy feeling, like she were the fly and a web was being woven around her. 'How did the party go?' asked Zara, with a slight pout.

'Good. Really well. Val did a top job. Everyone really enjoyed it.'

Zara was frowning. 'Was it not marred by my absence?'

Bugger, thought Pauline. 'Obviously people were disappointed you weren't there. *Everyone* asked after you.' She may have exaggerated somewhat.

'And Toby?' Zara fixed her with a steely eye.

Pauline swallowed hard. She knew she'd never last a

minute under interrogation by Zara or anyone for that matter. 'Toby?'

'It was his party.' Zara gave a hearty chortle. Her breath seemed to be sucked from her. 'Ow that bloody hurt.'

Had the parrot enjoyed himself? Pauline wasn't sure. Zara was waiting for a response. 'He was in seventh heaven,' said Pauline, sending up a little prayer that he wasn't in actual heaven.

'That's good.' Zara seemed to settle a little. 'Where's Jackie? I need my meds.'

'She'll be up in a minute.'

'Can you set my phone up for video conferencing? I need to get in touch with Jules and Alina. You'll need to prop it up somewhere. I can't hold the blasted thing.'

Pauline did as she asked. Using some books and moving the bedside cabinet she lodged the phone at a suitable angle and moved closer to the door. She could see an opportunity to escape. 'Did you want Christian to bring you up some breakfast?'

'I can hardly slide down the bannister to get it myself can I?' She was far more disagreeable than usual. Pauline put it down to the pain.

'Okay. I'll ask him to send up your usual.' She turned to leave.

'Hang on,' said Zara, stopping Pauline in her tracks. 'I can't live like this.' Zara waved a hand up and down the bed.

'It's temporary, Zara.' She did have a tendency to be a drama queen but then that was an occupational hazard. 'It only happened last night. Today and tomorrow are bound to be the worst but after that, you'll start to heal and then you'll feel better. You'll see.' She really hoped that would be the case.

'It's not just the physical issues...' Zara's shoulders drooped. 'The job in London was a disaster because I couldn't remember my lines. I went over and over them but they refused to stick. I ended up convincing the director to cut my character from two scenes so I could cope.'

'It's good you found a solution.'

'But don't you see? That's it. That's the end of my career. Nobody will work with me now if I can't remember lines. Even the scraps will dry up. It's over. I'm over.'

Pauline's heart broke a little for her friend. 'I'm so sorry. Maybe it's not as bad as you think.' Although Zara was shaking her head. 'I'll get you a cup of tea. Everything looks better after a cuppa.'

'Can you get me some tablets? They're in the bathroom cabinet.'

'I'll get Jackie. That's her department.' Pauline made for the door.

'Do you remember the conversation we had at the Café de Paris?' Pauline froze. Zara beckoned for her to return to her side of the bed.

Pauline remained where she was. The distance, although short, was a comfort. 'It's hardly one I'm going to forget.' Pauline's skin prickled. She'd tried to push that day to the back of her mind to join the other dark secrets that resided there.

'That time we talked of might be approaching sooner than either of us thought,' said Zara.

Pauline walked out and didn't look back.

53

JACKIE

Pauline returned, looking like a startled rabbit who had just been invited to a barbecue by Mr Fox. She walked slowly into the living room.

'Everything all right?' asked Val.

'The last time I saw someone that pale they were being warded off with crucifixes and garlic,' said Jackie. 'But then this is France and they're not that fond of tourists.'

'Jackie. Shh,' said Val, waving at her to be quiet. 'What is it?' she asked Pauline.

'Zara.' Pauline paused. She had little colour in her cheeks and her lips were white.

'Bloody hell, she's not dead is she?' asked Jackie.

'No, but for a moment I thought she was,' said Pauline, sitting down. Brian trotted over to greet her. 'Brian here almost gave us both a heart attack.' For a moment Jackie thought how handy that would be. It would avoid the looming issue of Zara's wishes about her demise. Although it would present her with a whole new set of issues, not least of which where she would then live. She needed Zara to hang on a while yet, at least until she'd got herself another job or a rich man. Both seemed to be eluding her.

'I've asked Christian to take her up some breakfast but she needs some painkillers too. She's in a bad way. Can't you do something, Jackie?' Pauline's expression pleaded with her.

'Call a doctor out,' cut in Val. 'Then at least we're covered.'

'And waste their time when we know she'll send them away? Bit pointless,' said Jackie.

The glass doors opened and Walter breezed in. 'Morning, ladies, how's her ladyship?'

Jackie loved Walter's flippant approach to his employer. It mirrored her own feelings. 'Awake and demanding breakfast and painkillers.'

'Almost back to her old self then,' said Walter, sitting down uninvited. Jackie saw Val note his actions.

'Not really,' said Pauline. Brian jumped off her lap and went to investigate the new arrival. Brian sniffed around Walter's shoes and then rubbed around his shins. 'I'm worried about her. Her wrist is swollen, she says everything hurts and she looks generally unwell.' With the absence of a cat to stroke Pauline wrung her hands in her lap.

'I need to call the vet for an update on Toby,' said Val getting to her feet.

'And then tell Zara,' added Jackie. She wasn't picking that one up – she was going to have enough on her plate dealing with Zara as it was.

Val nodded and left the room.

'Any chance of a cuppa?' asked Walter.

'Talk about while the cat's away,' said Jackie, although she was quite in awe of Walter's attitude. She was discovering that they had quite a few things in common.

'I'll get you one. If you keep an eye on Brian.' Pauline pointed to the cat.

'So...' Walter looked around the room. 'And then there were two.'

'The best two,' said Jackie.

'Absolutely. We had a good time at the party. Didn't we?' He was watching her closely.

'I enjoyed myself.' Jackie had a feeling she knew where this was going.

'I was wondering if you fancied going out for lunch sometime?'

Christian appeared. 'Jackie, Zara is asking for you... I say asking but she's raising her voice and swearing quite a bit.'

'Not really selling it, Christian. But okay I'll go and sort her out.' She got to her feet. 'Haven't you got a marquee to take down, Walter?' she asked.

'Not before I've had a cuppa. Let me know about lunch,' he said.

She nodded and left. She liked Walter; he seemed like a decent guy. But men his age usually came with a lot of baggage and he didn't have the sweetener of being a millionaire. For now she'd continue to seek out someone rolling in money and failing that some young blood while she still could. She'd sent Raphael a few text messages and each time he'd replied. He could be a nice distraction if she could get him interested.

Jackie could hear Zara's ranting as she went up the stairs. She popped her head around the bedroom door. 'Is it safe to come in or are you going to shoot flames from your nostrils and burn me to a crisp?' she asked.

Zara slapped her hands onto the bedcovers and flinched. 'I've had enough, Jackie. I can't stand this. I need a wee and I can't get out of bed.'

Zara being a diva was one thing, but Zara in genuine distress was completely different. Jackie walked in. 'We can manage that.'

Zara smirked. 'You know you slept in your make-up?'

'I've not looked in a mirror.' Jackie shrugged and pulled back Zara's covers.

'You look like a toddler has been finger-painting on your face in the night.'

'Thanks. Now did you want a wee or not? Because if you do some manners might be nice.'

Zara fixed her with a death stare. Jackie matched her. There was a long stand-off. Zara cracked first. 'Please.'

Jackie eased Zara's legs out of bed carefully, noting the bruising and what made Zara wince. Her ankle was a dark purple down to the sole of her foot. Jackie positioned herself ready to ease her upright. 'On three I'm going to gently pull you up. Okay?'

Zara bit her lip. 'Okay.'

Jackie counted down but as soon as any weight was on Zara's ankle it crumpled and Zara yelped. Jackie held her weight, what there was of her. 'Bad idea. Back we go.'

'No, I need a wee.' Zara was looking desperate.

Jackie didn't have a bedpan handy. A flash of inspiration struck. 'Cross your legs. I've an idea.'

Jackie dashed off and returned a few minutes later with the ice sculpture tray and the bucket. She held them up as if presenting Zara with an Oscar.

Zara's mouth fell open. 'What the hell?'

54

VAL

A few days after the party Zara summoned Val to her bedroom as pretty much everyone had been that morning. The party was a distant memory but the damage to Zara appeared to be lasting. If anything she was in more pain and increasingly hostile. They had ordered in a few essentials including a commode and a wheelchair, which Zara was less than impressed by and which had caused a number of heated discussions. Thankfully Toby had made a full recovery and was scheduled to return home.

Val had taken to bringing up Zara's mail in the hope of her receiving something from Wendy. There had been no word from her since she'd been a no-show for lunch with Zara. And whilst there didn't appear to be much more to the story than that, it still wasn't something Zara was keen to go over as she was trying to erase everything about the day of her accident. It didn't stop Val wanting to know more and craving an opportunity to contact her.

'Here's your post. How are you feeling?'

'Crap. Open it for me?' Zara's wrist hadn't improved. The bruising had faded but she couldn't grip anything with it. In the hope of giving her a little independence, and a way to contact Alina and Jules, they'd set up an Echo so Zara now had Alexa to shout at. Pauline had bought her a two-handled beaker so she could have a drink without someone helping her but that had been hurled across the room in a fit of temper and frustration.

Val opened two letters and passed them to Zara along with her reading glasses. Val opened the last package. It was a book and there was a card with it. Zara's eyes left the letter she was reading and darted in Val's direction. 'Who's that from?' snapped Zara.

Zara was tetchy most of the time. They both knew the situation couldn't continue but Val wasn't about to do Zara's bidding. Val put the book on the bed next to her and pulled the accompanying card from the envelope. It was a postcard from Haiti but nobody had written on it. 'It doesn't say.'

Zara took it from Val and studied it closely. She placed the card on top of the book and sighed deeply.

'Everything all right?' asked Val.

'Yes.' Zara pasted on a smile. Something she appeared to be finding harder and harder to do. 'What are your plans for today?'

'I'm still looking over the contract for that property portfolio you were interested in. Gabriel is going to drive Pauline over to collect Toby.' Pauline seemed to have assumed the role of animal carer. 'Then this afternoon we're all walking to Beaulieu-sur-Mer. Did you want to come in the wheelchair?'

'Absolutely not! The paps would have a field day.' Zara cleared her throat. 'I adore Beaulieu-sur-Mer; it's such a pretty little place. The magnolia trees, the galleries, the martinis. So many happy times taking that stroll. Hand in hand with Alistair, my last husband. We were happy you know.'

Val couldn't let the comment go unchallenged. 'Didn't you go to court over custody of a painting?'

Zara waved her hand dismissively. 'We *were* happy… until the divorce.' Zara's eyes glistened. 'Do something for me?'

'If I can.' Val was rather cautious about giving a firm agreement without knowing exactly what was being asked of her.

'This afternoon in Beaulieu-sur-Mer, go to Gran Caffe for me and order a martini. All of you. And drink to me.'

'I can bring you one back if you like?' Val wasn't one for dramatic gestures and if Zara wanted a martini this was an easy solution. She knew Zara was struggling being stuck in bed but any attempts to move her had been met with fierce opposition.

'No, just a toast in my name would be nice.'

'Sure. Anything else? Now I mean. Tea?'

'I'll have a Buck's Fizz please,' said Zara, awkwardly opening the cover of her new book.

Val pressed her lips into a flat line. Was this an argument she wanted to have? They'd barely cleared the breakfast things and Zara was talking about alcohol. It also wasn't advisable with the tablets she was taking. But then her quality of life had taken a nosedive since the party. Could half a glass of champagne do much harm?

Zara looked up. 'Everything all right?'

'Yes. One Buck's Fizz coming up.'

Jackie reluctantly took the drink up to Zara while Val busied herself with sorting out a drawer in the office. It was starting to become her domain now that Zara was bedridden. It was a lovely room with a view over the pool, framed by pink bougainvillea. When she heard someone call 'hello' she went to investigate. She found Walter in the living area brandishing a pot plant.

'Just popping up to see Zara,' he said.

Jackie came sweeping through with a face like thunder. 'I swear I'm going to swing for her,' she said, doing a full lap of the room.

'You need to ignore her,' said Walter. 'Half the time she's high as a kite on those drugs you give her. She doesn't mean what she says, you know. I never pay attention and nor should you. I do what I think is best for her.' He got no response other than Jackie looking like she now wanted to lynch him instead. He smiled and carried on through with his plant and disappeared upstairs.

'It's easy for him. He doesn't live here. I'm at her beck and call twenty-four-seven.'

Jackie was having to do more, that was true, but she wasn't exactly rushed off her feet. Val couldn't let that go unchallenged. 'Are you though?'

Jackie swivelled in her direction. 'Yes. I barely get a moment to myself. She wants her pillows fluffing, or help to get up, and she needs tablets every few hours so I can hardly clear off for a weekend.'

'We're going out this afternoon,' said Pauline, entering the room and picking up a cushion to fluff.

Jackie momentarily brightened. Val felt she needed to elaborate. 'Zara wants us to go to Gran Caffe and all drink martinis in her honour.'

Jackie threw up her arms. 'See. She's controlling every bloody thing. It's driving me crackers.' She stormed out into the garden and Val saw her get out her phone.

'I feel for Jackie. She does have more to do than us. Should we offer to step up, do you think?' Pauline was watching Jackie out of the window.

'I think our assigned duties are pretty clear. She knows what she signed up for.'

'But Zara has only given me about three pages to type up since the party.'

'You're picking up Toby this morning and you sat and read to her the other day. I think we're doing fine. Actually someone has sent her another book so you'll probably be back on reading duty again soon.'

'I don't mind.' Pauline smiled.

The doors opened and Jackie walked back in. 'Could one of you two please cover for me tonight? I've got a date and boy do I need a break.'

'I'm sorry,' said Val. 'I've got tickets for the theatre.' She'd been looking forward to it.

Jackie swivelled in Pauline's direction. 'Pauline?'

'Who's the date with?' she asked.

'Does that make a difference as to whether or not you'll cover for me?' Jackie put her hands on her hips.

'No. I was interested, that's all.'

Jackie's expression changed. 'You're a lifesaver, Pauline. Thank you. It's Raphael.' She fluttered her eyelashes.

'Seriously?' Val was astounded. She knew Jackie was keen to be in a relationship but one with Raphael was never going to amount to anything. She wasn't sure whether to be dismayed that Jackie never learned from her mistakes or be in awe of her unwavering optimism.

'I never joke about men. We've been sending flirty messages since the day we went to Monaco. And we're finally going out to dinner.'

'Isn't he a bit...' Pauline twisted her lips.

'Gorgeous?' said Jackie.

'Too young for you?' said Val.

'Don't be all judgemental, Val. It doesn't suit you... Actually it does but don't do it all the same,' said Jackie.

'I think Val's just concerned, Jackie. I mean that is a big age difference,' said Pauline. 'Maybe someone a little older would—'

'I have standards,' cut in Jackie.

'But no age restrictions it would seem,' said Val.

'Age is just a number.' Jackie brushed her hair off her face. 'I'm going for a swim before Zara starts shouting again. Anyone going to join me?'

Val shook her head.

55

PAULINE

The vet was pleased with Toby's recovery and Pauline was immensely relieved. Toby squawked most of the journey back to the villa, which Pauline took as a good sign even if Gabriel didn't. The parrot was soon settled back in his newly sanitised cage with some broccoli. Toby seemed happy to be home. Brian less so. Toby screeched at him from his cage and Brian glared back from the safety of an armchair.

Brian had quickly got used to having the run of the villa although it had taken quite a lot of patience and cooked chicken to get him to use the cat flap. He seemed to prefer meowing at the glass doors in the living room until someone opened them for him. Brian was not impressed with Toby or the fact he got shooed every time he tried to jump on the top of the cage.

'Mexican stand-off?' asked Val, from over her book.

'I don't think they're going to be friends,' said Pauline. 'The best we can hope for is that they don't kill each other.'

Pauline had checked the security of the cage and was pretty sure it was Brian-proof but she still didn't like the idea of leaving them alone together. 'Maybe I shouldn't go out.'

'Pauline, you can't watch over them all the time,' said Val, putting her book down. 'They have to get used to each other.' Pauline couldn't see that happening. 'How about Toby has a change of scenery and spends the afternoon in the office?' suggested Val.

Pauline pulled her doubtful face. 'I don't think his telephone skills would be great. He'll just swear at everyone.'

Val ignored her sarcasm. 'You know what I mean. I think it's the simple solution.'

'Okay, but if he makes premium-rate calls then it's on your head,' said Pauline, going to get his cage.

As they walked along the promenade to Beaulieu-sur-Mer, Pauline mused over how she'd ended up agreeing to cover for Jackie for the evening. Being alone with Zara put her on edge but she'd been careful to keep doors open because she was keen to avoid a repeat of the Café de Paris conversation. If she was going to be alone in the villa with her, that made it a little more difficult. She'd gone over and over how the conversation might develop and even when the discussion was one-sided and in her own head, Pauline still seemed to come out of it agreeing to things she didn't want to. She appreciated Zara's fear of going into a home but she couldn't understand her fear of the press. But then she'd never had to deal with it. She wanted to be supportive and spend time with Zara so perhaps she needed to be ready for any uncomfortable conversations. She needed to stand firm and if that didn't work she could always retreat downstairs with Brian and Toby.

Beaulieu-sur-Mer was a tiny place, making it easy to find Gran Caffe. As instructed Val ordered three martinis and they took them to a table outside. Jackie took a few photographs although Pauline wasn't sure if they were for Zara's benefit or her followers on social media.

'You could film the toast to show Zara when we get back,' suggested Pauline.

'Good idea,' said Jackie, with her phone poised. It wasn't always obvious, but Pauline could see that, underneath the brash exterior, Jackie cared.

'Okay.' Val cleared her throat and they held their drinks aloft. 'We all have a martini and we're here to raise a toast to our good friend, Zara Cliff, who sadly can't be here today.'

Jackie started to laugh. 'Bloody hell, Val. That sounds like she's snuffed it. Try again.'

'Right.' Val scowled at Jackie. 'To Zara, our companion, our friend and one of the girls. Cheers.' They all clinked glasses and took a drink.

'Whoo,' said Pauline as it caught the back of her throat. It was pure alcohol and a lot stronger than she'd been expecting.

One martini turned into two and then Pauline declared she was out while she could still walk unaided. They had a mooch around the little town and then made their way back along the now familiar walk to St Jean Cap Ferrat. Pauline didn't tire of the view, the sound of the ocean or the floral scents in the air. She was truly starting to feel at home and that brought a sense of calm over her.

Jackie was telling a story about some guy she'd dated

who had fancied himself as a bit of a Tom Cruise character from *Cocktail* as they walked back into the villa.

'Up here!' called Walter with panic in his voice.

They all stopped laughing and rushed upstairs.

'What's wrong?' asked Pauline although she hung back a fraction to let Jackie into the bedroom first.

'She needs a wee and she won't let me take her,' said Walter, looking flustered.

'Bloody man has been here all afternoon. He won't leave me alone,' snapped Zara.

'Was that all?' said Jackie, flopping down on the end of the bed. 'Bloody hell, Walter. We thought—'

'It was something more serious,' cut in Val. 'But thankfully it's not. We'll take it from here.'

'Thank you,' said Walter. 'Bye then, Zara.'

'Harrumph.' She turned her head away from him.

Walter beckoned to Pauline as he reached the door and she followed him outside. 'There's something up,' he said.

'Well there has been since the party,' said Pauline. 'It's all her injuries and being stuck in bed.'

'It's more than that. She's agitated. She wouldn't let me read to her. Even shouted at me when I picked her book up. I think maybe she's scared.' He didn't seem sure of his own words.

Pauline almost laughed – perhaps she should have stopped at one martini. 'Zara's not scared of anything.' Then she thought of her deteriorating health and the obvious pain she was in. 'Actually there is one thing. I think she's scared of getting worse. Don't worry about her, Walter. We'll take care of her.' They looked back into the room where Jackie and Val were helping her onto the commode.

'Shut the bloody door!' yelled Zara and Pauline hastily pulled it shut.

'Some flowers were delivered for her,' said Walter. 'I left them downstairs because... well I didn't like to leave her for long.'

'Don't worry,' said Pauline. 'I'll sort those out.'

Poor Walter was obviously concerned. Zara was lucky to have people who cared about her, even if she didn't appreciate them.

The early evening ritual of getting ready reminded Pauline of their time together when they were younger. At least now they didn't have to share a bathroom but the dashing about, sharing make-up and helping with each other's hair was still the same. Jackie was excited about seeing Raphael and wanted her hair blow-dried so Pauline had volunteered. She got a little vicarious pleasure from it and it was quite fun.

Jackie had then insisted that they do the same for Val as she had a big night out at the theatre. 'Shall I see if I can get another ticket?' said Val to Pauline when she switched off the hairdryer.

'Thanks but it's really not my thing and someone should keep an eye on Zara.'

'I bloody heard that!' shouted Zara from the next bedroom.

'Nothing wrong with your hearing aid then,' called Jackie, as she skittered across the landing.

'Bloody cheek!' called Zara although there was laughter in her voice and it was lovely to hear.

'You not going to ask me if I want a ticket to the theatre?' asked Jackie, brandishing a hair straightener.

'Sorry,' said Val. 'You're welcome to come. I just didn't think culture was your thing.'

'I'm kidding. The only culture I'm familiar with is what used to grow in my old fridge.'

Laughter filled the first floor. Getting ready together seemed to have lifted them all.

56

JACKIE

When Jackie left the villa she was already on cloud nine. She knew she looked amazing and she had a date with a hot young man. Life was good. She still had money issues – her credit card statement had virtually screamed at her that morning – but she had high hopes of finding a job. And if that failed she was going to ask Zara to loan her some money. That might then encourage Zara to help her job-hunt too or to pay her for the additional hours she was working. She'd not signed up for being on hand twenty-four hours a day.

As she strolled past the marina she saw Walter chatting to someone by the yachts. She paused for a moment to see if she could see Raphael. They were meeting at the restaurant but she wasn't opposed to some extra Raphael time if he was about. She changed track and walked down past the yachts, their rigging tinkling in the light warm breeze. She loved this place. It had snuck up on her and mugged her. The weather, the people, the wealth – it was all intoxicating.

'Good evening, fair maiden,' said Walter, spotting her and immediately striding over.

This was a good opportunity. She'd not got back to Walter about the lunch date and she had a prime opportunity to let him down lightly. 'Hey, Walter. Is Raphael about? We've got a date.'

Walter looked like he'd walked into a glass window. Maybe she hadn't been as gentle as she could have been. 'Dinner date,' she said, although she didn't want to lessen its status at all.

Walter seemed to recover. 'Raphael left not ten minutes ago but—'

'He's probably sprucing himself up for me.' She felt a shiver of anticipation run through her.

'Jackie, I'm sorry but he left here with a girl. A holidaymaker. I don't think he's—'

'Don't, Walter. I know this must be hard for you but don't.' She didn't want to hear it. He was bound to want to put her off Raphael. And the girl was probably just a customer. She turned on her high heels and went back the way she'd come with her head held high. She'd go and wait for Raphael at the restaurant as per the original plan.

'Jackie!' Walter called after her but she ignored him. She got her phone out of her bag. Dropping Raphael a quick reminder text wouldn't hurt.

The restaurant had their booking and the table was nice. Raphael wasn't there but then she knew from Walter that he'd not long since left work so that was understandable. She ordered herself a white wine spritzer and a jug of water.

She didn't want to be plastered before her date arrived. Tonight she was going to pace herself on the alcohol front.

When the waiter proffered the menu again she felt she couldn't refuse a third time. She smiled pleasantly and took it from him. It wouldn't hurt to have a little peruse. It was in French but thankfully there was a translated version on the opposite page. She mulled over her choices. It was difficult to avoid garlic in France. She settled on the seafood linguine, as it was moderately priced, although she wouldn't order until Raphael arrived. She wasn't sure who would be paying so the middle ground was the safest place to land.

She checked her watch. He was forty minutes late. She checked her phone. There was no response to her previous text. Had he even read it? Warmth was radiating through her body; ceiling fans were never as good as air conditioning. She composed something casual but clear and then rewrote it a few times until it barely sounded like she cared that he was late. She deleted it and went with her first draft.

The waiter came to take her order and she had a decision to make. She asked him to wait five more minutes and he grumpily agreed. She saw him talking to a fellow waiter and from the gesticulations she could tell she was being ridiculed. Walter's words rang in her ears. Raphael had left with a girl. She ran her lip through her teeth. She'd been a fool.

After a further ten minutes she had run out of options. She called the waiter over, explained in laboured English that she'd got the wrong restaurant, paid her bill and left.

Jackie wasn't given to tears. She was made of stronger stuff than that but she was pissed off, sweaty and hungry. It wasn't a good combination. She stopped at the little seaside café near the marina, taking good care that Walter wasn't still lurking there. She ordered some chips and ate them walking home in good old British style. She garnered a few odd looks from passers-by but she didn't care.

The more she walked the crosser she became. Why were men always doing this to her? More importantly why did she let them? She dialled Raphael's number. It went to voicemail. She hadn't expected him to answer but it wouldn't stop her giving him a piece of her mind. But this time she was going to be civil and dignified.

A polite voice asked her if she'd like to leave a message. 'Raphael, it's Jackie. But then you know that because you're screening your calls. Anyone with an ounce of decency would have let me know they weren't going to show up. Standing someone up is bloody rude in any language. Forget the excuses, you had your chance and you blew it. Consider yourself dumped. Arsehole.' Well, she almost managed to keep it civil.

In her heart she knew she'd done all the running with Raphael. Worn him down. She was getting too old for this. And at that moment she felt old. Who was she kidding? Mainly herself she decided. She wasn't a teenager anymore and her pulling days were over. Perhaps she needed to retire from the dating scene unless of course a millionaire landed in her lap.

When she reached the villa she was in no mood for Zara. Was it wrong of her to sneak in quietly and go straight to her room? Definitely, but Pauline had already said that she would cover for her, why waste that opportunity? She took off her shoes. Checked the living area. There was no sign of anyone. Toby was still in the office otherwise he would definitely have sounded the alarm. She tiptoed upstairs. She'd made it, home and dry.

57

VAL

The Salle Charlie Chaplin was a cinema cum theatre and was a short leisurely stroll from the villa. It was lovely to have something like it on her doorstep. Although she had been spoiled in London, with its array of theatres, everything was still a bus or tube ride away. An evening out required effort and pre-planning. And whilst she loved the buzz of London it was a grubby place, frequently too loud and littered with crime, making her increasingly aware she had to be on red alert. Women of advancing years were sadly an easy target.

Cap Ferrat truly was a beautiful, tranquil place. The mood was always easy-going and the crime rate was virtually non-existent. It was a small tight-knit community with plenty of security around every electric gate. However, Zara had wetted her appetite for finding her daughter and there was no doubt that would be easier to do were she back in England. It was a quest she had admitted defeat over a few years previously but with the new information

Zara's private detective had dredged up she had a renewed sense of purpose.

Val was seventy-one years old and nobody knew how much time they had left or if those years were going to be kind and comfortable ones, health wise. She wasn't a doom-and-gloom merchant, far from it. She was a positive individual but you also had to be realistic. Zara's health hadn't been great but she had very quickly taken a turn for the worse after a simple accident. One that Val did feel a tad responsible for, as she had brought in the new cleaners who had polished up the stairs. Perhaps her advancing years was simply an excuse but she felt she had to find a way to convince Wendy to meet her, and if her age was a bargaining chip she could exploit she wasn't afraid to try it.

One meeting, that was all she wanted – just to see Wendy again and to see the person she had become. She didn't dare to hope that she could get to know her. Even if that one meeting was a disaster and she never saw her again, at least it would provide Val with a picture of her daughter to savour and perhaps an opportunity to put forward her side of the story. She knew her ex-husband would not have painted her in a good light. At least she'd feel that she'd tried. It would be up to Wendy if she wanted to take it any further. Perhaps then, at last, Val would be at peace with her past.

Val had sent an email to the address Zara had used to make the arrangements for the lunch with Wendy, which had all turned to nothing. It was an anonymous sort of email address and Val had no idea who was monitoring it or even if anyone still was. But it was all she had. The email she had sent had been short but hopefully pleasant enough.

She had shared her details and asked Wendy to get in touch when she was ready. She hoped that was sooner rather than later, although after a few days she was now wondering if she would ever get in touch at all. With each day it seemed less and less likely.

She had a soft drink in the theatre bar before making her way through to her seat. She'd not booked her ticket that long ago and it was a small theatre so she was seated towards the back. She found her seat, settled herself down and felt that little squiggle of excitement in her gut – she loved live theatre, it was incredible. This was slightly different as the performance was all in French but she was open to that as a new experience. The lights dimmed, the curtain rose and she was instantly transported into the story.

About twenty minutes in she was aware of someone's mobile phone ringing. That was irritating. She joined the people near her in scowling and rolling her eyes until she realised it was coming from her bag. Val was mortified. She made profuse hushed apologies in English and French, pulled her phone from her bag and switched it off. The call had been from an unknown number anyway.

She tried to tune her attention back in to the play but her mind was wandering. Who would be calling her at that time in the evening? In fact who would be calling her at all? Any friends back in the U.K. she had regular arranged FaceTime calls with and anyone she knew was already in her contacts list. It must have been a sales call or some sort of fraudster telling her someone had withdrawn money from her bank account. That must be it. She focused on the actors on stage. She had to concentrate hard because they spoke fast.

But what if it had been Wendy? Could that have been a

call from her? She pulled her phone from her bag, switched it to silent and checked her email. Nothing. She let out a deep sigh. She looked at the actors on stage. She was no longer sure what was going on. Val watched for a moment but her mind was elsewhere. She excused herself and left the theatre.

Outside she was grateful for the fresh air. She was being ridiculous. There had been no response from Wendy so why on earth would she be calling for a chat? She wouldn't be. Val took a deep breath and started the walk back to the villa. Perhaps a quiet evening with a book was in order.

The house was silent when she got in. She made herself a cup of tea, picked up a blanket and a magazine from the table and took it into the garden. She didn't even have the concentration level required for a book – her brain was preoccupied with what-ifs and maybes, all of which ended with Wendy.

She switched on the garden lights around the patio. They were just enough to read by. She wrapped herself in the blanket and flicked through the glossy pages of the magazine. Zara had many magazines; she said it was for research. She liked to see who was in the news and who was taking up the most column inches. It didn't really interest Val and before long she found herself nodding off.

58

PAULINE

Zara spent the evening agitated and rather shouty. Pauline had been hoping for an early night but that hadn't happened. She tried to keep herself busy and had been rearranging flowers into a couple of vases. She took one vase upstairs with her and tapped on the door.

'Sodding well come in,' barked Zara.

'Flowers,' she said with a smile, hoping it would defuse things.

'You send those to funerals. Do they think I'm already dead? I might as well be. Nobody knows I exist anymore.' She drew in a long, laboured breath and huffed. 'I want to die, Pauline. I'm not being melodramatic. I'm quite sane and quite sure. I want this pain, discomfort and embarrassment to end. Will you help me?'

Pauline swallowed hard. She couldn't look at Zara; instead she concentrated on the flowers. 'I always think flowers brighten up a room.' She hurried over to the windowsill and made a space for the vase.

'Pauline, please don't ignore me. I'm asking... no I'm begging for your help.'

'I can't.' Pauline's voice was barely a whisper even to her own ears.

'If I could stand up and walk and my hands weren't utterly useless I'd take an overdose myself. Or possibly dive over the balcony. Drowning would also be an option although I don't like getting my hair wet. Is the cooker gas or elec—'

'Stop!' Pauline couldn't stand it. She knew Zara was trying to lighten the situation but it was far too serious a subject for that.

Zara's eyes filled with tears and she stretched out her hands towards her. Pauline couldn't deny her friend some affection. She took her hands in hers and felt the swollen joints and contorted bones. 'Pauline. I know what I'm asking you—'

'No, you don't,' said Pauline. How could she? Zara didn't know what was buried in her past. What she would never be able to come to terms with. She knew exactly what Zara was asking her and worst of all Pauline knew she could do it and that was what scared her the most.

'Please.' Zara's voice was gentle.

Pauline pulled her hands free. 'I'm sorry. Can I get you anything?'

'If you won't get me a large bottle of pills, I'll have a look at that book someone sent me.' She sighed and resignedly sank back into the pillows.

Pauline let out a breath. 'Sure. Which one is it?' She scanned the bookshelf.

'It's a cosy mystery apparently.'

Pauline pulled a couple from the shelf and showed them to Zara. 'One of these?'

'*The Lifeline*. That's the one.'

Pauline was about to pass her the large book but couldn't see how Zara would be able to hold it. 'Wait a minute I've got an idea.'

She had a root around the kitchen and returned with the cookery book stand, a tray and a cup of tea in the two-handled beaker. They found that if they didn't highlight the beaker, Zara didn't hurl it across the room.

'Here,' she said. Putting the tray on the bed and setting up the cookery book stand 'Does that work?' she asked, reaching for the book.

Zara placed her hand protectively on top of the hardback. 'No, it's fine.'

'But this might be easier,' said Pauline. 'Or I can read it to you?'

'I said, I'll be fine.' Zara's tone had changed.

Brian entered the room and immediately started to retch. 'Goodness. I'm so sorry.' Pauline scooped him up and popped him in Zara's en suite. 'Don't want him vomiting on your carpet.' At least a tiled floor would be easier to clean. 'I wonder what's wrong with him. He ate his dinner fine.' She shrugged her shoulders at Zara and tried to ignore the sound Brian was making in the bathroom.

Zara's gaze was on the windowsill. 'He's not been alone with those has he?' She nodded at the large vaseful of flowers.

'Not those but there's another vase of them downstairs. There were loads and I thought they would brighten up the living room. Why?'

Zara looked apprehensive. 'Darling, lilies are highly poisonous to cats.'

'Are they?' Zara nodded. 'Oh poor thing.'

Zara's expression intensified. 'When I say highly poisonous I mean just drinking the water they've been in can be fatal.'

'Seriously?' Pauline was instantly alarmed. 'I had no idea. Oh my goodness. Brian!' She opened the bathroom door to find Brian crouched on the floor. He didn't appear to have been sick but now she was panicked. 'What do I do?'

'Get him to the vet as quickly as possible. Call Gabriel. And, Pauline, I don't mean to be all doom and gloom but there is no antidote.'

'Good grief.' Pauline's stomach plummeted to the floor. She scooped up Brian and rushed from the room.

'Bye and good luck,' called Zara.

59

JACKIE

The next morning Jackie stepped out of the shower and dried herself. She wasn't usually up at this time. She'd ended up having an early night, which was definitely not her usual thing but she did feel better for it. Her evening had been spent ignoring Zara's shouts for Pauline whilst doing a face pack and stalking Raphael on social media. She put on some cropped trousers and a T-shirt and decided to check in on Zara before going down for breakfast.

The room was in darkness. 'Open blinds,' she said. Now she'd mastered the technical side of the villa she loved it. 'Morning. I had an idea. Perhaps we could get you in that wheelchair. Now hear me out,' she said quickly before Zara disagreed. 'If we wheel you to the pergola you can get some much-needed fresh air and as a bonus you can wave to bloody Felicity perky bottom. I thought that might...' As the sunshine filled the room and threw light across the bed Jackie froze.

It wasn't the first time she'd seen a dead body. Far from

it. But it was the first time one of her friends had died. She knew without even checking that Zara had gone. She walked round to the side of the bed. Moved the tray with its propped-up book to the floor and gently closed Zara's eyes.

A strange mix of sadness and relief overwhelmed her. All the times she'd bitched about Zara echoed around her skull. But her friend had been in pain and this had been what she wanted. 'You're at peace now, darling,' she said, patting her cold hand.

She went downstairs and found Val and Pauline already having breakfast.

'Well, how did it go?' asked Val.

For a moment Jackie wasn't sure what she was asking. 'Oh, Raphael. He stood me up.' She had no energy for bravado.

'Swine,' said Pauline. 'I had a nightmare of an evening. Brian has been kept in overnight at the vet's. I've hardly slept but I just rang and they—'

'What's wrong?' asked Val.

How on earth was she meant to tell them? She'd broken the news to relatives more times than she cared to remember but then that was part and parcel of working in a care home. This was different. She pulled out a chair and sat down.

'Jackie?' Pauline looked concerned.

'I'm really sorry but Zara died in her sleep.' Saying it out loud didn't make it seem any more real.

Pauline gasped. 'No.' She started to cry and pulled a tissue from her sleeve.

'When?' asked Val, blinking more than normal as if fending off tears.

'I've just found her. Jeez did you think I'd left her there all night?'

'I was simply checking. What should we do? Are there official steps we should follow?' asked Val. Always the practical one.

'There are in the U.K. I guess it's something similar over here. I'll call her doctor and I assume they'll come out and certify the body.' It felt wrong to refer to Zara in those terms. They sat in silence for a few minutes. The only sound was Pauline's muffled crying. Jackie wished she could cry. Perhaps the tears would come later when it had properly sunk in. Right now she felt like she was doing her job and she wanted to do it properly for Zara. It was the last thing she could do for her.

'Are you okay?' asked Pauline, moving her chair closer and patting Jackie's arm.

'A bit shocked maybe.'

'Should we see her before the doctor gets here?' Val rose to her feet.

'If you want to.' Jackie didn't need to; she'd have to show the doctor through anyway.

Pauline blew her nose. 'What's she wearing?' she asked.

Jackie gave her a look. 'The press won't be round for photographs.' Although as she said it she had a feeling they may well turn up outside. They could be a macabre bunch.

'I know but she'll want to look her best.'

Val squeezed Pauline's arm. 'It's fine. She won't be buried in her nightdress if that's what you're worried about. Shall we go up together?'

They left the room and Jackie decided she should probably make a few more people aware. She stopped by the kitchen and told Christian who offered her a brandy for the shock as he necked one himself – she declined. He agreed to tell the other staff and seemed to think they should all have the day off. Jackie wasn't sure who was in charge anymore but it sure as hell wasn't her. She went to the office to make a few phone calls. Toby was sleeping but he watched her with one eye. Was she meant to tell the parrot? She'd leave that one to Pauline. Jackie got hold of Zara's doctor who said he would be out within the hour. Next she rang Alina who cried down the phone for a bit while Jackie sat there awkwardly listening.

'I'm sorry to ask but do you know what we do about the staff and... well... us?' She knew it sounded heartless but this situation wasn't something they had thought through. The idea was that they would look after each other at the villa but presumably that villa would now need to be sold. Jackie's mind was racing. She had no job, no income and she was about to be made homeless. Maybe she *would* have a small brandy for the shock.

There was a loud sniff from Alina. 'The will is in the safe at the villa. Well a copy anyway. The original is with her solicitor here in the U.K. Would you like me to contact them?'

'Yes, please. And daft question but who is her next of kin? I mean I know she had a few husbands but she divorced them all. I don't know what that means for who needs to be notified.'

'There's a nephew,' said Alina with confidence.

'Okay, that's good. Someone needs to let him know and I guess he'll arrange the funeral and everything.' And in her head she added *and our eviction*. Jackie swallowed hard.

'Actually,' said Alina, leaving a gap as if considering whether to continue or not. 'Zara couldn't stand him. She said the details are all with the will. She left lots of instructions about what everyone should wear, what she should be buried in, who should attend the funeral and memorial service. She was quite particular about it. I had to type it all up. Why don't you have a look in the safe?'

'Because I don't know the code and anyway that doesn't feel right.' Things were kept in a safe for a good reason – because they were private. Although she had to admit she was itching to know what the will said. She was holding on to a tiny shred of hope that Zara had left them all a few quid. Otherwise she was screwed.

60

VAL

Val watched Pauline tidy up around Zara and straighten out her bedcovers. It somehow hadn't seemed real until she'd walked in the bedroom. Val took her time before looking at Zara. She could have been sleeping – she looked so peaceful. There were no tears on Val's part but an ache inside told her what she was feeling. Zara had been unhappy and had wanted the pain to stop. Now she had her wish. That was how Val chose to see it; viewing it that way made it a little easier to bear.

Pauline returned a book to the bookcase and broke down in sobs. Val put an arm around her shoulders to comfort her. 'This isn't right,' she said. 'I feel bad that we didn't do more. Make her see a doctor or something.'

'We couldn't force her. And I believe she was ready to go,' said Val.

Pauline nodded. 'I think she was too. But it doesn't make me feel any better about it.' She blew her nose and turned to face the bed. 'Should we say something?'

'If you want to.' Val wasn't really one for ceremony and in this situation talking to a corpse seemed positively ludicrous but then if it helped Pauline to process the situation she was happy to oblige.

'Um. Zara…' Pauline turned away. 'I can't face her.'

'Then tell me whatever it is you would like to tell Zara,' said Val.

Pauline rolled her lips together. 'Okay. Zara, you've been a great friend to me. You brought fun and laughter into my life when I needed it the most. You bought me Brian and he's given me something to live for. And moving here has…' Pauline paused and blinked. 'It's over isn't it? We'll have to move out.'

'Not today,' said Val. 'Finish your goodbye and we'll deal with one thing at a time.' It had already crossed Val's mind that she'd be heading home to her noisy neighbours but at least she had somewhere to go.

They finished their goodbyes and went back downstairs. Val walked into the office to find Jackie trying to open the safe and Toby headbutting his mirror.

'What on earth are you doing?' she asked.

'Exactly what Alina told me to do. She said there's a copy of the will and some instructions in the safe so I'm trying to get it out. Apparently Zara had quite clear views about what she would be buried in and who should and shouldn't come to the funeral.'

Val felt bad for her hasty assumption. 'I'm sorry.'

'It's okay,' said Jackie, although her expression said otherwise. She returned to fiddling with the barrel.

'You need to return it to zero, if you've made a mistake,' said Val. 'Let me have a go.'

Jackie reluctantly passed her a scrap of paper with the code on and stepped out of the way.

Pauline came in. 'I made tea and I brought sugar because that's meant to be good for shock I think. Christian is going home.'

'Yeah, I think I said they all could,' said Jackie.

Val felt the barrel lock click into place. She turned the handle and the safe opened. It wasn't a big safe but it was crammed. 'I suggest we find the will and then put this all back. It will probably have to be couriered to the solicitor in the U.K. but for now it's safest here.' She was talking as she moved things out of the safe and onto the nearby desk.

'I don't want to hurry you or anything but any sign of a will?' asked Jackie, leaning forward to peer inside for herself.

Val carried on removing items. Numerous cheque books – who even used those anymore? – but it was an indication that there were quite a few accounts to be sorted out. There was her current passport and a number of old ones with the corners clipped off. Some insurance policies and a few share certificates. She took out a jewellery box and some random keys and there, almost at the bottom, was a copy of the will. Val pulled it out and paused.

'That it?' asked Jackie. Val could tell she was itching to snatch it from her.

She nodded and opened it out on the desk so they could all read it. Alina had been right: there was a lot of detail about what Zara wanted. Along with the key information they were all dying to know.

'Have I read that right?' asked Jackie, sitting down in the office chair with a thump.

Val reread it herself to check before saying, 'That she's left the villa to the three of us? Yes, you read that correctly.'

61

PAULINE

Pauline was crying again. This time it wasn't sorrow or guilt – it was relief. Her hands were shaking and she was grateful when Val guided her into a seat. 'Are you sure?' she asked.

'Right there in black and white. Well, a nice shade of posh cream,' said Jackie, leaning back in the big swivel chair and looking quite chuffed as she slowly spun around.

'We shouldn't be pleased about this.' It all felt wrong to Pauline.

'Why ever not?' Jackie sipped her tea and then winced. 'Blimey, Pauline, how much sugar is in here? I'll be bouncing off the walls like a toddler on Haribo.'

'Because what have we done to deserve a place like this? And didn't you say she had a nephew? Surely he'll contest the will. And he'll win because he's a blood relative and—'

'Whoa, steady on,' said Jackie, although now she looked a little tense. 'You're panicking.' Jackie was right; Pauline

298

could feel her heart pumping hard in her chest. 'He's only a nephew,' continued Jackie. 'And people threaten to contest wills but they don't really go ahead and do it, do they, Val?' Jackie looked at Val.

Val was reading all the details but she lifted her head at the sound of her name. 'Not often and only if they feel they have a cast-iron case. He's been left the Belgravia property and a portfolio of investments. I doubt he'll be too upset.'

'See,' said Jackie, relaxing again.

'It says here that we inherit it for our lifetimes.' Val tapped the paper.

'What does that mean?' asked Pauline attempting to pick up her tea but her hands were too shaky so she left it. Maybe she'd be the next one using a two-handled beaker.

'We can live here rent-free but we are responsible for keeping it in a good state of repair and for paying all the ongoing bills. And when the last of us dies the property reverts to the estate and is...' she paused as she turned the page and read ahead '...split between the beneficiaries – her nephew again, the Actors' Benevolent Fund and Variety, formerly the Variety Club of Great Britain.'

'Hang on,' said Jackie, twisting in her seat and having to hold on to the desk to stop herself rotating again. 'We have to pay for the upkeep. Does that include all the blooming staff? We can't afford that. And what the heck are the rates like over here? This isn't right. Zara always said... well, implied that we'd be looked after. That was the whole point of us coming here.'

'Did you read the bit about the money?' asked Val, pushing the will in front of Jackie.

Jackie scanned the page. 'It just says an investment portfolio.'

'That when I updated it last week was worth in the region of six million pounds.'

'Holy crap!'

'What?' Pauline was having palpitations. Too much money wasn't a good thing. She didn't need something else to worry about.

'It's an estimate of the value of that specific investment portfolio. But we don't get that much,' said Val. 'We receive what it earns.'

'For heaven's sake. This is frigging confusing.' Jackie sipped her tea again and pulled a face. 'Is there any more of that brandy?'

'I think after the first glass it stops being medicinal,' said Val. Jackie glared at her.

'Here you all are,' said Walter, cheerily popping his head around the door.

'Feck off!' said Toby.

Walter ignored him. 'How's her ladyship this morning? Looks like the west border sprinkler is on the blink again. Don't want her petunias wilting or she'll have my guts for… What's up?'

'Oh, Walter. I'm so sorry,' said Pauline. 'Zara died in the night.'

'No. The poor old girl.' He rubbed his palm over his face. 'She seemed fine yesterday afternoon. Well, she was cantankerous, which was good form for Zara. What happened?'

'Probably her heart gave out,' said Jackie. 'She was on

a lot of medication for a number of ailments any one of which could have been what took her.'

Walter leaned against the doorframe. 'Goodness. That's such a shock. Has the doctor been?'

'Not yet. I've let him know,' said Jackie and Walter nodded. 'Christian and the other staff have gone home. You should have the day off too. We're not sure what's happening about pay and everything – we're literally just trying to work that all out.' She nodded at the will spread out on the desk. 'This is a copy of Zara's will.'

A smile spread across Walter's face, which Pauline felt was misplaced. 'I don't get paid,' he said.

All three women stared at him. 'Why ever not?' asked Val.

'It's my hobby. I absolutely love gardening. Zara had a massive row with her gardener so I said I'd take a look and the rest is history.' Walter was still grinning. 'I had no idea you all thought I was one of the staff.' He shook his head.

'Sorry,' said Pauline, feeling awful. She hoped she hadn't treated him any differently because of her assumption.

'You're a right mug,' said Jackie, sitting up straight. 'You could have been raking it in – you spend hours out there.' She shook her head.

'Because I enjoy it. Anyway, what's the will say? That bloody nephew doesn't get anything does he?'

'The house in London and an investment portfolio,' replied Val. Walter's eyebrows danced in surprise.

'We get to live out our days in this villa rent-free,' said Jackie, having a little swivel in the chair.

'That's good,' said Walter.

Pauline didn't know if she'd ever be able to feel happy about that. It was as if they were crows picking over bones for what they could get. None of this felt right.

'It is. There's a massive catch though,' said Jackie, with a pout. 'We have to pay all the bills. At least we don't have to pay for you. Maybe Zara has seen you right.'

Val looked up from the will. 'I'm very sorry, Walter – there's no mention of you here.'

62

JACKIE

The doctor who came spoke perfect English, which made things a lot easier than they might have been. Jackie answered his questions and then handed him over to Val. The two then conversed in French and Jackie zoned out. He issued a death certificate then and there, and said they were free to call the funeral director. Val took this on board as she had already set up a spreadsheet and was transposing information from the will into it and ticking off tasks. The London solicitors were sole executors but it didn't seem to stop Val wanting to put her oar in. But if she was honest, Jackie was happy for her to take charge on this occasion. The doctor offered his condolences and left. Jackie heaved a sigh of relief.

She joined the others in the study. Toby screeched as she entered. She still hated that parrot. She wondered if Zara had left instructions for him too.

'Can't we move him back to the living room?' she asked

Pauline. And let him take his chances with Brian, she thought.

'Okay. Give me a hand,' said Pauline. The two of them manoeuvred him out of the office and he swore at them for the whole excursion.

Val almost had her nose on the computer screen when they returned. 'I've googled a few things,' said Val. She seemed to be positively thriving in the wake of Zara's demise. 'And we need to give the funeral director the outfit Zara wants to be cremated in.'

Pauline gave a little shudder. 'Which one was it? Did the will say?'

'Yes, her nineteen ninety-five BAFTA nomination gown by Karl Lagerfeld,' said Val, reading from her spreadsheet.

'And which one is that exactly?' asked Jackie, glancing at the death certificate as Val moved it out of the way.

'Absolutely no idea,' said Val. Pauline shrugged. All eyes were on Jackie.

'How the hell would I know?' Jackie loved clothes but she had no idea about designers of that ilk although she could spot a pair of Louboutins at fifty paces. Her mind wandered to shopping. She was keen to understand if there was any money coming her way and Val seemed to be being quite cagey in that regard. It was tricky because Jackie didn't want to appear money-grabbing and give off the wrong impression but it didn't stop her wanting to know if she could go on a spending spree at some stage and obviously pay off her credit cards, again.

'We could watch that awards ceremony in the cinema room. She's got them all on DVD,' pointed out Pauline.

'Rather you than me.' Jackie wasn't going to waste her time watching reruns of old awards.

'I think that's quite a good idea,' said Val. 'Jackie, can you deal with the funeral director when he arrives? I'm quite busy here.' She returned her eyes to the computer screen.

She was liking the idea of Val assuming charge less and less but there was little to be gained by arguing over it. 'Fine. What are we doing about lunch?' She was already missing having Christian on hand. She had got used to being waited on surprisingly quickly. It wouldn't be the same if they had to let the staff go. She liked the fully inclusive experience; to be downgraded to self-catering would be a let-down.

'I'm sure there's enough food in the fridge for you to rustle us something up.' Val gave her a smile. Jackie gritted her teeth.

'I'm going to watch the BAFTAs,' said Pauline and she gave Jackie's arm a squeeze as she passed as if to say 'it's not worth it' and it wasn't.

Jackie had just finished making some sandwiches when the funeral director arrived. He was very French and rather brusque. His minimal English didn't help the situation. He explained that they needed to declare the death at what sounded like the local council but thankfully he explained that as the funeral director he could do it if he saw some identification and the death certificate. After he'd got what he needed from Val, Jackie showed him to the bedroom and was going to leave him to it but something made her pause in the doorway. He would be taking Zara away and that felt more final than her actual death. Zara had been such a huge personality it was hard to see her energy snuffed out. They may not have always seen eye to eye over things but that didn't mean Jackie didn't love her any the less.

She now felt a bit like Batman without The Joker. No adversary to spar with made her feel a little bit useless. She hadn't realised she was crying until she sniffed back a tear rather unattractively and the funeral director looked in her direction. She swallowed hard and took one last look at her friend.

'Bye, matey,' she said. 'I did all I could for you. Rest easy.' And she left him to it. She made hot drinks for the others including Walter, who for some strange reason had decided that he needed to fix the sprinkler system today, and then found herself drumming her fingers in the living room.

'I've found the dress,' said Pauline. 'I had to watch quite a bit because you didn't really see much of Zara. The shots on the red carpet were of her in the background while they interviewed Liz Hurley and then there was a brief head shot when they read out the nominations.'

'And the winner is…' said Jackie.

'It's a black and white one.'

Jackie smiled at Pauline. 'I fear we may need to narrow it down a bit more. Come on let's have a root through her walk-in wardrobe.' Truth be told Jackie had been itching to have a look through Zara's things. They walked to the stairs and then had to stand back as two men were bringing down a large black mass on a stretcher. It was Zara.

Pauline reached out and clutched Jackie's hand tightly. It was very strange to watch them take the body bag out of the house and know that Zara was inside. The funeral directors were respectful, but it struck Jackie that leaving your home the same way the recycling did was quite the reality check.

63

VAL

Val had spent most of the day deciphering the will and its many addendums. She'd spoken to the London solicitors who had yet to assign someone to the case, which was understandable given at that stage Zara's body had only recently left the villa. Val knew she hadn't interacted with the others much. Concentrating on the will had been her way of coping. Focusing on something she knew and understood was, in its own way, comforting.

She was understandably upset about Zara's death but she still had so many unanswered questions about her daughter. And now her friend was no longer here she'd never get any firm answers.

When Val eventually emerged from the office Jackie, Pauline and Walter were sitting in the garden drinking champagne. She went out to join them although felt hesitant about joining what looked like a celebration.

'We're toasting, Zara,' said Walter, as if anticipating her reaction.

'I think she would approve. Don't you?' said Pauline. 'She loved a glass of champagne.'

'And gin,' said Jackie.

'And a cocktail,' added Walter.

'Yes. She probably would approve,' agreed Val.

'She definitely bloody well would,' said Jackie emphatically, finishing her glass and lining it up for refilling.

Walter poured Val a glass and handed it to her. 'Thank you.' She noticed the others had left Zara's peacock seat empty. It was as if they were waiting for her to join them. She pulled up another garden chair.

'When's the funeral?' Pauline asked her.

'I don't know. I assume her nephew will sort that out,' said Val.

'I doubt it,' said Walter. 'You've got six days from death to cremation or burial.'

'Six days?' Val was taken aback. Nobody had mentioned that.

'That's how it works in France.' Walter shrugged.

Val stood up. 'I'd better get onto the nephew and—'

'Sit down, Val,' said Jackie. 'It's been a tough day for all of us and you've worked non-stop. He can wait twelve hours.' Walter's expression said different.

'I'll have a drink and then I'll call him.'

'I've told Toby,' said Pauline. Val smiled in response.

'Bloody hell, Pauline,' said Jackie. 'He's a sodding parrot.'

Emotions were running high and the fact that Walter was watching them all indicated that it hadn't passed him by. 'She loved having you all here, you know,' he said, drawing their attention. 'Before you came she was full of it. She was thrilled to have you all back in her life. The Girls she called you all. She got everyone who worked here together and explained.'

'Explained what exactly?' asked Val.

Walter took a sip of champagne but looked slightly uneasy. 'That things maybe hadn't worked out well for you all and she wanted to help.'

'I guess that's true for me,' said Pauline, looking at the others.

'Me too,' said Jackie, with a shrug.

'Not for me. She sold this idea as a way for us to look out for each other. That we were the ones doing *her* a favour and stopping her from ending up in a nursing home.' Walter looked taken aback. 'I own a house in Richmond and have made good pension provisions,' said Val, trying not to show her irritation at being labelled a charity case.

'Well, that's good then.' Walter sipped his champagne. 'Zara was a funny one. If you could get under that mask she was a lovely woman.' Looks were exchanged but nobody else spoke.

Jackie's stomach growled and broke the silence. 'I'm starving,' she said.

'Shall we order a takeaway?' suggested Pauline. Walter put his glass down.

'You fancy joining us?' asked Jackie.

'I've got nothing to go home for,' said Walter. 'Sounds good to me.'

Val rang and left a message for Duncan, Zara's nephew, and also Alina. Someone was going to have to move fast to get everything arranged for the funeral, especially if they were to meet Zara's lengthy and detailed demands. She left the others to choose the takeaway. Only in Cap Ferrat could you get the local bistro to deliver shrimp risotto, spaghetti vongole and tarte au chocolat. They ate outside and Brian joined them. He was fine and had been given a clean bill of health from the vet. He was particularly keen on the shrimp. As more champagne was poured the tension seemed to ease a little with each glass. Conversation turned to the will.

'What does it all mean?' asked Jackie. 'Actually I'm only interested in what impacts us. Sorry, I didn't mean to sound heartless. I just meant you only need to explain that bit.'

Val finished chewing her mouthful. 'The villa will be held in trust. The investment portfolio will pay for the upkeep, bills and the staff but nothing else. Basically we can live here until we die. When the last one of us goes it's sold and the money goes to charity and the nephew.' She felt that was fairly succinct and sufficiently layman for them to understand.

Jackie leaned back in her seat. 'So despite there being millions in that blessed portfolio I'm still going to need to get a sodding job?'

'Looks that way,' said Val.

'I might be able to help there,' said Walter.

'Go on, I'm all ears.' Jackie spiralled spaghetti onto her fork. 'Do you know some way to get at the money?'

'No.' He shook his head. 'But I know a lot of people locally so I could ask around about work for you,' he said.

Jackie looked disappointed. 'Right. Thanks.'

They ate in silence for a while. The quiet only broken by Brian's meows for more shrimp.

64

PAULINE

The following day Zara's death was headline news. Every paper across the globe had mention of it somewhere. Jackie was wowed by the level of publicity, exactly as Zara would have been, but to Pauline it felt like the eyes of the world were on them. That their anonymous little corner of France was now under the spotlight. The irony wasn't lost on her either. Zara, who had craved this level of attention her whole life, had finally achieved it with her death.

Things seemed to be moving fast and Pauline was still trying to process what had happened. Everyone in the house was fraught and there was an undercurrent that nobody was acknowledging. She found some comfort in spending time with Toby and Brian. Although even that had to be done with each creature separately as they were definitely not getting on. Val had called the staff together and explained that their jobs were safe and they had all seemed happy to hear the news.

Zara's nephew wasn't interested in having anything to

do with arranging the funeral and had given his apologies but he was away on holiday so wouldn't be able to attend any hastily planned one anyway. Which seemed awful to Pauline but who was she to judge?

Whilst the French six-day rule had been a bit of a shock, and it was causing Val a great deal of work, it was actually a relief to Pauline. She hoped she would be able to draw a line under things after the funeral.

She was ferrying tea to Val when someone knocked at the door and she went to answer it. They had received a few floral arrangements already, all of which she had scrutinised for lilies after the last scare.

A short, bearded man scanned her up and down. 'Oh, hello,' she said.

There was a long delay before he spoke. 'You are English?'

'Yes.'

'This is the home of Deidre Shytles?'

'No, I'm sorry,' said Pauline. Thinking what an unfortunate name that was.

'Hang on!' called Val from the office and she came to join them.

'Why do you ask?' Val regarded the stranger.

'Because, madam, I am Inspector Richard.' He flashed an official-looking card at them. What on earth were the police doing there? Nausea came over Pauline in a wave. It was suddenly difficult to breathe. 'I would like to speak to you about the death of Deidre Shytles.'

A sense of relief washed over her. He wasn't there for her. 'I'm sorry, there's nobody here of that name.'

Pauline went to repeat that he'd got the wrong house but Val was already beckoning him inside. 'Come through.'

They convened in the living room and Jackie came in from her sun lounger, wearing a hastily thrown on kaftan.

'Can I get you a cup of tea?' asked Pauline. The police officer sneered his response. 'Coffee then?'

'*Non.*' Now she didn't feel like she could get one for herself but she was starting to feel that she may need one. 'I wish to understand some details about the death of Miss Deidre Shytles.'

'Who?' said Jackie through a spluttered laugh. The inspector glared at her. 'I'm sorry but that's a comedy name if ever I heard one.'

'It's Zara's real name,' said Val.

'You're having me on,' said Jackie.

'No,' said Val. 'Didn't you realise?' Pauline and Jackie shook their heads. 'I thought you knew. Zara Cliff is a place in Jordan – that's where she got the name from.'

Jackie looked stunned. 'Huh. Is that so? You'd be ace on *Pointless.*'

The police officer was looking confused. Val explained. 'Deidre Shytles was an actor. Zara Cliff was her stage name. She kept it a closely guarded secret.'

'I'm not surprised. The press would have had a field day with that one,' said Jackie. 'Was she born a Shytles or did she marry one?'

'Born,' explained Val.

The inspector made a noise somewhere between a tut and a cough.

'I'm sorry. How can we help you?' asked Val.

'I would like to understand exactly what happened on the evening of Miss Shytles's death.'

'She died in her sleep,' said Jackie.

He fixed Jackie with emotionless eyes. 'Did she?' asked the police officer and he jotted something down in his notebook.

'Is there a problem?' asked Val.

He looked around the room as if seeking the answer to her question. 'There are some… how would you say… anomalies surrounding her death.'

Pauline felt her heart start to race and her chest tighten. She reached for Val and held her hand for support. The inspector noticed.

'What anomalies?' asked Val.

'I cannot go into any details. This is just an inquiry at this stage. If you would answer my questions.'

'What the hell does that mean?' Jackie was looking agitated.

'Calm down,' said Val, and she appeared to be trying to communicate something with her eyebrows.

'He can't demand information from us without explaining what he wants it for. That's data protection or something.' Jackie was waving her arms around.

'I'm sure if we help the inspector he will leave with all the information he needs,' said Val, calmly. 'Inspector, we will help you in any way we can. What do you need to know?'

'Who was here on the evening that she died?' He looked around the room.

'We were all out,' shot Jackie. 'Zara was here on her own.'

Pauline opened her mouth but it felt too dry to speak. She needed to explain about her evening. How she'd been there apart from rushing Brian to the vet's but Val caught her eye and gave an almost imperceptible shake of her head so Pauline kept quiet.

The inspector wrote something in his notebook, looked up and then wrote something else. 'And is there a will?' he asked.

'I believe her solicitors in London have a copy and that they are the executors. Her P.A. has all the information,' said Val. 'We can give you her details.'

He wrote this down too. 'I see.' His long pauses were making Pauline sweat. 'And is there anything else any of you would like to share with me?' He looked at each of them in turn but nobody spoke. Pauline was sure they must all be able to hear her heart beating. It was thumping so hard in her chest it was making her light-headed. She really did need that cup of tea.

65

JACKIE

Jackie had poured herself a brandy even before the inspector had left the villa. She heard the door close and let out a long breath. The encounter had unnerved her far more than she liked to admit. 'Thank goodness he's gone,' said Jackie, slumping onto the sofa. She was exhausted. The nervous energy that had been fuelling her had made a rapid departure with the police officer.

'Why be dishonest?' asked Val, striding back into the living room.

'I didn't know Zara wasn't her real name,' said Pauline, her arms wrapped around herself like a hug.

'Shytles,' said Jackie, with a grin.

'Not that,' said Val, stabbing a finger at Jackie. 'Why on earth did you say we were out all evening?'

'I didn't say *all* evening. He just assumed that was what I meant,' said Jackie, feeling defensive.

'But we weren't all out for the whole evening. I came back earlier than planned. And Pauline went to the vet's.'

'I didn't know that,' said Jackie. She'd not really thought about the others. It had been a knee-jerk reaction to the inspector's question. She'd panicked. 'You could have told him that. I didn't stop either of you explaining. You chose not to correct me.'

'Because as soon as we start contradicting each other we look like we have something to hide.' Val's voice was escalating.

'Calm down, Val. He's gone. It's over.' Jackie sipped her brandy and tried to look like she didn't care less. Usually she found that easy but not at that moment.

Val paced the room. 'Goodness me, Jackie. You realise they don't investigate a death for no reason? This could be serious.'

'Show us your knickers,' said Toby.

'Will someone please shut that ruddy parrot up,' said Jackie and Pauline went to cover the cage. Toby screeched in protest.

'Maybe it's routine in France. We don't know how they do things over here,' said Pauline, looking hopefully at Val.

'He said there were anomalies. Which I believe means there's something suspicious about her death. That's the only explanation. And now, thanks to Jackie, we have all given false alibis.' Val stared Jackie down. 'Is there something you want to share?'

'What?' Jackie looked incredulous. 'Oh, come on, you're not serious?' She shook her head. 'You think I killed her?'

Val stopped pacing. 'Did you?' Jackie went to speak and Val stopped her. 'Actually I don't want to know.'

'You're the one who went all cagey when he asked about the will,' pointed out Jackie. 'You directed him to the solicitor in London when there's a copy in the office. Why do that if you've got nothing to hide?'

'Because I didn't know if I needed to buy you some time.' Val threw her arms up.

'Stop it!' Pauline's voice was almost a shout. 'I think there's something I should tell you both.' Pauline returned to the sofa and sat down. 'She asked me,' she said without looking at either of them. 'Zara, asked me to... help her take her own life. That day in Monaco when you left us at the Café de Paris. She talked about what a wonderful life she had had but that she couldn't bear to be seen by her fans as a decrepit old woman. She said when the time came she didn't want to languish in a nursing home or a hospital. She wanted to die here on her own terms.' Pauline swallowed hard. The silence filled every corner of the room. Even Toby was quiet.

'Bloody hell, you too,' said Jackie, knocking back the rest of the brandy and pulling a face. It was a relief to know she hadn't been the only one. At least it would stop Val pointing the finger at her.

Val and Pauline both stared wide-eyed at Jackie. 'When did she speak to you about euthanasia?' asked Val.

'Not long after we moved in. She virtually told me it was in my job description.'

'And?' said Val her eyebrows raised. 'Did you do anything about those requests?'

'Hang on. If she asked me and Pauline. I'm guessing we're not the only ones. She could have asked anyone here. Like Christian or one of the housemaids or even you.' Jackie wasn't going to be the only one under suspicion. She stared Val down. 'Did she ask you, Val?'

Val puffed out her chest. 'Yes, she did ask me. And I obviously told her no.'

Jackie relaxed back into the sofa. 'We only have your word for that.'

'You're not serious?' said Val, her jaw visibly clenched.

'Why not? In fact, you're a solicitor so you know your way around the law far better than either of us do. And…' Jackie was finding her rhythm '…you're a diabetic. Insulin injection in the hairline. That's pretty much an undetectable way to kill someone. Apart from when it shows up during a post-mortem.'

'You're in fantasy land now,' said Val, scratching her neck and leaving a red mark.

Jackie's brain started to race. 'Shit. Is that why the inspector was here? Do they think we murdered her?'

'They've found something,' said Val, at last sitting down on the edge of the sofa. 'He wouldn't have come out here for a casual chat. Something has triggered him to ask questions.'

'He wasn't exactly *The Sweeney* though.' He hadn't looked like a policeman at all. He looked more like an accountant to Jackie. But then maybe she'd been watching too much *CSI*.

'Because he doesn't look the part you think he won't arrest us?' Val shook her head.

'But we're old ladies. Surely they wouldn't arrest us.' Pauline was wringing her hands.

'You speak for yourself.' Jackie slowly crossed her legs.

'There's no age discrimination when it comes to crime,' said Val. 'And no expiry date. If you commit an offence and they find out then you have to face the consequences.'

'Ah,' said Jackie sitting forward. 'And that's the key right there. *If* they find out.' She looked at each of them, expecting some agreement.

'Oh no. Oh no. Oh no,' repeated Pauline and she started to rock to and fro in her seat.

66

VAL

Through the night Val found herself working up defences and cases against all three of them in her mind. It was impossible to relax. She'd not been in this situation before. In the end she got up and decided to go for a walk even though it was early. She took the steps down to the promenade and was surprised to find flowers and notes tied to the gate. It wasn't Princess Diana level but it was certainly a gesture Zara would have cherished. It reminded Val that other people cared about Zara and also that if the press got wind of the anomalies the police had spoken about it would likely be front-page news.

Walking usually cleared her head. The fresh sea air was good for rebalancing her mind. But not today. She was at Beaulieu-sur-Mer and she'd barely started to sift through all the things that were worrying her. Most of all she wanted to know what the anomaly was. What had triggered the police to ask further questions about the death of an eighty-year-old woman with a lengthy list of health issues? Maybe it

was because she was famous. But then that had appeared
to be news to the inspector. Or possibly it was because she
was wealthy. Perhaps he simply wanted to be sure that
she had died of natural causes.

Val took a moment to catch her breath. She had clearly
been walking at quite a pace. She took a drink of water
from the bottle she now carried with her all the time. She
looked out to sea – it was spitting up a white froth. The
rolling surf reminded her of the worries tumbling over in
her own mind. She needed to work out how she was going
to play this one.

Val had just made it up the steps and on to the terrace when
Jackie came out of the house. 'You can stop panicking; she's
here,' she called over her shoulder. 'Pauline thought you'd
done a bunk. So did I to be honest,' said Jackie, taking a seat
and helping herself to some hot water and lemon. The staff
had stuck to their routine. Val found something comforting
about that.

'Why would I leave?' asked Val.

'I don't know. You tell me.' Jackie held her gaze.

'I've got nothing to hide.'

'No? You said you left the theatre early. Why was
that?'

Val threw up her arms. 'This is ridiculous. And you're
not helping Pauline's stress levels. You're aware that her
mental health was hanging in the balance before she came
out here?'

Jackie didn't have a chance to respond as Pauline came
scurrying over with a bunch of flowers in her hand. 'Oh,

thank heavens. I thought something had happened to you too.' Pauline gave Val a brief hug.

'Pauline, try to relax. It's all fine.' Val shot Jackie a warning look in case she was considering contradicting her. 'What's with the flowers?'

'In all the panic of getting Brian to the vet I forgot to destroy the lilies that made him sick.' She dropped the hand holding the flowers to her side.

Val paused for a moment and studied the blooms. 'They're amaryllis.'

'Are they?' Pauline scrunched up her features.

'And as far as I know they're not poisonous,' added Val. This called into question Pauline's whole reason for taking Brian to the vet. Had she tried to fabricate an alibi?

'Woo-hoo!' came the call from the promenade below and they all turned in that direction. Felicity paused her walk but continued to do an odd sort of walking-on-the-spot jig. 'Awful news about darling Zara. You must be devastated,' called up Felicity.

'Utterly,' called back Jackie.

'Such a character,' said Felicity. 'My sincerest condolences to you all.'

'Is she having a dig?' Jackie stage-whispered to the others.

'I don't think so,' replied Val, in equally hushed tones. 'Thank you,' Val called back.

Felicity raised a hand and then continued on her way.

'Bloody Felicity perky bottom,' muttered Jackie.

'I still like her,' said Pauline.

'I'm glad we're all together,' said Jackie. 'I've been thinking.' Val had to work hard not roll her eyes. 'I think we should do some investigating of our own in case that inspector comes back.' She nodded at Val as if sharing something insightful.

'What are you talking about?' Val's patience was wearing thinner than usual.

'I mean draw up a list of who we think might have killed Zara,' said Jackie.

Pauline gasped. 'They don't know that. Do they?' Her eyes darted back and forth.

'Calm down, Pauline,' said Val, although she knew her tone was anything but calming. 'Nobody is saying she's been unlawfully killed.'

'Ah.' Jackie held up an index finger. 'But if he comes back and is looking for someone to pin it on. Then wouldn't it be a good idea if we had a list of suspects we could present to him?' Jackie looked very proud of herself and her suggestion.

Val leaned against the pergola wondering why Jackie was keen to identify who might have killed Zara when they didn't even know if someone had. 'You're suggesting that we provide a smokescreen. Send the inspector off to ask questions of others and thereby detract attention from ourselves.'

'Exactly.' Jackie made a tick in the air with her finger. 'Think about it. Christian made all her food. He could have slipped something in her meals.'

'Was she poisoned then?' asked Val, watching for Jackie's reaction and any tell-tale signs of guilt.

'How would I know?' Jackie shrugged. 'I'm just saying he had an opportunity.'

Val didn't like where her train of thought was leading her but both Pauline and Jackie were making her question things. The sound of someone at the front door made them all freeze. Val composed herself. It could be anyone. Before any of them had made a move to answer it, Inspector Richard appeared in the garden – evidently having been let in by one of the staff.

'Good morning, ladies,' he said, but there was no cheer in his words. 'I would like you all to accompany me to the Police Municipale to answer some further questions.'

67

PAULINE

Pauline couldn't keep a limb still. She daren't even ask for a glass of water for fear of spilling it. She was in a small room with a large window. It wasn't what she had imagined all the many times she'd run through this scenario in her mind. There were no bars at the windows. In fact it was unlike every police drama she'd ever seen. There was no cheap-looking table and plastic chairs. This room had a low blue sofa, a matching chair and a coffee table with a box of tissues on top. There was even a picture on the wall. She'd been told to wait and that Inspector Richard would be with her momentarily. That had been at least twenty minutes ago. Her mind was overwhelmingly loud in the quiet room.

She ran the events in the villa garden back through her mind. Val had taken charge of the situation and asked lots of questions but Inspector Richard had provided little in the way of answers. Jackie had shouted a bit until both Val and the inspector had told her to calm down. Pauline had stayed sitting – unable to move or to engage. Fear controlling her limbs. Pauline's ears had buzzed and at one stage she'd thought she was going to faint. After some insistence from Val the inspector had confirmed that nobody was under arrest and shortly afterwards she'd found herself in the back of a police car with Val and Jackie.

The door opened and the sudden interruption made her jump. This was it – the moment she'd been dreading for so long. Inspector Richard walked in and Pauline's mind filled with Val's last words. 'Don't admit to anything. Don't give them anything they can use against you. Don't say anything at all.' She'd also rattled something off in French to the inspector but Pauline had no idea what that had been.

He sat down in the chair and placed a buff-coloured folder on the coffee table. She tried to read what it said on the front but it was in French.

'Would you like a drink of something? Coffee? Water?' he asked.

She shook her head. *Don't say anything at all.* She would have liked a cup of tea but the French weren't big tea drinkers. She wondered when she'd next get a cup of tea.

'Can you confirm that you are Pauline Crozier.' She nodded. 'Can I call you Pauline?' She nodded again.

Don't say anything at all.

'Pauline, I have a few questions I wanted to ask you? Is that all right?' It wasn't all right. It was far from all right. Nothing was ever going to be right again. She clasped her hands together in a vain attempt to stop them from shaking. The police officer noticed.

'Are you afraid, Pauline?'

She nodded and then shook her head. Idiot, she thought.

But then which was the safest answer? The truth, that yes, she was absolutely terrified. Terrified of saying the wrong thing, of being arrested, of letting the others down. Or lie, that no, she wasn't afraid, which would imply what? That she was regularly interviewed in police stations, that she was as hard as nails, or that she was enjoying a lovely morning out?

The inspector looked interested. 'Which is it, yes or no?'

He was waiting for a response. She went with honest. She nodded. 'What are you afraid of?'

What was she afraid of? For one thing being presented with a question she couldn't answer by shaking or nodding her head. How was she meant to respond when Val's words were still echoing through her skull.

'Okay. I understand,' he said, relaxing back into the chair. 'This is your first time in a police station. *Oui?*'

She was relieved to return to the yes and no questions. She nodded.

'It is okay. Really. We are not trying to… how would you Londoners say it? *Stitch you right up.*' He mimicked an accent so appalling even Dick Van Dyke would have been embarrassed. The inspector chuckled. Pauline tried to smile but it was beyond her current emotional capabilities.

'You can talk to me, Pauline. I wish you and your friends no harm at all. I just want to get things straight in my mind.' He grabbed at the air in pinching motions with both hands. 'I want to picture what went on the evening Miss Shytles… your friend Zara died. And once I have that you can return to the villa and everything can go back to how it was. Is that okay?'

She had to admit he did seem quite nice. She nodded.

'Good. If you could actually talk to me that would be really helpful too. *Non?*'

'Okay,' she said, almost startled by the sound of her own voice. She didn't want Val to be cross with her but she also wanted to leave the police station as soon as possible.

'Formidable. Where were you the evening Zara died?' He leaned forward and rested his forearms on his thighs and watched her closely.

She took a steadying breath. All she had to do was take her time and think before she answered anything. Surely she couldn't get into any trouble that way?

68

JACKIE

Jackie needed a gin. A very large gin. How the hell had she ended up in a bloody French police station? But she knew the answer to that one. Bloody Zara. She knew she shouldn't think ill of the dead but it was hard not to when you were wondering if you were ever going to see the outside again. She wished Val was with her now. That thought alone worried her. Val knew what to say and what not to say. She had authority in these sorts of situations. Jackie knew she just came across as bad-tempered and irrational, which was certainly not a good combination when police were most likely looking for a killer.

The door opened and in walked Inspector Richard. Jackie stood up. 'Is this going to take long? Because I have plans. Things I will need to rearrange.' She'd left her phone behind. That had been Val's doing. She said they'd only be confiscated if they took them to the police station.

'Would you mind taking a seat please?' he asked, sitting down on a grubby-looking sofa that sagged in the middle.

She reluctantly sat next to him. He got up and moved to a nearby chair. Was that to unnerve her? Because it had worked.

'Please can you confirm that you are Jacqueline Heatley.'

'I am. And I am a British citizen and I have rights. Bear that in mind.' She wagged a finger and then stopped.

'Indeed.' He looked irritated with her already. *Way to go, Jackie.* She really needed to keep her attitude under control. It had always got her into trouble. And this time it could be serious. 'I would like to ask you a few simple questions so that I can get a clear picture of the events that led up to your friend's death. Okay?'

'There were no events,' said Jackie. 'She went to bed. She died in her sleep.' She stopped herself from adding *The End*.

'Can you tell me your relationship with Zara?' He got himself comfortable in the chair. Was he expecting *Jackanory*?

Keep it brief, she told herself. 'We were friends.'

'But you live in her house.'

'Yes. She invited us all to stay with her.'

'For a holiday?' he asked.

She was tempted to say yes. That would be far easier to explain. But Val had already reprimanded her for lying to the police. 'No. We all used to live together when we were younger. And we thought it would be fun to do it again now.' He raised one eyebrow in a disbelieving fashion. 'And Zara was concerned about her health and I have nursing experience.'

She could tell it was the wrong thing to say as soon as she'd said it. He shot forward in his seat. 'You are a nurse?'

'Not exactly. I used to work in a nursing home. I'm a carer.'

'Do you have a good knowledge of medications?'

Oh shit. 'Only the basics.'

'Do you know what medication your friend was taking?' He pursed his lips.

'I thought you wanted to know about the night Zara died?' She tilted her head at him.

He smiled. 'But you tell me there is nothing to know. That she died in her sleep.' He put his fingertips together to make a bridge. He was an annoying little upstart of a man.

'Exactly. So you're wasting everybody's time.' She stood up. She wasn't sure why, apart from the obvious fact that she wanted to leave.

'Please be seated, madam. I promise I only need to understand a few facts and then you will be free to go.'

Her pulse was starting to race. She needed to calm down. She retook her seat and checked her watch. She didn't see what time it was; she was merely making a point.

'Her medication. What was it for?'

She cast her mind back to the drugs list she'd drawn up. 'Arthritis, cholesterol, depression, high blood pressure, oedema, Alzheimer's and her heart.'

'That is quite a lot. *Oui?*'

'Yes, it is but I've seen people on…' He'd perked up again so she shut up. He waited. 'Yes, it is,' she repeated.

'What was wrong with her heart?'

She thought for a moment. Aspirin had been prescribed but it was her who had made the assumption it was for her heart. That low-level amount usually was. 'I don't know.'

'Then why were you giving her the medication for it?' He narrowed his eyes.

'Because it had been prescribed by her doctor. Look...' She pointed at him and then thought better of it. 'When I moved in, her bathroom cabinet was overflowing with tablets. I went through it all and I ticked it back to the most recent prescriptions. Then I catalogued it all and made sure she got the right dose of everything at the right time. There's even a book I can show you where I wrote every dose down.'

'Could she not take the tablets herself?'

'No. Her arthritis in one hand was extremely bad so she couldn't grip.'

'And the other hand?'

'She... um.' Was she meant to tell him about the fall? How would she explain that they hadn't got her any medical care? He'd not met Zara; he didn't know what a force she was. What were the others going to tell him? Surely he would be comparing stories. Unless of course they weren't saying anything at all. She was starting to sympathise with Pauline and her anxiety – this was overwhelming.

'Yes?' He was waiting for a response.

Jackie knew as soon as she mentioned the fall it was going to open up a whole new can of worms but then if they had Zara's body they probably already knew that something had happened.

'She had a fall. A couple of weeks ago. She slipped on the stairs.'

'And did she hurt herself?' She bit the inside of her lip. This was not looking good. 'You are her carer. You have a medical background. I'm sure you could tell if she had any injuries that would need hospital attention. *Non?*'

'We called an ambulance. But she refused to go to hospital.' His eyebrows arched at this. 'You can check their records.'

'I will. Please continue.' He waved his hand.

'That's all I'm saying.' She folded her arms and stared at the wall.

69

VAL

Val was worried about the others. Pauline had been barely coherent when they'd got out of the police car; she'd been shaking uncontrollably. She knew Pauline was delicate mentally but today had shone a light on the fragility of her mental health. Perhaps it was the grief that was highlighting her reactions but Pauline was responding in an extreme way. But then it was easier for Val; she was used to dealing with the police and being in police stations. Many people would go their whole lives and never set foot in one. Let alone a French one. Not being able to speak the language would lend an additional level of uncertainty. At least she had been able to translate the mundane conversations she had overheard in the reception area.

Pauline was a loose cannon and someone she wanted to protect both for her own sake and for the rest of them. Val feared she could admit to anything under pressure. She hoped the advice she had given her would help. Anyone could see she was fragile so any intense questioning was unreasonable. A fact she had pointed out to the inspector in French before he had taken Pauline away.

Jackie was the opposite – she was full of bolshie overconfidence and was liable to shoot her mouth off and get herself and everyone else into a whole heap of trouble. She'd always found Jackie difficult at the best of times. Putting them both in this situation was stretching their relationship to the max. The more someone asserted their authority, the more Jackie would push against it regardless of whether or not that was wise and with no thought for the consequences for herself or anyone else. And even if Jackie did think about it, Val was certain, she would always put her own interests first.

Val had been waiting a long time, which was either a police tactic or a very bad sign that the other interviews were taking an age. She wondered if they were going to interview anyone else from the villa. Whilst she didn't subscribe to Jackie's tactic of throwing everyone else under the bus she was interested to see how far the inspector was going to go. That at least would give her an indication as to how serious this was. Was he just a bored police officer with too much time on his hands, fed up with the usual tourist pickpocketing and looking for a juicy case to make his name or had they really identified something untoward about Zara's demise that they felt compelled to investigate further?

The door opened and the inspector walked in. Hopefully now she was going to find out. He looked how she felt – drained. He pulled a chair out on the other side of the standard-issue police table. 'You are Valerie Chapman.'

'I am.'

'You are familiar with police procedures?' He placed a case file on the table and straightened it.

'I am.'

'Why is that?'

'Because I was a solicitor in the U.K. for over forty years.' She was oddly relaxed in this situation. She hadn't specialised in criminal law but she knew the drill. All she had to do was to give herself the same advice she would to someone in the same situation. Only she had the additional advantage of knowing for a fact whether she was guilty or innocent.

'*Bon*. Then perhaps we can be straight with each other.'

'I would welcome that,' she said. What she meant was she would like him to be straight with her so that she was better informed. The answers she gave would be no different either way.

'We will not be able to release your friend's body for burial for a few days because we are performing *l'autopsie*.'

'Why are you doing that?'

'There is an—'

'Anomaly. Yes, you said. What is that anomaly exactly?' He wanted them both to be straight. It seemed only fair that he went first.

He rubbed his hand across his chin and regarded her somewhat cautiously as if deciding whether to show his hand or not.

'There is a rash on your friend's body. It is unusual and we are trying to ascertain what it is.'

'Thank you. I appreciate your openness. Where is the rash?'

'I cannot divulge that.' The openness was short-lived

but at least she had something. She knew the reason why the police had been alerted. A reason why they were all in a police station being questioned. Clearly the rash was something unusual and implied foul play. Now all she had to do was make sure nobody could be charged with anything.

70

PAULINE

Pauline was so grateful for the two-handed beaker cup she could have cried. The sweet tea was like nectar and she was hugely relieved to be back at the villa. She'd also popped one of her antidepressants and it was beginning to work. Val and Jackie were pacing up and down the living area, making Toby screech.

'That bloody bird,' said Jackie, glaring at him flapping his wings extravagantly.

'Feck off,' said Toby.

'Listen,' said Jackie approaching the cage. 'You are on very dodgy ground, sunshine. If you're not nice...' She mimed cutting his throat and he squawked back at her.

'Stop it!' Pauline rushed over and put the cover over the cage. 'He's sensitive. He knows there's something wrong. Unlike us he can't articulate it.'

There was a scratching from inside the cage followed by, 'Feckers.'

'I can't believe I'm the one saying this but I think we

all need to calm down.' Pauline returned to her seat and indicated that Jackie and Val should do the same.

'I am calm,' said Val, although her eyes were darting about. 'Let me start a new spreadsheet and let's cross-reference what the inspector asked us and our responses.' She got to her feet.

'Oh hell no. Let's *not* do that,' said Jackie. 'He asked me what Zara's drugs were for and who could access them. And about her injuries.'

'He asked me where we all were,' said Pauline. 'What does it mean if he asked different things?' Although she wasn't sure she wanted to know the answer.

'It means he's fishing for something,' said Val. 'He said Zara had a rash and I think that's why he's asking questions. Did either of you notice any rash on her body?'

'Where?' asked Jackie.

'I don't know. Just on her body.' Val shook her head. Nerves were fraying before Pauline's eyes.

'I didn't notice anything but then she was pretty well covered up in bed. There wasn't anything on her hands or face,' said Pauline.

'Same,' agreed Jackie.

'So, Jackie, what could a rash mean somewhere else on her body?'

Jackie pouted. 'I have absolutely no idea.' As Val rolled her eyes Jackie picked up her phone. 'But Dr Google might.'

Some minutes later Pauline was wishing she was able to unsee the things that had popped up on Jackie's screen. Without any specific information about what the rash looked like or where it was on her body it was virtually impossible to glean anything useful about what might have caused it.

'Maybe she changed her perfume,' said Jackie, with a shrug and she put down her phone.

'I suspect they know the rash means more than a simple allergy. The good thing is that they don't have anything concrete to go on, otherwise they would be doing more,' said Val.

'Exactly.' Jackie luxuriated on the sofa. 'I don't know what we're getting ourselves all stressed about.' She looked at Val. 'Actually, it's you who's getting all stressed.' She narrowed her eyes. 'Why would that be I wonder?'

Val puffed out a breath. 'I'm not going over and over this ridiculous accusation of yours, Jackie. Pointing the finger at each other is going to get us nowhere.'

'Ladies, you're back,' said Walter, letting himself in through the sliding doors. What happened?' His eyes were bright as he sat down and regarded them all with interest.

Jackie leaned forwards. 'The police think—'

'Uh-uh,' cut in Val, shaking her head. 'Why do you want to know, Walter?'

'It was a bit of a shock seeing you carted off in a cop car,' he said.

'We weren't carted off,' said Jackie. 'We were helping them with their inquiries.'

'I assume it was about Zara?' He looked hopefully from one to the next.

Pauline was starting to feel jumpy again. Even if the police had stopped asking questions, other people were going to continue to. The staff and the neighbours would be talking. Gossip would be spreading. Rumours like that would easily snowball. Before she realised it she was starting to panic again.

'Pauline? Are you okay?' asked Walter.

She shook her head. Her chest was tight and her pulse was racing. Her tablets weren't as good as she thought. Anxiety had her in a tight hold.

'Pauline struggles with anxiety,' explained Val.

'I don't struggle,' said Pauline, through gasps. 'In fact, it's the one thing I'm incredibly good at.' She took another panicked gasp for air.

'Get a paper bag,' said Jackie and Val dashed off.

'I'm okay,' Pauline managed to squeak out.

'There's nothing to worry about,' said Jackie. 'Val is overreacting as usual. She thinks she's on a case again. She's just reliving her glory days. It's all done and dusted.'

'The police must have had a reason for carting... taking you to the station,' said Walter.

'Here,' said Val, coming back with a paper bag. Pauline took it gratefully and began to breathe into it.

'Deep breaths,' instructed Jackie, from across the room. Pauline did as she said.

'Walter, you seem rather interested in the police. Perhaps you visited Zara the night she died. Is there anything you'd like to share?' asked Val.

'Whoa! Don't go sticking this one on me. I had nothing to do with any of this.' He folded his arms.

'Leave Walter alone. I saw him at the marina that evening,' said Jackie.

'Yes, that's right. There's my alibi,' said Walter.

'I didn't know you needed one,' said Val.

There was a harsh rap on the door, making them all jolt

slightly. Apart from Pauline whose backside momentarily left the sofa – she was exceptionally jumpy even for her.

Val went to answer the door but it wasn't her who walked back into the living room.

'Good afternoon,' said Inspector Richard.

71

JACKIE

The inspector asked Walter to leave and the women to sit down although he was the only one who looked anything near to comfortable. For a moment Jackie felt she would have quite liked Walter to stay.

'I wanted to make you aware of some facts that have come to light.' Inspector Richard paused to look at each of their reactions. Jackie clenched her jaw.

'The will – it reveals that you are all substantial beneficiaries.'

'Are we?' Jackie threw her hands up. Zara would have been proud of her acting skills.

Val shook her head. 'It's true Zara has been generous. However, our status here remains unchanged. We were living here gratis with Zara; we simply continue to do so.'

'You were aware of this recent change to her will?' He locked eyes with Val.

'If you are implying we have a motive I disagree.' Val stared him down.

'Motive?' He gave a Gallic shrug. 'I did not mention motive.' Jackie heard Pauline's heavy breathing increase. She moved to sit next to her and held her shaking hand.

He turned to Jackie and she understood what people meant by the phrase *my blood ran cold*. 'I also have discovered that you, Miss Heatley, were dismissed from your last job. That is correct?'

This was all she needed. 'It was a misunderstanding.' The words seemed to stick in her throat.

He waved her words away. 'Are you aware of who it was that alerted your employer to the... additional funds you were obtaining from the patients?'

'A relative I presume.' Jackie didn't like the smug look on his face.

'They received an anonymous telephone call.' He went silent.

'Like I said. A relative.' Jackie lifted her chin and met his gaze. 'I don't know what you're implying but it was simply the odd few-quid tip here and there.'

'Then perhaps you would be surprised to hear that that telephone call was made by Zara's personal assistant?'

'Why would Alina do that?' Jackie raised her hands. 'What the hell have I ever done to her?' Jackie couldn't believe it. She'd loved that job. She'd not even met Alina until she moved to France. What was going on?

'How would Alina even know about that?' said Val, her voice even. 'And more to the point, Inspector Richard, how would you have got hold of that information?' Jackie didn't like to admit it but Val was very good at what she did.

Inspector Richard gave a one-shouldered shrug. 'I had a colleague ask Zara's personal assistant a few questions. And she was most helpful. In fact, she had useful information to impart about the property next door to your own, Ms Chapman.'

'What about it?'

'Do you know who the owner is? I will tell you. It is Zara. Or more importantly a company she set up. And it was her P.A. who hired some actors to rent the property.'

Jackie laughed. She couldn't believe what she was hearing. 'Bloody hell. The whole noisy neighbour thing was a set-up to make you leave?' Val looked stunned and Jackie could see tension in her jaw. She would be hopping mad at being outmanoeuvred by Zara.

He turned to Pauline who froze under his gaze. 'And, Mrs Crozier. Your cat. It was a gift from Zara?' She nodded. 'It was also her P.A. who contacted your landlord to inform them of your breach of tenancy.'

Pauline drew in such a deep breath she almost swallowed the paper bag. Her eyes were wide with shock. Jackie's brain was fizzing. Zara had wrecked their lives to get them to move in with her. This was huge, although she was also a little impressed with the lengths Zara had gone to, to get her own way.

'Bloody hell,' said Jackie, and a sigh whistled through her teeth.

When the inspector left Jackie felt a huge sense of relief of a level only usually experienced by removing her bra at the end of a long hot day. But unlike those moments this time Jackie was shaking. She had never been in a situation like this before – with the exception of the time she and

Tracey Fordham had been caught stealing sweets from the corner shop and the owner had called her parents. Now she thought about it the look on her father's face when he had collected her that day wasn't dissimilar to Inspector Richard's. Although this was obviously a lot more serious. She didn't like to admit that it was freaking her out.

'I can't believe bloody Poirot ransacked the place,' said Jackie. She brushed her hair off her face and then did it again because she didn't know what to do with her hands.

'It's called searching the property,' said Val, in her usual irritatingly calm way. 'And I'd hardly call taking the contents of the drug cabinet and some CCTV footage a search. In fact he specifically said he didn't want to have to get an order to search the premises. He's being clever about how he's handling this.' Val rubbed her chin as if in deep thought.

'He's trying to outwit us,' said Pauline, who was sitting on the sofa cuddling Brian close to her chest like a baby.

'That won't be bloody hard,' said Jackie. 'Zara outwitted and manipulated all of us. The conniving cow.' Jackie snorted. 'I should have bloody well known. She always got her own way.'

'And now she's got Inspector Richard thinking one of us might have killed her.' Val ran her lip through her teeth.

'Don't do that – you'll get lipstick on your dentures,' advised Jackie. 'I guess with everything Zara did it looks like we might all have reasons to want to kill her.' Things were starting to spiral out of control.

'They're still not the strongest of reasons. He needs more than that for a full-blown investigation. Which is probably why he's downloaded copies of the CCTV footage from the night Zara died.' Val looked tense.

'He took the book where I wrote down all the medication I gave to Zara. What does that mean?'

Val spun around. 'Was that totally up to date and accurate?'

'Yeah... well... sort of.'

'Sort of?' Val was scowling at her.

Jackie had started out well with recording the drugs she administered to Zara. She'd mainly done it to show Zara and the others that she was a professional and for the first few days had diligently jotted everything down. But as she'd got into a routine she knew it had slipped a bit. 'I think so. That was my intention but nobody was going to check if I missed the odd dose. It wasn't like I was expecting it to be used as evidence against me.'

'Fair enough.' Val held her palms up. 'We need to work out what his next move is going to be and prepare for it.'

Jackie didn't like the sound of that. 'Okay serious question.' Val and Pauline both gave her their full attention. 'Should we head back to the U.K.?'

Pauline turned towards Val and Brian swished his tail at the disruption to his comfortable position. 'Should we?'

'Absolutely not,' said Val. 'That looks like we are running away. And not to put too finer point on it... exactly where in the U.K. would you be running to?' She raised an eyebrow at Jackie.

'Good point, well made.' She put her hands on her hips but it felt too confrontational so she folded her arms instead.

'But it's a good sign that he hasn't asked for our passports.' Val nodded to herself.

'This has all got out of hand.' Pauline started to rock and that was Brian's cue to leave although it took him a few moments to prise himself from Pauline's arms. 'I'm going to end up in prison.'

'Pauline, stop it.' The same thought had gone through Jackie's head and having it confirmed wasn't helping.

'I am. I know it.' Pauline continued to rock.

'Pauline,' said Val softly. 'If we all stick together that's not going to happen.'

Pauline looked up with frightened eyes. 'It is, because that's what happens when you kill someone.'

72

VAL

The sliding doors opened and in marched Walter. 'Has the copper gone?'

'Yes,' said Val.

He nodded at Jackie. 'You okay?' he asked, looking concerned.

'I think so,' said Jackie. Val shook her head. They needed to keep everything contained. Letting on to anyone that things weren't one hundred per cent fine wasn't a good idea. Jackie spotted Val's gesture. 'Actually, I'm okay. Thanks.'

'That's good then.' He shut the doors behind him. 'It's a scorcher today. It must be thirty-two degrees out there.' He wiped his dirty hands on his work trousers. 'Now, I think the washer I fitted to the sprinkler has done the trick but only time will tell. You'll need to keep an eye on it because...' He paused and looked at the three women all staring at him. 'Did I miss something?'

Val was torn between answering Walter's question and the need to know more about Pauline's confession, which she was still reeling from. Pauline's words had caught her off-guard and she was having to rethink the situation.

Walter was looking at each of them, expecting an answer. 'The police took some things with them,' she said flatly. Walter immediately looked interested. Which was the last thing they needed. 'Just Zara's medication. Nothing exciting,' she added.

'Right.' He didn't look convinced. 'You know I can help. Don't you?'

'In what way?' asked Jackie.

He pursed his lips. 'I've been kicking around here a while so I know people.'

'If this is like Jackie's *I once knew a hit man* then that's not helpful, Walter.' Val didn't want to be rude but she really needed him to leave so she could question Pauline further. Pauline was not looking good. Her complexion had taken on a grey hue and she was still rocking a fraction whilst staring straight ahead.

'Hitman?' Walter was looking puzzled.

'Long story, messy ending,' said Jackie.

'Anyway,' said Walter, perching on the arm of one of the sofas. 'The neighbours might be useful for a start.'

'How the hell can a jewel thief and a hedge fund manager help us right now?' said Jackie, looking rather cross.

Walter's brow furrowed. 'I don't know what Zara told you but...' He blinked. 'Anyway, that side is a lawyer. I trim her bush.'

Jackie hooted a laugh. Despite everything even Val cracked a smile. 'I'm a retired solicitor, Walter, so we're covered on that front. But thank you,' she said.

'Not a bog-standard solicitor. How do I explain it?'

Walter jiggled his head. 'She's the sort of lawyer who used to get some seriously dodgy crooks off. So if you're in a tight spot she's the sort you want in your corner. No offence,' he said pointing at Val.

'Thank you. Some taken,' she replied. It was hard not to be offended when your professional credibility was being undermined. 'But I think we're—'

'Hang on a minute.' Jackie held up her hand to stop Val. 'Let's not be hasty.' She gave an almost imperceptible nod of her head towards Pauline who was still not in great shape. 'Surely, it wouldn't do any harm to have a chat to this lawyer woman.'

'Shall I pop round now?' asked Walter.

Whilst Val wasn't keen on having someone else involved she did want to get rid of Walter.

She brightened her features. 'That would be good. Thank you, Walter. Perhaps we could catch up with you tomorrow. Today has been somewhat trying. I'm sure you understand.'

'Right you are,' he said. 'And try not to worry.' He crouched down to get in Pauline's eyeline. 'We'll sort this all out.' Pauline didn't respond until Walter patted her on the shoulder and she jumped out of her skin. 'Sorry. Didn't mean to startle you,' he said.

'It's okay, Walter. We'll see you tomorrow then. Bye,' said Val, beginning to walk with him to the door in an attempt to encourage his departure. He said his goodbyes and left.

When Val was sure he was long gone she moved to sit next to Pauline. 'Are you okay?' she asked.

'Well, I doubt it,' butted in Jackie. 'She's just confessed to murdering someone.'

Val waved a hand to try and shut Jackie up. 'Pauline,

do you want to talk to us about it? I promise we'll do everything we can to help you.'

After a lengthy silence Pauline looked up. 'If I tell you doesn't that make you a party to the crime or something? Because I don't want either of you to get into any trouble.'

'No,' said Val. 'That's only if we withhold any evidence. You're fine to tell us.'

'Hang on,' said Jackie. 'You're not going to rat her out to Inspector Clouseau are you? Because before you spout a load of ethics at me I want to remind you that friendship comes first. *The Girls* come first. You have to promise that.' Jackie stared her down. Her gaze made Val feel uneasy. She wanted to agree with Jackie but a lifetime of living and breathing the law made it difficult.

'For goodness' sake, Jackie. We're not children. This isn't *The Famous Five.*' Val turned back to Pauline.

'Promise,' said Jackie, her tone stony.

Val openly sighed. She couldn't promise not to tell the truth if questioned. She quickly constructed something that might placate Jackie and not go against her ethics. 'Right. I promise I won't volunteer any information to Inspector Richard or any member of the police force. Are you satisfied now?'

Jackie appeared to be mulling over Val's words in her head. At last she nodded. 'Okay. And that promise is binding right?'

'We have to trust each other,' said Pauline, her voice sounding wobbly and almost childlike. 'If we don't have that then...'

Val took Pauline's hand. 'We do have that. You can trust

us completely.' Val looked to Jackie and she reached over to take Pauline's other hand.

'We're all in this together,' said Jackie.

And whilst it made Val very uncomfortable she had to agree.

73

PAULINE

Pauline was struggling to keep her limbs still. Whilst she was terrified of sharing her secret there was also a part of her that wanted to be rid of living with it day in and day out. She'd thought she would be able to cope with what she had done. Maybe even convince herself that it was going to make things better, but it hadn't worked out like that. The initial feeling of relief was soon replaced with guilt and fear. She'd been instrumental in another person's death. There was never any justification for that. The truth had gnawed away at her. At her soul and her sanity. And she wanted it to stop. Inside her own head was the worst place to be.

Val and Jackie held her hands, which was comforting and calming. They were patiently waiting for her to explain but it was actually quite difficult to articulate how you'd come to a point where watching someone die had seemed like an acceptable thing to do. There was no excuse. She was a monster.

'Just tell us what happened?' asked Val, giving her hand

a squeeze. Val made her feel safe but she knew she couldn't protect her from this, however much she might want to.

Jackie was on the edge of the sofa, like she was watching the climax of a soap opera. 'What did you use? Drugs or a poison?' asked Jackie.

'Jackie,' admonished Val with a scowl and she shrugged.

Pauline cast her mind back to the day it happened. It played out in her mind like a film. She'd seen it many times and could recall everything – she was haunted by every detail. Her mouth was dry. 'I came home and I knew straight away something was wrong. Just a sense. I can't explain what or why. But I knew.' Val nodded for her to continue. The pictures loomed large in Pauline's mind. Seeing someone in that much pain that their features were distorted was like a horror film constantly on a loop in her mind. 'It was awful. The sound. Like something was squeezing the air from their lungs. Rasping. Desperate to cling onto life.' She gave a shudder. 'I could have got the medication from the cupboard. I could have called an ambulance or run and got a neighbour. But I didn't. I chose to do nothing.' She looked at their rapt faces and took a deep breath. 'I turned around, picked up my shopping, walked out and I shut the door. I left him to die.'

'What? I'm confused,' said Jackie. 'Zara had a fit. Is that it?'

'Wait,' said Val. 'Who are we talking about, Pauline? Who did you see die?'

'Zara,' said Jackie. 'Bloody hell, Val, I know you're the oldest now but please try and keep up.'

Pauline shook her head. 'Not Zara. My husband, Ivan. He had a heart condition and I just walked out and left him to die. I walked around with my shopping for hours. And when I got home there was an ambulance. He'd managed to hit redial on our phone and it had called his mate who had come over and found him. It was too late though – he was dead. And I knew that because I saw him taking his last breaths but I did nothing. I let him die.'

'So you killed your husband *and* you killed Zara? Anyone else?' Jackie let go of Pauline's hand and leaned away. 'The thing I said about us all sticking together did not include if one of us was a serial killer. You think you know someone but—'

'Jackie!' Val's tone was sharp. 'When did this happen, Pauline?'

'The seventeenth of August Twenty-Fourteen.' It was etched on her brain.

'You feel responsible for your husband's death because he had a heart attack and you didn't get some medication that may have helped or call an ambulance. Is that correct?' asked Val.

Pauline took a shaky breath. She wasn't sure when the burden was meant to lift but she wasn't feeling any different after sharing her awful secret. 'Yes. I could have saved him but I chose not to. I let him die. I killed him.'

'Hmm, that's not exactly murder though,' said Jackie. 'And didn't you say he was a bit of a bastard?'

'He was.' She'd known it then but somehow hadn't admitted it to herself. He'd done such a good job of convincing her that she was the one with all the issues, the one who caused all the problems and, at some point which she couldn't remember, she had started to believe him. She tried to form her thoughts in her head so she could explain in a more articulate way something she'd never told anyone before. 'He controlled every aspect of my life. He told me constantly how worthless I was. What a pointless life I led and how much of a disappointment I was.' She swallowed hard. That was the most she'd ever shared about her husband. 'But I know that's still no reason to kill someone.'

'I disagree,' said Jackie. 'He got what he was due. Open-and-shut case. You'd get away with that one for sure.'

She liked Jackie but this was most definitely an area where she was not the expert. It was Val's judgement she needed. Pauline looked into Val's eyes and saw only warmth. 'What's your professional opinion, Val?' she asked, and she held her breath.

'It would be a very difficult thing to prove this far after the event. Even then I doubt any police force would want to pursue it because no jury is going to convict you. You were living in an abusive relationship and suffering coercive behaviour. Walking away was a natural response. Seeing someone like that is also a huge shock. You wouldn't have been the first person to react like that. And there's no guarantee that the medication or ambulance crew could have saved him. It may well have been too late. You need to stop being so hard on yourself.' Val smiled and it caught Pauline off guard.

The emotion she'd had locked up for many years bubbled to the surface and she blurted out a sob. And that was the moment when she felt just a little lighter.

Jackie cleared her throat. 'So how did you bump off Zara?'

74

JACKIE

Pauline was blinking at her. The big doe eyes of the perpetually anxious. 'I didn't kill Zara,' she said.

'Now I am seriously confused.' Someone was losing the plot and Jackie was pretty sure it wasn't her. 'You said you killed her.'

'No.' Val shook her head. 'She said she had killed someone, which we have now established was her husband and that his death wasn't necessarily her fault.' Val turned back to address Pauline directly. 'You didn't kill Zara, did you?'

'No.' Pauline shook her head vehemently. 'But she wanted me to. She asked me to. Don't you see? As soon as the inspector finds out about Ivan, that's it. He'll assume it was me.'

'Well you have got form,' said Jackie.

'For crying out loud,' snapped Val, making Jackie recoil slightly.

Jackie held her palms up. 'Calm down. I was only saying.'

'And it's not helpful. I think we're back to square one.' Val let go of Pauline's hand and moved to the opposite sofa. 'Although it's not square one because things have changed. Zara is dead. The police believe she was murdered or at the very least assisted suicide but they are lacking evidence. On the face of it we each now have a motive for killing her because of her manipulation, although I would argue strongly that whilst what she did was underhand we have all benefitted from enjoying a luxury lifestyle so it's not the most solid of reasons. However, being able to enjoy that luxury lifestyle without being at Zara's beck and call now we have inherited could be seen as sufficient motive. And on top of that she actually *asked* each of us to help despatch her.' Jackie went to point out that they didn't know about Zara's actions but Val held up her hand to stop her and she carried on. 'And as soon as he looks at the CCTV footage he's going to know that at some point in the evening we all returned home and therefore we have no alibi for the time of her death.' She let out a long slow breath.

'We're buggered then,' said Jackie, feeling it was important to summarise their situation.

'Not necessarily,' said Val. 'But I do think we need to stick together. I think that is the key. Whether one of us killed her or not.' She held up both palms to fend off any statements to the contrary. 'We need to back each other up because then no single one of us can be held accountable.' She looked at Pauline and then at Jackie. 'Are we in accord?'

Jackie resisted the desire to quip that she'd never be seen dead in cord. 'Yes, like I said. The Girls have to stick together.'

*

The rest of the day was a bit disjointed. The meals arrived as usual and the staff carried on with their jobs but everything had shifted. Their whole reason for moving to live with Zara was now under a different microscope. Each of them had been tricked into going. Their home situations made untenable for her own benefit. It was a lot to digest.

Val had spent most of her time in the office pawing over spreadsheets. Pauline had had such a long bath that both Val and Jackie had gone to check on her. She seemed calmer but somehow more distant after her confession. Jackie had sunbathed and read some magazines. But it was difficult to concentrate. She'd been glad of all the pictures.

Until now Jackie had thought whoever had dobbed her into the nursing home manager had done her a favour. Set her off on a course she wouldn't have otherwise taken. But now it all felt different and not in a good way. She had enjoyed her job. It had given her a sense of purpose. The pay was crap but the residents were lovely. Some of them were coping with a lot of health issues and some had been abandoned by their family but she liked to think she had made a connection with all of them. She might have put on a blasé attitude but she had thought about some of the individuals a lot since she'd left. Wondered how they were. If they'd missed their little chats. She had.

She tried to read her magazine again but it was no good. She did a lap of the garden in search of Walter but he'd gone. As he wasn't being paid it seemed he did whatever hours he fancied. She went inside and found Val writing a list.

'I'm going to give Walter a ring and see if he got anywhere with that lawyer woman from next door,' said Jackie scanning the room for somewhere Walter's number might be written down.

Val looked up. 'We're not asking her for help.'

'But you know this is a stitch-up. Someone has killed Zara and all fingers are pointing at us. Someone who can get people off even when they *have* done it is exactly who we need in our corner.'

'Right now we don't need a lawyer. If the inspector had evidence he would have charged one of us by now. If we all stick together then he's got a problem.'

Jackie opened and closed a couple of desk drawers and huffed out a breath. 'I can't stay around here. It's driving me potty to keep going over everything.' She couldn't stop her mind from thinking about Zara's death. She wondered if either of the others had worked out about Zara's manipulation before the inspector had told them today.

'Then go for a walk.' Val returned to her list.

Jackie spotted an address book under some papers Val had strewn across the desk. 'I might see if Walter wants to go for a coffee.' Val twitched an eyebrow but didn't respond.

Jackie returned to her sun lounger and thumbed through the address book until she found Walter's details. She gave him a call. 'Hi, Walter, it's Jackie. I know you've finished for the day but I wondered if maybe you fancied a walk and a coffee. Only if you're not busy. I just need to get out.'

'I'd love to. Give me half an hour to get home and showered and I'll be round.' He sounded bright and enthusiastic. She hoped she wasn't giving him the wrong impression having spurned his advances in the past but she did very much enjoy his company. They were similar souls and it was nice to feel she could relax with him, not be constantly trying to impress or flirt – flirting was exhausting. She needed someone to talk to but realised she only had the girls and right now they were the last people she could confide in.

'Brilliant. I'll see you soon.'

'No worries,' said Walter, sounding like he really didn't have any. Oh, how she wished she could say the same.

75

VAL

Val hadn't slept well. Her brain wouldn't switch off. Part of her quite liked being back in solicitor mode apart from the fact it was her own defence she was building. She had a cup of tea on the veranda and Brian joined her. He liked it outside when it was cooler and tended to snooze in the comfort of the air conditioning in the afternoon. She'd never really had time for pets but she quite liked Brian. You had to admire his take me or leave me attitude. He certainly seemed to help calm Pauline down, even if he had the opposite effect on Toby.

Pauline's revelation had been heart-breaking. That she had suffered mental abuse by a man who was still haunting her long after his demise was tragic. But it did make Pauline vulnerable to scrutiny. Val feared how Pauline would fare if Inspector Richard decided to interrogate her. The key piece of information Val wanted to keep from him was that at some point Zara had asked each of them to administer euthanasia for her.

One line of inquiry Val had considered pursuing was trying to establish who else could have helped Zara on her way. It would have to be someone who knew where the CCTV cameras were as she'd checked the files herself and nobody else had been picked up. Which would mean they had gone to a lot of trouble to not be seen on camera.

She decided to take a stroll and headed across the gardens and out the back of the property. As she descended the steps she could hear chatter. The voices were low enough that she couldn't distinguish exactly what they were saying but she did know they were speaking English. It instantly made her curious. It was early for tourists to be about. She took the last few steps cautiously and looked through the gate.

There were about four men all stood chatting. This wouldn't normally alarm her apart from the fact they all had cameras with seriously long lenses. She rushed back up to the house and onto her balcony. As soon as she stepped outside she saw the cameras all point in her direction. 'Bugger.'

She dashed through to Jackie's bedroom. Walked across the room instructing her blinds to open.

'Bloody hell,' said Jackie, pulling up an eye mask and blinking rapidly.

'For crying out loud.' There were more journalists on the road outside the property. She could even see a television van.

'My thoughts exactly.' Jackie rubbed her palms over her face.

'What's going on?' Pauline appeared in the doorway.

'The bloody press are here. That's what's going on. The place is surrounded with reporters and cameramen. I'll warn the staff. You two keep away from the windows and whatever you do don't leave the property.' She marched to the door.

'You can't keep us under house arrest,' said Jackie, swinging her legs out of bed.

Val spun around. 'Do you seriously want your picture on the front page of every newspaper?'

Jackie shrugged. 'Might be fun.'

'With the headline: *Is this Zara Cliff's murderer?*' Val tilted her head in challenge.

'Oh, well, maybe not.' Jackie put on her flip-flops and they all went downstairs.

Val made a few phone calls and it turned out that the staff already knew the drill should the press turn up. 'No comment' was the order of the day. Val called Jackie and Pauline into the office. 'I'm going to call Alina, ostensibly to inform her about the press. But I also thought it might be a good opportunity to ask her about the things Zara had her do that persuaded us to move here. What do you think?'

'Some answers would be nice,' said Pauline. She looked brighter today, which was good to see.

'Too bloody right they would be. I've been talking to Walter and he thinks we're due some sort of compensation.' Jackie nodded sagely.

'Yes, well, the gardener would be an authority on that.' Val couldn't hide her sarcasm. 'Shall we call Alina then?'

'Definitely,' said Jackie, and she pulled up a chair.

Val put the phone on loudspeaker and dialled Alina's number. 'Let her speak. I don't want to scare her off. Okay?' Pauline nodded. Jackie pouted, which Val took as her agreement.

Alina answered the call. 'Good morning, Zara Cliff's office. Alina speaking – how may I help you?'

'Hi, Alina, it's Val. How are you?'

There was a long pause. Jackie opened her mouth and Val put her finger to her own lips to shush her and thankfully Jackie remained silent. 'Oh, Val. Hello. I'm fine, thanks.'

'That's good. I wanted to let you know that we've had an influx of reporters here. The place is under siege. Anything we should do?'

'Not really. The story is all over the international press this morning.'

'What story?' hissed Jackie.

'Have you got a copy we could look at?' asked Val.

'Just Google "Zara Cliff murder" and you'll find them all,' said Alina.

Pauline gasped and put her hand to her mouth to stifle it.

'Murder is sensationalist. Alina, you know we had absolutely nothing to do with Zara's death don't you?' said Val.

Another long pause, which made Jackie pull a number of different athletic facial expressions and wave her arms around. As there was no response Val tried a different tack. 'Has anyone been in touch with you about it?'

'I had an officer come and interview me.'

'We wondered if that might be what happened,' said Val. 'The inspector said you may have taken some actions that led to us moving here.' More silence. 'Look, we're not blaming you...' Jackie unhelpfully mouthed, 'Oh yes we are,' in true panto style. Val waved a hand at her. 'But it would really help us to understand what Zara said to you and what her motivation was for instigating all the things that happened to each of us.'

There was a deep sigh from the speaker. They waited for her to reply. 'She was terrified of being seen by her fans as anything other than the fabulous Zara Cliff. She felt she could improve each of your lives and in return she would be able to carry on living hers. With Zara you didn't really ask too many questions. I'm her second P.A. in a year. I didn't want to lose my job. And now it looks like I'm going to anyway. No Zara, no job.'

'You lost me *my* job,' snapped Jackie, leaning into the phone.

Val held her hands up. 'Carry on, Alina.'

'Look I'm sorry. But as Zara said to me at the time. Two of you had broken the rules with taking money and having a pet so it was only a matter of time before someone made people aware. I do feel bad about hounding you out of your house, Val, but that private investigator...' Val snatched up the receiver, which took the call off loudspeaker. She didn't want more secrets to tumble out – that would muddy the already murky waters.

'Yes, I know all about Zara digging around my life. But the bottom line is that, aided by you, she manipulated each of us.'

Alina was quiet. 'What's she saying?' asked Jackie.

'Shhh,' said Val.

'I know it wasn't the right way to go about it and I'm sorry for the part I played but Zara did truly believe that moving to France would be best for all of you,' said Alina.

'That wasn't really her decision to make,' said Val. 'But I understand the pressure you were under. Hopefully you appreciate that we are in a really difficult position regarding Zara's death. If there's anything else you can tell us that could help we would be very grateful.'

'There's nothing else. She just said that when the time came she wanted to be with the girls.'

76

PAULINE

Pauline had experienced an erratic night's sleep. Although she certainly felt relieved after sharing her secret with Val and Jackie it had unlocked unwelcome memories. They'd always been there but this had let them run amok. She'd spent half the night going over everything. For Val to say her actions were justified meant a lot. She wasn't sure she'd ever get to feeling like that herself but it was good to hear someone of Val's profession say so. Perhaps it was even the start of her beginning to forgive herself.

Jackie's attitude was that Ivan got what he was due and whilst that was a little extreme it did help Pauline to think of it as karma. He had treated her badly; she knew that. But then she'd let him. She wasn't sure how that had happened. A gradual process of her losing friends and relying on him had whittled her down to a shadow. She despised that version of herself for being weak. And yet at the time it had felt like it had taken all her strength to get through the day. She was glad those days were behind her and now Ivan's death was out in the open she could think about giving herself permission to move forward with her life. That was assuming Inspector Richard didn't have any other ideas.

Maybe today was a good one to look at the tablets she had and sort them out. Like Zara, she'd accumulated quite a few and if the inspector did decide to do a full search of the property he might read too much into her having brought so many with her. She'd had them in case everything got too much and she needed to take an overdose herself but that wasn't something she would want to have to explain to the police. As the thought crossed her mind she hastily grabbed all the containers from her drawer and raced to the bathroom. She'd keep the latest ones from her GP. She knew it wasn't wise to go cold turkey on antidepressants but the out-of-date ones needed to be flushed. In her haste she unscrewed a lid and the tiny white tablets spewed across the bathroom floor. She got on her knees and began quickly picking them up.

'Pauline, no!' yelled an alarmed Jackie appearing as if out of nowhere.

Pauline looked at the many pills now in her palm. 'Oh, it's—' But Pauline didn't get to finish her sentence before Jackie had hauled her to her feet and frogmarched her out of the en suite.

'What are they?' asked Jackie, concern etched across her features, making Pauline feel bad for worrying her.

'They're a mixture really. Sleeping pills, tranquilisers, antidepressants but—'

'Give them to me,' said Jackie, holding out her hand. 'Please.'

'I need this one packet.' Pauline held up the current antidepressants.

'I'll keep hold of all these.' Jackie's expression was so serious it almost made Pauline want to laugh. 'We can get through this. There are other options.'

'Jackie, I was about to flush the others down the loo.'

Jackie's expression said she didn't believe her. 'Then you won't mind if I do exactly that, will you?' Jackie waved her open palm at Pauline and she handed the pills over. Pauline stayed sitting on the end of the bed. Brian came to join her and from there they watched Jackie flush every last one away.

'Will you let me explain?' asked Pauline.

'You don't have to,' said Jackie. 'Come on, let's get some breakfast. Maybe do some Tai Chi and shout abuse at Felicity – that will cheer you up.' She held out a hand. Pauline stood up, tucked Brian under one arm and took Jackie's hand. It was good to have friends around her who cared, even if they had got the completely wrong end of the stick.

They found Val on the patio grumbling over her muesli and a selection of British newspapers. 'Don't read these if you don't want your blood pressure to go off the scale,' she said, slamming one down and picking up another. But it was too late – Pauline had already seen the headline. 'Zara Cliff Murder – The Plot Unravels'.

'What?' Jackie snatched it up and began reading. 'Three suspects were arrested on suspicion of the long-planned murder of national treasure Zara Cliff, we can exclusively reveal.'

Pauline took a deep breath and decided she needed to take control of her emotions or they would continue to rule her. She would go inside to get herself some tea and pastries to enjoy far away from the tabloids.

'And listen to this load of bull,' began Jackie.

'Do either of you want some tea?' She said it loud to cut Jackie off. They both shook their heads but didn't lift their noses from the print. She couldn't change what the newspapers said and worrying about it wasn't going to help the situation. Best to leave Val and Jackie to go over them and they could decide if there was anything to be done. She left them to it and instantly felt better.

She fed Toby and had a chat to him before sorting her own breakfast out. He seemed okay. As long as he had food and a bit of attention he was a happy soul. With so much going on they hadn't paid much attention to the animals and it seemed that Toby and Brian had called an uneasy truce. They both seemed fascinated with each other. Brian liked to sit with his paws underneath him on the back of the sofa and stare at Toby. And Toby seemed at his happiest when he had an audience – even if it was a cat. Toby ruffled his feathers, splayed out his wings and did a sort of bobbing head dance as if in time to music only he could hear. Pauline supposed it was a bit like cat telly for Brian and perhaps Zara's performing spirit lived on in Toby.

On her way back from the kitchen she was carrying a plate of croissants and a cup of tea when the doorbell sounded. Without thinking Pauline went to open it. She balanced the plate and cup precariously in one hand and opened the door.

A stylish woman in her late forties was standing there. She held her chin high and observed Pauline keenly. That was the moment Pauline realised her mistake. The press were still crawling around the property so they had the main gates shut to stop anyone coming in without buzzing the intercom first. But this one must have somehow bypassed the system.

'How did you get in?' asked Pauline, wondering how on earth she was going to persuade this reporter to leave.

'The gates opened for a car so I just walked in.' She indicated Gabriel reversing up the drive behind her.

Their plan had been easily foiled.

'Well, I'm sorry but you can't do that. I'm going to have to ask you to leave.' Pauline tried to sound like she had some authority although brandishing her breakfast might have been diminishing that somewhat.

The woman's stony exterior cracked a fraction. 'I'm here to see Valerie.'

'No comment.' Pauline stood up straight.

'Sorry?' The woman looked confused.

'I know you'll write what you like in your grubby little paper but all you're going to get from us is no comment.' Pauline tried to close the door.

'I'm not a reporter,' she said. Pauline sniffed. These people would say anything. 'I'm Valerie's daughter.'

'Nice try,' said Pauline. 'Val doesn't have a daughter.'

There was a small cough behind her and she turned to see Val. Her complexion was pale. 'Actually I do.'

77

JACKIE

Jackie read newspaper after newspaper. They were all full of the conspiracy theory that Zara had been murdered by the three of them working together. Where did they get this rubbish? Possibly even worse than that were the awful photographs that accompanied them. Someone had managed to snap a photograph of them in the back of the police car. Although it had been taken when they were being brought home that wasn't what the paper claimed. Maybe it was because it was through glass but the photo wasn't flattering. They looked like three old ladies being driven to a WI meeting. Jackie was oddly drawn to the photograph. Like the reflection you got in fairground mirrors. It was grotesque but fascinating.

The pictures she usually saw of herself were the ones she took at a flattering angle and then altered with the wonders of filters. This was a very different image. They all looked tired and downbeat with a distinct lack of make-up. That was it. She had no make-up on. That was always going to be unflattering. She tried to convince herself that was the issue. The truth was harder to deal with. That old haggard face was hers.

A door slid open and Pauline and Val stepped outside. Jackie barely noticed that they weren't alone.

'Val, do you think I look old in this photograph?' Jackie held up the newspaper. She was still holding it for Val to pass comment when she spotted there was another woman with them. Middle-aged and well-groomed but with a look of caution about her as she stepped gingerly outside.

A penny dropped. It was obviously the lawyer from next door. Jackie got up and held out a hand for the woman to shake. 'Pleased to meet you. We hear you're excellent at keeping people out of prison.' She felt opening with a compliment was a good approach. Val looked tense and Pauline appeared to be trying to signal something with a croissant.

'I'm Wendy. I'm—'

'Can you do anything about this?' Jackie picked up an offending paper and tapped the photograph.

'Jackie, this is Wendy,' said Val. 'She's not a lawyer she's m—'

'Right.' Jackie put the paper down. 'What is it that do you do exactly, Wendy?'

Wendy looked confused by the question, which didn't fill Jackie with confidence. 'Well, I'm a senior manager in human resources for an international car manufacturer,' she replied.

'Um, right.' Jackie studied the faces looking back at her showing varying degrees of unease. 'Sorry, I might be missing something but how is someone in HR going to help us?'

'Jackie.' Val swallowed hard. 'This is my daughter, Wendy.'

Jackie knew her eyebrows had shot up. 'Blimey, that's a surprise.' She stepped forward and gave the woman a welcoming hug and an air kiss. 'Probably not the best time to visit for a holiday but we'll do our best to make you welcome. She gathered up the newspapers and put them on the floor. 'You should have said she was coming, Val. But I guess it slipped your mind what with the police and... Why do you keep waving a croissant, Pauline?'

'Because we need to go and wave at Felicity.' Pauline widened her eyes and beckoned in a shooing motion for Jackie to leave with her.

'Hang on,' said Jackie, as a thought crossed her mind. 'You don't have any children, Val.' What was going on? She studied Wendy. There was something about her that reminded Jackie of a young Val.

'I'll explain,' said Pauline, guiding her out of her chair and across the garden. Pauline was speed-walking Felicity-style and Jackie had to stride to keep up with her. When they reached the pergola, Pauline spun around. 'Val's got a daughter,' she said in a low voice.

'Did you know she had kids?'

Pauline threw up a hand and almost lost a croissant. 'Nobody knew.'

'Val must have known.'

'I know that. But she has a child who is what? Late forties or early fifties. Which means, if my maths are right, she must have had her in the Seventies.'

'Wow, and she never said anything back then. That's huge.' Jackie was still trying to get her head around the fact that Val had a child, let alone the fact that she must have already been around when they were bright young things kicking up their heels in London.

'Exactly. Which is why I've left them to talk. And we can—'

'Woo-hoo!' They didn't have to look to know it was Felicity.

'Morning, Felicity,' called Jackie.

'I say, have you seen the newspapers?' Felicity jogged on the spot.

'Yes, thanks,' called back Jackie putting on a posh voice. 'They'll print any old shite won't they? Ha ha.' She turned to Pauline. 'That hurts my throat.'

'Then don't talk like that.' Pauline shook her head.

'Do we have a date for the funeral or are they not releasing the body?' Felicity shielded her eyes from the sun.

Jackie went to answer but Pauline waved a hand in front of her face to stop her and pointed. Felicity was no longer alone. Paparazzi were appearing like ants on a dropped ice cream. 'We'll let you know. Got to go!' shouted Jackie and she and Pauline ducked down out of sight. 'Bloody hell that was close. What do we do now?' she whispered.

'I've no idea,' said Pauline, surveying her limp croissant.

78

VAL

Val thought she had experienced nerves when she'd been up against some tough barristers but nothing compared to how she was feeling now. Her stomach was churning, she felt physically elated and sick all at the same time. She wasn't far off needing one of Pauline's paper bags. 'Can I get you something to drink? A cup of tea perhaps?' Val asked, desperate to distract herself from the emotions swilling around inside her.

'No, I'm fine.' Wendy was looking at her intently and it was unnerving.

'Have a seat,' said Val, pulling over a chair and sitting down opposite her daughter. 'How are you?' she asked and then felt ridiculous. After forty-seven years she had so many questions she wanted to ask but also no idea where to start.

'Confused. Scared. Thinking I've done the wrong thing. I don't know.' Wendy didn't look comfortable. Val wanted to scoop her up and embrace her but she didn't know if she was allowed. Seeing Jackie effortlessly hug her had been like a stab to her heart. She now realised she should have done that at the door but that wasn't her way.

'It's lovely to see you. You look... well.' It was a good job Jackie had gone because she would have been all kinds of sarcastic at her lame sentences and for once she wouldn't have blamed her. 'Look. I'm sorry. I'm terrified of saying the wrong thing. You talk.'

Wendy pressed her lips together. 'Dad died.'

'Oh, Wendy. I'm sorry to hear that.'

'Are you?' Wendy tilted her head in disbelief.

'Yes. Despite everything I never wished him any ill.' After what he'd done it almost surprised her but it was true.

'That's not what he said.' Val didn't like Wendy's tone. It felt like she was expecting a row. There was an underlying aggression in her voice. Val knew she should have expected this but now she was faced with the situation she was terrified of arguing with Wendy and her walking out. She needed to stay calm.

'I don't know what your father has told you. I hope it was the truth. But I understand that I hurt him and sometimes that distorts things.' Val hoped she'd phrased that in a way so as not to sound like she was calling him out as a liar without even knowing what he'd said but given he'd disappeared with Wendy and vowed that Val would never see her again she didn't have very high hopes of him having painted her in a favourable light.

'He told me how you neglected me. That you put your career first. And ran out on us. You never even sent me a Christmas or birthday card. You've not been in touch until your famous friend invited me for lunch. You couldn't even be bothered to meet me yourself. I think that's fairly straightforward.' As Val had feared, Wendy was ready for an argument. She could almost see the torrent of emotions waiting to breach the dam.

'I'm sorry, Wendy. That's not true.'

'You would say that. In fact, Dad even said you would deny it all. He was right about you. I shouldn't have come.' Wendy got to her feet.

'Why did you come?' asked Val, but she didn't give Wendy time to respond. 'There must have been a small seed of doubt. Something must have made you fly out here. You don't do that if you're one hundred per cent certain someone is bad to the core. Did something not add up?'

Wendy chewed her lip. 'I'm a mother.' Val couldn't stop the small sob escaping. She was a grandparent. Wendy continued. 'My son and daughter have recently gone to university and it broke my heart to watch them leave. And I cannot fathom how a woman could leave her child.'

'I didn't,' said Val. She wanted to say more but she needed Wendy to want to hear it, otherwise she was only going to challenge it all as lies. She waited. Her heart ached in her chest. 'If you've got a moment. I have some things you might want to see.'

Val took a risk in not waiting for Wendy's reply. She walked past her, went inside and prayed she would still be there when she returned.

Val was beyond relieved when she came back a few minutes later to find Wendy was still there, although she was on her phone and pacing up and down, which wasn't a good sign.

'I found what I was after,' said Val, retaking her seat and gesturing for Wendy to do the same.

'I've got to go,' she said into the phone. She ended the call and sat down. 'Look, I don't think this was a good idea. I guess my curiosity got the better of me and—'

Val knew it was now or never. 'This is your birth certificate. I've been trying to find you for the last forty-seven years but I think your father must have changed your name.' She pushed it across the table.

'What?' Wendy picked up the certificate. Her shocked expression said it all.

'Who is Mark Dempsey?' Wendy was shaking her head.

It was Val's turn to look confused. 'Your father.'

'No. His name was Mark Smith.'

A few things started to slot into place. It wasn't just Wendy's surname he'd changed; he'd also changed his own. No wonder she hadn't been able to find any trace of either of them. 'He must have changed both your name and his, Wendy.'

'This can't be right.' Wendy was still staring at the certificate as if willing it to change. 'Have you had this printed off the internet or something?'

'No. It's real. I don't know how he explained the name change to you? You must have needed proof for passports and marriage and such like.'

'I'm not married. I've had a passport since I was a child. It's always been in the name of Wendy Smith.'

'Ah. That explains it.' Once a passport was issued in a new name there was no need to show the change-of-name documentation for subsequent issues – only the previous passport. There was a pause and Val felt the need to fill it.

'This is a picture of you when we brought you home. That's the house we lived in behind us. You were two and we were potty training you. I came home one day and you'd both gone. He left this note.' She passed the old tattered piece of writing paper to her daughter.

Wendy was already shaking her head but as soon as she unfolded it her expression changed. 'This is Dad's writing.' Val nodded. She waited while she read the note that was etched on Val's brain.

> *You lesbian whore. I've read your diary and I know what sort of deviant slut I'm living with. It's over and I'm taking Wendy somewhere where you will never find her and corrupt her. I hope you rot in hell.*

Val waited. Unless Wendy really struggled with reading she had had time enough to read it a number of times. Val swallowed hard before she uttered the hardest sentence she'd ever have to voice. 'I was confused about my sexuality. I was attracted to a woman at work. I didn't do anything about it. Only wrote my feelings in my diary.'

'But he said you…' Wendy finally looked up. Tears were pooling in her eyes. 'You left us for some bloke at work. You said you never wanted me in the first place.' Wendy openly sobbed and Val went to her. Whether it was maternal instinct or simply the response to another person in distress she'd never know but she wrapped Wendy in her arms and they sobbed together.

79

PAULINE

'Erm, what's going on?' asked Walter, seeming to appear from nowhere and joining Pauline and Jackie in a crouched position under the pergola. 'I went round the other way but Val and some woman are bawling their eyes out and here are you two playing Twister without the mat.'

'Journalists,' whispered Pauline, and she pointed to the promenade.

'They won't hear you from up here,' he said.

'But they can see us,' said Jackie. 'And I can't cope with another bloody awful picture on the front page of every sodding British tabloid.'

Walter cringed and gave Jackie's shoulder a friendly squeeze. 'Yeah, that was a rough one.'

'Thanks very much,' said Jackie, giving him a shove and sending him toppling onto his backside. 'Whoops sorry. I didn't mean to push you quite that hard.' They both started to laugh.

'I guess I deserved that,' he said, dusting himself down. 'But you can't spend all day like this.'

He stood up and Jackie beckoned for him to crouch down again. 'Get down or you'll get papped too.'

'Maybe we could crawl back inside,' suggested Pauline, trying to think what would get them out of their predicament.

'In this dress?' Jackie indicated her delicate cotton sundress.

'Maybe not,' said Pauline, looking around for some other ideas. It was like being under fire but instead of weapons they were at the mercy of telephoto lenses.

'I've a suggestion,' said Walter. 'Follow me.' Walter set off in a strange stooped position and scrambled across the lawn towards the side of the house and garages.

'Where the hell is he going?' asked Jackie.

'I've no idea but I think we should follow him.'

'And look as daft as he does?' pointed out Jackie.

Pauline shrugged. 'Not much choice. We can't hide here all day.' With that she adopted the same stooped stance as Walter and followed him across the garden, hoping that Jackie would follow.

Walter was at the side of the house and stretching out his back when she caught up with him. She darted into the shadows like a burglar. Jackie wasn't far behind.

'This is ridiculous.' Jackie stroppily adjusted her clothing.

'You look great,' said Walter, admiring her.

'Was there another part to this plan, Walter, or is this it?' asked Pauline, realising that although they were away from the reporters and upright they were now trapped between the house and garage.

'This way,' he said squeezing between the garage and a large conifer. He disappeared from view.

'But isn't that next-door's garden behind the garage?' asked Pauline. Jackie shrugged.

'Psst. Come on,' he hissed, from the other side of the conifer.

'In for a penny, in for a pound,' said Jackie and she flattened herself against the garage wall and side-shuffled out of sight.

Pauline didn't feel that she had much choice in the matter and if it was the side where the lawyer lived she was away anyway. Although if she was honest she wasn't really sure who lived where. She just hoped they were friendly and had no big dogs. She inched her way along, pushing bits of greenery out of her face as she went.

'Mind the wire,' said Walter, offering her a helping hand and pointing to a low wire fence which she stepped over.

Pauline gazed around. They were close to another good-sized villa. It looked newer than Zara's and as if it had been squeezed onto the plot. The garden was small and heavily terraced but each level had something different – be that bushes or flowers – and a different colour dominated each area. They were well protected by a shapely high hedge and there were no paparazzi lenses – perhaps she could relax a little. 'This is like stepping through the wardrobe into Narnia.'

'You like it?' asked Walter, pulling his shoulders back.

'Do you do this one too?' asked Jackie, knocking something out of her flip-flop before returning it to her foot.

'I did this all from scratch, when it was a new build,' he said proudly.

Jackie was paying more attention to the villa. 'Well, this is fancy. Who lives here then?' she asked.

'Me,' said Walter.

For a moment Pauline wasn't sure what to say. How could Walter afford this? 'Oh, does a room come with the job?' asked Pauline taking in the large sweep around balcony and classy modern exterior.

'No, I own it. It's mine.' He looked puzzled. 'Didn't you realise?'

They both shook their heads. Walter was rich. This was a turn-up.

Jackie pointed a finger at him. 'You're the jewel thief!'

'Ah, no. That's where you're wrong. My business was importing diamonds for the jewellery trade.'

'Why would Zara say you were a thief?' asked Pauline. It seemed unnecessarily unkind if it was a lie.

'There was a mix-up once where I might not have declared everything I brought into the U.K. but that was sorted out with—'

'A bribe?' asked Jackie still scanning the building.

'A suspended sentence,' said Walter.

'Blimey, this is the Costa Del Crime,' said Jackie, with a chuckle. 'So do we get to have a nosey around the inside too?'

'Of course, come on in,' said Walter leading the way.

80

JACKIE

Jackie was still reeling from the revelation that Walter had money. He unlocked the door and tapped a number into the alarm box. Inside was as sleek as the stylish exterior. It was all white shiny floor tiles with the odd grey wall and carefully chosen ornament here and there. It had a sophisticated air of expensive about it, which Jackie instantly fell in love with.

'Your home is really nice,' said Pauline. 'And thanks for letting us hide out here for a bit.'

'My pleasure. Feel free to have a look around. I know you're dying to.' He nodded at Jackie whose head was on a swivel. 'I'll get the kettle on.'

She didn't need telling twice and it was pointless to deny her curiosity. 'Come on,' said Jackie, taking Pauline by the hand and heading up the wood and glass staircase.

'It doesn't feel quite right having a look around someone else's home when they're not accompanying you,' said Pauline.

Jackie didn't have the same issue as Pauline as she strolled in and out of the bedrooms. 'Three bedrooms,' she said in hushed tones. 'Two with en suite. And there's bathrooms upstairs and down. It's not as big as Zara's but I like it and it has the same view.' Every bedroom was painted white with the odd framed black and white sketch. Only one room had some family photographs, it also had a giant bed, so Jackie assumed it was Walter's.

They ended up in the kitchen, which was sort of a negative of the rest of the house in grey and black with white accents. Every kitchen gadget Jackie could think of was rowed up along one of the many lengths of shiny black worktop. Coffee machine, slow cooker, steamer, deep-fat fryer, blender, food processor and a sandwich toaster.

Walter caught her looking. 'Labour-saving devices. I love 'em,' he said. 'And I'm not much of a cook.'

'A sandwich toaster!' Jackie stroked it reverently. 'OhMyWord the times I would have killed for a cheese toastie these last few weeks. Christian looked right down his nose at me when I mentioned it. Didn't he?' She looked at Pauline to back her up and she nodded.

Walter handed them hot mugs of tea and showed them through to an area with large shiny dark green sofas and a ceiling so high it was on the next floor. 'You have a truly beautiful home,' said Jackie, taking it all in.

'Thanks. I helped to design it myself.' Walter sat on one sofa so Pauline sat on the other. Jackie joined Walter. She relaxed into the sofa and had another look at him. A full head of thick grey hair. Tanned skin and good teeth although there was no telling if they were all his own. He was in good shape – that was likely because of all the gardening. He was probably mid-sixties – older than she usually went for but otherwise he had a lot going for him. And more than all of that she liked Walter. She had been hasty to dismiss him as an option. Very hasty indeed.

'I can't believe you kept this secret from us,' said Jackie. 'Making us think you were just a lowly gardener.'

Walter's jaw tightened. 'I never deceived you. You simply didn't seem interested in knowing anything more.'

Jackie laughed it off but sadly he was completely right. She hadn't been interested in taking their relationship beyond friendship when she thought he didn't have money. But in her defence she'd been holding out for someone who could provide the much-needed safety net from life she had been seeking. She liked Walter, of course she did, but she had to admit she liked him even more now she knew he had a bob or two and could provide the level of security she craved.

'Sorry, Walter. We've not been ourselves since Zara went,' said Pauline. Brilliant, thought Jackie – play the grief card. She nodded her approval at Pauline who frowned slightly in response.

'Any developments from the police?' He looked at them both in turn.

'No,' said Jackie. 'But that inspector is like a terrier with a shoe. He won't let go until he nails someone. I think he's going to stitch up one of us.' It sounded dramatic but it was how she felt. 'I keep telling Val we should go back to England but she says we should stay put. It's all right for her – she speaks the lingo. I don't want to end my days in some rotting French jail.' Okay, she may have overdone the dramatics that time.

Walter snorted a laugh. 'That's hardly likely though is it?'

Pauline was stony-faced. He looked at Jackie. She shrugged. 'Who knows? I think we should flee. I might speak to Raphael about borrowing that boat.'

Walter smiled. 'The yacht is mine and you can use it anytime.'

Jackie spat her tea out in spectacular style. 'I'm so sorry.' She caught the dribbles on her chin.

'It's fine,' said Walter, going to fetch a cloth.

'He must be loaded,' whispered Jackie.

'Millionaire,' said Pauline, with a nod.

'Bloody hell,' mouthed Jackie. 'Thanks, Walter.' She took the proffered cloth and wiped down herself and the surrounding area.

He rejoined Jackie on the sofa. 'If you really think it's an issue I can sail you back to Blighty. I'm assuming you're allowed to leave France?'

'Inspector Richard hasn't said we can't.' Jackie was thinking over his offer. If she was honest she'd quite like to go on a nice long cruise on the yacht. The Caribbean maybe – was that far? Perhaps England was a safer bet. A hop across the channel wouldn't take long and then what? Buy a tent and pitch it on the top of the Dover cliffs? She didn't have many options back there. 'I like the idea of being a fugitive. Sailing around the seven seas escaping capture.'

Walter smiled indulgently. 'You're only a fugitive if you've done something wrong.'

'You know what I mean.' She gave him what she hoped was a seductive look.

Pauline coughed and broke the mood. 'Your tea is really nice.'

'Yorkshire tea,' he said. 'You can't beat it. You can't get anything decent over here unless you know where to look. Beaulieu has some good shops for British essentials.'

Jackie glared at Pauline for changing the subject. She was enjoying her little fantasy. There was a bang on the front door. 'Excuse me,' said Walter and he went to answer it.

'Crikey, Jackie,' said Pauline, her voice reproachful. 'You're not subtle are you?'

'What?' Jackie tried to look innocent.

'As soon as you realised he had cash you've been all over him. You weren't as keen when you thought he was a gardener.'

'Now hang on...' But she didn't finish her sentence. They both had tuned in to the voice of the person at the front door. Moments later Walter returned. He agitatedly ran his hand through his hair.

'I need to pop out—'

'Good morning, ladies,' said Inspector Richard. 'Such a surprise seeing you here.' He scanned them all as if checking for weapons. 'Mr Hewitt is coming with us to answer some questions.'

'You too,' said Jackie, with a raised eyebrow.

'It would seem so,' said Walter, picking up his house keys. 'There's a spare set of keys in the cutlery drawer. Can you lock up when you leave?'

'Of course,' said Pauline.

Walter paused for a moment. 'Raphael's number is on the noticeboard.' He gave Jackie the briefest of nods. With that he and the inspector left.

81

VAL

Val had cried with Wendy until there were no more tears. They were wary around each other and it would take time to change that, but at least they were in touch and they were talking, however stilted. There had been a rush of questions from both of them, keen to fill in the many blanks and missing pieces. There was so much Val needed to know but she couldn't catch up on so many missed years in a couple of hours. Wendy had seemed to swing from excited to quite cross at times, which was completely understandable. It also showed Val that she didn't know this person at all and that was the saddest thing about being reunited. The toddler she remembered was long gone. The memories she shared with Wendy had all been news to her. Her father had done an excellent job of erasing Val. Wendy had given her a whistle-stop update of her life and achievements, all of which had filled Val with pride she wasn't sure she was allowed to feel. Eventually they had exhausted themselves.

Wendy and her long-term partner were staying in a hotel in Nice and she needed to get back to them but she had promised she would visit again as they were staying for a week. Wendy had explained that she had lost her nerve about meeting Zara and Zara had left a message giving the villa's address and saying she was welcome anytime. When she'd seen in the papers that Zara had died she found herself wondering about her mother having such a famous friend. Her curiosity about Val had got the better of her and she'd decided to make the trip and meet her face to face although she confessed part of her intention had been to tell her what she thought of a woman who abandoned her child – something she now knew to be a lie her father had peddled.

There had been more tears as she'd left. Val's heart was overflowing. It ached for the toddler she'd lost but was already filling with love for the woman she wanted to get to know.

Her unexpected visitor had almost made her forget what was going on until she'd seen reporters swamp Wendy as she exited through the villa gates. She was now even more determined to find a resolution. To put an end to the police inquiries and lay poor Zara to rest.

Val scoured the villa and its grounds for Pauline and Jackie but they were nowhere to be found. She discovered Jackie's mobile on the table under the pergola and was starting to wonder if they'd been kidnapped. She couldn't think of any other plausible reason as to why Jackie would have gone anywhere without her phone. Unless they had done a runner. The thought brought her up short. Jackie was daft enough and Pauline easily swayed. Had they absconded?

Possibly in the style of Reggie Perrin? Val looked around for any abandoned clothes. But there was nothing.

She marched back inside. Her emotional high was starting to disappear like a wave crashing on the beach. Brian came up to her and snaked around her ankles. Surely Pauline wouldn't have gone anywhere without him. She took him through to the utility and fixed him some food. Christian was preparing lunch but, when asked, he confirmed he hadn't seen Jackie or Pauline either. She asked the member of staff making the beds and got the same response.

Val was chatting to Gabriel by the garage when she heard a very unsubtle 'Psst!' from the bushes. She made her excuses and followed the sound around the side of the garage.

'Val, it's me,' said Jackie, in a stage whisper. She was relieved and annoyed in equal measure.

'Jackie, what on earth are you doing and is Pauline with you?'

'Yes. We were talking to Walter and… actually do you think you could come over because I feel like an idiot talking to a tree.'

'What are you doing hiding behind a tree?' asked Val.

'I'm in Walter's garden. He owns the villa next door and it's super swanky. Not quite as big as—'

'He's been arrested,' interjected Pauline.

That was all Val needed to force her to find a way of getting past the tree and into the next garden. 'Hang on. I'm coming.' She emerged into the light after a brief wrestle with the conifer. 'Here's your mobile.' She handed the phone to Jackie.

'Mwah.' Jackie kissed the screen. 'I thought I'd lost it.'

'What's happened?' asked Val brushing bits of green twig off her chest.

'Walter's not been arrested,' said Jackie. 'Bloody Inspector Gadget turned up again and wanted him to answer some questions down at the station like he did with us.'

'What do you think it means?' asked Pauline.

Jackie started talking before Val could respond. 'It means we have the keys to his house, Raphael's number and Walter's permission to use his yacht to take us anywhere we want to go. And now would be a really good time because the police are otherwise occupied interviewing Walter. What do you say?' Jackie fixed her with wide eyes.

It worried Val that Jackie wanted to run. She'd only consider that if she was desperate or guilty or both. 'Hang on, slow down.' Val waved her hands. 'We are not doing a moonlight flit on a yacht. My daughter is here.' Val couldn't stop the huge grin spreading across her face.

'I'm so happy for you,' said Pauline, giving her a warm hug.

'Oh yeah. Me too.' Jackie stepped forward and the two women briefly embraced each other.

'Thank you,' said Val. It meant a lot that they were pleased for her.

'It's nice that she came all this way,' said Pauline.

'Zara tracked her down for me. She's staying in Nice so hopefully this is the start of us getting to know each other.'

'That's only going to happen if you're not banged up for murder,' said Jackie. 'I say we have a few days on the yacht and see what happens. If we're not here they can't arrest us.'

'But we can't abandon Walter,' said Pauline. 'Or Brian or Toby.'

'I agree,' said Val. 'I say we call that Plan B. We need to stop panicking. Let's go back to the villa and—'

'Did you not want a look around Walter's place first?' asked Jackie, jangling the keys. 'It's really swish.'

'No, Jackie. You can't go poking around someone's home.' Val was amazed by Jackie's lack of moral compass sometimes.

'He said we could.' Jackie looked put out.

'And we should probably wash up the cups,' said Pauline.

'She's right.' Jackie pointed at Pauline. 'Come in and you can update us on this mystery daughter you've been keeping secret for umpteen years whilst we wash up.' Val didn't have time to protest as Jackie was already heading back inside the house.

Val had a brief scan of the gardens. They were neat and well kept. Walter clearly had a passion for gardening. But the question now was whether the police taking Walter in for questioning was just standard procedure or did they have some other reason?

82

PAULINE

Pauline and Val did the washing and drying up because Jackie was busy having another nose around Walter's home. Val was the most animated Pauline had seen her in a long time and looked so happy to have been reunited with her daughter. It was a lovely ending to a sad story thanks to her ex-husband. It seemed it wasn't just Pauline and Jackie who had chosen badly on that front.

Pauline managed to persuade Jackie to stop snooping and she reluctantly went with the majority decision to return to their villa and wait for news of Walter. The sun was high in the sky and it was hot. Pauline realised they needed to negotiate the conifers again but thankfully Val agreed to go first. They all rowed up like they were awaiting a firing squad and side-shuffled through the vegetation and along the side of the garage like arthritic crabs. Val suddenly stopped. Pauline did the same. Jackie wasn't paying attention and stomped on Pauline's foot.

'Ow.'

'Shhh,' said Val waving at them with an outstretched palm. 'There's people at the house.'

'What people?' asked Jackie but she was already pushing past Pauline.

'Hey.' Pauline was rammed up against the garage wall and now had a face full of Jackie's ample cleavage.

'Sorry.' Jackie peered past Val. 'That's the police.'

Here we go again, thought Pauline. She waited for her pulse to quicken but it didn't. There was a flicker but she wasn't heading for a panic attack, which both surprised and delighted her. Why wasn't she panicking? Maybe the police visits were becoming the norm.

'What do we do now?' asked Jackie.

'Let me have a think,' said Val.

'Maybe move so I can breathe?' suggested Pauline.

'Sorry.' Jackie clumsily reversed past Pauline, treading on both her feet this time, until she was able to exit the conifers. Pauline followed and Val eventually emerged and brushed herself down.

'Plan B?' said Jackie, putting her hands on her hips.

'Don't be hasty,' said Val. 'We don't know what they want.'

'But we know they've got Walter.' Jackie threw up her arms. 'That bloody grass – he's gone and ratted us out to the cops.'

'Calm down. You sound like you're in a bad Seventies police drama,' said Val. 'We don't know that he's said anything.' She narrowed her eyes at Jackie. 'Unless you've given him something he could have revealed to the police?'

'No. I'm going on the fact that there are hordes of them swarming all over our place. They were in and out of the villa and they were even roaming around the garden. They wouldn't do that without a good reason. Without new information. We can't go back,' said Jackie. 'I'll call Raphael.' She pulled out her phone.

'Hang on, don't go all *Thelma and Louise*,' said Pauline.

'That was a car not a yacht,' pointed out Val.

'I know but the theme was the same. Anyway, let's go back into Walter's place. It's cooler in there and we can sit down and come up with a proper plan.' Pauline was proud of her calm approach.

'That's actually a good idea.'

Val appeared surprised and Pauline was a little hurt by that but she'd take the praise anyway. 'Thank you.'

They looked at Jackie and waited. She huffed out a breath. 'Okay. But only because I need a stiff drink.' She marched off to Walter's front door.

Pauline made them all a cup of tea even though Val said she didn't want one and Jackie was trying to find something alcoholic. Tea was the British answer to everything. It's raining – have a cup of tea. Your dog has died – have a cup of tea. You're about to be charged with murder – have a cup of tea. Pauline mused over why a nation relied on the hot drink so much. Perhaps it was the comfort of a warm drink in a country that was frequently experiencing unfavourable weather. Or maybe it was something to do with your hands when you were stressed and otherwise might be pulling out clumps of your hair. But she concluded it was something we could all do on autopilot so required virtually no thought and not thinking was often the best thing in times of crisis.

She ferried the drinks to the table by the sofas and Val uncovered some coasters. 'Where's Jackie?' asked Pauline.

'Still in search of—'

'Hey! You two. Come and see this,' called Jackie.

Val and Pauline looked at each other, got up in a synchronised motion and went to find their friend.

'Down here,' called Jackie.

They found an open door and a set of spiral steps. Jackie was at the bottom waving up at them. 'It's a drinks cabinet only it's in the floor. How good is that?'

Pauline peered inside. 'Like a modern cellar then?' She noted the racks full of wine that lined the walls all the way down.

'Choose something and come and join us on the sofa. We need to agree what to do next,' said Val.

'But what if I take something and it's like uber expensive? I've seen it in films. They pick an old dusty bottle and it turns out to be the person's pension plan.' Jackie looked pained as she craned her neck.

'Then don't select a dusty one,' said Val, turning away.

The sound of voices outside made Pauline freeze. Val swivelled back and put her finger to her lips. They both listened.

'What is it?' called up Jackie watching them from below.

'Shhh,' they whispered in unison.

'It's the inspector,' said Val who had twigged it about a millisecond after Pauline who was already descending the steps to join Jackie.

'Hey what are you doing?' Jackie shuffled to one side but there really wasn't anywhere for her to go in the tiny space.

Val joined them and pulled the door to. The light automatically went out.

'Oh brilliant,' muttered Jackie. 'Are we really going to hide in here?'

Pauline didn't have an answer. She was glad of the darkness because this time she was definitely starting to panic.

83

JACKIE

'Is now a good time to say I need a wee?' asked Jackie, in hushed tones. Maybe she had a touch of Pauline's nervous bladder.

'No,' said Val in a sharp whisper. 'And be quiet I'm trying to listen.'

'I do really need one.' She felt it was important to explain her predicament.

Val didn't respond. 'I think you're going to have to wait,' said Pauline.

Jackie huffed by way of reply. She'd been chuffed to bits when she'd discovered the wine cellar. It was ingenious the way it had been dug into the floor like a giant corkscrew. She guessed there was quite a bit of money tied up in the bottles she was now surrounded by.

Through the silence she could hear muffled French accents. Was this it? The end of the road? She was glad the others had joined her even if it was cramped. Despite it being pitch-black in there it was good to know she wasn't alone.

They were in it together. Just like they'd been all those years ago. Maybe now was a good time for her to acknowledge that she was older than she cared to believe. Her bladder reminded her again.

Jackie turned around, shuffled back until she could feel the cold metal of the staircase on her legs and sat down on the bottom step. She wasn't sure if that made her bladder feel better or worse. She wished she'd chosen a bottle of wine before the lights had gone out. She felt along the shelf in front of her. Her arm nudged a bottle and it gave a little tinkle as it touched another.

'Seriously,' came Val's irritated voice through the darkness.

Jackie sighed deeply. Why didn't they ever listen to her? She should have called Raphael and gone on the yacht without them. But she knew she wouldn't have done that. The Girls stuck together - that was what they did. She should have been more persuasive. They could have been in Monaco by now. Instead they were trapped. Stuck in what was basically a posh hole. Didn't they find Saddam Hussein in a similar sort of set-up? she wondered.

'Psst,' said Pauline quietly.

'Not helping the wee situation,' replied Jackie, crossing and uncrossing her legs.

'Can you hear anything, Val?' asked Pauline. All Jackie could hear was Pauline's heavy breathing.

'I can hear voices but they've moved away so I can't hear what they're saying.'

Jackie had another tentative feel along the wine racks. The bottle tops were facing her so she could try to determine which were corks and which were screw top. She had twisted herself into an awkward angle when she at last found a screw top. She carefully pulled it from the rack and undid it. She sniffed the contents. Heavy and fruity. Definitely a red. If they were going to be trapped here for a bit she could at least enjoy herself a little. It might be the last alcoholic drink she would enjoy for a while. She tried desperately hard not to be despondent but the newspaper headlines had put the wind up her. The police would want to take action sooner rather than later and they were sitting ducks. She still wasn't entirely sure that one of them hadn't helped Zara on her way.

'Is the plan to hide here until Dick Tracy has cleared off and then get the yacht?' asked Jackie. It was met with silence.

Eventually Val spoke in a whisper. 'We can't run away.'

'Then what are we hiding for?' asked Pauline.

It was a good question. If one of them had done for Zara then it was likely they'd all be implicated. And if none of them had, then someone had stitched them up like kippers. Either way it wasn't looking good. Jackie thought back on her time at the villa. She'd enjoyed being back with the girls again. There had been a couple of niggles but overall it had been a lot of fun. And even if this was where it all went pear-shaped they had had a pretty good adventure together. It was a shame she didn't have anyone to tell. She wished now she'd at least sent a postcard to her brother.

Time ticked by. The further Jackie got down the bottle the more she was facing up to her mistakes. She'd been rubbish with men her whole life. Or they had been rubbish with her. Whichever it was, the result was the same. She'd never managed to find and hold on to a good one. A picture of

Walter flashed into her mind. She had another mouthful of wine and this time she savoured it. Walter was a decent guy, if you could ignore the fact he might have dobbed them in to the police. But before that he had been nothing but decent and she had dismissed him just because she'd thought he was a lowly gardener. She didn't like herself very much for that. She also felt a little bit cheated. It was as if life had tricked her out of him. Like it had given her a test and she had failed it spectacularly. If she'd only given him a chance maybe she could have had something special – and she didn't mean his villa.

Not having a decent relationship was one of her regrets in life. Although she despised the idea of ageing, she liked the idea of growing old with someone who cared about her. Someone she could share funny moments with. Maybe that had been the pull of living with the girls again. The chance to share things. Perhaps it was validation. Confirmation that you existed and mattered because someone else was there to verify it. Or maybe she didn't like getting drunk on her own.

The voices were audible again. Jackie took another slug of the wine. It tasted good. She hoped it wasn't really expensive – she wouldn't want to upset Walter. Pauline's breathing was sounding worse. Jackie guessed she was having another panic attack. She reached behind her in an attempt to comfort Pauline. However, it appeared that a hand touching your leg in the dark was a bit of a surprise.

'Argh!' Pauline squealed, only managing to curb the volume towards the end.

'Bloody hell, Pauline,' said Jackie. The door above them opened and the lights flickered on. They all blinked as they tried to adjust to the sudden brightness. When she could at last focus Jackie saw Inspector Richard staring down at them. The game was up.

84

VAL

'I have been looking for you ladies. I have to say it did not occur to me to look for you here.' The inspector's lip curled as he spoke.

'Hiya,' said Walter appearing next to him. He was smiling and for a moment Val wondered why. But then he hadn't been detained long at the police station, which would indeed be something to smile about.

'Judas,' hissed Jackie from the bottom of the stairs and Walter frowned.

'Would you like to come out?' asked Inspector Richard. Val led the way and the others followed. Like schoolgirls going to detention they trailed after him.

'Woman needing to pee,' said Jackie, taking a detour via the downstairs bathroom.

The others took seats on the sofas. They sat and looked at each other while they waited for Jackie.

'Sorry. When you've gotta go,' said Jackie. She went to

put the bottle on the table and Pauline hastily shot a coaster underneath it.

Inspector Richard viewed them all. 'I would like to ask—'

'No comment,' said Val firmly. They were prime suspects without alibis; this was their only option now. She nodded to the others and they all repeated the phrase.

The inspector looked surprised. He pouted for a moment and then continued. 'We have searched the villa next door.'

'We know,' said Val. 'I trust you had the required authority to do so?' She stared him down. It was a minor point but it might help them in court if he'd not followed due procedure.

'Indeed.' He nodded. 'And I have found some things of interest to us.'

Fear gripped her stomach. This wasn't good.

Jackie tipped up her wine bottle. 'Would you like a glass for that?' asked Walter.

'No, I'm fine,' she replied.

'What did you find?' asked Pauline.

The inspector turned his attention to her and smiled. 'Firstly in one of the bedrooms we found this.' He pulled an evidence bag from his jacket pocket. Val leaned forward to see there was another bag inside containing white powder. This was all they needed.

Jackie looked up. 'It's mine.'

'Jackie,' hissed Val.

'It's okay. It's not drugs.'

'Are you sure?' asked the inspector opening the first bag and licking his finger. 'I can easily check.'

'I beg you not to do that,' said Jackie.

'Because it'll get you arrested?' suggested Inspector

Richard with an arched eyebrow and his damp finger still poised over the open bag.

'No, because it's my mother's ashes and I have no idea what bit of her you're about to lick.'

The police officer quickly resealed the bag. 'We will have the substance properly checked.'

Val blew out her cheeks. 'For crying out loud, Jackie. Why is she... in a plastic bag?'

'I couldn't afford a fancy urn so had an argument at the funeral parlour and ended up putting the ashes into a few ziplock bags. I sent one to my brother, one to her favourite bingo hall and that one's mine. I was going to do something with them but what with everything I just hadn't got around to buying an urn off eBay, that's all. We can't all afford big send-offs.'

Val's jaw tightened. 'I wasn't even invited to my parents' funeral. After you told them I was gay they never spoke to me again.'

Jackie looked like she'd been slapped. 'Val, I am truly sorry. I didn't know.'

'Why would you?' Val shrugged.

'Jeez. No wonder you hated me.'

Val's resolve softened. 'I never hated you, Jackie.'

'You should have. I would. I was a mouthy little sod and I was showing off when they visited. If I'd thought for a second they'd react like that... Please know I'm really sorry.' She reached over and squeezed Val's hand.

'Apology accepted.'

The inspector cleared his throat and they all focused back on him. 'We have also found some seeds. Can any of you tell us where these may have come from?'

They all looked at Walter who shrugged. 'What sort of seeds and where did you find them?' he asked.

Inspector Richard put another evidence bag on the table this time containing some yellowish pip-like objects. 'I do not know exactly. I was hoping you could tell me.' The inspector watched Walter closely.

Walter glanced at the seeds. 'No idea what those are. I don't grow anything from seed. Everything I've planted next door has been plants. Oh, hang on apart from the grass seed I keep in the storeroom. I use that for patching up the lawn from time to time.'

The inspector shook his head. 'Even I, who am no gardener, can tell this is not grass seed.'

'Why are these seeds of interest?' asked Val. The inspector must have felt they were significant, otherwise he wouldn't have asked.

'We have some toxicology results on your friend and they are unusual.'

'And are those results connected to the rash?' asked Val.

'It would appear that is a possibility,' he replied.

Val put two and two together. 'She was poisoned by something plant-based?'

'It would appear so. Can you tell me anything about that?' He returned the bags to his jacket pockets.

'Nothing at all,' she said.

His gaze travelled to Jackie. 'No comment.'

Pauline shook her head.

'Beats me,' said Walter. 'Was it in her food?'

'That is something we are talking to her chef about.' He stood up all of a sudden, making them all flinch slightly. 'I would like you to inform me if you think of anything relevant. Please do not leave the area.' He looked pointedly at Walter. 'I will see myself out.'

They waited until a few seconds after the door had shut. Pauline sighed deeply.

'Well, that was like old times,' said Walter. 'Anyone else need a drink? Jackie, I assume you're still all right necking my Château Gazin?'

'Crap. I couldn't see the labels in the dark. Is it super expensive?' She had the decency to look guilty.

'You're okay – only about fifty quid a bottle.' Jackie's eyes went cartoon wide. 'What does everyone else want?'

'Tea, please,' said Val. 'I'd also like to know what happened at the station.'

'Don't worry. You ladies are all okay. They're still fishing.' He got out some mugs. 'They asked a few things about what I did as Zara's gardener. They'd seen me on the CCTV that afternoon and wanted to know what I was doing and which of you I had seen at the villa.' His eyes briefly darted to Jackie. 'They don't have anything substantial.'

'It sounds like they've found the cause of death,' said Val.

'I bloody knew there was something about Christian I didn't like?' said Jackie. 'I mean who doesn't like toasted sandwiches?'

'But why would he kill her?' Val knew reasoning with Jackie after most of a bottle of wine was probably pointless. 'He wasn't named in the will. As far as we know they got on well. There's nothing for him to gain. He has no motive.'

'Ahh,' said Jackie. 'Only as far as we know.' She upended the wine bottle but it was empty.

85

PAULINE

Pauline was the first to leave. She wanted to get back for Brian and Toby. She left Jackie and Val, who were both quizzing Walter about the other regular staff at the villa. Pauline was exhausted. Stress was certainly good at burning calories; she'd lost quite a bit of weight in the last week alone. She scuttled down the side of the garage and let herself in the patio doors. She hadn't really thought about the police searching the house but now she was confronted with the aftermath. Either that or they had been burgled. She scanned the living room. Everything that was previously in a drawer or a cupboard was on the floor. Nothing was broken but it wasn't where it should be. She puffed out her cheeks.

Toby squawked and drew her attention. Even his cage was on the floor. 'What on earth did they think they'd find under your cage?' she asked.

'Knickers,' said Toby.

She spent a few minutes straightening out the living room

and went through to the kitchen to find Christian sitting at the island surrounded by the contents of the cupboards. 'Are you okay?'

'They think I poisoned her,' he said, without looking up. 'Do you know what an accusation like that can do to a chef?'

'I would imagine it's not good,' said Pauline, picking up a jar of rice and then realising she had no idea which cupboard it went in.

'It's okay. I will sort this.' He looked up. 'I did not kill her with my food.'

'Of course you didn't,' said Pauline, pulling up a chair. 'I don't think that was what they were implying. Just that maybe someone put something poisonous *in* her food. But not you.' She wasn't sure that was any better but at least he smiled briefly.

'Poor Zara. This place is not the same without her.' He was right. She was so vibrant and colourful and now it was as if that colour had been bleached from the villa. They both stared at the blank white wall.

'I miss her,' said Pauline. 'I also miss working with her. She was writing her memoirs. Well, she was dictating it and I was typing it. I was enjoying that.'

'There are plenty of others in Saint Jean Cap Ferrat who would like to think they had a book in them. I'm sure you will find work.'

She'd not really thought about carrying on but now Christian had sown the idea Pauline quite liked it. 'Thank you. I'll think about that. Come on, you tell me where these all go and we'll have this sorted in no time.'

★

Pauline was upstairs when Val and Jackie returned. She could hear Jackie swearing long before she appeared in the doorway of Zara's bedroom. 'The bastards have only trashed my room. What's that all about? Why me?'

'I'm assuming it wasn't just yours, Jackie,' said Val.

Pauline shook her head. 'It was the whole place but Christian and I have pretty much sorted everything. I didn't like to intrude on your personal things so I didn't do your rooms.'

'Oh,' said Jackie. 'Well, as long as I've not been singled out.'

'Thank you,' said Val. 'You could have waited and we'd have given you a hand.'

'It wasn't nice. I wanted to get everything back in its place as soon as possible. Although I've not done the office. That's a right mess.'

'Leave it. I'll tackle it tomorrow. I might even be able to work out if they've taken anything. I don't suppose they left a receipt for what they took?' asked Val.

'Not that I've seen. But I think there is something missing in here.' Pauline pointed to the bookcase.

'Really? What?'

'Zara had a book she was reading. Creepy-looking cover. And I can't find it.'

'Maybe she lent it to someone,' said Jackie, poking her head back around the door.

'It was here the morning we found her and now it's gone.'

The next morning Pauline and Val tidied up the office while Jackie had a lie-in. When she did emerge she swore blind she didn't have a hangover and was interested in buying more of the Château Gazin as it was the first time she'd not had a stonking headache after drinking red wine. She'd even gone to do her own version of Tai Chi on the patio to prove how un-hungover she was.

The pages of Zara's memoirs that Pauline had already typed out had been liberally scattered across the floor. Pauline wondered if the police had found what they were searching for as she picked them up and made a small stack of the pages. Who would read it now? There wasn't enough to make a book. It was a shame because what she had typed out had been interesting and funny – just like Zara. Grief gave her a little shake. The investigation had barged to the front and losing Zara had somehow taken a back seat. Pauline took a wobbly breath. She missed Zara. Despite her getting her evicted, the fix they were in and everything that had happened, she still missed her friend.

Val was sorting financial papers into some sort of order. 'Do you think the police will be back?' asked Pauline.

'I hope not.' Val twisted her lips.

The phone rang and Pauline answered it. '*Bonjour.*' Her French had improved a little in the weeks they had been there and she could hold a conversation as long as the other person didn't speak too fast or use words she wasn't familiar with.

'*Bonjour.* It is Inspector Richard. Who am I speaking to please?' Her heart started thumping.

Pauline put her hand over the microphone. 'It's Inspector Richard,' she whispered to Val.

'Okay. Don't panic,' said Val. 'Put him on speakerphone and let's see what he wants.'

86

JACKIE

Jackie's head was full up but this time it had nothing to do with Zara's demise and everything to do with Walter. The attraction she had felt for Walter had been clear but as usual she had messed things up. She had been so focused on finding a long-term solution to her problem that she hadn't realised it was under her nose. Now she felt like a fool. But worse still there was no way for her to start a relationship with Walter without him thinking the only reason was because of his money. She was furious with herself and she needed to calm down.

Yoga was meant to be good for helping you to relax and de-stress so she thought she would give it a go. She had put on the closest thing she had to a gym kit – crop top, sarong and flip-flops – and headed out to the pergola. If she kept down low she was out of sight of the journalists. The irony of Zara getting all the press attention she wanted after she had died had not been lost on Jackie. Although the tiny insight into Zara's world and what it meant to have long lenses hunting you down had not been half as much fun as she'd always imagined it to be – quite the opposite. The photograph of her in the police car would always haunt her.

Jackie had her phone on the ground in front of her, as she tried to balance on all fours whilst sticking her bum in the air. 'Downward dog, my arse,' she muttered to herself. It was far harder than it looked, although that may have been down to her not doing any exercise of any note in the last thirty years. Apart from a brief liaison with a personal trainer called Fabio who, it turned out, was actually trying to sign her up to a fitness programme rather than date her. Another useless male in her dating history. So much for yoga bringing you peace – she was getting quite grumpy.

'Woo-hoo!' called a familiar voice.

She huffed out a sigh. That was all she needed. Jackie knew she wasn't visible from the promenade. Well, she hoped she wasn't because if she was then all they could see would be her bum stuck in the air. She tried to stand up but she was now in a particularly awkward position, a bit like doing the wheelbarrow race on her own. Her arms had locked and her back was twinging. Jackie went onto her knees and eventually got to her feet.

'I thought there was someone there,' said Felicity. 'You're still in residence then. Any news?'

'We've not been arrested if that's what you mean,' called back Jackie with a beaming smile.

'Ha,' Felicity gave a dry laugh. 'Of course not. Any date for the funeral?'

'Soon,' said Jackie. 'My people will call your people. Must dash. Toodle-pip.' She snatched up her phone and darted back to the villa before the conversation could be continued. As she came through the doors Pauline was on her way out.

'Quick. Val asked me to come and get you. The police are on speakerphone.'

'For heaven's sake,' said Jackie. 'I've had enough of this. It's like cat and bloody mouse. I'm going to tell him,' she said and she marched through the living room with Pauline racing after her.

'I'm not sure that's a good...'

But she wasn't listening. Jackie strode into the office. 'Is that him?' she said, pointing to the phone.

'Jackie, let me—' started Val but Jackie shut her up with a wave.

'No, Val, this has gone on long enough. Inspector Richard? This is Jackie speaking.'

'Hello Ja—'

'Yeah, yeah. Listen up. I, no, *we* have all had enough of this. We have been very patient and cooperative. We've been beyond helpful to you, with the possible exception of hiding in Walter's wine cellar but that was a minor error of judgement.' She waved her hand. 'Anyway, the point is you are harassing us.'

'*Non—*'

'I'm still speaking,' said Jackie, forcefully over the inspector. She was not in the mood to hear his excuses. She felt quite empowered. Val waved at her to stop but she ignored her. No doubt Val would have fourteen good reasons why this was a bad idea but she didn't want to hear them. This was how she felt and he needed to know. She was fired up. 'For too long we have done as you've asked and you've kept us in the dark and treated us like criminals. We are

British citizens and should have been given more respect. You've still not told us when you will release Zara's body so we can't even arrange her funeral. And quite frankly it's out of order. I want to make a formal complaint.' She folded her arms. She was quite proud of sticking up for herself and her friends. It felt good. She moved over to stand in between Val and Pauline. She took their hands in hers and gave them a squeeze.

'I see,' said the inspector. 'I am sorry you feel that way. The investigation, it was necessary—'

Here we go, she thought, he's going to justify what he's doing. 'Right. Listen to me. If I've not made myself clear. Let's try this. You need to either arrest one of us...' Pauline gasped next to her but she ignored her and carried on – she was on a roll. 'Or you need to leave us alone.' There was silence. 'Got it?'

He cleared his throat. 'Would you like to explain, Ms Chapman, or shall I?' he asked.

87

VAL

Val quickly made gin and tonics and took them outside to where the others were sitting waiting expectantly after they had ended the call with the police. She was the proverbial cliché with both good news and bad to share.

'Come on, out with it,' said Jackie. 'He's got something on one of us hasn't he?'

'Oh no,' said Pauline, taking her drink from Val and immediately having a big swig.

'No, it's actually the opposite,' said Val, bypassing Zara's chair and sitting in another. 'We are all off the hook.' Val was still trying to process what the inspector had told her.

'Hang on,' said Jackie. 'Completely? Are you certain?' She didn't wait for a response. 'Because I've watched enough cop shows to know that they like to lure the baddies into a false sense of security and then bam.' She slapped her palm on the table.

Pauline jumped. 'I wish you wouldn't do that. But I echo

the sentiment.' She fixed Val with a solemn stare. 'Are we really in the clear?'

'We are.' Val didn't know how else to say it.

'Thank heavens for that,' said Pauline, taking another swig of her drink.

'Steady on,' said Val, guiding Pauline's drink back to the table. 'Don't overdo the celebrations.'

'What are we celebrating exactly?' asked Pauline. 'Poor Zara is still dead. Someone killed her even if they no longer think it was one of us.' She looked at Jackie and then back to Val. 'I'm assuming it wasn't one of us.'

'Well, it definitely wasn't me,' said Jackie. 'I know you all thought it was but it wasn't.'

This was the part Val had been worried about sharing. 'It wasn't any of us. It was Zara. She took her own life,' said Val. The others looked stunned. They stared at her without blinking for a few moments.

'That can't be right,' said Jackie. 'Her hands were buggered up; she couldn't even hold a glass of water. And there were no tablets when we found her.'

'Because she took oleander seeds,' explained Val.

'I'm not sure I'm following?' Pauline leaned forward.

'The seeds of the oleander plant are highly poisonous. It's what gave her the rash. Chewing just a few seeds was enough to stop her heart.' Val took a sip of her drink. It was too early to be having a gin and tonic but it was welcome and seemed oddly appropriate given Zara's predilection for the tipple.

'She poisoned herself?' Pauline was shaking her head. 'That's awful.'

'Hang on.' Jackie waved a finger in circles. 'Do we have

oleanders growing here?' She looked about the garden, although Val doubted she had any idea what an oleander plant looked like.

'No, but they do grow in the area apparently,' said Val. 'They're a warm climate plant.'

'Is that why they hauled Walter in?' asked Jackie.

'I expect so.' Val put down her glass.

'How come old Inspector Dick doesn't think it's one of us who gave them to her?' asked Jackie.

'Because they found remnants of them inside a book in Zara's bedroom,' said Val. 'They had been taped to the back inside cover.'

'We could have hidden them in there,' said Jackie.

She was being deliberately awkward. 'I don't know why we would do that and surely if that were the case we would have got rid of the evidence as soon as the police showed an interest, not left the book sitting in full view.' Val tilted her head in challenge. She quite like a reasoned argument, not that this was one of those.

'Okay. Good point.' Jackie flopped back in her seat.

'Maybe she'd always had the book and the seeds,' said Pauline.

'It came in the post. I was there when she opened it,' said Val. 'She didn't seem to be expecting it. But I guess she must have asked someone else to help her take her own life.'

'That's the end of it then,' said Jackie, although Val wasn't sure if she meant it as a question or not.

'Maybe. Maybe not. The police are keen to find out who sent the book and the seeds. Apparently they found the envelope the book came in in the bins so they know when and where it was posted but he wouldn't give any details – only that we all have alibis thanks to the CCTV footage.'

'Whoever sent it effectively killed her.' Pauline shook her head. 'I wonder who it was.'

'Probably local if these seeds like sunny weather.' Jackie tipped her head back to place her face in the sun. 'Do you think the paparazzi will leave us alone now?'

'The inspector said he hopes to issue a statement later today. What he says will likely inform whether they stay or move on to the next big celebrity story.' Val wondered to what degree he would vindicate them of any wrongdoing. Sadly she was well aware of how unlikely this was.

'But why didn't Zara leave a note?' asked Pauline, watching Val from over her large gin glass.

'Hmm.' It was a good question. 'I suppose because she would have struggled to write one.'

'Because this is bloody Zara,' said Jackie with a dry laugh. 'Don't tell me she didn't plan this as the big dramatic climax she wanted. Think about it. She's dominated the world's press for days. This would be the perfect bloody send-off in her eyes.' Jackie chuckled and reached for her glass, which she raised in a toast. 'To Zara, for being a bloody brilliant friend and total drama queen to the very end.'

'To Zara,' they echoed.

88

PAULINE

Four days later Pauline was sitting alone turning the tiny white tablet over in her palm. Should she do it now or...

'You all right?' asked Val, putting her head around the utility room door.

'I forgot to worm Brian.' She held up the worming tablet.

'I'm sure it can wait. People are starting to leave.' Val pointed over her shoulder.

'Okay, I'll be there in a minute.' Val nodded and disappeared.

It had been a strange few days. They had all seemed to grieve at different times for Zara as the fear had ebbed away and the grief had taken up residence. But today had been her hastily arranged funeral and it had all gone to Zara's detailed plan. The great, good, and the extremely famous had all crammed into a tiny French church to hear biblical readings and Zara anecdotes, although Pauline had noticed that most of the stories had the teller at the centre – she guessed a lot of actors were cut from the same cloth.

They had all returned to the villa for the wake, which had lasted most of the afternoon, where a ridiculous amount of champagne had been consumed as per Zara's wishes. Brian meowed and looked hopefully at Pauline. 'This isn't a treat. It can wait until later.' He didn't like being shut in but she couldn't risk him covering all the designer black outfits in cat hair.

She slipped out, scooted through the kitchen where they were clearing up after the exceptional buffet and into the living area. Toby had been quite vocal during the round of impromptu toasts that had followed their return to the villa so after the third round of 'Show us your knickers', she had covered him up. She pulled the cover off the cage and he squawked his annoyance. 'Now behave or I'll put it back on,' she told him.

'Hello, girls,' he replied.

It caught Pauline off guard. 'Hello, Toby,' she said, smiling at him as he ruffled his feathers proudly. Perhaps he was capable of saying something nice after all.

'Feck off,' he added. Oh, well, thought Pauline, maybe she would try to teach him a few new happy phrases to replace the rude ones.

Pauline scanned the room. Jules was handing out his business card to all and sundry. He probably had quite a bit of space in his diary now Zara had gone. Alina had already found a new job working for some French actor but she had come to pay her respects. A multitude of famous faces, some botoxed rigid, were all chatting and the general vibe was refined party. Perfect, she thought.

When she found Jackie she was saying goodbye to Brian May. Pauline had a feeling of now or never. 'I love you,' she said. Brian blinked in alarm. 'I mean your music. Queen. Queen's music,' she clarified and he looked relieved. 'I named my cat after you,' she said, with a broad grin.

The musician returned to looking alarmed. 'Thank you,' he said stepping away.

'You take care now, Brian, don't be a stranger,' said Jackie, directing him to the exit. She returned to Pauline. 'Seriously, what is wrong with you?'

'Nothing.' Pauline preened herself. She felt empowered and the happiest she had in forever. 'I was brave and I spoke to Brian May. And he said thank you.'

'Shortly before he put a restraining order in place.' Jackie widened her eyes but gave her friend a congratulatory squeeze.

Val joined them. 'Wendy just rang.' She gave a little smile. 'We're going out for a meal in Nice tonight.'

'That's lovely,' said Pauline.

'It is. We're going to keep in touch, take baby steps, but hopefully we'll speak to each other regularly.' Val looked over the moon.

'I'm pleased for you,' said Jackie. She glanced over Val's shoulder. 'Look out.'

Pauline followed her gaze. Duncan, Zara's nephew, was striding over. He had managed to make the funeral after all. Although they all felt he was really doing a recce of the villa.

'Ladies, I need to make a move. Enjoy the villa. While it's yours.' He was obviously disgruntled that Zara had left it to them but the will was cast-iron and there was nothing he could do about it.

'It's ours indefinitely. The will was crystal clear on that,' said Val.

'Ha, of course. You're the solicitor. Well, then enjoy it for as long as you all live,' he said.

'Are you threatening us?' asked Val.

'Not at all. I've got no idea what it is three women of your age are going to do here.' He shrugged.

'I'm going to enjoy the sunshine and cultural delights,' said Val.

'We're going to have wild sex parties and drink champagne,' said Jackie.

Duncan recoiled.

'Reading mainly,' added Pauline and the others gave her a look that said she could have come up with something better. 'Do you like reading?' she asked him.

They all starred at Pauline like she'd lost the plot. Eventually Duncan raised his eyebrows. 'Yeah,' he said, in an odd voice like he was reading an autocue. 'I like thrillers.' He nodded at Pauline and turned to leave. 'Bye.'

They watched him go. 'What was that about?' asked Val.

'Buggered if I know,' said Jackie.

Val was staring after Duncan. 'What genre was the book the seeds came in?' she asked.

'A thriller,' said Pauline, followed by a sharp intake of breath.

'Everything all right?' asked Walter, sidling up and offering them a top-up of champagne.

'Zara's killer,' whispered Jackie pointing after Duncan.

'The nephew,' said Walter. 'I thought as much.'

'Did you?' asked Val, giving him a disbelieving look. Her phone pinged and she waved her apology before going to answer it.

'Based on what exactly?' asked Jackie.

'Intuition,' said Walter, tapping his nose.

'Because you've been on the wrong side of the law?' she asked.

'No, because Zara always said he couldn't be trusted and who better to go to when you're looking for someone to bump you off?'

'But his own aunt.' Pauline gave a shudder. How could anyone send someone to their grave so casually?

'You look good,' said Jackie to Walter. Jackie's tone caught Pauline's attention because Jackie seemed almost shy.

'Sometimes I make an effort.'

'You don't need to. You've aged like a fine wine. Most likely you've got better with age whereas I've aged like a biscuit.' Walter's eyebrows pulled together in question. 'I've gone soft and now nobody fancies me.'

'I wouldn't be so sure about that,' said Walter, with a coy smile.

The moment was interrupted by some mourners joining them. They said goodbye to a few more people and the staff started to tidy up around them. 'Shall we head outside?' suggested Pauline.

Jackie put on her sunglasses and they acknowledged the few remaining stragglers before taking seats under the pergola and admiring the now familiar view.

'My feet are bloody killing me,' said Jackie, kicking off her shoes.

Val returned and took a seat. 'That was Inspector Richard arranging when to return the items they removed.'

'Everything okay?' asked Pauline.

Val pouted as if taking a moment to consider what she

was going to say. 'Let's just say Duncan might find he has a police escort to the airport.'

'You didn't?' said Pauline, covering her mouth, although she was full of glee for what Val had done.

'Well, I doubt they can charge him with anything but if it makes him think he's a wanted man in France then the last thing he'll want is anything to do with this villa.'

'Amen to that,' said Walter, raising his glass and they all leaned over to clink it.

'You're pleased we're staying then?' asked Jackie.

'I've had worse neighbours,' he said, with a wink. 'I hear one of them is a jewel thief.'

Jackie thumped him playfully on the arm and he caught her hand and held on. 'I've got some more of the Château Gazin in for the next time you wanted to hide in my cellar.'

There was a moment where they held each other's gaze – so much so that Pauline felt she was intruding.

'Well, I might just do that,' said Jackie, a smile playing on her lips.

'Sorry to interrupt,' said a lightly tanned Jules hovering nearby.

'Come and have a seat,' said Pauline, looking around for another chair.

'I can't stop. I've a flight to catch.'

'Ooh off to top up that tan?' asked Jackie, giving him the once-over.

'No, I got this in the Caribbean. I'm on a flight back to London in a couple of hours. Anyway I wanted to say…' He seemed to look at each of them in turn. 'I'm truly sorry.' He paused as if expecting a response. They all waited.

'It was a privilege to get to know Zara. She would have loved today.'

'She pretty much planned it all herself,' said Val, modestly.

'That was her,' said Jules. 'It was her way or the highway. I wish I...' His voice cracked with emotion, making Pauline want to comfort him.

'Oh, Jules. You did so much for her. She was very grateful.' Pauline wasn't sure if it was true but she hoped it would help. 'You should have no regrets.'

Jules rushed forward and hugged Pauline, which took her by surprise. 'Thank you,' he said, with a sniff. He pulled away and rubbed at his tear-streaked face. 'I didn't feel I had a choice.' Jules seemed on edge.

'About what exactly?' Val fixed him with a steely gaze. Pauline had an uneasy feeling. Maybe it hadn't been Duncan who had sent the book after all. 'Here,' said Jules handing Pauline an envelope. Before she could say anything he was gone.

'Well open it,' said Jackie.

Pauline pulled out the typed page and scanned to the bottom. 'It's from Zara.' She looked at the intrigued faces. 'Shall I read it?'

'Yes,' said Jackie, waving an arm to speed her up.

Pauline swallowed hard. 'My darling girls, if you're reading this then I am at peace. Thanks to Alexa I am dictating this to an answer machine as I face the end of my life. Please do not mourn me for too long. I have had the most marvellous life. I longed to be on the big screen and for the world to know my name but once I achieved that I spent the rest of my life playing a part. It wasn't until we were all together again in London that I truly realised how hollow my life had become.

The real me was one of four girls sharing a house in London and I wanted to be her again. And for a short while, I was. I want to thank each of you for making that happen and for you to know how special you are.

'Jackie, you are a beautiful woman inside and out and I hope one day you recognise how lucky a man would be to share their life with you. Don't ever undersell yourself.

'Val, you are the strongest and smartest woman I know. Staid and dependable – this is not a weakness. You are rock-solid and I hope one day soon Wendy is lucky enough to have you in her life.

'Pauline, you are kindness to a fault. Don't let anyone put you down, especially not that little voice in your head.'

Pauline swallowed hard before carrying on.

'If my actions have upset any of you then I apologise, but I do not regret getting The Girls back together. My only sorrow is that I didn't do it sooner. I had hoped we would share a few more years but that wasn't meant to be.

'My body has failed me on all fronts. I have had to watch myself wasting away and it was killing me, but sadly not fast enough – please insert laughing emoji here.' Jackie chuckled. Pauline carried on before the tears blurred her vision too much. 'I am sorry too for asking each of you that very difficult question. I understand why you all said no. Thankfully this dear boy said yes. I hope you understand I had to exit as I had lived – burning brightly rather than fizzling out. My time with you has been the happiest of encores. With all my heart I love the girls you were and the amazing women you have become, and I will always be proud to call you my friends. All my love. Zara.' Pauline looked up at the teary faces. 'There are three kisses.'

Jackie sniffed back a tear. 'We could have done with that buggery letter a week ago.'

'Does it say Jules sent her the seeds?' asked Walter.

'As good as,' said Val, wiping a tear with a hanky.

Pauline checked the letter again. 'Oh there is another line. P.S. You must destroy this after reading and please do not read it aloud. Whoops,' added Pauline. Walter took it from her, whipped out a lighter and lit the edge of the letter. They watched it furl and burn to ash.

'Woo-hoo!' came the call from the promenade.

'Hello, Felicity,' called back Val.

'She was here a moment ago,' said Pauline, pointing into the living room. She'd offered her a generous fee to help write her autobiography, which Pauline was going to give some serious consideration to.

'That bloody woman is everywhere,' said Jackie.

'I couldn't find you all to say goodbye,' said Felicity. 'Well done. Zara would have approved. She liked a Cockney knees-up.'

'The cow,' said Jackie, under her breath.

'Anyway enjoy the evening. I expect I'll see you tomorrow,' said Felicity.

'I'm sure you will, darling,' called Jackie.

They stood for a moment and watched her speed-walk away. The sun was starting to kiss the ocean, making its surface flash like a thousand paparazzi cameras.

'Right,' said Jackie, when Felicity was out of earshot. 'Once more for Zara.'

They all raised their glasses and chorused, 'Bloody Felicity perky bottom.'

Discussion Points and Book club Questions

The questions below are designed to get the discussion flowing at your next book club meet-up.

1. What is the significance of the title?
2. The book follows four friends, Zara, Pauline, Jackie and Val, but is told from only three of their points of view. Why do you think the author chose to write it this way?
3. What were the key strengths and weaknesses of each of the main characters?
4. You learn more about the characters' backgrounds as you read further into the novel. Did your opinion of any of them change? If so, how?
5. How does the way the characters see themselves differ from the way others see them?
6. Was Zara wrong to get The Girls back together? If so, why?
7. What do you think they each gained by being reunited?
8. Friendship is a strong theme throughout the book. How does the friendship between the main characters influence their decisions?

9. What surprised you most about the book? Why? Were there significant plot twists and turns? If so, what were they?
10. Did you suspect any of the main characters of any wrongdoing? If so, why?

Acknowledgements

The biggest of thank yous to all of the fabulous team at Aria but especially Thorne Ryan and Laura Palmer for helping me to wrestle this book into shape. You are definitely honorary members of The Girls now! Thanks to my agent Kate Nash for her unending support and patience. Special thanks to Tatiana Boyko for the stunning cover.

Thank you to Heather Guppy for useful boating references and trying to track down 1970's sailing courses!

Thanks to the party people (Phillipa Ashley, Jules Wake, Sarah Bennett and Darcie Boleyn) for keeping me sane while I wrote this. And to the fabulous Christie Barlow whose writing retreat helped me nail my edits!

A warm hug of a thank you to all the members of the Friendly Book Community Facebook group – you really are the loveliest and most supportive bunch of people.

Much love to my family and friends for helping me keep one foot in the real world – I couldn't do this without you.

Big shout out to the booksellers, book bloggers, librarians and especially to you the readers – thanks so much for choosing my book. If you enjoyed reading this please tell your local book group and if you have a moment to leave a review that would mean the world. Thank you.

About the Author

B ELLA OSBORNE has been jotting down stories as far back as she can remember but decided that 2013 would be the year that she finished a full-length novel. In 2016, her debut novel, *It Started at Sunset Cottage*, was shortlisted for the Contemporary Romantic Novel of the Year and RNA Joan Hessayon New Writers Award.

Bella's stories are about friendship, love and coping with what life throws at you. She likes to find the humour in the darker moments of life and weaves these into her stories.

Bella believes that writing your own story really is the best fun ever, closely followed by talking, eating chocolate, drinking fizz and planning holidays.

She lives in The Midlands, UK with her lovely husband and wonderful daughter, who thankfully, both accept her as she is (with mad morning hair and a penchant for skipping).